William Faulkner famously said 'The past isn't dead. It's not even past.' *The Burden* explores, with sensitivity and skill, the way in which events that took place decades ago can impact on the present. Its unsentimental treatment of childhood as a time of confusion and uncertainty is especially acute. Many readers will see elements of themselves in this emotionally engaging novel.
Miles Salter, Director of York Literature Festival

The Burden is a fascinating amalgamation of diverse characters, woven into a luxuriant tapestry of plot lines from Alzheimer's to single motherhood, abandonment to alcoholism, and all whilst being portrayed through various periods of the characters' lives. The many surprises along the way were more than enough to keep me interested and I was curious to know exactly what this 'burden' was. What I love about N.E. David's writing is I never know what to expect next and he doesn't stick to only one genre. It's always hard to follow a good first novel, but the author has managed it more than capably.
Susan Buchanan, bestselling author of *Sign of the Times*

N.E. David's new novel *The Burden* is a pleasure to read, a witty and moving portrayal of the innocence of childhood, the responsibility we feel for our family, and the secrets that they keep from us. Every page is filled with evocative prose and fascinating characters that will tug at your heartstrings and make you smile.
Rob O'Connor, Creative Writing Tutor at the University of York, Centre for Lifelong Learning

I read this book in one go – couldn't put it down, in fact – and found it totally absorbing. Having inherited his father's restless spirit but not his charm, it's small wonder that Frank Johnson is such a tragic character. Will he believe the bitter irony of his situation as revealed to him on the final page? How might this affect the rest of his life? One can only hope for a sequel.

Maggie Cobbett, Former Chair of Ripon Writers Group

The Burden

A Family Saga

The Burden

A Family Saga

N.E. David

Winchester, UK
Washington, USA

First published by Roundfire Books, 2015
Roundfire Books is an imprint of John Hunt Publishing Ltd., Laurel House, Station Approach,
Alresford, Hants, SO24 9JH, UK
office1@jhpbooks.net
www.johnhuntpublishing.com
www.roundfire-books.com

For distributor details and how to order please visit the 'Ordering' section on our website.

Text copyright: N.E. David 2014

ISBN: 978 1 78279 936 8
Library of Congress Control Number: 2014954853

A CIP catalogue record for this book is available from the British Library.

Design: Stuart Davies

Printed in the USA by Edwards Brothers Malloy

We operate a distinctive and ethical publishing philosophy in all
areas of our business, from our global network of authors to
production and worldwide distribution.

Part One

Thursday 15th September

One

"Hello?" said Frank, for the umpteenth time that day.

At the Focus Do It All store on Clifton Moor, the staff telephone was mounted on the wall in the narrow corridor that ran from the rest room to the manager's office. It was prone to being knocked off its hook by every passer-by and it needed only the slightest of touches to send it clattering downwards. At first it was regularly replaced, but the staff had got tired of the constant bending and soon left it to dangle upside down from its cord, where it clicked and purred ineffectually.

In the eighteen months he'd worked there, and more particularly in the year since his mother had gone into the nursing home, Frank had lost count of the number of times he'd stooped to retrieve it and press it to his ear, expecting to hear news that might affect him. His anxious monitoring was met by a continual buzzing and after each check he would put the receiver carefully back on its hook. More recently his experiences had caused him to work exclusively at that end of the store and he'd unofficially appointed himself as an expert on plumbing. The aisle was located adjacent to the corridor so he could remain as close as possible to the telephone during working hours.

His perpetual fear was that Elisabeth might be taken ill or that she'd fall and break her hip and he dreaded the thought of her having to go into hospital. Worse still, it might be Sheila, the care-home manageress, her prissy little voice saying *I'm afraid I've some bad news, Mr Johnson,* and although he tried to banish this terrible thought from his mind, it surfaced with such monotonous regularity that it coloured his every act. Far more likely it would be some relatively trivial matter. *We're having trouble with your mother again, Mr Johnson – she's refusing to take her medication.* Or *She's locked herself in the toilet and says she won't come out until you get here. We've tried everything short of breaking the door down but she won't budge.*

So on the morning when the telephone did eventually ring and he rushed to answer it, he was surprised to find it was his sister who'd called him and not some carer or social-services official.

"Hello?" he repeated. "Who is this?"

"It's me – Pat."

His brow creased into a frown.

"Pat? What the hell do you want? I thought I told you not to call me at work."

"I know – but it's important."

"Important? How important? It's nothing to do with Mother is it?"

"No, it's not. But something's come up…"

"Oh, I thought it might have been the nursing home."

His voice reverted to its natural grudging tone. It was as if he continually needed to remind his sister of the great responsibility he'd assumed. As far as Pat was concerned, looking after his mother was a chore to him, a fact she must not be allowed to forget. God forbid she should ever think he enjoyed it.

"Anyway, what do you mean – 'something's come up'?"

"Something's come up and I need to speak to you about it."

Frank looked nervously up and down the corridor. A few steps away, the door to the manager's office was ajar but there was no one in sight.

"Well, go ahead, I'm listening. But you'd better make it quick."

"I'm afraid it's not that simple."

"So what is it then?"

There was a pause as Pat gathered herself.

"It's Dad."

"Dad?" This was truly a surprise. "D'you mean Geoffrey?"

The word 'dad' had no personal meaning for Frank. In his view he'd never had a father. His assumption was that 'parents' coalesced into a single object – his mother – and he struggled to cope with the idea that he might have two. *Geoffrey…* Even to give credence to the name was an event of considerable signifi-cance, let alone to have spoken it aloud. A thousand latent thoughts buried deep in the mud of time began to bubble slowly upwards and for the moment he was struck dumb. A protracted silence ensued. His sister eventually broke it.

"Frank? Are you there?"

"Yes, I'm here. So, what does he want?"

"He doesn't *want* anything," Pat insisted. This, of course, was a lie. But in the face of her brother's aggression she felt the need to go defensive. "It's just that he's not very well."

"Pah!" Frank scoffed. "Not very well? So what?" That meant nothing to him – his mother was 'not very well'. *Tell me something new.* "And?"

"I just need to talk to you about it, that's all." Pat waited patiently for a response. Then, when there was none: "Look, I can tell now is not a good time."

"No, you're damn right it's not."

"Why don't we meet somewhere? I get off at twelve. What about the coffee shop at Tesco, say around ten past?"

She'd obviously prepared her suggestion in advance and in the light of her pleading it seemed he didn't have much choice. Besides, whatever it was, whatever 'thing' was affecting his father, whatever had caused Pat to break his long-standing instruction not to contact him at work, perhaps it was better to face it now rather than let it fester. He reluctantly decided to agree.

"Very well then."

And yet he still felt the concession had been wrung out of him.

At the same time, the door to the shop opened behind him and his supervisor's head appeared.

"Frank? I've been looking for you all over. You've got a customer."

Frank clapped his hand over the mouthpiece. "I'm coming."

Only a couple of words but they were enough to make the head disappear. Bastards!

Always snooping. Couldn't they leave him alone for just a few seconds?

He returned to the phone. "Look, I've got to go."

"I'll see you at Tesco then? Just after twelve?"

He was on the point of saying *If you must* but there was a click and she'd already gone.

Frank replaced the phone carefully on its hook and waited for a moment before returning to the store. *Geoffrey's come back...* Geoffrey, the man in whose shadow he'd lived for the past fifty years had suddenly resurfaced. Why now? Why after all this time? He searched for a plausible reason and could think of none. But the fact was that he had and not even the need for Frank to immerse himself in the world of copper pipe and brass fittings could distract him and prevent whatever process had begun from continuing to its sad conclusion. For no good would come of it, of that he was certain. He turned and made his way thoughtfully down the passageway that would take him back to his place of work.

Whilst he'd been talking, someone had closed the door to the manager's office. Suddenly, the corridor had become eerily quiet and he felt quite alone. Halfway between the telephone and the exit he stopped. An old dryness in his throat had returned and he knew then, without even looking, that his hand had begun to shake just a little.

Unlike Frank, Pat had never had a problem with her father – not in the beginning, not later, and certainly not now. Oh, Geoffrey could be difficult, she'd discovered that, but no more so than any other human being. People in general were difficult – which is why she'd spent so much time learning how to deal with them. It was what she did for a living. She was supposed to be managing an electrical goods store, although in truth she was managing the people.

But Frank was of a different mindset. She'd concluded it was because she and her brother had followed such dissimilar paths in life. Frank was restless, always staggering from one disaster to the next, heavy with the smell of his own self-defeat and leaving behind the inevitable trail of destruction. She, on the other hand, had settled down almost immediately after leaving home to what Frank had once dismissed as 'the dull niceties of family life'. Although in recent years, since the boys had gone to college and she'd been left on her own with Terry, she'd started to experience pangs of disquiet.

But these were issues that were in no way attributable to Geoffrey. She and Terry would have to resolve things between them – but it had induced in her the feeling that there was more to life than the raising of children and the maintenance of a home and she'd begun to look outside it for answers. When Geoffrey had called it had awakened something in her, something akin to the realisation that there was a world beyond the kitchen door, the daily grind of work and the weekly expedition to her mother's house to sit and drink tea on a Saturday morning. For the first time she'd found she had 'family' and the temptation to explore it had been irresistible.

It was natural that she should be the one to keep in contact. Wasn't it always the women who stayed in touch? Weren't they the clay that bound the earth of life? *We're a family*, her mother had said, *and we stick together, no matter what*. And now, with Elisabeth out of action, it was she who'd become responsible and had shouldered what her mother had mysteriously described as 'the burden'.

But if that had been her intention, then her father was not an easy prospect to cultivate. Sometimes he would disappear completely, only to resurface much later, demanding attention. Her mother had warned her – *He'll give you a hard time, I should sup with a very long spoon if I were you*. It was then that she realised just how much Geoffrey was the progenitor of the same restless spirit that infected Frank (*So that's where he got it from, it certainly wasn't Elisabeth*) although her brother would never have thanked her for saying so.

In the end, she'd come to tolerate Geoffrey's approaches instead of encouraging them, partly through frustration and partly because she had more pressing needs of her own. On the occasions it had become a nuisance, she'd reminded herself it was familial duty rather than love that moved her. In fact, she could never claim to have liked him but a degree of acceptance had grown up between them. For the last few years they'd traded Christmas cards in the way that distant relatives often do, habitually and with no meaningful contact in-between.

He'd never suggested meeting. She'd have been surprised if he had. His life seemed full of its own importance and he appeared to have no immediate need of her beyond her role as messenger. Latterly, as soon as the idea of entertaining him in her own home entered her head, she instinctively recoiled from the prospect. Geoffrey, she'd discovered, was an acquired taste and she'd resolved to abide by her mother's advice and keep him at arm's length. But now he was ill and his latest communication had sounded like a cry for help.

That she'd thought to involve Frank must have meant she'd considered things serious. She was well aware of her brother's views (she'd heard them often enough) and his statements on the subject left no one in doubt as to his feelings.

Do not, under any circumstances, let that man anywhere near me. Do not invite him into our home. And above all, do not let him anywhere near my mother.

Rather than expressions of wish, coming from Frank they amounted to commands. He'd served in the Army and professed not to have been a stranger to violence so they carried the threat of retribution. The benefit of such strongly-voiced opinions was that at least you knew where you stood on the matter. Frank's adopted position was more than a line in the sand – it was a defensive rampart and any move against it was bound to provoke a response. One day he might flare up at the slightest thing, the next he would lie in wait to make a surprise attack. Pat had learnt to live with her brother's outbursts but for all her managerial skills she'd not yet found out how to control them. He would always come back at her, she could be sure of that – but she never knew how or when.

Today she was faced with the prospect of giving him news that he would certainly not want to hear. How would he react? Badly, she suspected, but the weight of family duty pressed on her and pushed her forward. And as she kept reminding herself, if he couldn't hear the truth from his elder sister, then who else could he hear it from?

The coffee shop at Tesco was a halfway house, lying almost equidistant from their respective places of work, although in practice it was further away for Pat. As manageress of Comet Electrical she was obliged to cross the access road to reach it, whereas all Frank had to do was stand at the entrance to Do It All, look out over the car park and there it was. It might even have paid him to stay there and watch for her arrival so he could ensure she got there first. At least it would have saved him from waiting.

As brother and sister they might have met there regularly, getting together over lunch or after work for a coffee and a chat. But despite the fact they were family, they were not socially connected and they used the place solely as a parleying ground, a piece of neutral territory where they could thrash out whatever business there was to be conducted between them. As far as Pat could recall, the last time they'd got together like this had been when Elisabeth had gone into the nursing home. That had been at her brother's instigation, although she'd had to coax his purpose out of him – these things did not come naturally to

Frank. But when he'd finally managed to tell her what had been going on, she'd instantly given her support.

You can't go on like that.

I know – but I don't want to let her go, Pat.

It was the closest she'd seen him to tears and one of the rare occasions he'd ever called her by name. That had been just over a year ago – now it was her turn to bring something to the table.

The access road was busy with lunch-hour traffic and she was running a minute or two late. Frank was already there, slumped in a window seat and staring out over the car park, looking sullen and resentful as if he were some errant child hauled up before the head teacher. The scowl on his face said it all. *Let's just get this over with.*

Pat queued for orange juice and a sandwich. She'd hoped to use the time to compose herself but there was a problem with her change and she arrived at her seat still flustered. She set her tray down in the empty space between them.

"Can I get you anything? Tea? Coffee?"

Frank shook his head. He wasn't in the least bit hungry and when it came to the matter of drink, he'd ideally have liked something stronger. Pat could tell he was already on edge.

"So what's this all about then?"

He snapped it out before she had a chance to settle. But she'd known there'd be no preliminaries, no polite enquiries as to health or children – Frank didn't do small talk.

"Look, I know you might not want to hear this…"

That much she'd prepared in those few precious moments in the queue – but Frank was already ahead of her.

"If it's anything to do with Geoffrey, you're bloody right I don't."

"Well I'm sorry, but we can't simply bury our heads in the sand and pretend that nothing's happened." She'd determined to remain calm in the face of any provocation. "We've just got to deal with it."

Frank breathed a sigh of frustration. Deal with it? Why did they have to 'deal' with it? Couldn't they just leave it alone? Although it didn't surprise him, coming from his sister. For some reason she always had to 'deal' with everything – sometimes Pat could make mountains out of molehills. As far as he was concerned, it wasn't a problem.

"So what's it got to do with me?"

"Well, he is your father."

In contrast to her earlier lie, this was an obvious truth – and for Frank, an inconvenient one. *Yes, in name only,* he thought. But out of the modicum of respect he held for his sister he outwardly relented.

"I suppose you'd better tell me what's been going on then."

The invitation came at an inopportune moment for Pat. She'd just taken a bite of her sandwich and was forced to launch into her story with her mouth full of tuna mayonnaise and salad.

"You know that Dad and I had been in contact." She brushed the crumbs neatly from her lap. "Well, last night I had a phone call." Her latest training course with Comet had been Key Concerns for Negotiators. This was Stage 1 – Preparing the Ground.

"A phone call?"

"Yes."

"He rang you?"

"No…"

"But you said you had a call."

"Yes."

"So did he call you or not?"

"No, *he* didn't, it was the hospital."

"The hospital? What hospital?"

"The hospital he's been taken into."

"Which hospital is that?"

"Oh, for goodness sake, Frank, I can't remember. Somewhere in Norfolk."

As if it really mattered!

She airily flapped her hand – his persistent questioning was getting her confused. Her meagre amount of preparation meant it was all going wrong and the story was coming out in fits and starts. Somehow they seemed to have skipped Key Concerns for Negotiators, Stages 2, 3 & 4 and progressed straight to Stage 5 – How to Deal with Stress. She took a deep breath and tried to compose herself.

"Norwich I think. I wasn't exactly taking notes at the time. I've got the details at home if you really need them."

Which of course he wouldn't – he was merely intent on scoring points.

"But they rang you?"

"Yes."

"He must have given them your number then."

"Well, yes, I suppose he must have…"

Her words slowed as she saw the trap he'd been leading her into. It was infuriating how he did this to her every time. She was supposed to be the professional, the one who was trained, whereas he came from the shop floor, untutored, but he could so easily destroy her, knocking her down through his flagrant disregard for the rules.

"You want your head tested, letting him do that!" First blow to Frank. Now he could sit there and smirk while he let her continue. "You were saying?"

"Yes, as I was saying…" *Before I was so rudely interrupted* "…the hospital rang." Her mouth was finally empty of sandwich and she could resume her speech with confidence. "Apparently he was taken in on Monday. He'd not been well the week before, there'd been several spasms and he'd been passing blood. Things got worse over the weekend so they thought it best to admit him straight away. The nurse told me they think it's bowel cancer. On top of that, he's diabetic and as you know, he smokes like a chimney."

Frank squirmed awkwardly in his chair. *As you know?* Why should she assume he knew anything at all? He wasn't privy to his father's affairs in the way that she was. And did she really have to catalogue all the gory medical details? Couldn't she just say he was unwell? And yet even that small amount of knowledge was enough to make him feel uneasy.

Pat sensed his discomfort and took the opportunity to press home her advantage.

"He's not well, Frank. He's dying."

"So? What do you expect me to do about it?"

"You could at least show some sympathy!"

But Frank was not the sympathetic type – certainly not as far as Geoffrey was concerned – and she was foolish to expect it. Under the circumstances, the best she could hope for was his bare acceptance of the facts.

"Look, I don't suppose there's very much any of us *can* do. The nurse I spoke to seemed to think it was terminal – a matter of weeks, she said, rather than months. I can tell you're not the slightest bit interested…" (Frank had turned away and was looking in the opposite direction) "…but I thought I ought to make you aware of the situation, that's all. It didn't seem right you hearing it from anyone else."

How could he object if she put it like that? Although who else he might hear it from, she had no idea.

"Well thank you so much for taking the time and trouble to let me know – I'm really grateful." For Frank, sarcasm was a well-practised art. "No doubt you're intending to go down there and fawn over him."

"Well, no, actually…"

Pat baulked at the idea. Just as she'd dismissed inviting Geoffrey to come to stay with her, going to visit him was equally unattractive. She had a store to run, there were meetings planned and there was always Terry to think of.

"So is that it then?" her brother continued. "Is that what

you've dragged me all the way over here to tell me? Geoffrey's dying, whoopee do. You can't have imagined I'd be the least bit concerned about *that*. Or is there something I'm missing here?"

There *was* more, but Pat needed a little extra time before broaching the subject.

"I'll be keeping in touch, of course, talking to the hospital, making sure he's getting the right kind of care. And if he's in there for any length of time, someone's got to see to it that his house is secure."

"Oh really... I trust you're not counting on me to get involved – you can find someone local to do it." Then Frank's face clouded over as a thought occurred. "Have you said anything to Mother, by the way?"

"Of course not!" It was more than she dared without his approval.

"Good. Let's keep it that way, shall we. My only worry is to make sure she doesn't find out. You know how much any mention of Geoffrey upsets her."

Did it though? Pat couldn't say that she'd noticed. It seemed to her that whenever she'd had cause to visit the nursing home, Elisabeth had remained totally immune to anything – Geoffrey included. An aura of imperturbable calm surrounded her that Pat found difficult to penetrate. She felt as if she were knocking at the door of a house where she knew the occupants were in but where they failed to hear her call – or simply refused to answer. But it was more than her life was worth to mention it to Frank as it would only draw a predictable tirade of abuse. *Well, you wouldn't notice would you? You're only ever there once a month, how can you expect to know what goes on? I'm the one that's there every day. I'm the one that sees what goes on. I'm the one she relies on.* And of course it was true. He *was* there every day, serving his obsession with the health and wellbeing of his mother as if it were the only thing in the world that mattered. It was the core of his 'I do more than you do' game, the game he used to justify his existence and continually put her down. Today, she decided to let it pass. There would be other, more suitable occasions on which to challenge it.

"Very well, if that's what you want. You don't think...?"

"No!" snapped her brother. "Definitely not. End of story!"

They stopped to collect their thoughts. Outside in the car park the world busied itself, ferrying its baskets of shopping. A clash rang out as two trolleys met head on. A young woman, more concerned with the text message she was sending on her mobile phone, hadn't been looking where she was going. *Sorry!* Viewed from the febrile interior of the café, there was an air of normality about it that Pat found refreshing.

Frank, meanwhile, couldn't wait to leave. "I've got to be getting back." He was already standing up, his body angled toward the exit.

"Yes, me too."

Pat scooped up her purse and then, judging it to be the most propitious moment, i.e. when he was on the point of departure and least likely to make a scene, she nervously delivered the message that had been at the forefront of her mind since it had been entrusted to her the night before.

"He wants to meet you, you know." Then, hurriedly, as if she felt the need to explain herself: "It's not me saying that, by the way. He made me promise to tell you. He wants you to go and see him."

Halfway across the café Frank came to a halt, his back toward his sister. He looked down at the floor, then closed his eyes and audibly exhaled.

Whatever it was that Pat had promised, he did not want to hear it; neither did he want to hear about Geoffrey, or hospitals, or visits, and the thought of assuming any responsibility in the matter appalled him. Better to escape now while he was still unscathed and in the absence of any further pressure he could pursue his usual strategy when it came to such things and ignore it. Given time and patience and a little bit of luck, this would all go away and he and his mother could be left in peace.

He shook his head, but he did not look round. Behind him lay hatred, fifty years of pain and the taint of a man he despised. He would not be travelling in that direction and just at that moment, even the prospect of returning to work was preferable by comparison. He took a deep breath and resumed his progress toward the way out.

Two

When he arrived home that evening, Frank struggled to open the door to the house. The news about Geoffrey had caused the shake in his right hand to worsen and although he was successful in finding the key and drawing it out of his pocket, there was a problem when it came to fitting it into the lock. After two or three failed attempts he grew tired of the exercise and resorted to grasping his wrist with his left hand to steady himself. It didn't help matters that he was desperate to get inside, off the street and away from prying eyes, where he could abandon any form of pretence.

It had been a difficult afternoon. Following the interview with his sister he'd returned to the store where he'd found it impossible to concentrate on work. His mind seemed to hover partway between York and Norwich and for the time being the technical requirements of the plumbing department were beyond him. He was acutely aware that despite spending a good half an hour in the coffee shop, he'd had no lunch and the constant desire for something to drink gnawed at an empty stomach. The flash point had been reached when he'd been incapable of deciding whether 12-millimetre metric pipework was compatible with old-style half-inch couplings, and in an uncontrollable fit of temper he'd lashed out at the display stand with his boot, sending several lengths of 2-metre copper pipe and numerous boxes of fittings crashing to the floor. Fortunately, no one else had been present to witness the incident, a fact that gave him the opportunity to blame it on a customer. His supervisor's reaction was nevertheless the same.

"Well, you'd better get it cleared up…"

He'd spent the next hour on his hands and knees in the aisle searching for missing parts.

On the drive home he found he was sweating and had to take a tight grip on the wheel to stop himself trembling, although things were palpably different once inside the house. As soon as the door closed behind him and he stood alone in the hallway he could relax and any pressure to behave immediately disappeared. It was as if the weight of social normality had been lifted from his shoulders and for the first time since answering the telephone that morning, the quivering motion in his hand had ceased. Not that long ago, he'd have rushed to the nearest cupboard, pulled out a bottle of whatever he could find and drunk himself into an incoherent state before collapsing somewhere on the living room floor. But those days were gone.

There was actually no alcohol in the place – his mother had seen to that. In one of her more lucid moments before going into the home, Elisabeth had extracted an undertaking from him that whilst she was away, he would not lapse back into any of his former habits. *You will promise me now, won't you, dear?* And out of reverence for her and his desire to stay clean, he'd consented.

The alternative was to go to the off licence and then sit on a park bench like some wino, clutching a brown paper bag. But he'd been 'dry' for over two years and to go back to that kind of behaviour now was unthinkable. Besides, it meant leaving the safety of the house he'd only just succeeded in entering.

Because to Frank, it was more than simply a home – it was a sanctuary, a place of refuge where he could escape the iniquities of the world and be himself. Whatever problems he may have suffered over the years, be they in his job (when he had one) or in his personal life (when he did not), this was where he could find the calm and comfort that arose from being in the presence of his mother. She might no longer be there in person, but she remained there in spirit and her aura continued to inhabit the rooms in her absence.

Hardly anything had altered since her departure. In the sitting room, a pair of high-backed chairs surrounded the television set and the old gas fire (there was not enough space for a sofa), while over the mantelpiece hung a garish print of the kind that had been fashionable in the 1960s. A layer of dust had begun to form on the clock but Frank had been reluctant to touch it. One day, he was convinced his mother would come back home – and when she did, he wanted her to find things just as they'd been before she went away.

He stood for a minute in the hallway, his feet planted squarely on the carpet and his back resting against the doorframe. Then he hung his keys on one of the brass hooks next to the coat stand, pushed himself forward and slowly mounted the stairs before crossing the landing to his mother's room. Every time he got home, his first act was to look in and see if she'd returned.

But today she had not, and the room was empty.

And yet the sense of her remained. The counterpane that covered her bed had been smoothed down and he imagined her reflected in the set of silver-backed hairbrushes that were laid out neatly on the dressing table. A faint trace of eau de cologne still hung in the air but it could not disguise the familiar smell of her – that smell like fine, dusted flour that had stayed with him since he'd been a child and had always described her presence. She'd been away for a year now, but for him these were things that would never fade, no matter how long she might be absent.

He paused in the doorway. It was still early evening, his neighbours had not yet come home from work and the house had the silence of a chapel. Had he been Catholic, he might have bent his knee and crossed himself for this was as close as he got to praying.

He returned to the landing and pulled open the door opposite. His own room was far simpler than his mother's and did not contain enough to become untidy. A single bed, a wardrobe, a set of drawers – what more did a man want? His desires amounted to no more than he needed to survive and the years of deprivation in the Army had taught him to be frugal. Walls were intended to support the roof over his head, not to be decorated, and as such required no adornments. A door was there to be closed and keep out draughts, not to be hung about with clothing. And besides, his regular bouts of unemployment had meant he'd no possessions with which to clutter the place and what with the rent and the expenses of the nursing home, even if he'd had the inclination, there'd been no opportunity for extravagance.

He took off his overalls and changed into a set of casual clothes. His stomach had started rumbling, reminding him that he'd eaten next to nothing since breakfast. In a moment he'd go down to the kitchen and prepare himself a simple meal, just as he'd done every day for the last twelve months, and eat it alone at the small square Formica-topped table pushed against the wall next to the fridge.

But he knew that once his tea had been consumed and the resultant debris cleared away, he'd still be left with a hollow emptiness that only a stiff drink or the company of his mother would assuage. And since the first was now denied him by his own decree – *No mum, I promise* – he'd automatically seek the latter, and having taken the keys from the hook where he'd placed them earlier, he'd start up the car for the last but one time that day and drive the two or three miles to the nursing home on the other side of town to see her.

Three

The Blue Cross Residential Care Home was housed in a late nineteenth-century property in one of the older, more prosperous areas of the city. It had once been staffed by professionally trained nurses but was now populated by a disaffected body of care assistants and NVQ trainees who had resorted to accepting the National Minimum Wage for the sake of looking after elderly women in their dotage.

The building had barely changed since its conversion and it consequently suffered from all the disadvantages of Victorian architectural planning. Its high ceilings meant high heating bills, the sash-framed windows gave rise to draughts and the siting of the kitchen facilities meant it was constantly permeated by the smell of boiled cabbage. Its sole redeeming feature was the fact that its walls were painted white both inside and out, so it had a bright external appearance and its rooms took on a light and airy feel. When he'd first come to see it, that had been the main reason Frank had chosen it and through the medium of his daily visits, it was now as familiar to him as the house he'd just left – its sounds, its smells, the repetitive nature of its monotonous routine.

In the beginning the staff would seek his identity on arrival, but after a while this formality had been dropped. Today it would be just *Good evening, Mr Johnson*. Or, if he were on a late shift and he'd come in before going to work, *Good morning. My, you're in early today*. At first, they'd mention his mother by name, but now that had gone too and these days it was no more than *She's in the day lounge* or *The last time I saw her she was on her way to her room*.

The first person he'd come across would invariably be Sheila, the manageress. Her office was immediately next to the entrance, partly for convenience and partly, he suspected, so she could keep an eye on whoever was visiting. She was probably in her thirties, on the short side, a little stocky perhaps but nevertheless busy in her black skirt and jacket, a large set of keys dangling from her expanded waist. If she was not in the foyer, he'd often find himself bumping into her in a corridor and it was at these chance meetings that they'd discuss whatever business they needed to conduct. *Is everything alright, Mr Johnson?* Or *There's something I've been meaning to speak to you about...* In fact, apart from their initial interview when he'd sat immobile in front of her, almost unable to speak, he'd only been into her office the once and that had been an occasion he was unlikely to forget.

But tonight the foyer was empty, Sheila was nowhere to be seen and he made his way unchallenged. It was just after seven and Elisabeth would already be back in her room. The evening meal was served on trays in the day lounge rather than in the dining room and when the plates had been cleared away, the residents would stay seated in front of the television or at the recreational tables strewn about at the back. For the first few weeks after her arrival Elisabeth had followed the same practice as the others, but then she'd begun to get restless at the sound of their idle chatter and one evening she'd demanded to be taken straight back to her accommodation after dinner.

Later on, his mother had confided in him as to why. *They talk such a lot of nonsense in there, Frank. I can't be doing with it.* So nowadays she was accustomed to spending the evenings alone in the quiet of her room. The only company she would allow at these times would be Frank's – or Pat's, if she could be bothered to turn up.

Elisabeth's apartment lay in the middle of a long passageway. As Frank rounded the corner leading into it, her carer emerged from her room and passed by in the opposite direction. He was wearing his usual cheeky grin and clutching a package beneath his arm.

Frank didn't like Danny – but then Frank didn't like anyone much. In Danny's case it was probably on account of his youth, his spiky blond hair and the way he wore his trousers at half-mast to expose the whiteness of his socks. Or perhaps it was the little silver earring he sported. *He wouldn't have lasted five minutes in the Army,* thought Frank. And according to his mother, Danny was not to be trusted.

Frank stopped briefly outside her door and looked at the inscription on the nameplate. *Mrs E. Johnson.* At some point in what he hoped was a dim and distant future, that wording would change. He shuddered at the thought, tapped gently twice, called out "Mum?" in his softest voice, then pushed the door open and went in without waiting for a reply.

She was exactly where he'd expected her to be, sitting with her back to him in the only comfortable seat the room contained, looking out into the garden. The window faced west, catching the light from the fading sun, and all he could see of her above the top of her chair was a mass of silver hair. An attempt had been made at brushing it (was that what Danny had been doing?) but it had the consistency of wire wool and tended to retain the waywardness that was such a characteristic part of her, as if it were an element of her spirit that refused to be conquered.

"Mum?" he enquired gently, as he'd done outside the door. But there was no reply or movement of the head which might indicate she was aware of his arrival.

"Mum?"

He called again, louder this time, and approached the chair, gripping the narrowness of her shoulder. Beneath her nightdress he could sense the frailty of her body, a parchment of dry skin pulled taut over old bones. At last she acknowledged his presence, reaching up with her hand and plying his fingers. She seemed so desperately vulnerable but despite all her weakness, she managed to give off an extraordinary warmth.

His grip tightened as he squeezed gently in reply, then stooped to plant his customary kiss on the top of her head.

"I was just looking at the birds..." she began.

"What birds?"

"The blackbirds. Out there. In the garden."

She removed her hand to point and the precious moment of contact was broken.

Frank manoeuvred round her and went to the window, pulling aside the net curtain and looking out for himself.

The main advantage of the room was the view it afforded of the grounds of the property. Immediately outside was a large patch of lawn bordered by trees and a mass of shrubbery. Frank had chosen it specifically for this purpose. The alternative had been something closer to the day lounge and although larger, it looked out over the busy road at the front. Elisabeth had always shown an interest in nature (it was she who'd organised the bird feeder in their small back yard at home) and he'd thought it would be a source of pleasure for her and help to fill the long hours of the day. He'd been proved right and now that she no longer frequented the lounge after dinner, it was making her evenings more bearable.

Frank stared out into the garden, shading his eyes against the sun's last rays. Try as he might, he could see no birds. It would have been helpful if he could as it would have given him a clue as to his mother's state of mind. In recent weeks that had become something of a lottery and whenever he came to visit, he never knew whether she would be in the same world as he was or one of her own making. Like a boat cast off on an ebbing tide, she seemed to be drifting further and further away from the shore.

He wondered whether her birds were real or imaginary. Whichever it was, he'd come to the conclusion he should go along with it – to contradict her and tell her she was seeing things would be to upset her unnecessarily. And anyway, she might even have been right.

"Ah yes..."

He let the net curtain fall back into place and turned to face her.

She was dressed as if preparing for bed and he noticed that her feet were bare. On top of her nightdress was a quilted dressing gown but the pop socks she wore during the day had been removed. It was normal practice that when residents returned to their rooms after dinner they changed into their nightwear. Sometimes his mother needed help – but she should have been wearing slippers, so whoever had assisted her had probably forgotten to put them on. Either that or Elisabeth had taken them off herself, it was impossible to tell. He knelt down in front of her and took her feet in his hands. They felt like blocks of ice.

"What's happened here?"

"He's taken them."

"Who's taken them?"

"That boy."

Danny. If Elisabeth was to be believed, Danny was capable of anything. Frank could cheerfully have strangled him, the aggravation he caused his mother. *One day I'll swing for you.*

And yet he could hardly believe the boy's job was worth a pair of old slippers. After his mother's derogatory comments, Frank had seen to it that there were no items of value in the place. There was never any money in the room (residents had no need of it) and any possessions of any significance were still at home, waiting for Elisabeth's return. There had to be another answer – his mother had lost them or, as was more likely, she'd put them somewhere 'safe' and had simply forgotten about them. Besides, she did have form as far as slippers were concerned. That was how it had all begun.

Not long after he'd started working at Do It All, Frank had arrived home to find Elisabeth waiting by the front door, dressed in her street clothes. It was a Friday, he'd just finished his shift and he'd arranged to take her to the supermarket for the monthly shop. They were out for no more than an hour and as soon as they returned, they took all their purchases into the kitchen and began putting them away. It was while he was stowing the milk in the fridge that Frank came across his mother's slippers, placed neatly side by side on the middle shelf.

At the time he'd thought nothing of it and had put it down purely to absent-mindedness on her part. He was equally guilty of such small faults – he could think of countless times when he'd gone upstairs to look for something only to discover that when he got there he'd completely forgotten why. And yet, as soon as he went back downstairs the purpose of his mission would come back to him. He could hardly accuse his mother of anything untoward.

His suspicions were fully aroused a week or so later. His mother's slippers had now been joined by a tube of toothpaste. Added to which, his breakfast cereal had begun to bear a marked resemblance to the type of nuts and seeds found in bird food, while out in the back yard, the bird feeder was full of muesli.

He resolved to say nothing about it but these occurrences caused him to monitor Elisabeth's behaviour more closely. Over the course of the next few months his observations revealed other disturbing traits, but it was not until these became of a personal nature that he decided to take action. The appearance of odd items in the fridge and the substitution of bird food for cereal were problems he felt he could deal with, but matters of female hygiene were not. He prided himself on being his mother's protector and provider and so agonised about it for days, but in the end he felt compelled to talk to his sister about it. Sitting in the comfortable surroundings of the coffee shop at Tesco, Pat's response had sounded rather facile.

"That's unacceptable, Frank. She'll have to go into a home."

An easy answer for her – far harder for Frank.

She was quick to come to judgement, Pat, especially when it concerned their mother. It angered him to think she gave so little thought to the matter whereas he was forced to face up to it every day. It was all very well for her to talk the way she did – she wouldn't have to deal with the disruption, never mind the expense. But in truth he'd known it was the only way forward, both for his own sake as well as his mother's. The rest, as they say, was history. And now, a year later, here was Elisabeth, up to her old tricks again.

He'd discovered that the best thing to do was to try and follow her lead. It appeared to be the path of least resistance but in fact it was much harder than it looked as his natural incli- nation was to correct her at every turn. That would only serve to confuse her and add to her distress, so he'd decided on the route of appeasement. His strategy had been reinforced by the comments of the consultant psychologist who'd attended her initial assessment meeting. With his half-frame glasses balanced on the tip of his nose and his sharp pinstriped suit, he'd cut an imposing figure.

"In her condition, your mother needs constant reassurance, Mr Johnson. Try not to contradict her too much, even though she may obviously be in the wrong. That may seem strange to you but it will help her to gain confidence if she feels what she is saying is right. At this stage we need to try and induce a positive frame of mind. That way she is likely to make progress much more quickly."

Frank had thought his advice contradictory. How did you put something right if not through constant correction? That's how things were handled in the Army. But that approach had left him with a problem and unlike his sergeant major, these people were supposed to know what they were talking about. So now, when Elisabeth mislaid something and afterwards pointed her finger at 'that boy' he was minded to play along and give his usual reply.

Ah, yes…

But there was one subject on which he was not so ready to comply. It had arisen the first time he'd visited her in her room after she'd been installed. He was still unfamiliar with the place – as were the staff with him – so he'd had to be escorted through the building and he'd agreed to meet Sheila in the foyer especially for the purpose.

"Your mother's doing fine, Mr Johnson."

She'd thrown this back over her shoulder as she bustled down the corridor in front of him, her set of keys jangling at her belt. It was welcome news, but when she opened the door and ushered him into his mother's apartment, there was a shock awaiting him.

"Now then, Mrs Johnson," Sheila had announced. "Here's your son come to see you."

"He's not my son, you know!" his mother had retorted from her armchair.

It had really upset him. How could she possibly come up with something so hurtful after all that he'd done for her? Any thought of passive agreement flew straight out of the window – he was not going along with that, never mind what any fancy therapist might think.

"You can't say that, Mum, you know it's not true."

And he'd looked straight round at Sheila in an appeal for help. *You see what she's like? You see what I have to put up with?*

Later on, he went back to the foyer and waited outside Sheila's office until she returned. He was desperate to speak to her and paced constantly up and down, mumbling to himself under his breath. When she did at last arrive and realised the state he was in, she took one of the keys from her belt and opened the door to admit him rather than let a scene develop outside.

"Steady on, Mr Johnson." She motioned him to the chair in front of her desk. "Take a seat. Can I get you a cup of tea?"

She knew what she was doing. As like as not, he wasn't the first relative she'd had to deal with in this condition.

But Frank was indifferent as to tea. A glass of brandy would have been more acceptable although it was as well there was not one on offer.

"So what was all that about?"

He didn't need to elaborate as she must have known precisely what he was referring to. She sat down and arranged her elbows on the desk in an attempt to get the situation under control. People were far less excitable when they were all sitting down. Had she been there, Pat would have done exactly the same.

"It's something we see quite a lot of I'm afraid, Mr Johnson. I wouldn't worry about it unduly if I were you – your mother's not the only one. We have plenty of instances where residents don't acknowledge their family. You see," and she leant purposefully forward, "when someone comes here for the first time it can be quite traumatic. They're suddenly thrown into a new set of surroundings and they have to mix with a completely different set of people. It's potentially confusing – and if they're already in a fragile state of mind to begin with, then, under the circumstances..." She sat back and let him draw his own conclusions.

"You mean she simply doesn't know who I am?"

"I wouldn't go so far as to say that, Mr Johnson. She probably remembers your face but she can't always place it in the right context."

"And will it always be like that?"

The thought that he might be mentally parted from her for an indefinite period was almost unbearable.

"No, it may vary from one day to the next depending on her state of mind."

"You mean one day she'll know me and the next day she might not?"

"Exactly."

"I see..."

Or so he thought. He'd always imagined she'd be there for him in every sense, but now it seemed she wasn't. And just like the advice from the psychologist, the whole idea sounded utterly implausible. How could a mother fail to recognise her own flesh and blood after all these years? It beggared belief.

The irony of it was that whenever Pat arrived – Pat, who merely put in the odd appearance once a month; Pat, whose tokens of affection were no more than a bunch of grapes or a pot plant – whenever *she* turned up, she was greeted with open arms as if she were the long-lost daughter. Whereas he, despite his constant round of daily visits, had to make do with his mother's occasional acceptance. It was as if the familiarity that had grown up between them had turned to a form of contempt. By comparison, it made the matter of the disappearing slippers pale into insignificance.

In the meanwhile, this current crisis would have to be dealt with. The offending articles would have to be found and reunited with his mother but in such a way as to spare her from embarrassment. A surrogate culprit had already been identified and for Elisabeth's sake this perception might have to be reinforced, be it right or wrong. For all the trouble he caused, sometimes Danny was a convenient answer to a lot of Frank's problems.

If her slippers were still in the apartment, locating their whereabouts would not be too difficult. There were only so many places where they could be – under the bed, in a drawer, at the back of the wardrobe (she couldn't reach the top) or behind the curtains. There was no kitchen – cooking facilities were deemed to be dangerous – and hence no fridge where she could have stored them as she'd done at home.

He decided to begin the search in the small en-suite bathroom.

"What are you doing?"

Elisabeth's eyes had followed him across the room.

"I'm looking for your slippers."

"He's taken them."

"Who's taken them?"

"That boy."

It was a repeat of the exchange they'd had no more than a few moments before. It had become typical of their conversations over recent months, the same phrases gone over again and again in endless repetition. For Elisabeth of course it was fresh each time, and in her goldfish bowl of a room she swam helplessly round and round, unable to recall anything beyond her last and progressively decreasing circuit. At least it got her talking – far better that than she should sit there in silence, brooding.

He found them in the waste bin beneath the sink. How they'd got there he would find out later but for the moment he contented himself with retrieving them and taking them to her. He thought this would please her but all he got for his pains was a dissatisfied frown.

"Oh, I don't want those! They're my old ones – I threw those in the bin. I've got a new pair." She assumed an expression of exaggerated pride.

"A new pair?"

"Yes, I got them from one of the women in the day lounge. She's got arthritis or something. Anyway, her feet got all swollen up and she had to take them off so I thought I'd make use of them. Huh!" Her tone changed to one of contempt. "She's a silly old biddy, if you ask me. Fancy leaving a new pair of slippers lying around like that!"

Gradually, he was eking the story out of her. This was why he needed to be there every day, in constant attendance. He only had to turn his back for a second and look what happened.

"So where exactly are these new slippers then, Mum?"

"He's taken them."

"Who's taken them?"

"That boy."

Given practice and with the addition of a few decent jokes, they could have made a comedy sketch out of it. He could have played Abbott to her Costello in a variation of the old routine about the names of the players on the baseball team.

So, who's on first?

That's right.

Ok, but what's the name of the player on first base?

No, Watt's on second. Hoo's on first.

Wait a minute, I asked you that! I'm confused, let's start again. So, who's on first?

That's right...

He'd heard it once and laughed – but in his mother's case it wasn't remotely funny.

He knelt down beside her and fitted the slippers onto her feet.

"Well, you'll have to make do with these until I can get your new ones back."

And just like the birds in the garden, whether these new slippers were real or imaginary he never really knew, but it was important to maintain the pretence. If necessary, in a day or so he'd go out and buy another pair. If that's what it took to make her happy...

Because making his mother happy was Frank's primary objective. In the course of his visits he would naturally seek her company and ensure she was alright, but these occasions were far more satisfactory if he could leave her with a smile on her face. Then he felt he'd done as much as he could. She seemed happiest when talking about times gone by and she would willingly recount events from long ago of which he had no personal knowledge. It was a potentially dangerous ploy. She'd doubtless been through much pain, but here and there pockets of joy could be found and the secret was to get her to latch on to them.

Sometimes he marvelled at her powers of recollection. In respect of the present her memory was a tangled mass of narrow country lanes, cul-de-sacs and dead ends through which no progress could be made. But her distant past was like an open road, a highway along which she could travel with considerable ease. And once she'd set off down it, the views it afforded could be quite revealing. It gave him a lift to hear her talk about them and once she'd got started, he could sit and listen to her for hours.

He was encouraged in his efforts by the remarks of the consultant psychologist.

"Like many women her age, your mother is a treasure trove of memories, Mr Johnson," he said, peering over the top of his half-frame glasses. "There's a great store of knowledge buried deep within her. If you can succeed in unlocking it, the mental exercise she will derive from it will benefit her immensely."

Once he'd got her settled of an evening, if she seemed in the mood he would try and set her going down this route. It was helpful if he could create a scene within which she could tell her stories, and so he'd turn on the standard lamp and draw the curtains in an effort to create the right atmosphere. In the winter, he'd light the gas fire for warmth. Then, when all was carefully prepared he'd try and initiate a conversation, usually by saying *Do you remember…?* as a means of sparking her off.

They'd reached that stage now and with the business of her slippers resolved, he deemed it appropriate to begin the process and set about organising the lamp and the curtains in the usual way. The sun had gone in and the light was fading, but there was no need as yet for the fire.

He'd got as far as *Do you remember…?* when he realised it was on the tip of his tongue to say *Geoffrey* and he stopped abruptly before he could complete the sentence.

Geoffrey… The name he must not mention. In an unguarded moment he'd been a split second away from disaster – all because he'd not been concentrating – and the subject which had been lurking at the back of his mind had suddenly leapt forward to occupy the space at the front.

Elisabeth twisted round in her chair.

"Do I remember what?"

"Nothing…" He hesitated, trying to gloss over his mistake. "I was thinking of something else, that's all."

"So don't you want to talk tonight then, dear?"

She seemed disappointed. The lamp, the curtains, all had led her to believe he was about to lead her on one of her nightly trips down memory lane, and suddenly he'd backed out of it.

But the moment had gone and he knew that any chance they might have had of connecting that evening had disappeared. They could have discussed a dozen different subjects – the house, Pat, her grandchildren, even life in the caravan – but there were areas he was anxious to steer clear of. Paramount amongst them was Geoffrey and in his current state of mind, Frank didn't trust himself to avoid it. After she'd broken her news that lunchtime, he'd told his sister that Elisabeth was not to be informed, whatever the circumstances. He would do anything to protect her and yet, here he was, ready to blurt it out at the first available opportunity.

"I'm sorry, Mum. I'm feeling rather tired to be honest. I think I'll give it a miss tonight if you don't mind."

"Well, if you must…"

It was a feeble excuse and he was rather ashamed of it although had she known what he was thinking, she might have forgiven him more easily.

In an effort to compensate, he made a special trip to the day lounge to fetch her a cup of tea and set it down on the occasional table next to her. It was still there when he left, cold and untouched and there was no sign of the smile he so dearly cherished. They parted on good terms, nonetheless.

"Goodnight, Mum."

"Goodnight, dear."

She proffered her cheek for a brief kiss and he enjoyed one last squeeze of her hand before closing the door behind him.

Standing alone in the car park, Frank stared implacably at the surrounding hedge then smashed his fist onto the bonnet of his Ford Fiesta. *Damn!* Why did this have to happen? He thought she'd be safe, she was in a nursing home for christsake, a place where she couldn't be got at. What more could he do? He'd sworn to protect her, lay down his life for her if he had to, rather than let anything spoil what they'd managed to achieve. And yet somehow he felt that he'd failed her.

This time he'd been lucky, he could see that. He'd come within a fraction of saying something he knew he'd regret – next time it might not be so easy. Pat's phone call had pushed open a door into what had been a locked and shuttered room. A shadowy figure stood before him. It carried a sickly disease that had infected him and whatever happened, he must not pass that on to his mother.

He tried to block the image from his mind on the drive home. He no more wanted to be reminded of it at Balfour Terrace than he did at the nursing home and he turned the radio up full blast in an attempt to shut it out. As soon as he got in, he did his rounds as normal, switched off all the lights and went straight up to bed. It was only just after nine o'clock but it felt more like midnight. He was brutally tired but there was too much on his mind to allow him to sleep and he lay awake until the early hours, gazing up at the ceiling.

In the morning he could look forward to another dreary day amongst the copper pipes and fittings of the plumbing department at Do It All. But here, even though he'd shut every door and window tight, he could not prevent the thought of his father from entering the house. His name ran through his head like a dripping tap *Geoffrey, Geoffrey, Geoffrey* and he knew now, as he'd always known, that there'd be no peace until the matter was resolved, one way or another.

Part Two

Elisabeth

One

They think I'm crazy.

It sounded absurd – but the belief was never far from her mind. Who could blame them? She was elderly, female and living in a nursing home – what more proof did they want? All they saw was an old woman, infirm, sometimes unsteady on her feet and to all intents and purposes, losing her marbles. Nobody ever thought to ask her how she felt, what she was thinking – she might just as well have been in prison for the way that they treated her.

Frank had tricked her – probably with the best of intentions, but he'd tricked her all the same. *It won't be for long, Mum, honest. It's just a temporary situation. I'll have you back in no time.* He'd made it sound like a holiday, as if she were going to a hotel. *Just a few days, Mum, that's all – until you get better. I'll look after you, Mum, you can count on that.* But Frank had said a lot of things and had made a lot of promises, not least of which had been his commitment to giving up his little habit. *No, Mum, I won't touch a drop – not while you're away.* The funny thing was, for all his fussing and insistence, she hadn't actually felt unwell.

She remembered she had a house – she had a very clear picture of it – but she couldn't recall how to get there. Once, she'd tried to go home, had packed all her belongings into two carrier bags and walked smartly through the front door, determined to make her escape. But as soon as she'd got into the garden, she couldn't find her way out and had wandered about the rose-beds searching for an exit. It was Danny who'd come to rescue her. *Now then, Mrs Johnson. Out for a little walk, are we?* Another of his snidey remarks.

That above all else had convinced her she was never going to leave. She was never going back to Balfour Terrace and for all its defects, this was now her home, never mind what Frank said. It was shortly after her arrival but she'd been there long enough to know that the only way people left was feet first in a wooden box – only she wasn't going to tell Frank that. You had to be careful what you said to Frank.

Frank, her dear boy! Frank, who for all the trouble he'd caused her over the years was now the one she relied on – or so he kept telling her. Who else could she turn to? It was no good asking Pat. She had a job and two boys and a husband (although she struggled to remember his name) and that was enough for any woman. So it was Frank she'd come to lean on, just as he'd leant on her.

And yet she still worried about him, as if he were the one in the home. Despite the sincerity of his pledge, she was concerned he would somehow renege and return to the bottle, however involuntarily. Although it wasn't the fact of his drinking that bothered her, it was more the idea that if he did regress she wouldn't be there to help him. And as she knew from experience, when Frank was left to fight his battles alone, he rarely succeeded in winning them.

Even now, something was troubling him – she could tell from the evening before. He'd arrived at the same time as usual but he'd seemed flustered and unsure of himself. And when he'd laid his hand on her shoulder and she'd reached up to touch it, she'd detected that tell-tale tremor which meant he was suffering from the shakes. Something had unsettled him and he wasn't going to tell her about it. But Frank wasn't good at keeping secrets – living cheek by jowl in a small house had seen to that – and his attempt at concealment was futile. She'd already guessed the cause.

He'd started off on his nightly routine just as usual. The curtains had been drawn, the lamp had been lit and he'd got as far as *Do you remember…?* when he'd stopped rather abruptly. But even before he'd thought of it himself, she'd sensed the word *Geoffrey* forming on his lips: Geoffrey, Frank's old and ancient enemy, the symbol of all that was wrong in his world.

And did she remember Geoffrey? Of course she did! How

could she possibly forget? Once upon a time, they'd been married. And despite all Frank's tirades about his infidelity, his lack of responsibility and his general dereliction of duty, the memories she carried were much, much warmer and she looked back on those times with fondness. She'd been young and impressionable and far more importantly, in love, and she could not expect Frank to understand. For instance, it would shock him to know that in one of the zipped compartments of her purse, she still kept a photograph as a reminder.

It had been taken at Weston-super-Mare in the summer of 1950. Now tinted sepia with age, it showed the two of them, her and Geoffrey, walking briskly along the promenade arm in arm. Her hair had been jet black then – not the mass of silvery white it was now, all tangled up like a bird's nest. She'd continually tried to brush it flat but there'd been a curl to it she'd never been able to eradicate. She'd taken a lot more care over her appearance in those days.

She was wearing a pleated summer skirt and a pair of tennis shoes, and slung over her shoulder was a box camera of the type that was popular at the time. She'd always been on the short side, five foot four at the most, and in her low-heeled pumps the top of her head barely protruded above the height of Geoffrey's shoulder.

He was tall and possessed of an athletic build – handsome too, brown from the summer sun and with a mop of floppy hair he was always pushing back from his forehead. In those days it was fashionable for men to wear an open-necked shirt and cravat – no wonder she'd fallen for him so. She'd just turned twenty and he was twenty-seven although she didn't know it at the time. Even if she had, it wouldn't have made a scrap of difference – she was head over heels and oblivious to considerations of that kind. Besides, as an older man, it made him all the more attractive.

The picture had been taken by one of those photo johnnies who patrolled the promenade. You'd be minding your own business when suddenly one of them would leap out in front of you, brandishing a camera like the one she was carrying, and proceed to snap away at you. Once they'd captured your image, they'd force their card on you and tell you that the print would be available the following day if you'd care to collect it for just a few shillings. And perhaps for a bit of fun they must have gone to look for it in the photographer's shop window for her copy carried a stamp on the back with the words:

Further Copies or Enlargements
Can be obtained Winter or Summer
From JACKSONS PHOTOS LTD
WESTON-SUPER-MARE

Exactly when it was taken she couldn't be sure – they'd spent a lot of time together in Weston-super-Mare that summer.

Two

It had begun on the night of her birthday. She was not quite 'coming of age' but it was the next best thing and she'd arranged with her friend Millie to go out somewhere and celebrate. She was working as an operator at the Telephone Exchange in Bristol and earlier that day, during a lull in traffic, they'd called each other to finalise their plans. Millie was a receptionist at the BBC on Whiteladies Road and their respective positions gave them ample opportunity to chat. Sometimes they'd spend hours on the phone, just talking.

The news that afternoon was dramatic. Millie could hardly contain herself and Elisabeth knew immediately that something was afoot as her friend's normally dispassionate voice had degenerated into a high-pitched squeak.

"Lizzie? You'll never guess what!"

"What?"

"We're in luck. There's a party tonight! How bizarre! Some of the gang are getting together at Freddy's place in Clifton. It's not that far from the office and it sounds such fun. Do say you'll come."

"Of course I'll come."

Elisabeth was always happy to oblige. Millie was the one with the contacts – you never met anyone new stuck inside the Telephone Exchange.

"Oh well done, Lizzie, you're such a sport. I do so want to be there and you know a girl can't go anywhere on her own these days. There might even be some celebrities. They say Charles Cochran's going and he's awfully famous!"

Charles Cochran was not a name Elisabeth was familiar with but it was not reason enough to deny her friend. Millie continued squeaking.

"Good, that's settled then. I'll meet you at the bus stop as usual. Is seven o' clock alright?"

"Yes, seven will be fine."

They were just on the point of discussing what to wear when a light began to blink on the switchboard and Elisabeth had to hurriedly cut off.

"Millie? I'll have to go, there's a call coming in. See you tonight at seven. How exciting!"

And for a girl who was used to the odd night at the cinema, it *was* exciting. What more could she ask for on her twentieth birthday? An evening out with her friend, the prospect of meeting some interesting people – there could hardly be anything better. The only problem would be with her father.

Arthur Johnson was both a civil servant and a Presbyterian, and this heady mix of bureaucracy and puritan beliefs meant he was a strict disciplinarian. In his book it was simple – rules were rules, birthdays or not, and if you broke them you were damned for eternity. The idea that a woman, never mind his own daughter, should be allowed out at night unless in the company of a male member of her immediate family was anathema to him. And since Elisabeth was an only child and he was not prepared to take her himself, she'd have to stay in – he'd made up his mind on the matter. This edict came as no surprise to Elisabeth. It was not the first time her father had confused parenthood with tyranny.

But Elisabeth was nothing if not spirited and fought her corner admirably. If a girl couldn't go out for the evening at the age of twenty then when could she? Besides, she was going with Millie who was already twenty-one and therefore counted as an 'adult', albeit female. Brave words, but they had little effect on her father and to add to her distress, Dorothy, her mother, a timid little thing who pursued a policy of constant appeasement toward her husband, piped up and begged her not to go against his wishes. It was her mother's betrayal that decided her, and after a terrible scene in which she yelled that she wished she'd never been born at all and then there'd be no birthday to argue about, she stormed out of the house with her father's words ringing in her ears. *If you go now, don't expect to come back here. The door will be locked on your return.*

The suburb of Bristol where they lived lay at the foot of a steep hill. It would have been better for Elisabeth had she been obliged to climb it as the physical exertion might have slowed her emotions as well as her body. As it was, she turned down toward the Bath Road and the slight descent only served to accelerate her feelings. She arrived at the bus stop in floods of tears.

Millie was already waiting.

"Goodness me, Lizzie, whatever's the matter?"

"I've had the most frightful row."

"Oh really? Do tell me about it."

So she did, word for word, spinning it out between sobs into her already sodden handkerchief. Millie was appalled.

"Gosh, Lizzie, that's dreadful."

It was, but Millie could afford to talk like that. She was already twenty-one and could do as she liked.

As a way of marking her rebellion, Elisabeth insisted on sitting on the top deck of the bus up at the front. If she'd been with her father she'd have had to sit downstairs at the back. As to what might greet her when she got home that night she had no idea, and as the two girls enjoyed their elevated journey into town, their thoughts became fixed on the evening ahead.

The party itself was a complete anti-climax. Freddy's place was a run-down, one-bedroom flat on the ground floor in the seedier part of Clifton. It was easy enough to find. Someone had left one of the front windows open and the sound of a jazz dance tune from a cracked 78 was spilling out into the street. The same music bled out from beneath the door and as they stood in the corridor waiting for a reply to their knock, there were butterflies in Elisabeth's stomach.

Freddy himself answered, a young man in his mid-twenties.

Millie had made him sound suave and attractive but he was actually rather portly and squinted at them from behind a pair of National Health spectacles. There was a look of disappointment on his face as if he'd been hoping it was someone else.

"Oh, hello, Millie. I see you've invited a friend." He gave Elisabeth a cursory glance. "Hmm... I don't suppose you've brought anything to drink? We're running short and I don't want to go out unless I absolutely have to."

Millie shook her head.

"Well, I suppose you'd better come in anyway."

He stood to one side and ushered them in.

The door opened directly into the living area. It felt like a large room – probably because the furniture had been pushed back against the walls to create a space in the middle for dancing. But nobody was dancing at all, despite the continual encouragement from the gramophone in one corner. The other guests were mostly gauche young men like Freddy (only not so portly) and lay sprawled on the sofa and the adjoining chairs in what appeared to be a state of abject boredom. In contrast to the spirited sound of the jazz, the place was filled with a feeling of lethargy and either they had all exhausted themselves or, as seemed more likely, the party had never really got going to begin with. The reason for the open window immediately became apparent as all the ashtrays were full and the air was thick with cigarette smoke. Dotted about on various book shelves and side tables (and, Elisabeth noted, on the floor) were numerous empty bottles of wine. Whatever impression Millie might have given, it was not in accordance with her idea of the smart set.

Freddy took their coats into the one and only bedroom, then waved them toward the kitchen.

"You're welcome to whatever you can find. The glasses are in the cupboard over the sink."

And he simply left them to it. Elisabeth had the distinct feeling that if they'd brought alcohol, he might have been a lot more attentive.

But he was right and they were definitely running short. Glasses were easy to come by but the difficulty lay in finding anything to put in them. Elisabeth was not yet accustomed to these affairs and stood aside to let Millie rummage through the empties racked up on the draining board. After a moment or two her friend let out a loud "Aha!" and produced a squat-shaped bottle. In the base lurked an inch or so of clear fluid.

"What is it?" asked Elisabeth.

Millie sniffed at it gently.

"I think it's gin. Anyway, whatever it is, it'll do."

She poured the contents out into two glasses.

Elisabeth sniffed gently at hers. It smelt awfully strong and if she were honest with herself, rather disagreeable.

"Hadn't we better have something to go with it?" she asked. Although what one drank with gin, she really had no idea.

"Good thinking," said Millie and topped the glasses up with some orange. "Well, bottoms up."

She drained half her glass in one go and invited Elisabeth to do the same.

Elisabeth was cautious and confined herself to an exploratory sip. There was a burning taste at the back of her throat and she felt as if she wanted to wretch. As soon as Millie's back was turned she threw the contents of her glass down the sink and replaced it with pure orange.

"Shall we go through?" said Millie.

"If you like..."

And firmly clutching her glass of orange as if it were the one thing she could be sure of in this strange and unpredictable world, she returned to the sitting room.

The words 'sitting room' seemed particularly apt. Nothing had changed since their arrival and as every seat in the place was occupied, they were obliged to stand in a corner and observe proceedings. Not that there was a great deal to observe. The only entertainment was provided by their host who shuffled about the room quietly bemoaning the lack of alcohol and occasionally fiddling with the gramophone and recycling the pile of 78s. Celebrities – Charles Cochran in particular – were conspicuous by their absence, and a meeting of interesting people with interesting ideas it was certainly not. Even Millie was forced to comment.

"This is disappointing…"

The only event of any significance was when Geoffrey arrived.

They must have been there for an hour. Elisabeth knew it was a while because she recognised one of the jazz tunes repeated from the stack. At the same time there was a noise out in the street and the throaty roar of a sports car could be heard drawing up outside. Freddy went over to the window and poked his head out to investigate.

"Geoffrey's here! Thank God for that."

A moment later a pair of feet came marching down the corridor, the door opened and Geoffrey stepped into the room.

Elisabeth had heard of the expression 'making an entrance' but this was the first time she'd seen it in practice. To the untrained eye it appeared quite natural, but there was enough about it to suggest it was staged. Geoffrey was of imposing height and wore a long brown overcoat draped over his shoulders with the collar deliberately turned up. A white silk scarf hung nonchalantly about his neck and he looked the picture of an off-duty fighter pilot. More importantly, protruding from the folds of his coat each hand carried a bottle of wine. Their host welcomed him with open arms.

"Geoffrey! How nice to see you!"

"Freddy, dear boy." The voice was smooth but without being plummy. "I was just passing so I thought I'd drop in."

Elisabeth was so taken with his appearance that she failed to spot the obvious inconsistency. To be 'just passing' but to be simultaneously clutching two bottles of wine must have taken a certain degree of planning.

This was of no concern to Freddy however.

"Here, let me take those…"

He seized the bottles and made off in the direction of the kitchen.

Geoffrey called after him.

"Pour me one out while you're at it…"

While he waited for his drink, he took out a silver case and extracted a cigarette which he tapped adroitly on the back of his hand before placing it between his lips and lighting it up.

Elisabeth was mesmerised. Compared to the other party-goers, here was a man of the world and although his actions were occasionally contrived, they were certainly not awkward. He seemed perfectly at ease with himself and gave off an air of sophistication. After a while she forced herself to look away as she realised that she'd hardly taken her eyes off him from the moment he'd walked in. This must have registered with Geoffrey because as soon as Freddy had returned with his glass of wine and removed his coat and scarf, he made his way straight across to talk to them.

He began by addressing himself to Millie.

"Hello, I didn't realise you were going to be here. What a surprise!"

He made it sound as though she were the only person in the room. Elisabeth looked steadfastly into the distance, afraid of catching his eye.

"What on earth is that?"

He nodded in the direction of their drinks.

"We think it's gin," said Millie. "But it tastes awfully weak. I'm afraid we've rather drowned it."

"I should say you have by the look of it. Why don't you let me get you something decent?"

He caught Freddy's attention and motioned him to fetch two

more glasses of wine. His careful turn back allowed him to take in Elisabeth.

"Aren't you going to introduce me to your friend?"

"Of course. Elisabeth, this is Geoffrey Jones…"

Elisabeth's face reddened and unsure of exactly what to do, she resorted to shaking his hand. It felt dry and smooth whereas she was sure her own must have seemed like a piece of damp lettuce. Her confusion was further compounded as Freddy arrived with the drinks and she was obliged to let go and sort herself out.

She remembered little of the next hour, save that it seemed to pass very quickly. The listless background melted away and she lost sight of the gauche young men and their mood of indifference – for the moment she had eyes and ears only for Geoffrey Jones. He had a vibrant personality and his every word seemed to fill the room, and her, with life. He told her he was a sports reporter and his main interests were rugby and athletics. She recalled he made a point of saying he studiously avoided football, but in such a way as to avoid any hint of snobbishness. His next major assignment was at the Arms Park in Cardiff where Wales were going to 'put one over the English' by which she deduced where his sympathies lay.

But for all these asides it was clear that she was the real object of his interest and before long he had gone quiet and it was she who found her tongue. She was surprised to discover she was soon talking about herself, her likes, her dislikes – she even told him she worked at the Telephone Exchange, although how she managed to make it sound interesting, she hadn't a clue. And yet she must have done because she became aware he was listening intently to her every word. But this was the girl who earlier that evening had stood up so valiantly against her father, so perhaps it was no surprise that she could express herself with conviction.

After a while, Millie began to assume a rather bored expression. Elisabeth felt she'd only just got started, but out of the corner of her eye she caught her friend consulting her watch and mouthing words to the effect that they should think about leaving. She began making her excuses, but Geoffrey was having none of it. Why worry about missing the last bus home, he said, when all the time his carriage was waiting outside? And before they could raise an objection, he'd signalled Freddy to fetch their coats and they were piling out in to the street.

His car was a smart two-seater with a drop-down roof. It was a warm spring night so this was soon dismantled, and just as Millie had taken a back seat for most of the evening, she did so again and perched herself on the edge of the open luggage compartment. Elisabeth was awarded pride of place in the front although as they flew along the Bath Road at what felt like a hundred miles an hour, she had enough compassion to offer her friend a shoulder on which to steady herself. The effect of fresh air and two glasses of wine had made her a little light-headed and as they swept past Arnos Vale and on towards Brislington with the wind rushing through her hair, she felt an overwhelming sense of exhilaration.

They dropped Millie off first. Elisabeth suggested that she might get out there too and walk the last few hundred yards, but Geoffrey insisted on taking her further.

His motive became clear as soon as they were alone and he asked if she had a telephone number where he could call her. Of course she did! She had hundreds, and the irony was that he needn't have taken the trouble to enquire – all he had to do was pick up a phone, any phone, and dial zero or ask for the operator. If she didn't answer it herself then he had only to mention her name and someone would come and find her. The realisation made him laugh.

She persuaded him to set her down round the corner rather than directly in front of her house. She was in enough trouble already and the disturbance would only cause more. As his car roared off into the night she waited for a moment to compose herself, then smoothed down her skirt and headed for home.

Just as she'd feared, the front door was locked with the latch down. It was not that she'd missed her eleven o'clock curfew (there were still ten minutes to spare), but rather that her father was paying her out with his petty regulations. She tried her key a couple of times, then gave up and sank down onto the floor of the small porch where she sat and closed her eyes. Be it her father or the milkman, whichever came first, she decided to wait for events. There was no need for haste – she had plenty to think about in the meantime.

And that was how her mother found her, her head resting against the jamb, half asleep, when she came down the stairs to let her in. Maternal instinct had kept Dorothy awake until her daughter was safely home and as she ushered Elisabeth in, she pressed her finger to her lips.

"Shush! Don't let your father hear…"

Although what good would that do, now that the damage had been done?

Three

It was a week before she heard anything from Geoffrey. She'd almost given up hope so when he did finally call, it came completely out of the blue. Later, she was to learn this was typical of him. Days would go by and there was nothing. Then, suddenly, he'd be back in her life and the world was bright again.

In the days following the party, he was a constant topic of conversation with Millie. Was he in today? Yes, she'd seen him first thing that morning. Had he said anything? No, and she hadn't dare ask. They talked of little else and Elisabeth soon sensed that her friend was becoming tired of it and perhaps a little jealous, especially when Millie began to focus on the downside of his character. *I've been asking around. Apparently, he's got a bit of a reputation.* Why would her friend want to rake up such gossip? What business was it of hers? Besides, she didn't hear half of what Elisabeth heard – Millie was only a receptionist.

Elisabeth had just returned from her lunch break. She was on the point of donning her headset when she noticed that one of her colleagues was waving to catch her attention. Betty was in her forties and still single, although in her own words she'd 'been around the block a few times'.

"There's a gentleman here for you, dearie. Calls himself Geoffrey Jones. Are you going to take it?"

Elisabeth nodded and as good as ran to her seat while Betty held the line.

"Connecting you now, sir…"

And suddenly there he was, the same smooth voice in her ear with its promise of urbane sophistication. Was she well? What had she been doing with herself? She said she couldn't speak too freely and found a few carefully chosen words in reply. But then it was all about 'getting down to brass tacks' and the crux of the matter was that he'd managed to get an extra pass for the game in Cardiff on the Saturday. Would she care to join him?

His invitation threw her off balance. She'd imagined something romantic, a restaurant perhaps, or even a trip to the cinema. She naturally wanted to go – but how did one get to Cardiff? What time did the game begin? A mild panic set in as a flurry of questions ran through her head.

He was quick to put her mind at rest. There was a train from Temple Meads at midday and all she had to do was meet him at the station, he would see to the tickets. So could he look forward to her company? Well of course he could. She would be out on a Saturday afternoon – her father could hardly object.

When her shift was over and she was preparing to leave, Betty made a point of seeking her out.

"You take my advice and hang on to that one, dearie," she said, giving her a knowing wink. "He's worth a few pairs of silk stockings by the sound of it."

Elisabeth felt her face redden. Thoughts of silk stockings were far from her mind. She was more concerned with how to slip out unnoticed on a Saturday afternoon.

Her escape from the house proved easy. At eleven am there was no one about so she simply pulled on her coat and set off toward the bus stop. She'd left a note for her mother just in case, hidden in a place where Arthur wouldn't find it, to the effect that she'd gone out to watch a game of rugby. What she neglected to mention was the fact that she was going with a man and it involved travelling to another country.

She arrived at the station earlier than planned and found herself with time on her hands. He'd told her to meet him at the barrier, and although she kept consulting her watch in an attempt to conjure up his appearance, it was five to twelve before he showed up, striding purposefully through the main entrance, a raincoat slung over one arm and his briefcase dangling from the other. He was otherwise just as she'd remembered him – tall, handsome and incredibly self-assured.

"Sorry I'm late. Here, take these..."

And before she could even say hello, she suddenly had possession of his coat and his case while he dashed off to the ticket office. At the same time there was an announcement on the tannoy, *The train now approaching platform three...* and he was back at her side, clutching the tickets and recovering his abandoned belongings.

"Come on then..."

They barely had time to clear the barrier and get onto the platform before the train was upon them, preceded by a great whoosh of steam. And having hung about for the best part of half an hour, twiddling her thumbs, now she was all in a rush.

But that was the price you paid for his company. The moment he'd walked through the station entrance the atmosphere had changed. Suddenly, everything had become electrically charged and her person tingled with the feel of it. It was thrilling to be in his presence. But it was also unsettling – one never knew when it all might collapse and disintegrate back into nothing. She was filled with a nervous apprehension but still felt compelled to follow him.

The train was packed and they were forced to sit apart. As soon as they were settled, Geoffrey took out a notepad and a pencil and that morning's edition of *The Times* and spent the next hour compiling a series of notes.

Elisabeth contented herself with looking out of the window. Train rides for her were a rarity and therefore to be savoured. Life was all the more interesting for being viewed from a moving carriage. Soon, they were crossing the Bristol Channel and her heart started to lift as they passed over the border and into Wales. As far as she was concerned, this was a foreign land – it was the first time she'd ever left England.

They walked from the station to the ground. The streets were packed and at times the crowd became so thick they were hemmed in on both sides. She had no idea where she was going. She feared being lost in the throng and to avoid separation casually slipped her arm through Geoffrey's. He didn't seem to object.

At the turnstiles, Geoffrey produced a pair of press passes. They ascended into the stands and he led her to a small box overlooking the field of play. The box seemed suspended from the roof of the grandstand at a truly vertiginous height, and to look down at the crowd below was to induce a feeling of dizziness. But Elisabeth was determined not to be daunted. She quickly found a chair and confined herself to a forward view.

The stadium was full and the sun was shining, bathing the sea of upturned faces in a pleasant light. As the teams ran out beneath her, the crowd let out a mighty roar and 70,000 Welsh voices began their anthem. She felt her soul uplifted and looked round at Geoffrey as if to ask what she should do. She saw that he was singing too and it was only her lack of knowledge of the words that prevented her from joining him.

Then the game began and it was a relief when things quietened down.

Elisabeth knew little at all about rugby. As far as she could tell, the game involved a series of squabbles over the possession of an oddly shaped ball. As soon as one of the teams had got hold of it, they promptly kicked it back to the other and the ruckus started over again. It seemed a rather pointless exercise. But Geoffrey was enthralled and scribbled furiously on his notepad, stopping occasionally to make the odd verbal comment.

"Good Lord, that was a poor pass." Or, "I say, well played, sir!"

By the end of it, she was hardly any wiser than she was at the beginning. What had impressed her most was the singing.

When the game was over, Geoffrey still had work to do. While the crowd drained away, he completed his notes and asked Elisabeth to bear with him while he delivered his post-match report. After ten minutes or so he retreated to a small table at the back of the box and drew a hessian curtain in front of him. Before long there was the click of machinery, marked by a small red light, and then the sound of Geoffrey's voice, smooth and urbane, as he recounted the events of the afternoon into a microphone.

Elisabeth dared not move for fear of making a noise. It thrilled her to think that those same words would soon appear in the living rooms of thousands of people up and down country. It sounded so glamorous – and yet he'd made it all look so simple.

They walked back to the station in silence. The crowds had ebbed away but she still linked his arm. He seemed tired, as though the effort of his work had exhausted him, but it was she who felt herself dozing off on the train.

As they neared Temple Meads, she awoke with a start to find him staring at her.

"I'm dreadfully sorry – you must have had such a boring afternoon."

He sounded genuinely apologetic.

"No, not at all, I really enjoyed it."

"Oh, jolly good, I'm so glad. So what did you think of Jenkins' try?"

"I really can't remember…" In the process of coming round she felt confused, and she truly couldn't recall anything about it. "It's just that I'm really rather hungry." She'd had nothing to eat since leaving home that morning.

"Of course, how stupid of me. We must do something about that."

"Alright. What did you have in mind?"

She hoped it was the restaurant of her daydream but even a bite in the station buffet would suffice.

His reply surprised her.

"We'll go to my sister's…"

Many years later, it occurred to her that the purpose of the visit to Geoffrey's sister was to show her off. Or if not, then to present her as though she were a candidate in a beauty contest and to receive an opinion as to her suitability.

What was not admissible was the idea that he'd planned it in advance. Geoffrey made decisions on the spur of the moment and they were not always good ones. Sometimes they came off, sometimes they got him into trouble. On this occasion, the best you could say was that he got away with it – as he did with so many things.

But at the time her head was young and pretty and she was far more concerned with the prospect of meeting members of his family. As it turned out, Georgina proved immensely sympathetic towards her, if not towards her brother. But as well as the visit went in general terms, it did not pass entirely without incident.

Georgina and John lived in a rather grand flat in a converted Victorian mansion in one of the smarter areas of the city. Elisabeth knew Bristol well (she'd lived there all her life) but she was not quite certain as to the location. Geoffrey had driven at his usual breakneck speed from the station and while trying to remain within the car rather than be thrown out of it, she'd lost her sense of direction.

A flight of steps led up to an imposing front door. Below, there was evidence of a basement and what had once been servants' quarters. Geoffrey strode forward and pressed firmly on the bell. A light came on in the hallway, then the door opened a crack and a young woman's face appeared.

"Good Lord!"

Georgina was fashionably dressed with a large pearl necklace dangling at her throat. She turned and called out behind her.

"John? Geoffrey's here – and he's brought someone with him."

She turned back toward her visitors.

"Well, I suppose you'd better come in."

These were the self-same words that Freddy had used prior to his party. In the new world Elisabeth was entering, this casual style of invitation was clearly common practice.

The flat itself was light and airy and the interior well appointed. It had modern furniture and clever lighting but it still managed to retain a homely feel. An array of patterned cushions spoke of designer comfort. It made Freddy's place look like something out of the Ark and frankly, rather seedy.

John awaited them in the lounge, hands in pockets. And with thoughts of Freddy to the fore, Elisabeth could not help but continue the comparison. Here was the man himself, a few years older perhaps but no less portly and with his NHS specs exchanged for a private pair. So what did they do, he and Georgina, that they should appear so well-off? Were they doctors, lawyers? Everything about them smacked of bourgeois pretension.

"Can I get you a drink?"

John hurried to offer refreshments.

Elisabeth declined any alcohol and opted for a cordial. She did not want to risk a repeat of events at the party and feared the consequences of drinking on an empty stomach. As she took a sip from her glass, she began to wonder what she might say. Fortunately, it was her host who started things off, addressing Geoffrey directly.

"Well, old man, it's a while since we've seen you. What have you been doing with yourself?"

"We've been to the match."

"Yes, I heard your report on the radio. Good game was it?"

"On the whole – the forwards played well."

At this point, Georgina cut in and turned to Elisabeth.

"You don't mean to tell me that he's dragged you all the way to Cardiff just to watch a game of rugby?"

"Yes," she replied. "I'm afraid so."

"You poor thing!"

Was it as condescending as it sounded? Elisabeth didn't really think so.

"No, it was actually quite an experience..."

She wanted to tell them about the singing, but she lacked the confidence to do so. There was an awkward moment of silence while they waited for her, but then Georgina resumed.

"Geoffrey has many faults but he's developed the knack of timing his visits to perfection. You've come for something to eat, I suppose?" she said, turning to her brother.

"Well, if there happens to be anything available..."

"It's the only time we ever see him you know – when he's hungry."

This prompted Elisabeth to confess.

"It's my fault, I'm afraid. We haven't had anything all day. And when we got back to Temple Meads, I happened to mention that my stomach had started grumbling."

"Of course." Georgina patted her arm and shot her brother an accusing glance. "Now, if you'll excuse me, I have things to see to in the kitchen."

"Can I help?"

The thought of being left alone with Geoffrey and John and more talk of rugby had made Elisabeth inwardly panic.

"Please do," said Georgina.

Out in the kitchen, a pot was bubbling slowly on the stove.

Half an hour later they were all sitting down to eat. By now the two men had exhausted the topic of rugby and talk had moved on to food. The bubbling pot contained a casserole and this rapidly became the next subject of conversation. Besides the vegetables Elisabeth had helped prepare, there was also a little meat. This had cost Georgina her week's ration and she'd been forced to top up from the black market. Geoffrey expressed surprise.

"I didn't realise the black market was still in existence. The war ended years ago."

"You wouldn't know anything about it," his sister retorted. "You're not in the position of having to go out and shop."

"Well that's true…" Geoffrey was forced to admit.

"As long as there's rationing there'll always be a black market," said John. "The two are inextricably linked. The real question is – when's it going to end and what's the Government going to do about it? Attlee's going to have to go back to the country pretty soon – he can't get by on a majority of five – and if Labour get in again there'll be hell to pay."

"You say that," ventured Georgina, "but they seem to have done all right to me. I think we need a period of stability. We don't want to be chopping and changing all the time."

This exchange of views led on to a discussion about the relative merits of the parties and soon a vigorous debate was in progress.

At first, Elisabeth didn't speak but found herself drawn mentally deeper into the conversation. Events such as this did not occur in her house. In her house, her father dominated affairs and even to raise such subjects was taboo, never mind offering an opinion. But here they were, three people, each with a different perspective, openly discussing the issues of the day without rancour or recrimination. It was a novel and exciting experience and as the debate moved on, she found it was not just her thoughts that were quickening, but also her pulse. Finally, she could no longer contain herself and burst out with a comment of her own.

John had been saying that it was a shame Mr Churchill had been denied his opportunity in 1945 and the country should have been more grateful when she suddenly found herself speaking to the effect that just because he'd won the war, it didn't entitle Mr Churchill to run the country and one should really look more closely at Mr Attlee's achievements in terms of reforming the nation's institutions before rushing to judgement.

And yet as soon as the words had left her lips, she regretted them. She recognised them for what they were – a simple repetition of her father's socialist views which she'd assimilated without thinking.

There was a momentary pause while the group assessed her intervention. She wondered whether such comments were acceptable in this overtly middle-class company but she need not have been concerned. Georgina immediately came to her rescue.

"Well said!"

As a result, no one looked at her askance, no one even raised an eyebrow, and the debate promptly resumed.

With this encouragement she soon found herself in the thick of it, taking the occasional tilt in their intellectual joust. When they moved on to art and literature she got a little stuck, but she had read (although not widely) and her knowledge of books was at least an improvement over rugby.

The evening wore quickly on. She soon lost track of time and over three hours went by before there was a lull in the conversation. When she realised how late it was she looked imploringly at Geoffrey and tapped gently on her watch. Luckily, he got the message.

"Good Lord! Look at the time. We'd better be going."

John was sent for their coats while Georgina enlisted Geoffrey's help in clearing the dishes.

Elisabeth enquired if she could visit the bathroom.

"Of course. First on the right, just here." Georgina pointed to a door immediately adjacent to the kitchen.

Standing at the sink, washing her hands, Elisabeth caught the sound of voices. The partition wall must have been exceptionally thin or there was some unusual conjunction between the pipes and the ventilation system. But for whatever reason, Georgina's words were quite distinct.

You've got a damned cheek, I must say, turning up out of the blue like this. Then, after Geoffrey's muffled and probably apologetic response: *Another of your waifs and strays, I suppose. Well, at least this one's not married.*

More of Geoffrey's mumbling was followed by Georgina again. *She's got some spirit though, I'll say that for her…*

Elisabeth slowly dried her hands and checked herself in the mirror. Her cheeks were a little flushed and as usual, her mop of thick black hair needed flattening.

What should she make of these remarks? They'd clearly been aimed at Geoffrey rather than herself – but they were still a disappointment as she'd begun to count on Georgina as a friend. They were helpful in one respect. If she was not already aware of the risks she was running, she certainly was now. Her evening had otherwise been a triumph and out in the street, Geoffrey acknowledged as much as he opened the car door for her.

"You soon found your feet."

She had – and it excited her, no matter what his sister might say. As they raced back along the Bath Road, not only was the wind in her hair but it carried with it the exultant sound of 70,000 Welsh voices and the cut and thrust of intellectual debate. She felt exhilarated once more and the fact it was gone midnight by the time she reached home only added to her sense of having done something extraordinary.

A note from her mother lay waiting in the porch – *I've lifted the latch. But remember, no noise* – and as she crept indoors she was careful to remove her shoes before climbing the stairs.

In the morning, Elisabeth lay curled up under her counterpane, barely awake. It was a quarter to nine and Dorothy had come to her as emissary on behalf of her father. He was enquiring as to whether she would be joining him at church that day – if not, she could go to the Devil and he would not be responsible for the consequences.

Elisabeth turned to face the wall and pulled the counterpane further over her head. Tell him, she said to her mother, that she had already ridden with the Devil the night before and that it was a far more enlightening experience than going to church. Not wishing to exacerbate what was an already delicate situation, Dorothy declined to deliver the message in full and confined herself to a polite, no thank you.

Elisabeth snuggled down and away from her father's wrath. She had made her bed and was now obliged to lie in it. She knew she was playing with fire – but the problem was, it was so deliciously hot.

Four

And so it began – a round of engagements and a social life that a month before she could scarcely have dreamed of. Cocktail parties, dinner parties, gala functions – at Geoffrey's request she was in constant attendance. The invitations came thick and fast. Would she go to this with him? Would she go to that with him? In the course of the next few weeks she was bombarded. She was happy to accept and took any excuse to escape the stultifying atmosphere of home. The world had opened up to her and she was determined to make the most of it.

Her meeting with Georgina and John had been a test and having had passed it, she'd been accepted into the smart set. She found it particularly useful to be acquainted with Georgina. She seemed to know everyone – and if she didn't, she made it her business to find out. And despite the views she'd expressed that night in the kitchen, she took it on herself to befriend Elisabeth and give her the guidance and advice she needed.

With Georgina's encouragement she drank champagne for the first time in her life – and liked it. When she realised it was an acceptable and almost necessary social accomplishment for a woman to smoke, Georgina suggested she try menthol with a filter tip (Geoffrey's brand was Navy Cut and had a strong and acrid taste). As for dress, it was Geoffrey who paid for her wardrobe although his sister was the one to recommend what was fashionable.

But it was her mother who taught her to dance. On Sunday mornings when Arthur was at church, they pushed back the furniture in the front parlour and Dorothy led her through the waltz and the foxtrot as best she could. No daughter of hers was going out into the world unable to take to the floor when asked.

Her name began to circulate. Not in the highest places it's true, but amongst Geoffrey's friends and acquaintances she soon became well known. It wasn't long before she lost count of the introductions.

Elisabeth, have you met so and so?

So and so, this is Elisabeth Johnson...

She continually saw a question forming in people's minds. *So who exactly is Elisabeth Johnson?* She feared being discovered and dreaded the reply *Elisabeth Johnson? Isn't she the girl from the Telephone Exchange?* The answer she invariably heard – *Why, that's Geoffrey's girl* – placed her firmly at his side but not beyond it. To her colleagues at work she was, and always would be, Lizzie. But in her social life she was Elisabeth and it was important to maintain the distinction.

One night, clothed in a new evening dress and on her way to some black-tie function, she found herself wedged into the back of a taxi with Geoffrey on one side and someone new on the other. By then she'd become so used to it all that it came as no surprise to discover who he was and after Geoffrey had shaken hands, she was duly introduced.

"Elisabeth, this is Charles Cochran – Charles, this is Elisabeth Johnson..."

She thought of what Millie's reaction might be and it was at that moment she realised how far life had taken her from her friend.

And all the time, Geoffrey was beside her, tall and handsome, brushing back his mane of floppy hair, full of bonhomie and behaving as if he were the perfect gentleman. How long it would last, only time would tell. She'd met him in March and in April she'd come out like a spring flower, but it was June before matters were tested.

In all this time, her father had hardly spoken. Their paths rarely seemed to cross and it was as if they were studiously avoiding each other. Elisabeth took to eating in the kitchen but if by some strange accident they found themselves at the same table, he would raise his newspaper as a barrier between them. If he needed to communicate with her at all, he would invariably do so through Dorothy. *Tell your daughter that the churchwarden will be here on Friday evening and we will be in the parlour between seven and nine.* Or, *I have noticed that the light bulb in your daughter's room has expired. If she would care to take it out and leave it on the landing I will provide her with a replacement.* On issues of substance he remained inauspiciously quiet.

It began to distress her mother. Dorothy professed to be ignorant – *I don't know what's going on between you and your father* – but in reality it was obvious.

He could hardly turn her out – she had nowhere else to go. She'd no idea of how or where Geoffrey lived and the only plausible alternative was to go and stay with Millie. At first she considered this as a temporary means of escape, but as she climbed the social ladder their friendship correspondingly waned and now they were merely acquaintances rather than friends. In recent conversations, Elisabeth had even detected that her sense of envy had grown.

It was not as if Arthur were supporting her. Elisabeth's wages at the Telephone Exchange might not be enough to sustain her social lifestyle, but they were sufficient to ensure her independence at home. She paid her way, and her father knew it. It might seem hypocritical but he was not going to cut his nose off to spite his face. And so he stayed silent and ignored her.

It was this failure to recognise her that finally made up her mind. Having a man in her life seemed perfectly natural and after three months of Arthur's cold-shouldering, she came to the view that she may as well be hung for a sheep as for a lamb. So when Geoffrey made his proposition (as she knew he eventually would) her answer was already prepared. Yes, she would go away with him – if only to anger her father.

Geoffrey said he needed a break, a respite from his hectic life and the social whirl they were caught up in. He'd barely had a day off since Christmas and he claimed it was beginning to tell. He planned to go away for a few days. Would she care to join him? He was clearly not suggesting a long-term commitment. What he had in mind (with all its implications) was a couple of nights away in a hotel.

Elisabeth was under no illusions. This was no melodramatic elopement, a great romantic adventure from which she might never return – this was a weekend away somewhere where they could be alone together. Instead of a suitcase packed with all her belongings, all she'd be taking with her was an overnight bag and a change of clothes and in her heart she knew that on Monday morning, she'd be back at the switchboard, connecting people. If he'd dressed it up as something permanent – *Let me take you away from all this* – she wouldn't have believed him. Although something told her she'd probably have gone off with him, all the same…

It was just as the day of the rugby match. When she'd stepped off the train and announced she was hungry, he'd surprised her with a trip to his sister's. And so he surprised her now. They needed to go somewhere quiet, somewhere discreet to conduct their affair and she'd imagined the countryside with its fresh air and wide open spaces. It turned out to be Weston-super-Mare, the smell of ozone and the claustrophobic atmosphere of a seedy bed and breakfast.

On the Friday evening, Geoffrey arrived later than intended. He'd said seven, but it was more like eight before he got to the house.

Elisabeth was waiting in the shelter of the porch with her coat and bag at the ready. There was no problem with her departure. Her father had gone out to see the churchwarden and although her mother had begged her to think carefully, Dorothy had eventually become resigned to it. As the car roared off up the hill, she even came to the door to wave goodbye.

The trip took over an hour. It was no great distance, less than thirty miles, but rather than the prosaic journey along the A38, Geoffrey insisted on taking the back roads to show off his prowess as a driver. As her head swayed from side to side with each twisting corner, Elisabeth felt her eyes closing. Soon the tiredness engulfed her and she gradually nodded off.

She awoke with a jolt. It was still light and she was able to make out her surroundings. They'd come to a halt in a crescent-shaped backstreet of what she assumed must be Weston-super-Mare. They couldn't be far from the sea as the muddy odour of the Bristol Channel was already warming her nostrils. The houses forming the crescent were of a terraced two-storey construction (three if you counted those with converted lofts) and they exhibited a shabbiness which could at best be described as genteel and at worst tending toward dilapidation.

The one outside which they were parked was certainly not one of the best – although neither was it one of the worst. A crumbling sign hung from a post next to the pavement with a single word painted on it – *Vacancies*. Elisabeth's first thought was not particularly charitable. Now that Geoffrey was out of sight of his friends, he could treat her more as he thought befitted a working-class girl from the Telephone Exchange.

He'd already got out of the car and was busy carrying their luggage up the flight of steps to the door. When he saw Elisabeth was conscious he came down to help her out, then began pulling up the canvas hood and clipping it shut. They were clearly not going out again that evening.

Their arrival had alerted the landlady and by the time Geoffrey had finished portering and they'd reascended the steps, the front door was open and a figure awaited them. This was Mrs Beazley, a woman of about fifty and of slightly unkempt appearance. She looked more like the cleaner than the proprietress (although she no doubt undertook both tasks) as she wore an apron instead of a housecoat, a pair of fluffy slippers and her hair was wrapped around with a duster tied off at the front. A cigarette (from which she never seemed to inhale) dangled permanently from her lips. This caused her to speak out of the corner of her mouth and gave her face a crooked aspect. She paused briefly, looked at Geoffrey, then blinked as smoke curled into her eye.

"You'll be Mr Jones, I take it."

She pronounced the word 'Jones' with a great deal of suspicion.

"And you, I suppose," she said, turning to Elisabeth, "will be Mrs Jones."

She clearly thought this equally unlikely as she gave a derisive sniff which required considerable contortion of her features if she was not to dislodge her cigarette.

Elisabeth nodded, although if anything a little too vigorously.

"I'll show you to your room..."

Mrs Beazley turned and led the way inside.

They took their cases and followed her shuffling gait toward the stairs.

Part way down the corridor they passed an open door. Hearing the steady hiss of a gas fire, Elisabeth looked in. It was evidently the den Mrs Beazley permanently occupied. In front of the fire, roasting in its heat, lay an elderly and seemingly indolent dog, while next to it stood a small square card table with a green baize top on which was laid out a half-finished game of patience. A comfortable chair had been pushed back, the accompanying ashtray was full, and on the side rested a cut-glass tumbler filled with a golden-brown fluid.

Meanwhile, the room's regular occupant was puffing her way up to the first-floor landing and mumbling under her breath.

"My old bones. I shouldn't have to be doing this at my age..."

She paused to recover and took a key from her apron pocket which she pressed into Geoffrey's hand.

"Number 4... On the left... Can't miss it..." She spoke in short bursts now, alternating each phrase with a gasp for air. "Biggest room in the 'ouse... Honeymoon Suite I calls it..." She managed a throaty cackle and leered at Elisabeth, whose face promptly turned scarlet. "Bathroom's straight across the 'all... Water's on from six..." Then, consulting her watch, "Should be some left now if you're lucky... Breakfast downstairs at eight... Any questions?"

She stared at them enquiringly, the ash teetering on the end of her cigarette, and dared them to make a response. When there was none, she headed back toward the stairs, anxious to return to the comfort of her fireside.

"I'll leave you to it then. You know where I am if you want me."

As she passed she glanced directly at Geoffrey, and for a brief moment Elisabeth thought she detected a flicker of recognition. Perhaps this was not the first time they'd met, perhaps he'd been here before. Or perhaps, some years ago, the now unprepossessing Mrs Beazley had been one of his earlier conquests...

The room was of a good size and overlooked the street. It was dominated by a large double bed, but it also contained a chair and a settee in addition to the more conventional wardrobe and bedside table. As the reality of the situation confronted her, and confused as to what to do next, Elisabeth took up on Mrs Beazley's suggestion.

"I think I'll take a bath..."

And seizing her overnight bag went straight across the hallway and into the bathroom.

A slight nervousness had suddenly become apparent, and she prayed fervently there'd be enough hot water to justify her decision. Thankfully there was, and as she sank beneath the warm water she felt a sense of calm returning. Whatever was going to happen next, she had at least been able to prepare for it.

When she returned to the room in her nightclothes, Geoffrey had already tidied his things away and was waiting for his turn in the bathroom. As soon as he'd gone across the hall, Elisabeth removed her nightgown, folded it carefully across the chair and got into what she assumed was her side of the bed. Now all she could do was wait – it would not be long.

But as soon as her head touched the pillow, the effects of the hot bath took hold and the same sense of overwhelming tiredness she'd experienced in the car returned. Before Geoffrey could come back to claim her, her eyes fell shut and she went out like a light.

Five

This time she came to much more slowly, gradually sloughing off the layers of sleep. At last she became aware that she was not tucked up at home but in a strange room in a B&B some thirty miles away, a shaft of bright sunlight slanting in through the half-drawn curtains and across the double bed. She hadn't run away, she hadn't eloped to Gretna Green, and as far as she was concerned she hadn't done anything wrong. But whatever had happened the night before (and of that she was still not yet certain), in the eyes of most she'd already transgressed.

To her sudden consternation she discovered she was alone. The rest of the double bed was empty and showed no evidence of having been slept in. There was no sign of Geoffrey's clothing and looking round the room, she could find no clue as to his whereabouts although there was an impression left on the settee where a man might have lain down for the night. She went to the window and assured herself that his car was still there. He must be about somewhere…

Her fear was that having had his way with her the night before, he'd already abandoned her – but as far as she was aware she was still 'intact'. Or, worse still, as she'd been unavailable, he'd gone to seek out Mrs Beazley as a means of satisfying himself. Either way, it would be difficult to face, but she must do it. Inwardly panicking, she snatched her watch from the bedside table. It was already half past eight and she was late for breakfast. She dressed hurriedly and went downstairs.

Geoffrey was sitting at one of the tables in the dining room, calmly smoking. On the place mat in front of him lay a half-finished cup of coffee and an empty plate, the knife and fork pushed to one side. As he saw her approach he got up, pulled out a chair and ushered her into it.

"Good morning. Did you sleep well?"

His apparent composure only served to fluster her.

"Yes... Thank you... A little too well I think... I'm..."

She was on the point of saying 'sorry' as if that would alleviate any feeling of disappointment but thought the better of it.

"That's alright – you were tired. I'd have done the same myself if I were you."

He explained that he'd woken early (the couch had not been that comfortable) and had gone out to fetch the papers. Copies of *The Times* and the *Western Morning News* lay discarded on the floor next to the table. On his return he'd looked in on her but she'd still been asleep and rather than disturb her he'd decided to start breakfast on his own. He hoped she didn't mind.

"Of course not..."

How could she object?

They were interrupted by the arrival of Mrs Beazley. To Elisabeth's relief she looked equally as unprepossessing as she had the night before, the inevitable cigarette glued to her bottom lip as she moved amongst the tables.

"Mornin', dear. And what are you 'aving?"

Her greeting was cheery, if a little uninviting. Elisabeth resolved to check the contents of her breakfast carefully for ash, although when it arrived there was none. Nor was there any sense of relationship between Mrs Beazley and Geoffrey. Or if there was, it was so minute as to be imperceptible.

She ate her breakfast in silence and after Geoffrey had gathered up his papers, they went back to the room and got themselves ready to go out.

Returning there now, Elisabeth would find Weston-super-Mare a very different place than it was in 1950. Many of the buildings she would have known were swept away in the '50s and '60s and little of the old town remains. It was a popular seaside resort and of no strategic value, but it was bombed during the war and although hostilities had ceased some five years before, in 1950 it was still pockmarked with craters, waiting for the money and the motivation of its citizens to cover them over.

Despite these setbacks, the place continued to fulfil its objective of providing pleasure. That had become all the more important, as in those early post-war years there was increased demand for the recreation and enjoyment which had been absent for so long. In summer, Weston was thronged with people looking for a good time. Railway excursions from Bristol were especially popular, and on Bank Holidays in particular, day trippers in their thousands disembarked at Locking Road Station and flooded into town. On days such as these, the crowds were so thick along the seafront that it was difficult to catch any sight of the sea at all. And so when Geoffrey and Elisabeth stepped out of Mrs Beazley's B&B and into the summer sunshine on that Saturday morning in June, it was into a Weston-super-Mare that still bore the scars of a terrible war, but one that was packed with people trying to forget it.

Their first objective was to walk the length of the promenade (it may have been then that the photograph was taken) but when they returned to the Winter Gardens for a well-earned rest they struggled to find seats in the shade. In the afternoon, the queue for the bandstand stretched well around the corner and it took them half an hour to get tickets for the three o'clock performance. Later, when a short, sharp shower drove everyone inside, the cafés and tea rooms were full but they managed to find a corner in one into which to retreat. Cloistered together amongst the damp bodies and babbled conversation, Elisabeth felt a sense of intimacy growing between them.

She clung to him amongst the crowds, just as she had done in Cardiff and as she did in the photograph. She felt safe in his presence, as if his height and honed athletic build could protect her against the masses. He had an air of self-confidence and charm that confirmed in her the thought that of all the people in

Weston-super-Mare, he was the one she most wanted to be with. He always knew where to go and what to do. It all added to the impression that he'd been there before, although how many times and with how many other women she had no idea. She no longer cared and for the moment he was alone with her; he was her guide and she relied on him.

It was on this day more than any other that she imagined she was in love with him. Wasn't this what love was? This great feeling of comfort that arose from the knowledge that you could rely on someone, that they would protect you and look after you as he did? She wanted to be near him, to feel the warmth of his arm through the rough folds of his jacket, to take every opportunity to be pressed against him in the crush of the crowds. And when they were parted, even for a few brief moments as she waited for him outside the conveniences, standing alone on the pavement with nothing to cling to save a handbag and a camera, she felt such a sense of loss, as though it were part of herself that had been removed, that she yearned to have him back at her side and would not feel whole again until she did. For that was how it was – a feeling of great fulfilment when he was there and a desperate sense of emptiness when he was not. It must be love, she'd convinced herself of it, there could be no other explanation.

Her conviction grew as the day wore on. They kept close amongst the crowds but there were other factors at work. Deep in her subconscious lurked the realisation that whatever happened during the day, it was only a prelude to what would take place that evening. The night before she'd been excused and she couldn't count on it happening again. She was about to commit what her father would deem 'a sinful act' and for which there was no moral justification. But if she were in love, if union resulted from a deep emotional attachment rather than the mere abandonment of principles, wasn't that reason enough? Did that not excuse her?

After they'd eaten dinner and walked off their meal, Geoffrey suggested they head back to their accommodation. She found herself ready to comply and when they got back to the room and lay on the broad double bed together, she gave herself to him willingly and without restraint. She was pleased to discover it didn't hurt as much as she'd been led to believe (she'd heard the women at the Exchange talk about such things and she'd even discussed it with Millie) and once he'd broken through, there was a warmth and a power about it she found quite thrilling. Later, when his moment eventually arrived, she gripped him as hard as she could, but it was as much through the pleasure he afforded rather than any pain she might feel.

Afterwards, as she nestled close to him, her arm across his chest as he smoked his cigarette, she thought herself the luckiest woman in the world. Geoffrey was handsome, debonair and of a social milieu she found exciting and into which she'd been accepted. She *was* in love – of that there could be no doubt. Thoughts of Mrs Beazley and her father were banished and she went to sleep undeniably content in the comfort of her newfound happiness.

Weston-super-Mare was their favourite haunt that summer. Left to their own devices they would probably have gone every weekend, but their combination of working arrangements made it awkward for them to coincide. The athletics season had started and for at least two Saturdays of the month, Geoffrey's job required him to be at some event or another. Elisabeth was bound by her shifts and although weekend working meant more money, it soon became tiresome and inconvenient. That was until Betty stepped in. She understood things only too well.

"Don't you worry, dearie, I'll take care of it. I could do with a bit of extra cash. You go off and enjoy yourself. Make the most of it while you can. I know I would. If only I was twenty years younger..."

She gave a knowing wink to show whose side she was on.

As for Elisabeth's friendship with Millie, nowadays they barely spoke. Her calls were few and far between and as Elisabeth became more deeply engaged in her new world, she felt her old one slipping away.

Soon, the winding bends and hills of the trip to Weston-super-Mare were as familiar to her as the jolting bounce of her bus ride into town. Petrol rationing had come to an end. *Thank God for that*, was Geoffrey's comment. It wasn't cheap, but at least it was readily available so there was no waiting for coupons. The Honeymoon Suite at Mrs Beazley's seemed permanently booked in their name and over the coming months Elisabeth got to know Weston almost as well as Geoffrey did. When he went to fetch his paper – *I'll only be ten minutes, meet me outside the Post Office* – she knew exactly where he meant. If they were ever split up, they were to rendezvous at the Speak Your Weight machine at the entrance to the Grand Pier, and she'd learnt to find her way there on her own. Not that she wanted to be on her own, that was the point.

Her favourite occupations were seeing a Punch and Judy show or watching the lifeboat launch from the lifeboat station. She was amazed that such a slightly built craft could survive the descent down its ramp and every time it plunged headlong into the water she held her breath, waiting for it to reappear from the spray. Geoffrey preferred the putting green in the Winter Gardens and the dodgems on the Pier, but together they boated round the Marine Lake, he gently rowing while she relaxed in the sun. And on hot days, really hot days, he would persuade her to put on a bathing suit and they would take a dip in the open-air pool to cool down.

In the evenings, they'd go to a variety show or the theatre and arrive back at Mrs Beazley's late, giggling like children as they tried to fit the key into the front lock without too much noise. Then, creeping along the passageway, they'd attempt to pass Mrs Beazley's half-open door without waking her as she snoozed by the fire in the company of her dormant hound. Success meant they could reach the bedroom and begin to make love all the sooner. And to think that not long ago, she'd considered Mrs Beazley as a rival...

By the end of the summer, Mrs Beazley's attitude toward her had changed. She no longer glanced disdainfully at Elisabeth on arrival and her look of contempt was replaced with respect. They signed the register as Mr and Mrs Jones and it was as Mr and Mrs Jones that they were treated. To all intents and purposes, in Weston-super-Mare they were a married couple. And like any other married couple, they had their ups and downs. As the senior partner, it was Geoffrey who invariably led and for the most part Elisabeth was happy to concur with his suggestions. But on one particular occasion she came close to rebellion, and it led to a tearful scene.

It was August Bank Holiday and they'd managed to get the weekend off. The Honeymoon Suite was booked and in celebration they went out to a special dinner on the Saturday night. When they returned to the room, Geoffrey had a bottle of champagne and an ice bucket waiting. They made love as usual, not only that night but at Geoffrey's instigation again on the Sunday morning, this time a little too enthusiastically for Elisabeth's liking. She'd noticed that his appetite for sex had increased and it worried her a little. Afterwards, just when she'd have liked to lie in, and even to have gone back to sleep, he insisted on rousing her, telling her that she was to get up and get dressed as they were going out somewhere. He had a surprise trip planned.

Her hope was that he'd arranged an outing on the paddle steamer across the Bristol Channel to Penarth. It was something she'd set her heart on. She'd mentioned it on at least two occasions, but to no avail. Following the exertions of earlier that morning, the idea of a leisurely cruise over the water was quite appealing but after breakfast, instead of the walk to Birnbeck Pier she found herself seated in the car and hurtling south to some unknown destination.

After twenty minutes of hectic driving, she was alerted by the sight of a concrete runway appearing behind a linked-wire fence. This was Weston Airport. Further down at the entrance gate, suspended between two rickety poles, a banner flapped lazily in the breeze announcing *FLYING TODAY*. As they turned in, ready and waiting on the tarmac in front of her stood a light aircraft of what could only be described as flimsy construction, its propeller already turning. Her heart sank at the same time as her stomach rose, and their untimely conjunction produced an instant response.

"I can't possibly go up in that!"

"Of course you can!" retorted Geoffrey. "You'll enjoy it."

"I won't! Just look at it. The very thought of going up in it makes me feel ill."

"You won't be ill, I promise. It's not an acrobatic flight – we're just going for a quiet trip around the bay. It'll be fun."

But just for once, Geoffrey's idea of fun did not coincide with her own.

She wondered how much 'fun' he wanted for the day. Perhaps their union that morning hadn't been exciting enough and he needed more outrageous challenges to fuel his adrenalin. His failure to appreciate her anxiety annoyed her and she continued to protest.

"Oh, Geoffrey! Please don't make me go up in that thing. I shall be terribly sick."

But he did. And she was.

She spent the next half an hour in hell. Strapped into her tiny seat she dared not look out of the window, and as the plane banked left and right over Steep Holm and Flat Holm she wretched violently into the paper bag provided.

Geoffrey, meanwhile, sat calmly next to the pilot and spent the whole flight gazing out over the landscape and pointing out the sights. He seemed completely insensitive to her plight. She hated him for it.

Once they'd landed she gradually recovered but her underlying anger remained.

"I told you so!"

In truth, it was not just Geoffrey's indifference that had upset her. There was something else on her mind, something far more important. It wasn't the first time in the last fortnight she'd been sick in the morning.

Six

It came as no surprise to discover she was pregnant. She'd taken no precautions, she wouldn't have known how, she was ignorant of such affairs and there was no one she could talk to on the subject. It wasn't something she could bring up at home (her mother never spoke of such things) and she was no longer in contact with Millie. The only alternative was Betty but despite her willingness to help, it hadn't seemed appropriate. Her natural assumption was that Geoffrey was experienced in these matters and knew what he was doing. How naive she'd been! In the end, all she'd been able to do was cross her fingers and hope. Although as it turned out, that proved to be a particularly ineffective method of contraception.

The problem was how to tell him. It was not a question of whether, but rather of when. Left for any length of time, things would become obvious and so it had to be dealt with. Following her discomforting aeroplane ride, she'd almost blurted it out at the airport as a means of paying him out – *Now can you see?* – but she'd felt too ill and had managed to hold her tongue. To be on the safe side, she waited until she'd missed her second period, then, one evening in September after a night out in Bristol, rather than walk round the corner to her house as usual, she elected to stay in the car and break the news.

"Geoffrey, I'm expecting…"

"Expecting what?"

She thought it was plain enough but he appeared not to have caught on. Was he as ignorant as he made himself sound – or did he just not want to face up to it?

"A baby."

"I see…"

He sat back in his seat, staring out of the front window. He seemed neither shocked nor delighted.

"And how long…?

"Eight weeks."

"I don't suppose there's any chance you might be mistaken?"

"None."

His lack of emotional response astounded her. It was as if he were a doctor practising his bedside manner.

"So what do you propose to do about it?"

And now, rather than prescribe a solution, he was asking her for suggestions.

This last remark took the wind out of her sails and shattered any fragile confidence she might have had.

"Well… I don't really know… That's why I thought I'd talk to you about it…"

It didn't seem an unreasonable thing to say (there was no question he was the father) but his answer was exactly what she later came to expect from a man to whom responsibility was an anathema and who always looked to someone else to solve his problems.

"You'd better go and talk to Georgina…"

It slipped out so easily that she wondered if he'd prepared it in advance for such an occasion. Perhaps it wasn't the first time he'd been forced to use it.

So she was supposed to go and see Georgina. Georgina, his sister, who could say one thing to your face – *You poor thing!* – and then something different behind your back. Did he count on her for everything?

She wondered whether Geoffrey had any form of compassion for her. It was not that long ago she'd imagined herself in love with him and now there was doubt. But wasn't that what love was supposed to do – tear you apart? She despised him for his lack of consideration, but life was so empty without him. At that moment all she wanted was to be looked after and comforted and to feel that sense of guardianship he'd afforded her in Weston-super-Mare. But his arms were folded against her and she knew it was impossible. Just like her father, had a newspaper been available Geoffrey would have sat there and hidden behind it, such was his concern. He could make love to her with a passion she found alarming, but when it came to affairs of the heart and of conscience, he was cold and unfeeling. At the aerodrome she'd hated him as lovers do, momentarily, and in a way that made making up afterwards all the sweeter. But now, for the first time in their relationship, a flicker of contempt passed through her mind that was hard to dispel.

"Very well then..."

Inwardly, her spirit raged. She left the car and although she managed not to slam the door behind her, her cheeks were hot and flushed as she crossed the road. As soon as she got into the house, she sunk to her knees at the bottom of the stairs and promptly burst into tears.

He did at least accompany her to Georgina's. She could hardly go alone and unlike that first occasion when they'd arrived unannounced, this time they were expected. When Geoffrey rang the bell, his sister's voice was already in the hallway.

"The door's open..."

Elisabeth wondered what else might have been prepared and in particular, whether Geoffrey had given her secret away in advance. She could imagine what he might have said. *Look, Georgie, I'm in a bit of a jam. The stupid little bitch has gone and got herself knocked up...* She could at least be sure of one thing – all Georgina would have heard would have been his side of the story. She arrived feeling at a definite disadvantage.

She was the last to enter the sitting room. Geoffrey, John and Georgina were already standing by the coffee table. She was conscious that their eyes were all on her and her hand moved instinctively to her belly as if to protect its contents. It was as though the progress of the last six months had all been wiped away and they were back to when she'd first been brought round for inspection. In the intervening period she'd been lionised, but now her class and her condition had come between them and in the snakes and ladders of social climbing she'd tumbled back down to the start. She sensed she'd no longer be sitting in the backs of taxis with the likes of Charles Cochran.

Her suspicions that this was a pre-planned affair were soon confirmed. There was an awkward silence, then John piped up.

"Well, old man." He turned to Geoffrey, nervously jingling the coins in his pocket. "Fancy a quick half before we have something to eat?"

It was as if he were delivering lines in a play. It made Elisabeth feel sorry for him because whatever his main line of business, John was never destined to be an actor. For Geoffrey, of course, it was second nature.

Before anyone could object, the two men had fetched their coats and made a dash for the door, leaving the women to their business.

As soon as they'd gone, she was motioned into the kitchen. Georgina pulled on her apron, handed one to Elisabeth, then set about preparing the vegetables. It was a ritual they went through prior to every meal. Today there were carrots to be diced. Afterwards, lives would be dissected too.

Elisabeth saw no point in beating about the bush – much better to get it over and done with.

"I gather you're already aware..."

"Yes, I'm sorry."

Sorry? Why should anyone be sorry? It was a perfectly natural occurrence, being pregnant. Elisabeth wasn't sorry at all. All that was happening was that she was expecting Geoffrey's baby. Perhaps that was what Georgina was sorry about – not that Elisabeth was carrying a child, but rather the fact that it was her brother's. She resolved to be positive.

"Look, I'm quite capable of sorting this out on my own."

"I'm sure you are, sweetie, but if I can be of any help..."

"What do you mean, 'help'?"

"I have contacts. In the medical profession. I can put you in touch with someone. You know, someone who'll help you get rid of it."

Georgina despatched the last of the carrots and swept them into the saucepan with a flourish.

Get rid of it? What was she talking about? Elisabeth had no intention of getting rid of it. What she wanted was some practical advice on how to cope with what was about to happen to her – not a recommendation to some backstreet abortionist. The true purpose of her visit was now clear. Georgina wasn't there to help, she was there to persuade Elisabeth to fix it so Geoffrey could extricate himself from whatever hole he'd dug himself into. And in the meanwhile, while his beleaguered sister did the dirty work, he'd gone off up the pub with his brother-in-law.

Although the suggestion did not come as a complete surprise. In the week that had elapsed between the scene in the car and her trip to Georgina's, Elisabeth had taken time to compose herself and think about her future – or at least, to achieve as much composure as she could given the torrent of emotions that was running within her. To keep the child or not? To stay at home or leave? These were the questions that constantly occupied her mind. She'd suspected what Georgina would propose and the decision as to whether to go along with it had been uppermost in her thoughts. At first she'd been afflicted with a terrible doubt, but then, as each day went by and the baby grew within her, so did the conviction that she could not in all conscience 'get rid of it'. This was a living being, an integral part of herself that she could not just dispose of at the drop of a hat. Her motherly impulse was strong, she loved her baby now, even before it was born, and she was not going to let anyone take it away from her.

"I have every intention of keeping the child."

"That's very brave of you."

"Hardly…"

Elisabeth didn't see it that way. It wasn't duty that was driving her, it was instinct. What would have been brave was to have gone against it.

Her show of defiance caused Georgina to back off for a moment. Perhaps Geoffrey's victims didn't always resist so forcibly. Either that or his sister had grown tired of fighting his battles and had decided to relent. Then she started down another track.

"So, what do you propose to do?"

"I'll do whatever I must."

"He won't marry you."

"He will if you tell him."

Elisabeth had already worked that out. There was enough in the relationship between Geoffrey and Georgina to imply she had some kind of hold over him. She'd calculated that Geoffrey would listen to his sister and most likely take her advice as he rarely went against her judgement. And if Elisabeth was to get what she wanted – i.e. the child, Geoffrey and the social life to which she'd become accustomed – she'd realised she'd have to enlist Georgina's help in persuading Geoffrey, just as Geoffrey had tried to enlist Georgina's help in persuading her.

She possessed two principal weapons in the engagement. The moral right of the argument rested clearly on her side but more importantly, she'd recognised in Georgina a desire to reform her brother and to set him on the straight and narrow, rather than have him continually come running to her with his problems. Here, immediately at her disposal, was a God-given opportunity for her to use. She must have been at the end of her tether as she caved in far more easily than Elisabeth could have hoped.

"Geoffrey won't like it, you know."

An element of reluctance remained, but the intention was there nonetheless. Now the boot was on Georgina's other foot.

Half an hour had elapsed before Geoffrey and John returned from the pub. By then, Elisabeth had been relieved of her culinary duties and Georgina had installed her on the living room sofa with a glass of sherry.

"Here, take this. One of these won't do you any harm."

Soon there were voices in the hallway and the sound of coats being hung up. Geoffrey was first to come in. His trip out and a couple of beers seemed to have made him even more carefree and had instilled in him an unwarranted level of confidence. John followed behind, looking rather more subdued.

Georgina appeared from the kitchen, still clad in her apron. She deliberately caught Geoffrey's eye, glanced meaningfully in Elisabeth's direction and discreetly shook her head.

John had gone to the sideboard to fetch some glasses and was facing in completely the wrong direction, missing this latest development. He came back to sit down opposite Elisabeth. His subsequent attempt at jollity was completely out of touch with affairs.

"Well, I wonder what's on the menu this evening?"

Georgina had returned to preparing the meal, swiftly pursued by her brother.

This left John and Elisabeth facing each other across the coffee table. It was an unhappy combination. They had little in common and even less to talk about and sat in an awkward silence, punctuated by the odd nervous glance in the direction of the kitchen.

Elisabeth shortly excused herself and got up to go to the bathroom. She'd no real need, but for a few precious moments she could escape John's excruciating presence. And more to the point, she'd remembered that the seat in the bathroom offered a listening post through to the kitchen. Anxious to discover her fate, she pressed her ear to the party wall. Even then she only caught snatches but it was enough, Georgina leading the way while Geoffrey followed in her wake.

I can't go on fending things off all the time, Geoffrey.

Why not? You've done it before.

Yes, but there comes a point...

A saucepan rattled on the stove, then the flow of words resumed.

So what happens if...

It'll be all over town. Trust me, I know the type.

Elisabeth stiffened. Georgina's last remark was unfair and made her appear unworthy. But if that was what she had to do...

Another saucepan masked the debate, the voices fading in and out as they moved about the room.

Damn it, Georgie, must I?

Don't underestimate this one, she's different.

You think so?

I know so.

There was a lull and Elisabeth sensed the discussion was coming to an end. She crept back to the sitting room and resumed her place.

In her absence, John had arranged the wine glasses on the table and was busy selecting a prime bottle of red. This time his actions could not have been more in tune with events. No sooner had he pulled the cork than Geoffrey emerged from the kitchen with a rueful expression on his face and prepared to make an announcement.

"You'd better charge your glasses and we'll all have a drink. It would appear that I'm going to be married."

And so Elisabeth had her victory. But it was to come at a heavy price.

Seven

The wedding itself was a secretive affair. Rather than hold it in church, for the sake of expediency it was thought best to proceed with a civil ceremony in a registry office. A self-appointed committee was set up for the purpose, led by Georgina together with John and, when he could be persuaded to take any interest in the matter, Geoffrey. Elisabeth took no part in it and was happy to concur with whatever they suggested. She had no desire for a big wedding – her priority was simply that it should go ahead and she was not too concerned as to how. And besides, she was hardly in a position to make demands. So by common consent there were no bridesmaids, no flowers, no ranks of relations in silly hats, no reception and more to the point, no flowing white dress. All in all, it was no great society event.

The potential stumbling block was her parents. She was still under twenty-one and nominally required their consent. Her mother wasn't a problem. Dorothy would do whatever was needed to keep the peace at home and to please her daughter beyond it – it was from her father that she expected opposition. But this perceived threat proved more imaginary than real as Arthur had effectively disowned her. In his own words, since their conversation earlier that year he'd given up hope of her ever walking in the path of God and as far as he was concerned he'd washed his hands of her. She'd told him she'd ridden with the Devil. Now she could marry him into the bargain for all he cared and for all the good it would do her. She was already damned and going to Hell so another step in that direction would not make a jot of difference. As this tirade contained no hint of objection, Elisabeth took it as a 'yes' and continued with her intended course of action.

And so with this resounding denial of her prospects ringing in her ears, on a wet and windy morning in October, Miss E. Johnson became Mrs E. Jones. Or rather Mrs E. Johnson-Jones, for the committee had recommended that this particular style and ordering of her name was far more appropriate to her new station in life. Elisabeth felt it sounded rather chic. No one with a name such as that could be thought to work in a Telephone Exchange.

But that same afternoon she went back there, hanging her coat in its usual place with the others. This was not a time for celebration, dashing away in an open-topped car festooned with good-luck charms and clattering cans. The only concession to gaiety appeared in the form of her mother who materialised outside the registry office armed with a box of confetti and a desire to wish her daughter well – but that was as far as it went. There was to be no honeymoon either – the time they'd already spent in Weston-super-Mare was deemed enough for that.

A more important problem was the question of where they should live. For the immediate future things could stay as they were, but in the longer term something would have to be done – Elisabeth had no intention of having the baby at home. The committee proved of little help and it was left to Geoffrey to 'sort something out'. But as time went by it was clear that he was not sorting it out, and Elisabeth was on the point of taking matters into her own hands when something happened that completely changed the course of affairs. Geoffrey received a long-awaited promotion and was required to move to London.

He'd mentioned the possibility before. *They can't keep me down here for ever. One day they'll recognise my potential – it's only a matter of time.* The region was all very well but it didn't offer the scope for a man of his talents and he yearned for a bigger stage. He said he'd grown tired of Bristol, it was stuffy and provincial and he couldn't wait to get away. A vacancy had arisen for a sports reporter with the World Service and he was just the man they were looking for. Admittedly, it was not the dizzying heights inhabited by the likes of Charles Cochran, but it was a step in the right direction. And with the World Service – there could hardly be a bigger stage than that.

He began to talk of people and places Elisabeth had never heard of – Butterfield, Twickenham and the Calcutta Cup; Zatopek, White City Stadium and the Olympics in Helsinki. In recent weeks he'd become rather sullen and withdrawn at Georgina's table, but now he was buoyed up with enthusiasm and warmed to his subject once more.

"You'll take it then?"

Elisabeth casually slipped her question into the conversation, anxious to know his response and the effect it might have on her future.

"Of course I'll take it!"

She was not entirely displeased, although it might have been better if he'd consulted her.

Her concern was that he'd go off without her and leave her literally holding the baby. His bright new horizon seemed to have blinded him, and although this newfound motivation was preferable to introspection, she feared he'd use it as an excuse to escape from her as well as from Bristol. It only wanted the words *Why don't you stay here* to fall from his lips and in his current state of excitement he'd forget about her entirely and make off on his own. He'd claim his absence was necessary rather than deliberate but he'd have abandoned her all the same.

She could not afford to let that happen. She'd committed herself to a course of action of which Geoffrey was a vital part and she couldn't let him go. He was more than her passport to a better life; now there was a child to think of and she clung to him and to hope as strongly as she'd clung to him amongst the crowds in Weston-super-Mare. She began to use the words 'we' and 'us' instead of the 'I' and 'me' he favoured in the belief that if she said them often enough, they'd seep into his subconscious and eventually translate into reality. The tactic proved successful. He never asked *You'll be coming with me I suppose?* but the assumption grew up in everyone's mind that she'd accompany him.

Later on, she came to realise that in his own way he needed her. He craved support and attention and for all his outward worldliness and confidence, he was not as self-reliant as he appeared. He feared solitude and the thought of his own company, and in Bristol he couldn't function without the guiding presence of Georgina. In London, he'd ultimately be on his own.

Toward the end of November, Geoffrey disappeared for a week. He told no one where he was going or why, or when he'd be back. When he returned, he said he'd been to London – an assertion Elisabeth could verify by means of a discarded rail ticket. He said he'd met his new employers and he'd been 'having a look around'. But exactly what he'd been doing, how he'd filled his time or where he'd stayed remained a mystery. It all conspired to create in Elisabeth the unfortunate thought that somewhere in the great metropolis stood a sweeping crescent of terraced houses behind one of whose doors lurked a younger edition of Mrs Beazley.

Press him as they might, neither Elisabeth nor John nor Georgina could extract much from him about his trip. Their enquiries were met with an offhand response, and so when one evening he casually announced *Oh, and by the way, I've found a house,* the revelation came as a bombshell. Even then, it was akin to getting blood from a stone but they gradually eked it out of him.

It was a small house but it would 'do'. It was close to Kingston-upon-Thames and handy for the rail connections to Bush House. It was not to be bought but rather to rent, a situation which would 'see them alright' until they got settled. As to its features, what facilities it might have and whether it was suitable for bringing up a family, Elisabeth remained in the dark. Given Geoffrey's customary lack of attention to detail, it wouldn't have surprised her if he didn't actually know.

She spent December preparing herself, gathering together what few items she possessed in readiness for the move. Now that matters had been resolved she wanted to get on with things and start this new and better life she had promised herself. Christmas seemed like an irrelevance and she passed most of the holiday trying to avoid being in the presence of her parents, conscious of her swollen belly.

Time hung heavily on her hands in the last few days of 1950. She said her farewells – to Millie, to Betty and most painfully, to her mother and father, the one desperate for her to stay, the other for her to go. Finally, as the New Year began she found herself in the familiar front seat of Geoffrey's car, the hood raised against the winter, hurrying east. With her suitcase packed in the dicky seat, she carried nothing more than a handbag, a raincoat, an unborn child and an anxious sense of foreboding.

She was never to go back to Bristol. Nor was she ever to go back to Weston-super-Mare. Later, she would remember the days she'd spent there in the summer of 1950 – in the sun, with Geoffrey, tall and handsome, a man she'd believed herself to be in love with – and she would think them the happiest of her life. After that, apart from the blessing of children, it was all a downhill journey.

Her first disappointment was the house. There was no getting away from it, it was small, smaller than she could possibly have imagined. It was terraced – but so was her parents' house, the one she'd lived in all her life. That was broad and spacious but this house was narrow and wedged between others of a similar size. The image of a great sweeping crescent with loft conversions had stayed with her, but this was life shoe-horned next to life, a cheek-by-jowl existence.

Her most pressing question was: *Where will the baby sleep?* Upstairs there were just the two bedrooms. The one that she and Geoffrey were to occupy was of a reasonable size whilst the other was small and cramped. The place was allegedly furnished but the second bedroom had been left completely empty. As soon as she put her head round the door, the words formed in her mouth.

"We'll need to get a cot."

Geoffrey, standing behind her on the landing, waiting for her to complete her inspection, simply shrugged his shoulders.

"I suppose so…"

Downstairs, the kitchen could best be described as basic. It had a stone floor, a stone sink and in the corner, a plain wooden top for preparation. Above the basin, a solitary tap dripped incessantly. At least there was running water.

The presence of a gas cooker struck her as a luxury. As to how she should use it, she hadn't a clue. She'd never cooked in her life. The kitchen at home was her mother's domain and without Dorothy there to guide her, she was going to have to learn on her own.

She suddenly felt engulfed by an overwhelming sense of failure. The practical necessity of looking after a husband and a family were staring her in the face and she'd no idea of how to cope with it. Her belly ached, the cooker laughed at her, and the monotonous plop, plop, plop of the incontinent tap annoyed her to the point of distraction. In a fit of pique she went to turn it off, but she wrenched at it too hard and sprained her wrist. Next time she resolved to be more careful. It was no good looking to Geoffrey for assistance – he'd be spending his day at work.

One thing she did have at her disposal was time. And prior to Pat's birth, if anything she found she had too much of it. When Geoffrey quit the house to catch his train at seven-thirty she was left quite alone and the rest of the day stretched endlessly before her. The place would fall into a gloomy silence broken only by the sound of a motor car puttering down the street outside or the shuffling of a next-door neighbour. In an effort to break this dismal spell, she took herself out on a daily visit to the shops, even if there was nothing she required. She discovered a small library and each week returned home with an armful of books so she could spend her afternoons immersed in a constant stream of trashy novels – anything to fill the hours.

But this was not enough and she longed for some form of company. She begged Geoffrey to provide her with a radio so she might hear another voice in the house. He could hardly deny her that – he of all people would understand.

As to what he expected of her, that soon became clear – a clean shirt to go to work in each morning and a decent meal to come home to each night. So as often as not, she could always pass a few hours in the kitchen, washing, ironing or cooking.

And every day, the child grew bigger within her.

By the middle of March, Elisabeth was practically immobile and learnt the true meaning of confinement. She was confined as to what she could do and she was confined as to where she could go. Her twenty-first birthday slipped by without celebration. The house fell into disarray and her daily trips to the shops were curtailed. The sheer effort of getting there had become exhausting and she'd started to feel nervous about being away from home. If anything should happen while she was out...

She'd been booked into a hospital in Hammersmith. Once this had been settled she ceased to be concerned with the problem of giving birth and worried more about getting there. Between seven in the morning and seven at night Geoffrey was unavailable. If by chance he was at home, it was agreed he would take her in the car. If not, she was to get a taxi and to this end, a pound note and some change had been placed in a tin on the mantelpiece.

It proved a wise precaution as just before lunch on the first Saturday in April her waters broke and she was obliged to call a cab. Geoffrey was typically absent. He'd gone to see London Irish play Wasps, and while he watched thirty hearty men strain and heave over the possession of a rugby ball, a midwife at Queen

Charlotte's watched his far frailer wife strain and heave over the birth of their daughter. He arrived home that evening to find a hastily scribbled note left on the dining room table – *Gone to hospital* – and he belatedly made his way out again.

At eight o'clock that night, Pat was born – and life changed yet again.

The birth of a child – and particularly a first-born – is a momentous occasion. But for the mother, while the event brings great pride, it also brings a tremendous amount of work. Before, she'd had time – now Elisabeth had none. Every minute of every day was consumed with the business of childcare, from the moment she woke up in the morning to the moment she fell asleep at night. The pile of trashy novels she'd accumulated prior to her lying-in lay unread, the radio she'd pestered Geoffrey to acquire stayed off – save if some soothing music was required to lull the baby to sleep. Then, when she *was* asleep, it remained silent for fear of waking the child.

But when Pat was awake, it was Elisabeth who was desperate for sleep. At night, while Geoffrey slumbered on, oblivious to all around him, it was she who got up at two in the morning to give that all-important feed – and it was she who at two in the afternoon started preparing an evening meal as Pat dozed. There were times when she'd willingly have lain down beside her daughter – if only time had allowed.

So was this the better life that Elisabeth had yearned for? If not, she could hardly blame someone else – it had all been her own doing. It was she who'd allowed herself to become pregnant, she who'd put her foot down in Georgina's kitchen, she who'd forced Geoffrey's hand. What had begun a year before at Freddy's party now seemed part of a different world. Speeding down the Bath Road with the wind in her hair, the cut and thrust of debate around Georgina's table, the parties, the pop of a champagne cork, the trips to Weston-super-Mare – where were they now?

She might have felt resentful, angry that the benefits life with Geoffrey promised were denied her. And yet the thought never crossed her mind. Despite the drudgery, the endless hours of toil, the sleeplessness and overwhelming sense of exhaustion, she was fundamentally happy. She loved her baby to a degree she'd not thought possible. Every smile Pat gave was greeted with joy, every cry she made welcomed. And where the house had been dull and empty, now it was full of new life – what a difference it made to the silence that had preceded it! For all her deprivations, Elisabeth was content. Although the same could not be said of her husband.

A month after Pat was born, Geoffrey disappeared again. It was only a matter of days, but this time there was no explanation. He'd simply 'gone away' for a while.

At first Elisabeth put it down to disappointment on his part. During the latter stages of her pregnancy she'd realised how much he'd wanted a son. They'd discussed naming the child, but he'd shown no interest in her suggestions for a girl and had told her she could have what she liked. But if it was a boy...

She later dismissed the idea and began to blame herself. Since the birth of their daughter she'd given him little attention and was far more focused on her child than she was on her husband. Perhaps he'd gone off in a sulk and with this in mind, she determined to be more attentive.

The opportunity arose soon after he returned. Because of her condition they'd not made love since arriving at the house, but now he approached her and she allowed it. She was anxious to please him, he was her husband, they lived together under the same roof and slept in the same bed – there was no reason to deny him.

But it was not a happy experience. Her stitches had healed but she was still sore and she asked him to be careful. But he either failed to hear her or chose to ignore her plea and pressed on regardless. At one point she called out *Geoffrey, you're hurting,* but to no avail and rather than push him off, she turned her face to one side to disguise her pain.

Afterwards, he sat on the end of the bed, smoking one of his full-strength cigarettes and staring moodily out of the window. The curtains had been left open and a bright moon cast its gleam across the room, just as the sun had done that morning at Mrs Beazley's. Then, their lovemaking had brought pleasure and a closeness which had inspired her, but now it seemed like nothing more than a duty and for the first time since leaving the West Country, it dawned on her that from now on this was how it would be. Their romance had become as stale as his breath.

It boiled down to how long things might last. Would it be weeks? Or could they manage to see out the year? She began to suspect it was not going to be a lifetime, whatever vows they'd made – the idea he'd remain faithful to one home and one woman simply wasn't supportable. For twelve hours of the day he was out and about in London, with all its attractions. God only knew what he got up to.

The challenges of his new job sustained him for a while. From time to time he'd return from work enthused, excited by the thought of some project or another he'd been asked to take on. The Olympics in Helsinki was high on the list and as the time approached, a series of charts and timetables appeared on the dining room table. But apart from these flashes of interest, his mood was generally sombre and more often than not, depressed. Whatever Elisabeth's efforts, the house offered him little comfort and sometimes he'd go a week without speaking.

He paid scant attention to his daughter and preferred to sit out on the back step, smoking. Elisabeth might have understood had Pat been a bad-tempered child, but she was not. She was both bonny and good-natured and deserved far more from her father than she received. She learnt to talk without him, she learnt to walk without him, and she was always ready to greet his presence with a smile and a gurgle of pleasure although the sentiment was rarely returned.

Geoffrey's absences gradually became more frequent. Sometimes it was two days a month, sometimes it was two days a week, it varied. Whenever he returned he declined to be interviewed on the subject and snapped at her, saying it was a poor show when a man had to be questioned about his whereabouts the whole time. She soon learnt to hold her tongue, choosing to avoid his wrath rather than incur it. At the end of July he disappeared for a fortnight, gone, as he told her, to Helsinki.

It was not as though the place was quiet without him. Pat was always with her and her presence filled the house, her time and her heart. Despite the endless rota of domestic chores, Elisabeth embraced motherhood as easily as her hand slipped into a glove. Her only regret was that Pat had no sibling with whom to share her childhood. She began to yearn for another child and with this in mind, submitted gladly to Geoffrey's demands. Even when he'd been away and she could have chided him, she preferred to receive him warmly into her bed, anxious to conceive again.

But it was to no effect, and the ease with which she'd managed affairs the first time round eluded her. A year went by and then, miraculously, another, and yet still she could not get pregnant.

Finally, as if by divine intervention, her prayers were answered as one day, completely out of the blue, Frank arrived on the scene.

Part Three

Frank

One

"Watch out!" said Mr McGregor.

He was leaning against the gate at the edge of the field, resting his gammy leg.

Crack!

A noise like a whiplash rang out as the makeshift washing line tied to one of the concrete fence-posts snapped taut. Then, as the caravan next door pulled away, there was the sound of tearing metal as the small back window to which the other end had been secured was wrenched from its hinges.

"That's buggered it," said Mr McGregor, limping from one foot to the other.

The towing vehicle jerked to a halt and the owner of car and van jumped out to inspect the damage. His face had a florid complexion, a fact which helped hide any embarrassment.

"What the hell...?"

"You forgot to untie yer line," said McGregor, pointing at the offending article.

At the back of the van, the errant window dangled precariously, swinging between the line and the one remaining hinge, half on, half off.

"Damn it!" said the florid man, his face burning, and stamped his foot.

McGregor's response was to laugh, throwing his head back with his mouth wide open, exposing the rows of bad and blackened teeth.

The van owner scowled and began to untie the line. It was all very well for McGregor to laugh. He didn't have to bear the expense.

A small crowd was gathering, attracted by the commotion. From the van diagonally opposite Frank's an elderly couple appeared, their frail feet clad in carpet slippers. They shuffled across the grass and came to stand at the side of the gravel road.

The man was tall and thin, and while one hand held that of his wife, the other repeatedly pushed his spectacles back up the bridge of his nose then reassuringly patted her wrist. Shorter and broader, she stooped beside him. It was the first time Frank had ever seen them, and as far as he could remember, the last. After that there was only the glow of the light in their window which reminded him they were there.

Other unrecognised faces emerged from neighbouring vans and clustered round in groups. It was at times like these, unscheduled moments in the course of local history, that communities drew together. Rumours began to circulate.

"What's going on?" asked one.

"I dunno," replied another. "I only 'eard the bang. I thought t'was a firecracker going off."

"Hmm... Sounded more like a pistol shot to me."

"Look, there's McGregor. If 'e really wants to find out what's happenin', go ask 'im. 'E's bound to know."

The noise and the sound of voices eventually drew his mother out of their van. She came across to him, drying her hands on her apron, then stopped to crouch beside him and whispered.

"What is it, dear?"

Frank raised his hand and with an outstretched finger showed her the dangling window, the van, the man with the florid face, and finally, Mr McGregor.

"There," he said.

"Shush now," said his mother, guiding his hand gently downwards. "You mustn't point at people, it's rude. Besides, it isn't any of our business what goes on next door. You'd better come in now."

She took his hand and led him back toward their van.

As they reached the corner he looked back over his shoulder. The man with the florid face had got back into his car and was about to drive off, while the elderly couple hadn't moved. Mr McGregor was still leaning on the gate at the edge of the field, but his interest in the departing van had now ceased and to Frank's discomfort his eyes were currently directed toward him and his mother. Frank followed her up the step and into their van where he went to watch the rest of the proceedings, kneeling on the settee and staring out of the side window with his chin resting on his hands. The small crowd parted to allow passage and the car and the van, now freed from the line which remained tied to the concrete post, rocked and rumbled down the gravel road, the broken window clanging unceremoniously at the rear.

It was at that moment, looking out of the window and over the empty pitch next door, that Frank came to the conclusion he didn't much like Mr McGregor.

It was his first abiding memory – not just of the caravan site and all that it entailed, but of anything at all really. Prior to that there'd been a house, but he'd no recollection of it whatsoever. All that remained was a photograph, slipped in amongst the others his mother had kept of him. It showed him at the age of three, outside in a small garden, sitting astride a metal tricycle and wearing a woollen bobble hat. But there was nothing of the house itself or what had taken place within it. It had assumed an air of mystery and stayed like a locked room, unopened, a chapter in his life to which he had no access.

Elisabeth must have been in desperate straits to have moved. God knows how she'd coped. Her parents had refused to take her in and he'd no idea what they'd lived on. She couldn't possibly have gone to work, there was a home and two kids to look after. And if that wasn't enough, there was always the prospect of bumping into McGregor, prowling about late at night.

Later, when her days became free she could find employment, but she was initially tied to the van and to her family. Although now he came to think of it, it couldn't have been long after they'd arrived before she'd packed him off to school.

"So," said Mr Thorpe, looking down from on high, "this is Frank."

"Yes," said his mother, "this is Frank."

She still had hold of his hand, yet he felt there was a latent desire within her to propel him forward and into the care of another. He curled his toes up ready to resist and his new pair of sandals bit at his heels.

"Now then, Frank," said Mr Thorpe, bending down to meet him.

He leant forward to shake hands and Frank could see he was completely bald, the smooth curve of his pate glistening under the foyer's neon light.

"And are you looking forward to joining us at school?"

Frank shook his head. He was not looking forward to it one iota. He could not betray the fact and his gesture was probably too vigorous for his own good.

Mr Thorpe straightened to his full height, threw back his head and laughed. It was not a cruel laugh like McGregor's, but more the hearty laugh of a man who'd embarrassed himself, caught in a word-trap of his own making.

"Well," he said, trying to recover, "we'll have to see what we can do about that."

Although Frank didn't want him to do anything about it at all.

"Jonathon!" Mr Thorpe hailed an older boy who was passing by with a large book tucked under his arm. "Run along to 1B will you, and ask Mrs Williams if she could join us for a moment."

"Yes, sir."

Jonathon made an abrupt about-turn before disappearing through one of the swing doors that opened off the foyer. The door flapped ponderously behind him. Short of tugging his forelock, he could not have been more obliging.

Mr Thorpe beamed.

"Jonathon is one of our best students. As you can see, he's quite capable of operating without supervision." Mr Thorpe clasped his hands behind his back and twiddled his thumbs. "We try to run a progressive establishment, Mrs Johnson. I'm sure Frank will be very happy here."

Frank, meanwhile, was thinking quite the opposite.

Mrs Williams arrived. She was tall and thin and rather angular and not like his mother at all. Her nose stuck out like the beak of a huge bird and dripped incessantly so that every word she uttered was muffled by the constant application of a tissue or a handkerchief.

"You sent for me, Mr Thorpe?" she sniffled through her latest piece of Kleenex.

"Ah yes!" With every movement of his head, the neon light shining on Mr Thorpe's bald pate changed its pattern like a kaleidoscope. "I want you to meet Mrs Johnson. Mrs Johnson is new to the area, aren't you, Mrs Johnson?"

His mother nodded silently, although Frank wished she'd say something positive in their defence.

"And this," said Mr Thorpe, glancing downwards, "is Frank. Frank is going to be joining us soon, aren't you, Frank?"

Frank shook his head again but this time Mr Thorpe had prepared his reply.

"You see, Mrs Williams? He will have his little jokes, will Frank. I like a boy with a sense of humour. Adds something to the school don't you think? Why don't you take Mrs Johnson and Frank and show them the classroom he'll be working in. I'm sure he'd like that, wouldn't you, Frank?"

Frank's response was utterly predictable.

Mr Thorpe threw back his head and laughed for the second time, causing the kaleidoscope to dance violently up and down.

Mrs Williams sniffed.

"Follow me," she croaked, holding open the swing door and ushering them into the corridor.

It was a long, straight corridor, stretching as far as the eye could see. On the right, an acre of plate glass gave out onto the grey expanse of a playground. On the left, doors appeared at regular intervals, rather like cells in a prison block, each with its own porthole and individual number – 4B, 4A, 3B, 3A and so on. In front of them, Mrs Williams' pale summer sandals slapped the polished floor *clop, clop, clop* and with every passing step his grip tightened on his mother's hand as they moved further and further away from what he perceived to be the known world. By the time they reached their destination, her fingers were white where he'd squeezed out the colour.

Eventually they came to a halt in front of room 1B. Mrs Williams flung open the door and the babble that had preceded their arrival ceased. A sea of blank faces stared out at him and he felt their eyes searching every ounce of his person.

"As you can see, we've a pretty full complement." Mrs Williams clopped her way to the front and plucked another Kleenex from its box. "But don't worry, we'll find another desk from somewhere."

In contrast to the bravado of Mr Thorpe, her comment did not inspire confidence.

"Yes," said his mother. "Of course. I'm sure it'll be fine."

But it wasn't.

Two

It was all very well for Pat. She was older and didn't have the same problems as Frank. She'd gone to school straightaway, whereas he'd had to wait. And being a girl, she'd found it easier to fit in. Within a week she'd made a friend and got invited round for tea. Besides, she was good at things that he was not, skipping and running and the like, things which he somehow found awkward. He wasn't handicapped or disabled, he was always a strong and healthy boy. It was just that he was different.

Pat could already read and write. Her exercise books were neat and tidy and filled with a rounded copperplate script regularly punctuated by ticks – an achievement he could never emulate. She worked hard, talked a lot, played hopscotch with the other girls and unlike Frank, she didn't seem afraid of anything – a fact which became all too obvious when it came to the matter of cows.

He'd never actually seen a cow before. At least, not a real one. He knew what they looked like. Or he thought he did. There'd been pictures of them in the book of farmyard animals his mother had read to him when he was little. Corralled within the soft fabric pages of a fairy tale they'd seemed likeable, placid creatures and the *moo* they emitted was a gentle, unalarming noise. Even when you shouted it at the top of your voice – *MOO!* – as he did to make his mother laugh, it never seemed capable of violence.

But confronted in the wild, proper cows were altogether different. To start with, they were huge – far larger than you could ever have imagined – and when you stood next to one it towered above you, blocking out the landscape, its horns wider than you could spread your arms. And instead of the comforting call of the farmyard book, their cry was often a blood-curdling, raucous bellow that split the night as you lay huddled in your bunk. And they stank (a fact no book could ever convey), of poo mostly, or if not then a white milky smell that invaded your clothing whenever they were near. Proper cows were dangerous, proper cows were to be avoided and so if you had the misfortune to find one blocking your route home, it was a decidedly daunting prospect.

"Come on, Frank, you're lagging behind."

It was true, he was. His bag felt particularly heavy that day and he was not inclined to rush.

"I'll race you to the gate," said Pat, and she shot off down the cinder path at the bottom of the playing field, her pigtails flying out behind her. With her knees up high and her legs a blur, there was no way she was going to stop.

"Wait for me!" implored Frank, and he stumbled forward into a trot in a forlorn attempt to catch up.

His bag, a brown leather satchel handed down from his sister, banged against his thigh and impeded his progress. Fearful of being left alone, he made a concerted effort and struggled up the slight incline, panting. By the time he reached the gate, Pat had already opened it and stood ready to let him through. Had she been on her own, she'd probably have climbed straight over it.

"Hurry up, I've lots of homework to do."

He slowed to a deliberate walk so he could catch his breath. He had to exercise some form of control or else Pat would literally run off.

Beyond the gate, the field stretched away into the distance and over the top of the hedge on the far side, he could just make out the roof of their van. In-between lay the footpath, clearly marked and well trodden. All he had to do was follow it and he would be home. But there was a problem. This was no ordinary field, this was a cow field and thereby fraught with danger.

"I don't like it!" he moaned.

Pat sighed, depressed by his lack of spirit.

"Come on, it'll be alright. I'll be with you the whole way."

She took his hand to lead him forward but he defiantly snatched it back.

"I won't go!"

"You've got to go. Anyway, Mother said tea was at four o'clock and you don't want to be late."

It was a common theme. Mention of tea and Mother had a calming effect on Frank. Pat took his hand again. This time he allowed it and they began to move forward. Step by step, like burglars tiptoeing on a landing, they crept along the side of the hedge. At the point where the field opened out and you could see into the blind corner, Pat peered round as look out.

"It's alright," she announced. "There's half a dozen cows but they're way off." She daren't lie as sooner or later Frank would find her out. "If we go now, we'll be fine."

Frank chewed this over. What did it mean? It implied that if they didn't go now, they'd somehow be in trouble. How could that be? The cows were in front of them...

But before he could voice a response his sister was pulling him forward and they were off, she at a brisk walk while he followed behind at his steady trot, clinging to her hand. His knee thumped against the heavy satchel. It would be hopeless if she started running – he wouldn't be able to keep up.

Ten yards in, he was overwhelmed with an anxious curiosity and made the mistake of looking back over his shoulder. There, barely fifty feet away, stood a herd of the bovine giants, staring at him inquisitively. Even as he watched, one of them began to lumber towards him in a slow but certain gait. His sister had lied to him – this was not fine at all. He was seized with a fit of panic and urged her to move faster.

But Pat's attention was elsewhere.

"Mind where you're putting your feet!"

His eyes shot forward and in the nick of time he hurdled a cowpat, the satchel swinging wildly. With this disaster avoided he continued at full speed, only to be confronted by another.

While they'd been focused on cowpats, one of the beasts had got round in front of them and now stood between them and the far gate. Raising its huge head, it gathered its breath and let out a roar of triumph.

Brother and sister halted in the middle of the field. Pat muttered something unintelligible under her breath, while Frank began to cry.

"For goodness sake!" said Pat. "It's only a cow, it can't hurt you."

Only a cow! What did she know about cows? Cows were the worst thing in the world!

Meanwhile, the rest of the herd had gathered behind them and they were completely surrounded.

"I don't like it!" repeated Frank, the tears stinging his cheeks. His feet began to dance up and down as if he were about to wet himself.

Pat considered her options.

"Wait here," she decided and let go of his hand. This was a huge mistake. Her intention was to shoo the cow off and clear a path to the gate. She stepped intrepidly forward, waving her hands in the air and shouting. "Shoo! Shoo! Go on! Push off!"

And for a moment it looked as if this brave and selfless act would pay off as the cow shied away. But as soon as her hands went down it returned, unmoved, and they were back to square one.

Not to be outdone she tried again, more violently this time, running at the beast and hollering out loud. The effect was much the same, only now the cow circled her and suddenly she was outside the ring, leaving her brother within it.

"Frank?" she called from her position of safety. "Come on, Frank. Just run at them and they'll let you through."

But Frank could no more run at a cow than climb Mount Everest. He was rooted to the spot, his feet like blocks of concrete while the rest of his body trembled. His sister had abandoned him, he was trapped in his own worst nightmare and his reaction was to open his mouth and wail, long and loud, until his cries reached screaming pitch. And when Frank wailed, the noise could drown out the bellow of even the loudest cow.

People on the caravan site looked up from what they were doing. Elisabeth, recognising the sound of her son's voice, abandoned her cooking and rushed out to the gate.

"What on earth is going on?"

"Mum! Mum!" Pat arrived, breathless from her dash across the field. "It's Frank! The cows have got him and he's gone berserk!"

Elisabeth's hands flew up to her mouth.

"Oh my God!"

Quickly unfastening the gate, she joined her daughter in the field and together they ran toward the spot. The herd scattered before their determined advance and there was Frank, exactly where Pat had left him, knees shaking, eyes closed and mouth open, wailing.

"You poor boy!" Elisabeth snatched him up and began to comfort him, gently patting his back. "There, there..."

His little body throbbed against her and she could feel the tumult inside him.

Frank buried his head into the soft warm folds of his mother's neck. Here was the familiar smell of hair and flaky skin that filled his senses like dusted flour. With her arms wound tight about him, he could forget about cows and school and all the things that bothered him and rejoice in the fact that there was nowhere else on earth he'd rather be. His sobbing gradually subsided and soon it had reduced to the occasional convulsion.

Pat retrieved her brother's satchel and carried it back to the van, carefully brushing off the grass and mud it had accumulated in the course of their adventure.

Later, when they'd cleaned themselves up, Frank was awarded an extra portion of jam to go with the drop scones his mother had made.

"Why do you make such a fuss of him?" said Pat, after he'd gone to bed. "They were only cows, you know."

"I'd do exactly the same for you." Elisabeth was trying to read a magazine beneath the hissing glow of the gas mantle. "Anyway, he's a lot younger than you are."

"Humph!" said Pat and sucked the end of her pencil. But there was no real jealousy in her comment. She knew that she was loved too. Besides, there was no time to dwell on it – she'd a lot of homework to get through.

Of course there would be cows on a farm. They lived on a farm, McGregor's Farm, it said so on the letters that arrived in the postbox at the end of the gravel road. One of his chores was to walk down to the box and inspect its contents, looking for anything that might be addressed to them. Later, when the short cut to school through the field had been abandoned in favour of the road, he checked the box every day on his way home, learning how to flick open the rusty lid without trapping his fingers.

His mother expressed particular interest in the thin brown envelopes – not those handwritten on the front, but the ones printed behind a transparent window. As soon as they arrived, usually on a Friday, she would glance at the cover then slide them unopened into the pocket of her apron. And if for some reason they didn't come, there was an air of tension over the weekend you could cut with a knife.

At first they were labelled by name *Johnson* but when McGregor got round to giving them a number, 7, he found he could look for that too.

The numbers went up to 25. One Saturday afternoon, instead of kicking his heels in the van, he set himself the task of touring the site to count the pitches and found there were only 24. Checking through them again, he discovered there was no number 13. In the long dull days of childhood, this classed as excitement. More often than not though, the box was empty, but that was understandable. Other than the authorities, who'd want to write to them, stuck as they were in some backwater at the bottom of the hill on the road coming out of Keynsham?

The post was not his only job. His mother had plenty of tasks to dish out and as soon as he was old enough, he got more than his fair share. She only had to utter the words *Frank? Are you busy? Have you got a minute?* and he knew what would come next. Bring in the water, take out the slops, fetch this, carry that, he always had his chores. Things got worse when Pat went to big school and he was forced to take on the jobs she no longer had time for. *Frank? Leave your sister alone, she's got schoolwork to do.* Ah yes, she always was the clever one, Pat, in more ways than one.

His reward, at the tender age of eight, was to be called the man of the house. It was a title that did not always sit comfortably on his shoulders.

"Pay attention, class."

Class paid attention, noting the difficulty with which Mrs Williams extracted the next Kleenex from its box.

"In a moment we're going to go through some of our times tables," she mumbled through her tissue.

Class sighed in unison. Times tables was not the most popular activity for a Wednesday afternoon.

"But first I have an announcement to make."

Despite Mrs Williams' calculation to the contrary, this was not greeted with any more enthusiasm than the prospect of times tables. Announcements had a habit of being dull and rather boring. More often than not they related to some domestic arrangement such as a test of the fire alarm or the need to ensure the windows were closed before going home – they were rarely of any real interest.

"No doubt you will have noticed that a new member has been

added to our class."

Class had indeed noticed – and were wondering.

Frank looked round the room, a little puzzled. He'd not seen anyone new since his arrival.

"Frank?" Mrs Williams secured his attention. "Would you like to stand up and introduce yourself?"

No, thought Frank, he would not, and the shock of being singled out kept him rooted to his chair. Surely she couldn't mean him? But she did. He rose bashfully to his feet and inspected the toecaps of his new and pinching sandals.

"Now then, Frank. Why don't you start off by telling us your name?"

Frank looked bemused. What a silly question! Especially as she'd just given the answer.

"Frank, miss."

"Yes, but your other name."

"Johnson, miss."

"And how old are you, Frank?"

"Five, miss." Then, with an element of pride, remembering it was almost his birthday, "Nearly six!"

Class tittered, although Frank remained straight-faced. What was so funny about that? It was the truth, wasn't it?

Mrs Williams continued, undaunted.

"And what else can you tell us about yourself, Frank?"

"Nothing, miss."

"Nothing at all?"

"No, miss." Frank shook his head. There was really nothing to tell.

"There must be something, Frank," Mrs Williams persisted. She saw it as her duty to develop a child's capacity for self-expression. "For instance, perhaps you could tell us your favourite colour?"

"I haven't got a favourite colour, miss."

It was true. Frank didn't think in terms of colours. His world was black and white, like cows, or occasionally a muddled grey.

But Mrs Williams was not to be put off. Every child had a character, sometimes hidden deep inside, and it was merely a question of finding it.

"Now, come on, Frank – I'm sure you can do better than that. There must be something."

Frank blinked, as he was wont to do under pressure. He cast around his classmates but all he received was their eyes, just as he'd done on that first day, searching his person.

Mrs Williams, meanwhile, stood waiting.

In the end, he decided on the only thing he was sure of, the only thing that really mattered, the thing that defined him.

"I don't have a father, miss."

For a moment, this blunt statement of truth was met with complete silence. Then there was a snigger from one of the girls at the back of the room.

Silly old Frank! Fancy not having a father!

"Ah," said Mrs Williams, rather taken aback and reaching for the comfort of her tissue box. This was not the part of a child's character she'd particularly wanted to explore. She'd rather had in mind butterflies and rabbits and other more cuddly things. "Well, perhaps we can talk about that later. But thank you for sharing it with us, Frank. You can sit down now."

Frank sat down, relieved to have survived his ordeal. It had been painful – but it had been enough.

"So, class. Shall we get on with our times tables?"

Mrs Williams was anxious to move on.

But class was not. Class was buzzing with the implications of this latest revelation. How could you not have a father? Didn't everyone have a father? He looked quite normal but perhaps there was something different about Frank. Was he some kind of biological freak? The possibilities were far more interesting than times tables and it was a good ten minutes before Mrs Williams got them settled down.

Later on, she collared Mr Thorpe in the staff room.

"You should have told me…"

Mr Thorpe shrugged his shoulders – it was the first he'd heard of it. Parents didn't always give up their secrets.

Back in his office, he took out the file marked 'Johnson, F.' and in the section reserved for father's occupation he added the words *Not Applicable* and returned it to the drawer. As far as he was concerned, the incident was closed.

Three

It was a while before a new van arrived on the pitch next door. The grass grew long and unkempt and the bare patch where the previous van had stood became covered over. There must have been a problem. It was not like McGregor to leave a space lying empty when there was rent to be had for filling it.

He came across from the farmhouse to supervise, hitching up the belt of his corduroy trousers, the limp in his leg a reminder of an old war-injury or an accident with farm machinery that had disadvantaged him. He stopped in front of their van and stood with his back to them, looking up the gravel road, shielding his eyes from the watery sun.

Frank knelt in his usual place on the settee, his chin on his hands, staring out of the side window. It was a Saturday morning, there was no school and he was in need of occupation. He'd begun the day by helping his mother with the washing, holding the basket of wet clothes while she pegged them to the line which now flapped in the steady breeze. He'd reverted to the square of carpet at the back of the van to play with his cars and his soldiers but nothing had taken his fancy and he'd become a little bored. The low throb of an engine and the scrunching of tyres on the gravel road had soon drawn him away.

Outside, a caravan and its towing vehicle bumped and bounced toward them. It had rained during the night and the potholes in the road had formed into brown muddy puddles so each dip of the van's wheels was met with an accompanying splash.

McGregor raised a hand in recognition, then indicated where they should stop.

"Pull right up to the end..."

The rig comprised a substantial van pulled by a long, low estate car, the back of which was piled high with personal belongings. It came to a halt directly in front of their plot.

119

McGregor motioned in the direction of the empty space.

"You'll need to back 'er in there."

The driver of the estate, a muscular man in his mid-thirties, wound down the window and gave a sign of acknowledgement. Clamping his elbow to the outside of his door, he turned his head and the steering wheel in co-ordinated motion and slowly began to reverse. The engine cut in with a deep growl.

McGregor limped smartly to the back of the plot, his gammy leg trailing behind with the effort.

"Come on, then!" he beckoned. "You've another couple of yards to go yet."

Still tied to its concrete fence-post, the broken washing line trailed in the grass as evidence of the plot's former occupants.

The driver deftly see-sawed his steering wheel and carefully backed the rig into place.

"That'll do yer!" cried McGregor, slapping his hand on the back of the van as it reached its appointed spot. Brake lights flashed red and a handbrake was jerkily applied.

The driver leapt out to inspect his handiwork. There was a shaking of hands, a nodding of heads and a general air of self-congratulation. Compared to the previous departure, it had been a successful exercise.

On the far side of the estate, the passenger door opened and a woman got out, rubbing her bare arms in the cold morning air. She was of roughly the same age as the driver and had strong bony features. Frank thought how much like Mrs Williams she looked with her beaky nose, only she, of course, was much older. Reaching back into the car, the woman took out a wrap and pulled it round her shoulders.

At the same time, the rear door on the driver's side opened and a young boy hopped down from his seat. He was taller than Frank but not as tall as his sister (Pat was a good height for her age). The boy was of sturdy construction with a mop of unruly black hair that blew about in the wind.

Frank shuffled round on the settee. This was something to think about.

Further along in the kitchen, her hands in the sink and looking out over the same scene, his mother had already formed her opinion.

"They look like a nice family. Why don't you go out and play?"

Frank considered her suggestion then clambered down from the settee and began tidying away his cars and his soldiers. First, he would wait until McGregor had gone. But then, if there was nothing better to do…

"'Lo."

"'Lo."

Then there was silence, a period of assessment, waiting to see who'd blink first.

There was no fence between the plots and no formal boundary, just a rough dividing line where the grass had been cut and kept on one side and left unmown on the other. At some point someone would have to cross it.

Frank wriggled his toes and stared. Wind ruffled the boy's black hair. He was juggling with something in his pocket.

"Want to play jacks?"

"What's jacks?" asked Frank. He'd never heard of it.

"Here, I'll show you."

The boy drew out a set of six small metal pieces and a rubber ball. He extended his hand so Frank could see.

"There."

"What do you do with them?" said Frank. He still was none the wiser.

The boy looked around, searching for something. Then, seeing a flat patch at the side of the gravel road, he went down on one knee beside it. He scattered the metal objects on the ground, tossed the ball into the air and before it could bounce, swept three or four of the pieces up with a deft flick of his hand.

"See? That's what you do."

He gathered everything up and offered it all to Frank.

Frank looked at the ball and the metal pieces and shook his head. It was all too complicated and involved the rapid movement of hands. The boy seemed disappointed, but not hurt and screwed his face up tight as he thought of his next move. As the elder it was up to him to make suggestions.

"What about marbles then? Fancy a game of marbles?"

This time Frank nodded. Marbles were alright. Marbles were round and solid and predictable and far more reliable than jacks. Frank had some marbles. He ran back to the van to fetch them.

His mother had been watching affairs from the window.

"What are you doing?" she asked.

"Playing marbles," said Frank.

He ran straight past her and into the back of the van. Lifting up the cushion of the settee, he took out his toy box from the space underneath and tipped the contents onto the floor. His marbles were in a circular tin of the kind that had once contained cough drops dusted in icing sugar. He unscrewed the lid and counted them. There were twelve in all, rolling around. At the bottom of the tin there were still traces of the sugar. He put the tin in his pocket and ran back through the kitchen.

"Excuse me!" Elisabeth called after him. "I hope you're not going to…"

…*leave those toys in a mess.*

But it was too late and he'd gone.

Frank arrived back at the flat patch at the same time as his new neighbour. The boy was carrying a transparent plastic bag, knotted off at the top and containing an extensive collection of marbles. They were mostly the normal type, clear glass with a swirl pattern, but some were a solid white colour and a couple were quite large, a bull's-eye and possibly a gobstopper. Frank was impressed. He rattled his tin to show willing.

"Tell you what," said the boy. "We'll start from here." And with the edge of his shoe he drew a rough line in the ground at the end of the flat patch. "See that rock over there? That's the target." He pointed to the largest stone in the area, about a yard away from the line. Next to the rock was a large puddle. "Anything that goes in the puddle, you lose. Ok?"

Frank nodded. He wasn't worried about the rules, he just wanted to play.

"You can go first," said the boy, making a great concession.

Frank chose a marble and knelt behind the line. Positioning his fist, he gave a flick of his thumb and the ball sailed forward. It was a good shot, travelling the whole yard, but it lacked something in accuracy. There was a 'plop' as it landed in the water. Frank laughed. He'd gone straight into the puddle!

"Well, you've lost that one," said the boy, scratching his head. "My go."

He knelt behind the line and took his shot, only instead of trying for distance he dropped his marble deliberately short of the rock, then hopped forward and took another go, pinging the ball onto the stone.

"That's one to me," he said.

His tone was confident but without triumph, as if he'd been expecting to win.

Frank decided to copy his tactics and dropped his next marble short. He hopped forward on the rough road, only to find that the flat patch wasn't as flat as it looked and the place where his marble had landed was crooked and sloped. It was awkward but he took his shot nonetheless. There was a 'plop' as it landed in the puddle. Frank laughed again. He didn't mind. He liked going in the puddle, it was fun.

"Well, looks like you've lost another one," said the boy, the wind ruffling his hair. He was laughing too. Now they were both laughing.

Before long, all of Frank's marbles were in the puddle. After the last of them had gone in, they went over to look. Standing at the edge of the pool with their hands in their pockets, they could see the glass balls staring back at them like the eyes of dead fish.

"Well," said the boy, scratching his head, "I dunno what we're gonna do now."

Frank thought hard but nothing was immediately forth-coming.

The answer arrived in the form of a shout from the boy's van. The muscular man had appeared and was calling for him.

"Paul? You'd better come in now. Your mother's got you something to eat."

The invitation was accompanied by the tantalising smell of fried bacon.

Frank wriggled his toes for a moment, then asked the obvious question.

"Is that your dad?"

"Yup," said Paul. "That's my dad. Why?"

Frank was curious. He'd never been close to someone's dad before.

"What does he do?"

"I dunno," said Paul, shrugging his shoulders. "This and that. What does your dad do?"

Frank blinked – his question had rebounded on him. At the bottom of the muddy pool a dozen fish eyes stared up in expec-tation.

"I haven't got a dad."

"Oh," said Paul. "That's a bummer."

It was, but the boy didn't dwell on it. He was drawn more by the prospect of bacon.

"I'd better go."

He started to move off but there remained the matter of the sunken marbles. In the light of Frank's predicament he decided to be generous.

"You can have those back. We weren't playing keepsies anyway."

When he'd gone, Frank recovered his marbles from the pool, drying them off on his handkerchief and putting them back in the tin with the icing sugar. At the window of their van, he could see his mother waiting for him to come in.

But he didn't want to go in just yet. There was something joyous in his heart and he wanted to give expression to it in a way that the presence of his mother would not allow. Rattling the tin as loudly as he could, he ran round the van, mouthing under his breath, *Bummer, bummer, bummer, bummer, bummer, bummer, bummer, bummer.* Somehow he knew it was a bad word – a fact which only added to the pleasure of using it. Eventually he grew tired and went inside, heaving himself up the steps.

"You've been out a long while. What have you been up to?"

His mother had long since finished peeling the potatoes.

He declined to answer and pushing past her, went to the back of the van where his toys were still heaped on the carpet. He was out of breath and rather exhilarated. He'd made a friend, he'd learnt a new and interesting word and he'd got his marbles back. But more importantly, he'd told someone that he didn't have a dad – and this time, it had been alright.

"Well, this is very nice," said Paul's mum, perched on the edge of the settee, pretending to admire their van.

Her positioning made it impossible for Frank to kneel up and look out of the window as usual. He wanted to see if Paul was coming out to play, but Paul had gone to the breaker's yard with his father to find some spare parts for their car. Pat was off somewhere with the school to play rounders or netball or something, and as a result he was left alone, indoors, with just the two women.

"It's not ours of course, we rent it."

His mother was perched on the other side.

"Ah yes," said Paul's mum. "Of course. We own ours."

"I see," said his mother, sipping her tea.

To make matters worse, his mother had extended the table in honour of their guest, invading the space at the back of the van so he was reduced to crawling about underneath it to play with his cars and his soldiers. Although he couldn't deny it was fun, scrambling around, hidden from view, brushing against legs.

Zap! Zap! Zap! From his lofty fortress on top of the toy box, Captain Fantastic defended his position against allcomers. The opposing army was closing in and the fortress was under threat. Out of sight, from somewhere above in the heavens, came the rattle of teacups.

"You must be very proud," said Paul's mum.

Deep at the back of Frank's mind was a name which he thought corresponded to a flower. Was it Marigold? Or Anemone? He couldn't remember. In the end, he settled for Hermione. He suspected it wasn't a flower at all but it was as close as he could get.

"Yes," said his mother. "She's done very well. I wish I could say the same…"

Beneath the table her hand appeared, searching for his head and stroking his hair.

"Still, one can't have everything I suppose."

"Indeed," said Hermione and nodded in agreement.

She should know, living in a caravan.

"As to your suggestion," his mother continued, "I'd be pleased to take you up on it. It will make a tremendous difference. To be perfectly honest, I never did like the idea of them going across that field. The cinder path's all very well in daylight, but you've got to wonder whether it's safe – you know, in the winter months…"

"Think nothing of it," said Hermione. "I'll be taking Paul to school anyway so I'm hardly going out of my way. Besides, now that we're neighbours… What's it all about if we can't do each other a little favour now and then?"

"Well, thank you," said his mother. "I'm very grateful. If there's anything I can do in return…"

Beneath the table, Frank focused on extricating his hero from the predicament in which he'd placed him. Captain Fantastic unleashed a burst of deadly firepower, the opposing army withered before him and for the moment the fortress was safe.

His mother accompanied them on the first day, walking up the hill with them on the main road. They made an amorphous grouping. Pat strode on ahead, her pigtails streaming out behind her, anxious to put as much distance as she could between herself and the two boys. Elisabeth and Hermione brought up the rear, chatting whilst they kept an eye on their wards.

"Don't go running off, Pat. Wait for us at the crossing…"

Outside the school gate, his mother crouched beside him.

"Mrs Hutchins is going to bring you to and from school from now on," she said, her stiff fingers buttoning his coat. "So she'll be here to meet you when you come out. I don't want you to make a fuss. Mummy still loves you, but it means I can go out to work and things will be a lot easier at home. You do understand that, don't you?"

Frank nodded. He was ok with that. He was ok with Paul and he was ok with Hermione. And what's more, it meant he wouldn't have to face the cow field again.

"Now promise me you'll try your best and behave yourself at school."

"I promise."

"Good boy."

She kissed his forehead, the way she did when he went to bed.

"Go on now, off you go."

And he went into school.

"Pay attention, class," said Mrs Williams, and sniffed rather violently.

Class paid attention, noting that the box of Kleenex had been replaced by a small bottle of nasal spray. Mrs Williams had come round to the idea that prevention was better than cure although her theory had yet to be proven. Meanwhile, she kept the box of Kleenex handy, out of sight in the drawer, just in case.

"What I thought we'd do today," she continued, "is try something special."

Class held its breath. This was not necessarily welcome news. 'Special' might mean something good or it might mean something bad, only time would tell.

"What I want you to do," said Mrs Williams, between regular squirts of the spray, "is to think of something familiar, something you know quite well, and draw a picture of it. You can colour it in if you like."

This was obviously the good bit. Class liked drawing and colouring in.

"Then underneath, I want you to write down a word that tells me what it is."

This was clearly the bad bit. Writing was tricky and needed lots of concentration.

"Let me show you what I mean."

Mrs Williams advanced to the blackboard and armed herself with a piece of chalk. After a few short strokes the shape of an animal appeared and beneath it, the letters *dog*.

Class evaluated her performance. That it was a dog was presumably not in doubt. Mrs Williams had said so and the lettering underneath proclaimed it to be one. But frankly it could have been anything – a cat, a mouse, even a sheep – Mrs Williams was not renowned for her drawing skills.

She consulted her watch. She was keen to press on, sensing that another drip was forming.

"It's now twenty past nine. Let's see what you can get done before the break."

Desk lids clattered as pencils, paper and the occasional crayon were gathered from their hiding places. Taking advantage of the momentary commotion, Mrs Williams opened the drawer and surreptitiously sneaked a tissue.

Frank sucked at the end of his pencil and stared at his blank sheet of paper. *Think of something familiar,* she'd said. His head was full of images – sometimes he thought it would burst – and here was a chance to tip it all out onto an empty canvas. But where to begin? There was so much.

Suddenly it all became clear to him, and while the others were still contemplating their composition, his flash of inspiration drove pencil to paper and lines began to appear.

After break, Mrs Williams made a tour of inspection. As far as she could tell, the exercise had been largely successful. As she'd expected, there'd been the usual flurry of questions. *Please, miss, can I draw a giraffe? Of course you can, Tommy – you can draw whatever you like.* Freedom of expression was to be encouraged. Although in Lucy Prior's case this proved problematic as she was now faced with the prospect of spelling 'elephant', a difficulty which was causing some distress.

But these were isolated incidents. For the most part everything had gone smoothly – probably because the majority of the class had chosen to copy her example and illustrate a dog. And rather than the standard of the drawing or the writing, it was this failure of imagination that caused her to feel disappointment. Her hopes were, however, raised when she came to look at the work of Johnson, F.

Frank had avoided the obvious. He could easily have chosen a cow (they were certainly familiar things) but there were other, more pressing issues on his mind. And besides, he'd no intention of dignifying one of his greatest enemies by drawing it and calling it by name. Instead, he'd chosen to depict a caravan. You could tell it was a caravan because it only had one wheel, positioned firmly in the middle. On either side were two stick figures, one representing his mother, and the other, as far away from her as possible, representing Mr McGregor, complete with gammy leg. Somewhere in-between was the green grass of their pitch and the brown of the gravel road.

Mrs Williams was thrilled. Here was something inventive, here was a spark of real creativity! This was what she'd secretly been hoping for, and before Frank could give an explanation of his work, she'd snatched it up and was showing it to the class.

"Look everyone."

Everyone stopped what they were doing and looked.

"I want you to see what Frank has drawn. It's really very good."

Her praise was not misplaced. The colours were vivid and striking and the outline of the van was readily discernible. The word underneath, however, was not. At best it was a scribble and at worst, indecipherable. But then, Frank's lettering had never been of the highest quality. Not to worry, it was the effort that needed recognition.

"So, Frank," said Mrs Williams, oozing encouragement. "What word have you chosen for your picture?"

And even as she said it there was a sense of impending doom, of something unwanted looming on the horizon.

Frank blinked. He wasn't sure Mrs Williams wanted to hear his word. It had been on his mind for several days – ever since he'd first heard it in fact – but now he felt reluctant to come up with it. It had never occurred to him that he'd be forced to reveal it like this, in public.

"Frank?"

Mrs Williams was waiting. Frank swallowed hard.

"It's 'bummer' miss."

There was a stunned silence – then the inevitable snigger from one of the girls at the back. *Silly old Frank! Fancy writing a rude word underneath his picture!*

"Ah," said Mrs Williams, wishing she'd kept her tissues closer to hand. Now there was nothing to cover her confusion. This was not the part of a child's imagination she particularly wanted to explore. She'd rather had in mind 'house' or 'hearth' or something altogether more homely. "Well that's not a particularly nice word actually, Frank. Perhaps we'll talk about where you heard it later. Meanwhile, I think you'd better go and stand in the naughty corner until you've forgotten about using it."

Frank sloped off to the naughty corner, burning with shame. He hadn't meant to offend anyone – he was only doing what he'd been told.

"Now then, class, let's get on with our drawing."

Mrs Williams was anxious to move on.

But class was not. Class was still buzzing with excitement at this latest development. Someone had used a bad word during lessons – they'd even written it down on their drawing paper. What kind of person did that?

Frank stayed in the naughty corner until lunchtime. He'd not forgotten about using the word but they couldn't keep him there any longer. He went to the canteen for school dinner, then out into the playground – but nobody wanted to play.

Later, in the staffroom, Mrs Williams reported the affair to Mr Thorpe.

He scowled and lowered his eyebrows, wrinkling the top of his pate. Boys weren't supposed to behave like that in his school. Back in his office, he took out the file marked 'Johnson, F.' and in the section reserved for comments, added the words *Uses bad language. Subversive. Keep an eye on this one,* and then put it back in the drawer.

Four

Mooching around in his dinner break, Frank found an old tennis ball in the long grass at the edge of the playing field. He showed it to Paul on the way home.

"Nice one," said Paul, and bounced it on the pavement to test it out.

Back at the caravan site, his mother had not yet arrived home from work. In wet weather he'd sit in the Hutchins' van to wait, but it was dry so they went outside on the gravel road. They each took up their natural position outside their respective vans, Paul facing forward, Frank with his back to the gate and the cow field. Somewhere in-between, the puddle which had once contained Frank's entire collection of marbles was now just another pothole.

"Catch!" said Paul, and hurled the ball in Frank's direction.

There wasn't a hope in hell of Frank catching the ball. He could see it clearly enough and he held out his hands to receive it as if he were shielding his eyes from the sun. There was a thud as the ball hit him in the chest and bounced off to one side.

"Ha, ha, ha!"

Paul laughed and danced round in a circle.

Frank grinned. He liked it when he made Paul laugh. It gave him a warm fuzzy feeling. He ran off to fetch the ball and then went back to his appointed spot.

"Catch!" he cried and flung the ball in Paul's direction.

Only he wasn't as good as Paul and instead of flying into the air, the ball slid off at an angle and went straight beneath the van belonging to the elderly couple.

"Ha, ha, ha!" Paul laughed again and repeated his little jig. "You'll have to go and fetch it."

"Why do I have to fetch it?" asked Frank.

"You threw it. And if you throw it and it goes wrong, you have to fetch it."

They usually played according to Paul's rules. Frank didn't

mind. He didn't mind doing anything if it made Paul laugh. He crawled under the elderly couple's van, looking for the ball. It was dark and there was a jumble of wheels and brake wires and grass. Somewhere above him, the elderly couple sat quietly unaware in their carpet slippers.

"Here it is!" He emerged from beneath the van, knees muddied, and tossed the ball over. "Your go!"

And he ran back to take up his place in front of the gate.

Paul threw again, harder than before, and the ball sailed way over Frank's head and landed in the field. Frank turned and faced the gate, but he didn't move. There was no way he was going in that field, no way at all. He'd rather die than go in there.

"Come on," said Paul. "Aren't you going to fetch it?"

Frank shook his head.

"Why not?"

"It's full of cows," said Frank. "I don't like cows. You fetch it. You said that if you threw it and it went wrong, you had to fetch it. I'm staying here."

Paul ran down the gravel road and they both advanced as far as the gate, peering through the bars and into the field. The ball lay some five yards off, wedged in a grass tussock next to a cow pat. Away in the middle distance, the herd of cows munched placidly at the turf.

Paul surveyed the scene and considered his options.

"Hmm, that's a bummer."

Frank blinked. There was that word again, falling from Paul's lips as easily as rain fell out of the sky. He didn't have a problem using it and yet it seemed to cause Frank so much trouble. But what did it matter, out here, in front of a field full of cows with no one to bother him? Suddenly, he didn't care about Mr Thorpe and Mrs Williams and class and the naughty corner – all he cared about was that he and Paul were playing together and he was having a good time. With both hands clinging to the gate, he threw back his head and let it out as loudly as he could.

"IT'S A BUMMER!" he shouted.

"Ha, ha, ha!" laughed Paul in response.

Frank liked it when he made Paul laugh.

They stared through the bars of the gate for a while, then Paul began climbing over it. He hopped down into the field and, checking the coast was clear, ran out to fetch the ball then sprinted back to the gate holding it high above his head.

Frank jumped up and down and clapped his hands. Now they could resume their game. Soon, his mother would come home and the chores would begin.

He never thought of his mother as possessing any violent emotions. In all the time he'd known her she'd remained remarkably calm, and even when she scolded him it was in a soft and imploring manner which inspired his love and obedience. If she ever raised her voice, it was a matter of concern as it aroused in him the fear that he might thereby lose her affection.

Later on, when he was in the Army, it was the norm to be shouted at on every occasion, whether you deserved it or not. *I'm your mother now, you miserable sods!* was the sergeant major's favourite expression. It made Frank laugh. What did the SM know about his mother? She never shouted at him like that.

If ever she did become perturbed, it invariably provoked the same reaction in Frank. He was finely tuned to variations in her temperament and in the close confines of the caravan, it was impossible for her to hide her feelings. So it could not escape his notice that she always became flustered by the prospect of being in the presence of Mr McGregor, and in the hour or so that preceded his weekly visit an air of tension would permeate their van.

It would begin around six on a Friday. Tea was eaten and cleared away as normal. Pat would have an hour or so's homework to do, and on any other evening his mother would relax and read a magazine while he played with his toys and his sister sat at the table working.

But on Fridays the rent was due, and his mother could never seem to rest until McGregor had called and it had been paid. She'd move about the van inventing little tasks for herself, dusting a shelf or straightening the cushions, and she was forever looking at the clock. Every ten minutes or so she'd go to the jam jar in the kitchen where the money was kept to ensure it was there and it was right. She was never short but she was anxious to have the exact amount so as not to prolong things any more than necessary.

At about seven, there'd be a knock on the kitchen door and he'd be standing there, waiting for what he was due. After she'd paid him and he'd gone, there was a palpable sense of relief – it was as if their lives had been on hold and now they were able to resume. So on the night he came into the van, instead of the usual air of tension there was an atmosphere you could cut with a knife.

His mother must have been distracted (Frank thought she might have been ironing). On hearing the knock she usually fetched the jam jar before answering, but on this occasion she went to the door first and had to return for the money. McGregor must have slipped in behind her. He seemed surprisingly nimble for a man with his supposed disability, because suddenly there he was, looming before them in his check shirt, his corduroy trousers and his heavy working boots, literally filling the room. He'd brought the whiff of the farmyard with him and the white milky smell of cows was everywhere. As Frank looked up from his toys, he caught the look of horror on his mother's face.

"Why, Mr McGregor." Her voice was shaking a little. "I don't believe I invited you in."

"I don't believe you did," said McGregor. "I must 'ave invited myself. You don't object, I take it?" It was clear that she did and his attempt at politeness was false, but he gave her no chance to respond. "Anyways, a man's got a right to look around what's 'is, ain't 'e?"

His mother remained silent. Somewhere in the terms of their lease...

McGregor stayed solidly in place and began to survey his surroundings.

"Well, this is very cosy." He cast his eyes over the meagre contents of the van, noting the cushions and the covers Elisabeth had made in an attempt to brighten the place up. "A nice little family scene."

Frank was kneeling on the floor amongst his cars and his soldiers. McGregor bent forward in front of him, blocking out the light.

"And who's this?"

"That's Frank," chirped Pat from her seat at the table. "He's my brother."

Pat had no fear at all. She wasn't scared of cows and she wasn't scared of Mr McGregor.

"Well now," said McGregor, staring him in the face. "So this is Frank, is it? You're a fine young man. How d'ye like living on a farm then, Frank? Like it 'ere, do ye?"

Frank blinked. Frank didn't like it at all. Frank cowered in the corner and shook his head. Mr McGregor chuckled.

"What? A fine young man like you? And ye don't like living on a farm? Hah! You'll come to it. You'll come to it, you wait and see. They all do in the end. There's nothing like living on a farm."

But Frank was not convinced and stayed backed up against the settee.

Seeing his discomfort, his mother came to the rescue.

"Mr McGregor, this is really not convenient. I've work to do," she gestured in the direction of the ironing board, "and I really should be putting the children to bed."

Pat grimaced in protest. Frank, on the other hand, nodded hard.

"Another time, then."

"If you wouldn't mind."

"Oh, I wouldn't mind," said Mr McGregor, gradually retreating. "I wouldn't mind at all. In fact, Mrs Johnson, it 'ud be a pleasure."

After he'd gone, Pat started sniggering and fanned her fingers in front of her nose.

"Phew! I don't think I could stand much more of that!"

Frank and his mother agreed – but for a very different reason.

"Come on now, Frank," said Elisabeth, trying not to dwell. "It really is past your bedtime. Go and put your pyjamas on and clean your teeth, there's a good boy."

Frank obeyed, but he sensed there was a cut in her voice. It would be a while before her soft and imploring tone returned.

The following Friday his mother pretended she'd mislaid the key to the door and couldn't open it. She passed the jam jar out through a side window instead, a ploy that required McGregor to stand outside to receive it. Rather than become annoyed, he found it tremendously funny and throwing back his head, let out a cruel roar of laughter. He took the money and shoved it into his pocket without so much as a second glance, then stomped off back up the gravel road, still laughing, his gammy leg flapping like a hinge.

Five

It was an age since he'd last seen Paul. After breakfast on the Saturday morning he'd gone out to look for him, crossing the imaginary boundary and walking onto the pitch next door. But their van was all shuttered up, the place deserted and not a trace of him to be found. The long, low estate car he'd arrived in and which had spent the last fortnight jacked up off the ground with its wheels missing had disappeared, and in its place lay the scattered remains of discarded motor parts and half-empty cans of oil. Strewn around in the long and unmown grass, unwanted pieces of metal were beginning to rust. Left to his own devices, Frank took to running up and down the gravel road and jumping into puddles.

At five o'clock on the Sunday afternoon he was drawn to his familiar perch on the settee by the rumble of an approaching vehicle. Coming towards him was the estate car with Paul, his father and Hermione sitting in their usual places, towing a dilapidated saloon. The same deft reversing procedure was repeated, and very shortly the estate and the saloon were parked side by side next to the van. He jumped down from his seat and wanted to go out, but by then it was too late in the day.

After it had got dark and he'd snuggled down in his bunk, he heard the sound of voices, McGregor's amongst them, arguing. Eventually McGregor stormed off, his angry exit marked by his uneven gait across the gravel. It was just as he'd done on the Friday, only this time he wasn't laughing.

And now, here at last was Paul, coincidentally visiting the toilet block at exactly the same time as he was.

"'Lo."
    "'Lo."
    "So where have you been?"
    "Away."

Evidently, he didn't want to elaborate and Frank assumed that wherever he'd been and whatever he'd been doing was somehow deemed irrelevant to their relationship. His excursion must have contained little of interest for he looked rather bored and stood kicking the bare breeze-block wall with his shoe, scuffing the toe. Paul soon changed the subject.

"Whatcha' doin'?"

"Fetchin' water."

"Oh."

It was Frank's least favourite chore. His mother had given him a gallon can and an instruction to fill it half full (he couldn't carry any more) and bring it back straight away. The fresh-water tap was located in the toilet block in the far corner of the site. Going was fine, the can was light and he could run, but coming back was a different matter and he struggled under the heavy load. This would be the first of several trips it would take to fill the container under the kitchen sink. But then, he was supposed to be the man of the house…

Water cascaded from the tap and thundered into the can, splashing out onto the stone floor. Frank let the level rise to halfway then shut the tap off hard so it gave out a squeak. Paul showed no interest in proceedings and continued to kick at the breeze-block wall, his hands in his pockets, staring moodily downwards. Eventually he came out with what was bothering him.

"My dad says McGregor's an arsehole."

There ensued a silence, occasionally punctuated by a 'plink' as water went on dripping into the half-empty can. The tap never seemed to shut off properly no matter how hard you turned it.

Frank blinked. 'Arsehole'? Here was another word to add to his collection. Paul was full of interesting words – where did he get them from?

"What's an arsehole?"

Paul stopped kicking at the breeze-block wall and looked

round in surprise.

"You don't know what an arsehole is?"

Frank shook his head.

"Well, an arsehole…" Paul began to explain, but then thought the better of it. "Well, if you don't know what an arsehole is, I'm not going to tell you. Anyway, my dad says McGregor's one and that's it."

Despite his friend's failure to explain, Frank was elated at his discovery. So McGregor was an arsehole! And perhaps Paul was right, there was no need to delve into it any further, the word itself was enough. Arsehole… It had a ring to it. More than that, it had a resounding echo and within the hollow walls of the toilet block, it reverberated like a sounding board. Frank felt it multiply inside him, filling his throat, and suddenly, in defiance of McGregor and all that he stood for, he let it out at the top of his voice in the form of an abbreviated song.

"Arsehole! Arsehole! McGregor is an arsehole!"

Paul started to laugh and the sight of his little friend calling out in his support lifted his gloomy spirits.

With this encouragement, Frank repeated the tune and jumped up and down, dancing in a circle on the stone floor.

"Arsehole! Arsehole! McGregor is an arsehole!"

Somehow it seemed so apt.

Paul joined in, and with the two of them shouting as loud as they could, the block overflowed with their noise.

"ARSEHOLE! ARSEHOLE! MCGREGOR IS AN ARSEHOLE!"

Frank ran round the gallon can, jigging his crazy dance. Fired up by his friend's antics, Paul dashed into one of the closets and began leaping on and off the toilet seat. Frank turned all the taps full on and watched the water rush down the plugholes. Paul beat his fists on the toilet door and thumped out a rhythm to their song.

"ARSEHOLE! ARSEHOLE! MCGREGOR IS AN ARSEHOLE!"

Time after time they recited their newfound chant, until the walls of the toilet block shook. Finally they grew hoarse and with their throats sore and their voices exhausted they were forced to stop, collapsing into fits of laughter instead.

Frank felt he was going to burst with it all. There was something wonderfully rebellious in it, jumping and dancing and calling McGregor names, and by the end of it he felt a sense of freedom he'd not come across before. McGregor *was* an arsehole – there was no question about that, they'd proved it beyond any shadow of doubt. This newfound knowledge gave him added strength – to the extent that when he carried the can of water back to their van, he didn't have to struggle so. The thought sustained him through two more trips to the toilet block, and even after the container under the kitchen sink was full he remained buoyed up.

He went to bed early. He was tired but found it impossible to sleep. It was hard to drop off when their schoolboy chorus was still ringing in his ears. His head was in a spin – Paul, McGregor, school, Mrs Williams, not to mention cows – and much like the water in the sinks back at the toilet block where he'd forgotten to turn off the taps, it all went whirling round and round and round.

Frank didn't see much of Paul at school. Every morning they walked up the hill together, but once Hermione had brought them to the gate they broke apart and went their separate ways. But that was what happened at school, and he was no different from the other kids whose older friends or siblings dropped them as soon as they crossed the threshold.

Pat had certainly dropped him. She'd dropped him well before they got there, striding out up the hill on her own, anxious to meet with the group of girls who'd be waiting on the corner of the main road, leaving him and Paul to finish the journey alone. She'd no more have played with Frank than she would have done with Paul, such were the distinctions of her sex and her age. And so, in the two years before she moved on to big school, Pat and her brother grew further apart, she with her homework and her sports, Frank with his cars and his soldiers. When it came down to it, at school as well as at home, he couldn't rely on his sister.

Paul had his own mates, too. It hadn't taken him long to find them – and just like Pat, Paul found it easy to mingle. But where Pat's friends skipped and chatted, Paul's pushed and shoved and ran and shouted and played football. And being bigger than the rest, they pushed and shoved more than most. They had a leader, Dale, a tall rough-hewn crew-cut lad who continually called the shots. And when Dale was around, Paul did as he was told – he wasn't going to rock the boat.

But Frank wasn't in a gang. In fact, Frank wasn't in anything at all. Who wanted to play with someone who didn't have a father and who used bad words in class? He took to hanging round the edge of other groups, running in and out in an attempt to get himself noticed. When this failed, he'd sneak off and spy on Paul and his mates from a distance, watching their every move and wishing he might be one of them. But he never was and he never could be – Frank didn't do that sort of thing. But then, when it came to matters of school, Frank didn't do much of anything...

"Good morning, class," said Mrs Williams.

"Good morning, Mrs Williams," class responded.

The product of twelve months' training shone through as they spoke in neat and measured unison.

Mrs Williams sighed as an unusual combination of pride and intense tiredness overwhelmed her. It had been a long and exhausting year, and now, thank God, the end of summer term was finally in sight. Soon she'd be able to take that month off she'd been looking forward to and the prospect of a quiet sojourn in a white-washed Cornish cottage beckoned irresistibly. Salt-tanged breezes and the cry of seagulls wafted through her head, calling her to rest. There was still work to do, but with the rigours of the school concert behind her, all that remained was the production of the year-end reports.

"Now, class, what I want you to do this morning," she continued, "is to take all your exercise books out and put them on your desks where I can see them. Because today…" (she paused, conscious that she needed to imbue the situation with an appropriate element of drama) "…today, I'm going to conduct your assessments."

Class fell deadly silent. Class froze solid at mention of the word 'assessments'. Assessments were bad news. Assessments had *no* redeeming features. Assessments meant red biro and marks out of ten. Or not, as the case may be. There was widespread groaning and the begrudged opening of desks. Class felt depressed.

Mrs Williams decided to play her trump card.

"But this afternoon…" she said, with a distinct uplift in her voice, "…this afternoon, if it stays fine, we can all go outside and play."

Although relieved, class was not impressed. As if that were the be-all and end-all – they went out to play every break-time! But if that was the best she could offer…

Mrs Williams touched wood in the hope of securing good weather – and for the maintenance of her present state of health which had allowed her to get through her speech without the help of either her tissues or her nasal spray. She attempted a long intake of breath and revelled in the joy of a clear bronchial passage. If her luck held, today could be a drip-free day.

Frank sat stiffly at his desk and squirmed uncomfortably. This was not a happy occasion. The prospect of an assessment filled him with dread, although he didn't doubt that Mrs Williams would treat him any differently from the others. She'd look and see how they had done – but in his case, she'd look and see how he had not. He didn't imagine she'd be pleased.

He glanced quietly round at his classmates, seeking inspiration. Most were prepared and waiting, their books arranged in three neat piles, ready to be examined. Like them, Frank was waiting – but it could hardly be said he was prepared.

Later, when he was in the Army, it was a scene he'd remember with some clarity. It mirrored a similar predicament when he'd stood by his bed in the barracks waiting for the sergeant major, his kit (or as much of it as he could find) laid out for inspection.

You're a disgrace, Mr Johnson, a bloody disgrace. What are you?

A disgrace, Sergeant Major.

Yes you are, Mr Johnson – and don't you forget it!

He couldn't do otherwise when it was rammed down his throat at every available opportunity. But by then he was used to it and the criticism slid off like water from a duck's back. Now it was new and still painful.

He raised the lid of his desk and, one by one, slowly drew out his books. From the outside they appeared no different from anyone else's. Alright, they were tattered and dog-eared – they'd spent a considerable portion of their existence in the grubby depths of his satchel, a billet they shared with a number of leaky biros and half-eaten sweets – but that was nothing unusual. It was what was inside that was important.

A lot of the pages were blank – or at least contained no more than a dot or a dash or a pencil mark of some indistinguishable kind. Where there *was* evidence of work, it was patchy and incomplete and whereas the other children had laid out their efforts with some attempt at neatness, his were characterised by smudges, scrawls and scribbles. Where there was enough identifiable content to warrant appraisal, the pages looked like a giant game of noughts and crosses, 'X' marking the spot where he'd erred and 'O' representing the sum total of his achievements. That most prized of possessions, a tick, was a rarity and was usually for effort rather than accuracy. Frank was not a model student and the thought that after lunch he could go outside and play was hardly consoling.

Mrs Williams approached his desk with a degree of trepidation. One never knew what one might find when it came to Frank – a startling word, a great feat of imagination, or some unlooked-for revelation that would disrupt the surface of what was an otherwise calm and unruffled pond. She'd deliberately left him until last, a ploy calculated to enable everyone else to complete their task before Frank could throw them into disarray. Although she need not have worried, since at that moment Frank's mind was as blank as his pages and she found him staring out of the window and into the playground.

"Frank?" she enquired, nervous as to a reply. She could already feel a drip forming. "Are you with us, Frank?"

Frank turned his head in the opposite direction and said nothing. He clearly wasn't with them, he was somewhere else, somewhere beyond the playground, the cinder path, the cow field, and even the caravan site – but exactly where or why he'd no more idea than his teacher.

"Shall we look at your work, Frank?"

Frank neither shook his head nor nodded. Wherever he had been, wherever his thoughts had taken him, he had now ceased to care for her opinion, and instead of seeking it he spread his arm across the desk and lay his head on it, feigning sleep. There was no point in asking anymore, he already knew the answers.

Mr Thorpe sipped his afternoon tea and pored over the reports Mrs Williams had diligently prepared. They were mostly of an acceptable standard – *Shows good progress, has come on well this year* – and one or two were positively glowing in their approbation. The remarks appertaining to Johnson, F., however, were causing him some concern. They didn't surprise him – he was well aware of the problems and had reminded himself of the contents of the file – but now he was faced with a difficulty. The annual parental interview was looming and he was at a loss as to what he should say. His forehead wrinkled, drawing the smooth skin of his bald pate forward. Leaning back in his chair, he placed the tips of his fingers together and began to compose his speech.

Ah! Mrs Johnson. I'm sorry to have to tell you...

Six

It was all Pat's fault. If she hadn't been ill, he wouldn't have had to go. And if he hadn't had to go, then it might not have happened at all. Although, it was unlike her. She was supposed to be the strong one, the one who ran and jumped and skipped and was good at games while he was deemed awkward and fragile – yet it was she who was lying in bed, throwing up every half an hour.

The doctor, a fat jolly man with glasses, diagnosed gastroenteritis.

"It's nothing to worry about," he said, after prodding her about. "Let her rest. Forty-eight hours, seventy-two at the most, and she'll be as right as rain. As soon as she can keep something down, I recommend a diet of white fish boiled in milk. That usually does the trick."

He snapped his little bag shut with a decisive click.

It was ironic. Of all the things they could have kept in the larder, there was already a piece of white fish – but they'd run out of milk. And no sooner had the doctor left than his mother was calling out the dreaded words.

"Frank? Are you busy? Have you got a minute?"

Meanwhile, the doctor was waddling off down the gravel road toward his car. Looking at his retreating figure, Frank doubted that *he* lived on a diet of white fish boiled in milk.

His mother gave him a pail and a set of instructions. As was the norm when she wanted him to know that she relied on him, she crouched down to his level to deliver them.

"Your sister's quite ill. What I need you to do is go over to the farm and fetch some milk. Ask Mr McGregor. When he knows who it's for I'm sure he'll give you some."

Frank blinked, twice. The farm? McGregor? Milk? This was no ordinary errand. He had a strong suspicion it would involve cows.

"I don't want to. Why don't you go?"

Colour rose in his mother's cheeks.

"You know very well why I don't want to go. Anyway, I can't. I have to stay here and look after Pat."

Well, he could do that just as easily as she could. But there was no persuading her.

"Now, be a good boy and don't make a fuss. Mummy needs you to do this for her please." She buttoned his little jacket against the breeze. "Go on now. And when you get back I'll make you some drop scones for tea, I promise."

When she said it like that, how could he deny her? He took the pail and pledged himself, nodding. Wasn't he supposed to be the man of the house?

McGregor was standing in the yard with his hands on his hips. He was sporting a new check shirt and corduroy trousers and had adorned himself with a red handkerchief which he'd folded into a triangle and tied around his neck. He'd no cap on and his hair was black and sleek and combed straight back from his forehead.

It looked as though Frank was in luck. The cows were in for milking so although the parlour was full, the yard itself was empty. His insides were shaking, but he'd determined to take a leaf out of his sister's book and be bold. And hadn't he and Paul decided that McGregor was an arsehole and not someone to be scared of?

"Well, well, well, look'ee here," said McGregor, turning at the rattle of the bucket. "If it isn't young Frank. Now then, Frank, and what is it ye might be wantin'? Must be somethin' special, ye comin' all this way an' all."

Frank steadied himself and held out the bucket.

"We need some milk please, Mr McGregor."

"Milk, is it?" said McGregor. He took the pail and stared into it as if expecting to find something untoward. "Well, you've come to the right place, I'll give ye that. I daresay we can find ye a drop."

He made off in the direction of the milking parlour, swinging his gammy leg.

Frank followed close behind, listening as the farmer talked to himself.

"Milk, she wants, is it? Hah! I said 'e'd come to it. I said 'e would. They all do in the end…"

He disappeared into the parlour, his voice and the clank of the bucket echoing amongst the lowing of the cows.

Frank stayed well outside. Through the open doorway he caught a glimpse of a vast cavernous space filled with bellowing animals, their long hind legs kicking out. The smell of manure and rancid milk turned his stomach. There was no way he was going in there! Not in a million years!

Somewhere in the middle distance he could hear McGregor calling.

"Stand still, ye bugger!"

Then the man himself appeared, dangling the bucket half full of milk.

"Ye aren't comin' in then?" he asked.

Frank shook his head. Wild horses couldn't drag him.

"Well, 'ere's yer milk, anyways," continued McGregor. "It don't get no fresher than that. Still warm, see?" He made Frank feel the outside of the pail which was now tepid to the touch. "You tell yer mother," he went on, "you tell 'er that there's plenty more where that came from." Then, a thought occurred and he leant forward into Frank's face. "In fact, you tell 'er I've enough milk for 'er to bathe in if 'er wants." The idea seemed to amuse him and he continued on the same theme. "Hah! That's a good 'un! Yes, you tell 'er she can come and 'ave a bath in it if 'er likes. Oh yes – that's a good 'un! Bath in it! Ha! ha! ha!"

He threw back his head and laughed, then hitched up the belt of his corduroy trousers and stomped off back into the milking parlour, his guffaws echoing in the lofty space.

Frank recovered the bucket and made good his escape. The incident had confirmed what he'd already suspected. McGregor was not merely an arsehole, he was also deeply insane and he needed to put as much distance between himself and the farmer as possible. Halfway back to the van, he stumbled on the rough ground and some of the milk slopped out of the pail. But as McGregor had said, there was plenty more where that came from and there was certainly enough to boil a piece of fish for his sister.

For the first time ever, he actually felt proud of himself. Despite the lurking presence of cows and the impending madness of McGregor, he'd been brave, very brave, and the thought of the approbation he would receive from his mother sustained him beyond the weight of the bucket and the length of his journey home.

Back at the van, he handed over his prize and told his story. But he thought it best that there were some things his mother shouldn't know and he was careful to omit the part containing McGregor's invitation.

Apart from his visit to the farm, his sister's illness hadn't caused Frank any inconvenience. On the contrary, things had worked out well. Given Pat's germs, his mother had no desire to confine him to the van so he was constantly sent out to play. And since school was over and they were into their summer break, every day was a day off.

Paul was his constant companion and together they roamed the site, exploring its boundaries. Next to Frank's van they found a tree they could climb and from whose lower branches they could look safely out into the cow field. Behind the toilet block they built a den which served as a hiding place when anyone came looking for them. Beyond the block was a small stream that disappeared into a culvert under the main road, and when they discovered it was possessed of an echo, much like the toilet block itself, it became a favourite place where they could sit and shout out their chants. There were fish in it too, and they set about trying to catch them, at first with their hands then using jam jars. They played marbles (but never jacks) and sneaked beneath the van of the elderly couple, pretending to look for their ball. And in the course of these adventures they did all that you'd expect young boys to do – skinned their knees, got dirty, tore holes in their trousers, and so when they came home, there was always a comment from the welcoming committee. *Oh, Frank! Just look at you. I only washed that yesterday.* But at least he was out in fresh air.

Elisabeth had found a position in the kitchens of a private school some two or three miles off. The travelling was difficult but it meant she was free during holidays. This convenience came at a price – there were no wages when she was off and she continued to rely on the State. Money was tight so when the chance arose of some casual work, it was something to be considered. The problem was, it was on McGregor's farm.

She was initially against the idea. The money wasn't great, they might have to pay tax on it (not to mention the potential loss of benefits) and besides, it was a little too close to home. But Hermione was in favour and set about overcoming Elisabeth's objections. The money was better than nothing and she contended that McGregor would pay cash in hand and there'd be nothing to worry about. They could go together and take the children with them. They could make a packed lunch and have a picnic. They could get away from the constrained interiors of their vans and be out in the open – it would be almost like going on holiday. In the end, Elisabeth relented and they earmarked a week at the end of August.

They met in McGregor's yard early on the Monday morning – Elisabeth, Hermione, the boys, two of their neighbours and a couple of lads from the houses up the road. Pat had refused to join them so she'd been left in charge of the van, her nose buried in a book and with strict instructions not to wander off. *What did you think I was going to do? There's nowhere to go anyway – it's boring.* Unlike Frank, she couldn't wait to get back to school.

McGregor was in his element. On the dot of eight they heard the cough of an engine starting, then its steady *phut phut phut* announcing his arrival as he shot round the corner mounted on the seat of his tractor. Behind him, bouncing around with no load, was a two-wheeled flatbed trailer. The tractor jerked to a halt and the farmer got down, painfully extracting his leg from amongst the controls, then stood to survey his workforce.

"Well, this is a merry crew, a regular platoon and no mistake. Ready for some 'ard work, are we?" He saw the boy holding his mother's hand. "And here's young Frank, come to join us. Lookin' forward to a day out in the fields, are ye, Frank?"

Frank said nothing.

McGregor leaned towards him and softened his tone.

"I see ye aren't come over wantin' more milk, then?"

He glanced up at his mother.

Elisabeth looked deliberately away.

McGregor laughed, exposing his blackened teeth, then slapped his thigh and decided it was time to make a start.

"Right then, up you get."

He motioned them onto the trailer.

Hermione clambered aboard first and turned to assist the others. Frank had to be passed up, but Paul insisted on trying it for himself, although eventually he too had to be helped. Elisabeth came last, handing up the picnic basket and taking Hermione's arm. With them all safely aboard, McGregor dropped the clutch and they shot off in the direction of the fields, swaying and juddering along the bumpy tracks. *Hold on tight!* someone shouted.

McGregor organised the work, while his own hands stayed firmly on his hips. Not counting the boys, there were six of them all told, two to lift the bales, two to stay on the trailer and do the stacking and two to rake the hay left over at the edges of the fields where the baler couldn't reach. The bales were heavy and the work exhausting so the jobs were to rotate, an hour at a time.

The boys tried their hand at lifting a bale, but when they found it was beyond them they took to exploring the ditches and the hedgerows. They ran their sticks along the hawthorns, flushing out the blackbirds, and from a row of ancient alders a flock of startled sparrows were put to flight. They knew how to entertain themselves, a month turned loose on the caravan site had given them practice enough.

Each time the trailer was full, the makeshift gang climbed back on board and headed off in unsteady fashion toward the barn to unload. Elisabeth and Hermione thought it not worth disturbing the boys and they took it in turns to stay behind and mind them, Elisabeth watching from the gate while Hermione sat on a bale and smoked a cigarette.

It took all morning to clear the first field. At first the early cool of the day refreshed them, but as the sun rose high into the sky it grew hot and uncomfortable. Sweat trickled into awkward places. Necks and faces began to redden, and their initial joy at working in the open air evaporated as each bale they lifted grew heavier and each swing of the arm required more effort. Lunch came as a welcome break.

They took it in the shade of the alders and did their best to make something of it. Elisabeth spread out a cloth while Hermione unpacked the contents of the basket – meat-paste sandwiches, some tomatoes and a selection of fruit. They'd brought orange squash and there was pop for the boys, and even these small delights, taken in the open air and away from the confines of their vans, made the occasion seem special.

In the far distance they could hear the hum of motor cars on the main road, but the predominant sound was that of the countryside – a long silence broken occasionally by the cawing of rooks or the song of a skylark fluttering high above their heads.

When they'd eaten, they rested, and for a while everything seemed idyllic. But then it was back to work as they were forced to pack up and start clearing another field.

Soon, the boys began to grow restless. Initially it had been fun – the bumpy ride on the back of the tractor, the freedom to run across an open, cow-free field – and the ditches and the hedgerows had provided sufficient diversion. But as much as they'd enjoyed running their sticks along the hawthorns, there were only so many sparrows they could startle and so many blackbirds they could flush. The ditch bottoms were dry and barely afforded a decent footprint to look at, never mind yield anything of lasting interest. And they could stand and beat their sticks against the bank for as long as they liked but all they got back was a face full of dusty earth, and the nagging thought that they were wasting their time. It was not as if there was a stream to dabble in.

Then Paul hit on the idea of playing soldiers. The purpose of the game was to sneak off in one direction, hide behind a hedge or in a ditch, and then creep up on a selected opponent and surprise them with an ambush. For an hour or so this engrossed them and they roamed back and forth along the sides of the fields, jumping out on their victims with the minimum of warning.

"Bang!" cried Paul

"Bang!" cried Frank.

"Got you!" they chanted together, then laughed at their own cleverness.

Hermione and Elisabeth were natural targets, although none of the others were spared.

The afternoon wore on as the second field was cleared and the boys began planning their final attack. Hermione had gone back to the barn on the trailer to unload so the recipient of their attention was Elisabeth. They slunk along a ditch they already knew well, crouching low behind the bank beyond which they thought she was resting. Then, reaching the gate, they gathered themselves and suddenly leapt out into the open field, firing their imaginary guns in her supposed direction.

"Bang!" cried Paul.

"Bang!" cried Frank.

"Got you!" they chorused – and began to laugh.

But their plan had failed. Their assault was too late – McGregor had beaten them to it.

At the edge of the field stood the tractor, the trailer slewed at an angle as if it had been carelessly parked. The driver, easily picked out in his check shirt and red neckerchief, had already dismounted. He'd caught Elisabeth by surprise and had her pinned up against the bank, one hand clapped across her mouth while the other searched roughly inside her blouse. Unable to move or cry out, she was using her hands and arms as best she could, striking out against his face and chest in an attempt to combat his strength. The look of fear in her eyes amounted to panic.

Her assailant was enjoying her struggle.

"You can wriggle as much as you like, my dear," the boys heard him saying. "But you can't escape McGregor!"

Frank blinked and dropped his imaginary gun. These were disturbing scenes. McGregor was attacking his mother – but how had a man so disabled been able to trap her in this way? Was she a willing participant in the proceedings and were her struggles merely to add effect? His mother's eyes told a different story, but these were the thoughts that ran through his head. He was at once both afraid and confused, just as he'd been when trapped by the cows, and he remained similarly rooted to the spot. His companion seemed equally incapable of action, and so he and Paul stood and stared incredulously.

McGregor must have heard them as he immediately broke off and turned in their direction.

"So it's you, is it? Ye little buggers, come to spoil a man's pleasure. Just ye wait until I get hold of ye."

And he left off his enjoyment and set off toward them.

Frank blinked for a second time. His mother had been released, but McGregor's move only served to compound his agony. Was it now best to run? And if so, in which direction? His fear bred indecision and he consequently remained immobile.

The matter was taken out of his hands as Elisabeth freed herself and dashed toward them, her first thought for the safety of the children. She pushed past McGregor, one arm flailing, the other raised up to her face. And where his hand had held her mouth shut, she now clamped her own as if to prevent the horror of her emotions from leaking out. Grasping Frank by the hand, she yanked him away and together they stumbled hurriedly across the stubbly field. Paul followed as quickly as he could. Some way behind, McGregor hobbled in their wake, cursing and shaking his fist.

"Just ye wait! I'll catch ye! Ye little buggers!"

His voice began fading into the distance and he soon gave up the chase. On another day he might have been content to stand there, hands on hips, laughing his cruel laugh. But today, it seemed, was not a laughing matter.

They reached the end of the field and turned into the comparative safety of the lane. Elisabeth slowed to a brisk walk. She was out of breath and between each rapid intake came the sound of a muffled croak, her hand still clasped to her mouth, although now it was more in disbelief.

Frank trotted along beside her, looking continually up at his mother. He needed guidance as to what to do next, but none was immediately forthcoming. He sensed she wanted comforting but he felt particularly unable. He glanced across at Paul, but he too, seemed equally unsure of himself and so together, they made their way toward the farm in silence, save for Elisabeth's occasional sob.

As they entered the yard, Hermione caught sight of them from the barn and came out to meet them. Her face creased into a frown as Elisabeth's distress became apparent.

"What on earth's the matter?"

Elisabeth, who had now found a handkerchief to choke back her emotion, could do no more than give a short shake of her head and emit a few brief phrases punctuated by gasps for air.

"Can't speak... McGregor... Back there..."

She extended her free arm to indicate the general direction of the event. The rest would have to wait – she was in no condition to recite the full facts just as yet.

Hermione saw it was pointless to press her further and slipped a hand around her shoulder for support.

"Come on then, let's get you back to the van..."

Mention of the van raised Frank's spirits. In that direction lay hope and safety and despite all its shortcomings, there was no thought more appealing at that moment than to get inside it and lock the door.

He watched as Elisabeth nodded silently and they started off as a group toward the site. And just as on his first day at school when they'd walked down that long corridor and into a new world, he grasped his mother's fingers tight. Then, she'd given him up into the care of someone else. He wasn't going to let her do so now – this time he was going to stick to her like glue.

Back at the van, Hermione made tea while Elisabeth recovered. She thought she had a bottle of brandy but Elisabeth declined – this was not the time to let her brain become fuddled. Gradually, as the hot tea took effect, she began to recollect and tell her story, of how McGregor had surprised her and carried out his assault.

Hermione expressed disgust: *What a horrible man,* although not surprise: *I could have guessed as much.*

Pat, who'd spent all day obediently shut up with her books, was agog with disbelief: *I've read about people like that;* while Frank, who'd normally have played with his cars and his soldiers, sat quietly with Paul, not knowing quite what to do.

When Paul and Hermione had left and it was just the three of them, Elisabeth gathered her children together on the settee and put her arms around them. She was calmer now and much more composed.

"We're a family," she said, squeezing them closer, "and we stick together, no matter what."

Pat was embarrassed by scenes of this nature and sat rather rigidly, looking down at her hands clasped together in her lap. Frank, in contrast, gazed up at his mother in admiration. For all that she'd been though, he thought her quite magnificent.

"Now," Elisabeth went on, "I want you to promise me that you won't repeat a word of what you've seen or heard today to anyone – ever. Will you do that for me?"

"Yes, of course," Pat mumbled.

Frank nodded faithfully. At that moment he'd have done anything she asked, anything at all.

His mother drew him in and kissed his forehead, then his sister's. "I think we should all go to bed now and get some rest, don't you?"

When he was eventually tucked up in his bunk, Frank found it hard to drop off. In the small living area not ten feet away, he knew his mother was sitting there, weeping, and all the tears she'd held back earlier that day were now flooding out. He felt for her, as he'd always done, and he wished he could take away her pain. But he could not, and he was forced to lie there and listen and wait until she'd cried herself to sleep.

Seven

A week later, Frank went back to school. Needless to say he was not looking forward to it, although it made a change from the sombre atmosphere that had descended over the caravan site. He'd moved up a year and could at least escape the attentions of Mrs Williams.

His promotion had been far from automatic. Had it been left up to Mr Thorpe, it might not have happened at all. *Well, Mrs Johnson, under the circumstances I don't see how we can avoid keeping Frank down.* But Elisabeth had objected and through her intervention he'd advanced – but it was more by age than achievement.

After lunch on the first day he went out into the playground as usual, looking for his friend. Dale and his mates, Paul amongst them, were gathered in their customary spot on the grass verge near the entrance, laughing and skylarking about. Frank must have stared at them a little too long as someone shortly gave Dale a nudge and pointed in his direction. Dale broke off from whatever story he'd been telling and looked around, then walked across, beckoning his mates to follow.

Frank remained stock-still. There was no point in trying to head off. You couldn't outrun Dale and anyway, just at that moment his legs would simply not have taken him.

"Ah!" said Dale, bearing down on him. "What 'ave we 'ere? You're 'utchins' little mate, aint yer? Aint that right, 'utchins?"

Paul promptly looked in the other direction.

"Yeah, I thought so," Dale resumed. "We know all about you, don't we boys?"

The boys nodded in loyal agreement.

"You're the kid from the caravan site. In fact," (Dale paused to give effect to his forthcoming pun) "you're The Caravan Kid, that's who are are! 'Ere boys, come an' 'ave a look at this."

Dale's mates gathered closer, hemming Frank in.

"This 'ere's The Caravan Kid. 'E's a real cowboy! Only 'e aint no ordinary cowboy see? This 'ere's th'only cowboy that's afraid of cows! Can you believe it? A cowboy an' 'e don't like cows, ha, ha, ha!"

"I'm not a cowboy," protested Frank, in a moment of unlooked-for bravery.

"Oh!" Dale feigned surprise. "I see. So you aint a cowboy then?"

"No," said Frank, "I'm not."

Dale looked round at the assembled group and smirked.

"Well, if you aint a cowboy – then you must be an Indian!"

And he began to perform a war-dance round Frank's stationary frame, nodding his head backwards and forwards and waving an imaginary hatchet. Mingled with the laughter of his mates, Dale's war cries whooped across the playground.

Frank stamped his foot.

"I'm not an Indian, either."

"Ooh!" said Dale, coming to a halt in front of him. "We're a little touchy now, aint we? I tell you what then. If you aint a cowboy and you aint an Indian, you tell me what you are."

"I don't know," said Frank, confused.

"'E don't know," repeated Dale. "What do 'e think of that then, boys? 'E don't know."

The boys quietened down, waiting for the punch line. When it arrived, the joking would be over.

"I'll tell you what you are," said Dale, prodding a hefty finger in Frank's chest. "You're a gyppo. That's what you are, a fuckin' gyppo."

Frank blinked. It was the first time he'd heard the 'f' word and it came as a shock. And besides, he wasn't really sure what a gyppo was, although the way Dale said it, it didn't sound particularly nice.

"Yeah, that's what you are, you're a fuckin' gyppo. Just like your mate." Dale jerked a thumb in Paul's direction. "Aint that right, 'utchins?"

Paul continued to look the other way as a means of covering his embarrassment.

"An' I'll tell you summat else an' all," continued Dale, as if he'd just been given a reminder. "Not only are you a gyppo, but your mother is a fuckin' tart."

More words for Frank to swallow – and because they came from Dale, their meaning was bound to be unpleasant. But this time they involved his mother and struck a chord deep within, so whatever Dale was implying, he would naturally resist it.

"No, she's not."

"Course she bloody well is," insisted Dale. "We know all about it. McGregor 'ad 'is 'and up her skirt, didn't 'e? An' I'll bet 'e's 'ad 'er away an' all, aint 'e boys?"

The boys naturally agreed. It didn't do to go against Dale.

Frank squirmed as he recalled the scene to which Dale was referring. There was an element of truth in it that caused him disquiet – but his mother had surely been blameless, utterly blameless. And as if memory of the incident was not pain enough, now it was common knowledge.

He looked imploringly at Paul, desperately hoping for some form of support, but the eyes of his so-called friend steadfastly refused to meet his own. In a moment of rare intimacy with his mother, Frank had been sworn to keep a secret and he'd assumed that Paul had been asked to do the same. Evidently not. Tears welled up inside as he realised the extent of his humiliation and he felt their hot and salty tang on his cheeks.

This was just the reaction Dale had hoped to provoke and now he latched onto it.

"Aw, look boys. I do believe 'e's goin' to blub."

He pointed at Frank's flushed face.

Frank was indeed going to blub and there was nothing he could do about it. And as if on cue, his outburst induced a response from the boys which was rendered to the same tune as he and Paul had used in the toilet block to ridicule McGregor.

"Blubber! Blubber! Mummy's boy's a blubber!"

The words rang cruelly round the playground. He was filled with anger and a hatred boiled up inside and consumed him. He hated Dale – but his spiteful actions were to be expected. It was Paul who'd hurt him the most. He'd looked on him as a bulwark against all that was wrong with his life – school, cows and above all, McGregor. But his friendship had been no more than a sham, and now that this prop had been removed he felt crushed by the weight of the world and all its injustices.

At that moment, standing at the edge of the playground, his chest convulsed and shaking, what he wanted more than anything else in the world was to fall on Paul and beat him to a pulp – Dale too, come to think of it. But even if his spirit was willing, he knew his body was weak. There was no red mist to cloud his reason and so instead of venting his frustration on some external target, it pointed inwards and buried itself within.

He arrived home from school red-eyed and inconsolable. As hard as Elisabeth pressed him, he remained resolutely tight-lipped. A few days before he'd promised to keep her secret – now he would keep his own. In the end, she assumed it had just been a bad day at school and let it ride.

He took himself to bed early and let the tears flow into his pillow. The world was a horrid place. Paul had betrayed him, he'd been desperately shamed and worst of all, he'd failed to defend his mother. And as with so many things, he'd been a coward to boot. He was afraid of cows, he was afraid of McGregor, and today he'd been afraid of Dale. He was supposed to be the man of the house, but the shoes felt too big for him to fill. Now it was his turn to cry himself to sleep.

In the morning he awoke with a premonition of something untoward. Running into the living area, he scrambled up onto the settee and assumed his position at the side window. Next door, the pitch was empty. At some point in the dead of night, the

Hutchins, Mr, Mrs and young Paul, had all upped sticks and gone – 'done a runner' as he heard it described – and all that was left was a rectangular patch of yellowed grass where their van had once stood. They'd evidently been in a hurry for the site was still strewn with the rusted motor parts they'd failed to gather up, and in the corner the saloon car was left abandoned, jacked up off the ground with its wheels missing.

McGregor was reportedly furious. They'd not just left the place in a mess, but they'd gone owing a month's rent and he'd no idea where to find them.

Two days later, the rain began. It lasted over a week. At the start it was nothing unusual, merely a series of showers, but as the days wore on it became heavier and more persistent. It soaked the ground and after what had been a dry summer, the water table was firstly restored and then progressively raised. Grass squelched beneath the foot. Fields became boggy. Along the gravel road, the potholes were perpetually full and never seemed to drain.

Each morning before leaving the van, Elisabeth checked the children for raingear – a waterproof coat, some sort of headwear, both were insisted on, despite the protests. If it wasn't windy she put her umbrella up and sheltered them as far as the main road. Then, having safely crossed them over, she turned right towards the lay-by where her lift was waiting while Pat escorted Frank up the hill. Now that Hermione had gone, these were the new arrangements. Pat was not altogether happy about them.

"I don't see why I should have to do it."

She'd become used to her freedom and the incident with Frank in the cow field had stuck in her memory and she wasn't keen repeat it.

"Because he's your brother and you should look after him," Elisabeth had told her. "We're a family and we stick together, no matter what – remember?"

Pat shrugged her shoulders. It didn't leave her very much choice.

Matters came to a head over the weekend. On the Friday afternoon a violent storm began that was to last for thirty-six hours. The heavy showers turned into a torrential downpour and to make matters worse, on the Saturday morning the wind got up, lashing the rain against the van and trapping them all inside. Up in the hills, the sodden land dripped water into gullies which gushed and gurgled down towards the sea. On the plains, rivers rose to alarming levels.

The threat to the caravan site came from the culvert running beneath the main road. The stream that ran through it was not a problem – the brook flowed freely and had always stayed within its banks – but the culvert was narrow, no more than a large pipe, and was never intended to carry the weight of water which now descended. Rubbish had accumulated within it and never been cleared and this, combined with the debris that the swollen stream brought with it, now blocked it completely. The stream backed up and began to form a lake.

The vans by the toilet block were the first to be affected. Late on the Saturday afternoon the residents found the land below them flooded, the only exit being upwards toward the gravel road. Those who were sensible decamped and made alternative arrangements with friends or family. Those who were not, decided to stay put and were forced to deal with the mass of steadily rising water as it crept irresistibly through their doors and windows.

On higher ground, the owners were generally unaware of the danger. It had finally stopped raining and this had given rise to a false sense of security. As night fell and it grew dark, no one could see the approaching tide and the most natural thing to do was to draw the curtains and go to bed as normal. At the highest point of the site, in the corner above the gravel road, the Johnson family slept soundly. But even for them, it was only a matter of time.

Frank woke to the sound of strange voices and the beam of a torch being shone through his window.

"It don't look too bad up 'ere, John. What do 'e think?"

"Best get 'em out all the same – us don't want to take no chances."

It must have been the middle of the night as it was still dark and he instinctively felt he'd not yet had enough sleep. Beyond the voices lay an eerie silence, all the more distinct since for the last two nights he'd gone to bed with the noise of the rain thundering on the thin metal roof of the van above his head. Now there was nothing.

He felt disorientated. The storm had ceased, the wind had abated and had it not been for the presence of the storage cupboard directly above him, he'd have struggled to know exactly where he was.

There was a *thump, thump, thump* on the kitchen door, then the sound of his mother rising from her bed, the clatter of coat hangers as she took a dressing gown from the wardrobe and the padding of her feet through the van.

The voices started again.

"Sorry to disturb you, ma'am, but you're in danger of being flooded out. You'd best come with us if 'e don't mind."

Elisabeth felt the same sense of disorientation as she took a moment to reply.

"Come with you? Why...?" But then she must have seen the situation for herself and her maternal instincts cut in. "What about the children?"

"So 'ow many are there of you altogether?"

"Well... Three, I suppose..."

The voice turned as it called to its companion across the water.

"You'd better bring the boat, John..."

There was silence for a moment, then his door cracked open and his mother was in the room with him.

"Frank? I need you to get up and come with me."

Frank sat up and rubbed his eyes. It must be something important to be woken up at this hour. He slid out of bed and followed Elisabeth into the kitchen. He heard the sound of a match being struck then the hiss and dull glow of a gas mantle. He wasn't sure whether he was supposed to get dressed or not – but before he could decide on it, his mother had taken his coat from the wardrobe and slipped it over his pyjamas. There obviously wasn't much time.

Pat emerged from the other end of the van and stood yawning and stretching her arms.

"What's going on?"

"There's been a flood."

"Where?"

"Outside."

Pat went to the window and drew back the curtain, but beyond the van it all appeared pitch black.

"How did that happen?"

"I don't know. Now come and put your coat on."

While his mother began searching for his shoes at the bottom of the cupboard, Frank had a question.

"Where are we going?"

At that stage, Elisabeth had no idea. All she knew was it involved a boat and she was about to entrust the lives of her children into the hands of complete strangers.

"Somewhere safe…"

Or so she hoped.

She snuffed the mantle and the three of them gathered at the kitchen door.

As their eyes grew accustomed to the light, the scene outside the van gradually became apparent. From just below the level of the door, a dark, flat sheet of water stretched into the distance.

Next to their doorway stood a man in thigh-length waders, carrying a torch. On top of his head was a yellow fireman's helmet. Given the circumstances, it struck Pat as being quite incongruous. Alongside was a small flat-bottomed boat, manned by his colleague and equipped with a set of oars.

"Here," said the fireman, "let me help. I'll lift you across."

He stretched out his arms.

Pat went first and seated herself in the prow. "This is exciting."

Then it was Elisabeth's turn and she went into the stern.

"Steady, John…"

As the man of the house, Frank was left until last. But it was not a position that imbued him with pride – rather blind panic as the fear arose within him that he was about to be abandoned and separated from his mother as she sailed off without him. He was about to start running on the spot and letting out a wail when he suddenly found himself hoisted in the fireman's grasp and placed on Elisabeth's lap. A blanket appeared and was thrown over their shoulders. Behind them, the van door clicked shut.

"Away you go…"

The boat moved slowly off with the soft splash of an oar blade and the steady squeak of the rowlocks.

From her position in the bows, Pat had an unobstructed view. As they rounded the end of their van and the rest of the site opened up before her, she could see the extent of the damage. A pale moon hung overhead and down by the toilet block the tops of the vans protruding from the water shone with a dull light. Elsewhere, windows were visible, some half-submerged beneath an inky-black sheet, and here and there torches flashed across the surface, searching for survivors. To the left, the derelict shell of the saloon car discarded by the Hutchins seemed to float unsupported on the surface of the water, while to the right another boat was in attendance at the van belonging to the elderly couple. Still clad in their carpet slippers, they shuffled gingerly across their threshold, he tall and thin, while she, shorter and broader, stooped behind him. There was a brief flash of recognition. Somewhere beneath them, the gravel road let out toward the entrance.

Frank remained blissfully unaware of his surroundings. Snuggled down on Elisabeth's lap and with the comfort of the blanket surrounding him, he took no notice of the journey. He'd no idea of where they were going or why. All that concerned him was that he should be in the hallowed presence of his mother. With her arms about him, his head buried in the soft, warm folds of her neck and the smell of hair and flaky skin filling his senses like dusted flour, he could once again forget about cows and floods and Dale and McGregor and all the things that bothered him, and rejoice in the fact that there was nowhere else on earth he'd rather be.

Part Four

Pat

One

The day Frank came out of the Army, we decided to hold a party. We wanted to celebrate his homecoming, to give him a welcome fit for a hero – or at least, Mother did. Whether Frank really *was* a hero or simply just another soldier was always an unanswered question for me – but for the moment it was enough that he'd done his time. He'd served his country and good or bad, whatever effort he'd made would suffice. Anyway, that was what you did in those days – when a serviceman came home you threw a party and gave thanks for their safe return. It was probably a mistake – although my instincts tell me that what was to follow would doubtless have happened anyway. In my experience, the traits of human nature are ingrained slowly over the course of time rather than formed by a single event. You only have to look at Terry for example.

I suspect it was all Mother's doing. She had a habit of blurting things out without thinking and in typically generous fashion she'd have said: *We must do something for Frank when he comes home. We'll invite all his friends – and the neighbours, of course.* It was this same generosity of spirit that blinded her to the fact that Frank didn't have any friends. That had been why he'd signed up in the first place. I remember him looking at the poster. *JOIN THE ARMY AND SEE THE WORLD.* It held out the prospect of mates but none had been forthcoming and in the end the list of invitations boiled down to the neighbours and a few of Mother's former colleagues from the chocolate factory.

We tried tracking down people he might have known at school. For a while this had looked promising and one had come forward. Cyril was a delicate-looking lad who'd shared the same woodwork class as Frank at college. He'd become a joiner, but twenty years later he was just as delicate and with his hair thinning and in his late thirties, he'd never married. But then, neither had Frank. Even so, he seemed an unlikely companion for a man who was allegedly used to the rough and tumble of life in the Services. And so it was to prove.

The plan was that Mother would stay at Balfour Terrace and hold the fort while I collected Frank from the station. Mother didn't drive – she never had – and as yet Frank didn't possess a car so I was the only one who could go. I suppose I could have asked Terry – but that would have been like waving a red rag at a bull.

The last occasion I'd done it had been about three years before. I'd arrived home from work one evening to find a message on my answerphone. *I've got some leave and I'm coming home for a week. Meet me from the Plymouth train at half past three on Thursday. Don't tell Mum. It'll be a surprise.*

Frank was fond of surprises (of his own, that is) and he'd turn up out of the blue when you'd least expect it. We'd hear nothing for ages, then suddenly there he'd be, large as life and expecting everyone to dance to his tune. He said the Army didn't work regular hours and it was impossible to predict when he'd be home or for how long. *War doesn't take holidays, you know.* I suppose there's some truth in that, but I always suspected his lack of communication was due to laziness or his practised desire to maintain an air of mystery about what he actually did. If you ever pressed him on the subject, he'd grow touchy and defensive. *I'm sorry, I can't discuss that – there are issues of National Security at stake here.* And he'd invariably follow it up with his favourite joke. *If I tell you, I may have to kill you…*

True or not, I had my doubts – it was much more likely he'd spent the last six months guarding some wet and windy outpost on Salisbury Plain and making tea. The fact was, however you phrased it, you never did get a straight answer from Frank. In the end, I learnt not to ask.

None of this would have mattered but for the effect it had on Mother. I was prepared to go along with it (what was it to me if my brother wanted to play silly games?) but in her innocence, she believed every word of it. Not only was she blind to his lack of friends, she was blind to everything else about him as well. And if I ever questioned or pointed out any inconsistencies in his story, Mother would react and suggest I must be mistaken. If Frank had said he'd done something, as far as she was concerned, he had. To her, he *was* a hero – and by joining the Army and serving his country, he'd done something wonderful of which she could be immensely proud. He was her blue-eyed boy and nothing was to be said against him.

The clever thing was that Frank never actually lied. Everything Mother assumed about him came about through implication. Frank didn't deal in facts – other than the obvious. *I've been away. They sent us abroad – somewhere hot.* That way, he ensured the truth could never be tested. If he came home tanned and Mother chose to think he'd been in Saudi Arabia for instance, so be it.

Although he must have seen action at some point. You couldn't spend twenty-two years of your life in the Army and not be put to the test. At the very least he must have gone to Northern Ireland. Every regiment did its tour of duty and Frank's would have been no exception. It seemed strange he hadn't mentioned it specifically. It wasn't the most glamorous of postings but it was certainly one of the most dangerous – and knowing him as I do, I'd have thought he'd have wanted to make something of it.

And then there was The Falklands. There was a conflict thousands of miles away, and while the families of other servicemen knew the whereabouts of their offspring (went to the docks to wave them off in many cases) we heard nothing from Frank except for one brief message. *I'm on a ship – not sure where, possibly in the South Atlantic.* Given his customary vagueness, it could have been anywhere.

The last time he'd come home there'd been mention of the Gulf. *The Arabs are a weird lot – take the Yemenis for example.* And when Mother came to clean his room out afterwards, there were traces of sand spilt from his boots and onto the carpet. She'd made a point of showing it to me. *See? I told you.* But had he really been in the desert? Or gone for a walk on Filey beach? You could tell which version Mother wanted to believe.

There was one thing I did know. Three years before, when I'd met him from the train he'd been wearing battledress of the type used in warmer climes. His boots had been buffed to a shiny black and he had on a maroon beret, sloped to one side. He'd looked every inch the soldier and he wore his uniform with pride. I believe he thought himself part of a band of brothers and that he belonged. But it was more than that, it was a statement, a badge of honour. *I am a soldier – look at me and know who I am.* So if nothing else, no matter where he had or hadn't been or what he had or hadn't done, this fact alone enabled him to hold his head up and look his fellow man in the eye. He'd even brought his kitbag home on leave.

How things had changed. Now, as he stepped out onto the grey platform there was none of that. The uniform had gone, replaced by the nondescript garb of an ordinary civilian, and the bag in which he carried his worldly belongings was just a common holdall. His back was not as straight, his head was not as high and there was nothing to set him apart from the rest of the passengers. He looked tired and drawn and for the first time I noticed a touch of greyness about his temples. In the space of a few short years he'd aged and it seemed that in his departure from the Army, my brother had left something of himself behind.

"Frank?"

I thought he might fail to recognise me amongst the crowd on the platform. In those few short years perhaps I'd changed too. He turned but didn't smile, then he was standing next to me. Close up he looked even more haggard.

"Hi."

"Hi."

We didn't embrace. Time and distance had put a space between us neither of us felt comfortable in crossing. We weren't close. We never had been, not even as children.

"Well," I began, "long time, no see."

"Yeah, I guess so."

"How are you?"

"Fine."

His offhand replies were typical. Talking to Frank was like trying to extract blood from a stone. Nevertheless, I persisted.

"Good journey?"

"Not bad."

"Well, at least the train was on time."

He shrugged.

"I suppose so."

I got the impression he didn't care whether the train was on time or not. Now he was free from the constraints of Army life I suppose he could sit there all day without thinking – there were no fixed points on his horizon.

It was totally different for me. My existence was organised according to a strict schedule – the school run, meetings, personal time, family time, quality time – everything had to be juggled into place. On the last occasion I'd collected Frank from the station it had irked me that he could blithely assume I had nothing better to do at three-thirty on a Thursday afternoon than come and run around after him. At least I wasn't required to take an hour off work this time; although even now I felt compelled to take a look at my watch.

"Well, shall we get going?"

If push comes to shove, I thought, *I can always carry his holdall.*

And for the moment, that was the end of our conversation. There should have been catching up to do, gaps to be filled, but we had nothing of any consequence to say to each other. If you don't talk every day, you fall out of the habit until eventually there's nothing to talk about.

Besides, Frank had no interest in me or my family. He was uncle to my two boys, but he rarely saw them. As for my husband, Frank always professed to have forgotten his name. It took me a long while to convince Terry it wasn't a wind-up. Luckily, he believed me. I dread to think what might have happened otherwise.

At the core of this failure lay a mutual suspicion of each other's motives. He was my brother, but deep in my heart I distrusted him. I couldn't bring myself to believe he was what he affected to be and I took everything he said with a pinch of salt.

I'm sure he was aware of my feelings. As a result, he was guarded with me to an extent bordering on obsession, never wanting to let slip something he thought I might use against him. His great fear was that I'd succeed in persuading Mother of my views and this would destroy the precious relationship he enjoyed with her. And because I was 'on the spot', he saw me as having an advantage. How could he defend himself when he was never there?

How futile it all was – if only he knew how little his petty deceits bothered me. I would never dream of betraying him – Mother was the one piece of common ground between us. He raised the subject as soon as we were in the car.

"How's Mum?"

"Fine."

Now it was my turn to be guarded. I'd good reason not to elaborate. Mother had recently had a health scare of a kind often experienced by older women. She'd gone for tests and although these had proved negative, it was thought best not to tell Frank. *You see? I'm as fit as a fiddle. Now don't say a word. I don't want him worried unduly.*

I remember thinking how wonderful it must be not to be burdened like this. Frank was spared these concerns, but there were my children to think of too, so I always had something to worry about. Later, when Frank assumed control, things would change, but for the moment Mother's wellbeing was a duty we theoretically shared – although at present, I was the one doing the work whilst he merely asked the questions. Today he was easily satisfied and took to looking out of the passenger window, staring at traffic.

We'd not gone far, halfway home and waiting for a red light, when I realised there was something between us. I mean literally, physically, in the air – a scent, an aroma, a sweet heavy smell that Frank had brought with him – and in the pent-up space of the car it had become all the more apparent. In the years to come I would know with certainty it was alcohol, but for the moment I could only suspect as much.

So what? If my brother had indulged himself with a couple of beers on the train, it was really no more than he deserved. After twenty-two years in the Army he was entitled to a break. Even so, it was not entirely pleasant. I wound down my window for a breath of fresh air and we passed the rest of the journey in silence.

Two

To all intents and purposes the house in Balfour Terrace looked unoccupied. The downstairs curtains were drawn tight and if there was a light on anywhere at all, not a chink of it shone into the street.

I don't suppose Frank thought anything of it – he was probably used to coming back to a cold and dark billet. On the doorstep, he fumbled for his key, but before he could apply it the door was flung open, the lights came on, and there was Mother and half the neighbourhood all crammed into her tiny front room and chorusing out together. "Surprise!"

By the look on Frank's face, it must have been. He blinked, his face turned to stone and I noticed the slightest of twitches begin beneath his left eye.

I closed the boot of the car and followed him in carrying a tray of provisions. As I made my way through to the kitchen, he pulled at my elbow.

"Did you know about this?"

"I'm afraid so."

I waved the tray under his nose.

"You might have warned me…"

Of course I knew about it – how else could it all have been arranged? In those days Mother was still able, but the sheer volume of work was more than she could have coped with alone. Anyway, it had been a chance for us to do something together, mother and daughter in concert.

She'd wanted to put on a show and between us we'd made quite an effort. Terry had got the drink in but it was us women who'd prepared the buffet. Beyond that, the house had to be clean and tidy, and there'd even been time for a little decoration. There were greetings cards, some twenty in all, paraded along the mantelpiece, above which was strung a set of coloured letters spelling out the words WELCOME HOME. Out in the back yard, in the absence of a tree, we'd tied a yellow ribbon round the metal pole that supported the washing line.

Back in the parlour, Frank and Mother had found each other. There was a look of joy on her face and her hands were extended toward him.

"Here he is! My brave boy's come home!"

"Hello, Mum…"

His cheeks were burning. Stripped of his uniform, he must have felt strangely exposed. It was their first moment together for almost three years and I think he'd have preferred it to have been in private. They hugged, briefly, then broke apart as she wiped away a tear, holding him at arm's length.

"Why didn't you come to the station with Pat?" he asked.

"I wanted to give you a surprise."

"But…"

"Oh, never mind that now." She flapped a hand at him. "Let me look at you. I do believe you've put on some weight. Don't tell me the Army's been feeding you properly at last. It's about time! All the same, you still look as though you could do with a good meal." She glanced him up and down. "And where's your uniform? You know I like to see you wearing it. Last time you were here you had that nice sandy-coloured one with the brown patches. What happened to that?"

"It's finished, Mum. It's over. I'm not in the Army any more."

"Of course. Silly me." Mother gave a nervous laugh. "Well, I suppose I'll get used to it." She sniffed, then blew her nose and straightened herself up. "Now, come and meet some of the neighbours…"

I found Terry in the kitchen, his backside propped against the sink unit, a broad hand wrapped around a pint of beer. I bustled in, set the tray down on the drainer and proffered my cheek. He duly obliged with a peck.

"Alright, luv?"

"Yes, thank you. How are the boys?"

"Fine. I left them with a pizza and a couple of videos to watch – they'll be ok. Oh, and by the way, I made sure they had your Mum's number just in case. But I'll be surprised if we hear a peep out of them tonight."

"Good. Now excuse me, you're in my way…"

I elbowed him aside and ushered a selection of pastries into the oven.

Terry supped at his pint and continued unperturbed.

"Soldier boy's arrived then, by the sound of it. Where's he been this time?"

"He didn't say."

"He will."

Terry was even more sceptical than I was.

"For goodness sake, keep your voice down. He'll hear you."

"I'm not bothered if he does, I can handle him."

I was sure he could. My husband was a big man and solidly built, just like the houses he constructed. All the same, no one wanted to see things put to the test.

I spent the best part of the next hour or so in the kitchen slaving over a hot stove, then popping in and out of the living room with trays of food. So I wasn't privy to all that went on and I've had to piece the story together as best I can based on what I could glean from Mother, Terry, Cyril et al, but I'm pretty sure I've got the gist of what happened. I was certainly there when Mother introduced Frank to the Major. And the Major was enough to drive anyone to drink, never mind Frank.

"…and this," said Mother, pulling at Frank's sleeve, "is Mr Shuttleworth. Or should I say, Major Shuttleworth."

Frank turned to look. Major Shuttleworth was elderly and sported a white handlebar moustache, the edges of which were stained brown from the habitual use of nicotine. He wore a blue jacket and a tie which indicated membership of some formal organisation, probably the British Legion. A row of medals dangled from his chest and at the mention of his former rank, he stiffened and drew himself up to his full height.

"At your service, ma'am..."

There was a danger he was about to salute.

"Mr Shuttleworth was in the Army," said Mother. I always suspected she had a soft spot for Mr Shuttleworth – but that's another story.

"Ah!" he said, taking his cue. "That was a long while ago." He leaned forward and tapped the ribbons on his breast pocket. "Suez...1956...bad business...would've been perfectly alright if the French hadn't been involved...never could trust the French... Funny lot..." He began to reminisce in a ponderous, wistful fashion as if he imagined the rest of the world was interested. "We left Portsmouth on the 15th of May as far as I recall..."

Frank's eyes glazed over as if a dark cloud were obscuring his view. There was something on his mind and it wasn't Major Shuttleworth. He craned his neck to one side and whispered into Mother's ear so as not to attract attention.

"Mum... Can I get something to drink? It's gone seven and I've had nothing since lunchtime."

This was partly true. What he meant was he'd had nothing solid.

"Of course you can, dear. It's in the kitchen. Go and help yourself."

Frank made his excuses and side-stepped toward the door.

Major Shuttleworth detected a movement in the ranks.

"Ah! Strategic withdrawal, eh? Live to fight another day and all that... Good plan... Now, where was I? Oh, yes... Took us a fortnight to get to Port Said... Choppy seas in the Med apparently..."

But this was a story I'd heard before so I'd already slipped away and was back in the kitchen before Frank arrived.

I was having trouble with Mother's oven and the sausage rolls were taking their time. I told Terry about it.

"It's not as good as mine. These'd be fifteen minutes at home – I'll have to give them twenty here." I started fiddling with one of the controls. "I thought you were going to fix this."

I'm sure he'd said he would. He looked the other way, muttered something about 'old appliances' and sipped quietly on his ale. But that's Terry for you, always making promises.

At this point Frank wandered in looking like a lost soul, although there was a glint in his eye which betrayed his true intent.

"Aha!" Terry stirred slightly. "Look who's here. Hail the conquering hero comes."

I immediately turned on him and gave him a sideways glance. *Don't start that…*

Terry backed off but he still didn't shift from the sink. Even if Frank had offered, there was no way he'd have shaken hands. And with me watching over the pair of them like a hawk, Terry decided to forget the whole thing and cut straight to the chase.

"So what can we do you for, chief?"

"Drink," croaked Frank. "I need a beer."

"A man after my own heart," said Terry, trying to be jovial. "No problem. Here you go."

An open case of Tetley's stood behind the kitchen door. Terry reached into it and fetched out a tube, which Frank eagerly grasped.

"Would you like a glass…" Terry continued… *with that?* His latent question was rendered redundant as Frank ripped open the metal top and started drinking straight from the can.

Frank didn't need such niceties as a glass. A glass merely got in the way. If you were serious about your drinking, as Frank clearly was, you took the direct route. He upended the can and polished it off in one go. It made Terry slightly nervous.

"Steady on."

But Frank was not in a prudent mood. Consciously or subconsciously, he'd decided to get drunk and drinking was not an occupation that admitted of prudence – to be successful he had to go at it wholeheartedly. It might not look like it, but his form of drinking was a carefully planned journey, a path he'd mapped out for himself over the course of the evening. The next step was to find a bottle of whisky.

This, we discovered, was how he'd learnt to drink in the Army – a pint, followed by a chaser. The theory (as Terry explained to me afterwards) was that if you drank beer you got full but you didn't get pissed. If you drank whisky, you got pissed but you didn't get full. But if you drank beer and *then* whisky, everything would work out just fine. Sounds great, doesn't it? Personally, I wouldn't make it past the first pint.

This elegant technique had probably been perfected somewhere like Cyprus. Spending your days guarding a radio mast on a lonely mountaintop must be rather dull and in your off-duty hours, drinking was a practical relief from the tedium. At every opportunity your platoon would visit the bars in Limassol or Farmagusta, where at two or three o'clock in the morning they'd be found staggering down the main street, roaring drunk, their arms about each other's shoulders, singing.

There was a soldier, a Scottish soldier,
Who wandered far away, and soldiered far away...

But wasn't that why Frank had signed up? To have mates and moments like these?

JOIN THE ARMY AND SEE THE WORLD.

More often than not, I suspect that world had been the back of an MP's van and a night in alternative accommodation. And before long, what began as a pleasurable diversion turned into a habit and Frank became dependent. Beer and whisky, whisky and beer – what was the difference? They were his mates now.

The good news for Frank was that there was a bottle of the hard stuff readily available. Mother usually kept it in a cabinet in the sitting room, but for the purposes of the party Terry had brought it out into the kitchen. Frank clocked it straight away, took a tumbler from an overhead cupboard and sloshed it half full. He wasn't going to drink *that* straight from the source – there were limits to how low he could sink. Then he grabbed another can from the case of Tetley's and disappeared in the direction of the lounge.

I looked at Terry and raised an enquiring eyebrow. Last time Frank had been home, we'd seen nothing like this.

Now we come to the part concerning Cyril. I didn't know Cyril very well – hardly at all to be truthful. It had been difficult tracking him down but Mother was adamant we should have *someone* from Frank's past. He'd been reluctant to come but had succumbed to her powers of persuasion on the grounds that he was 'ready to sacrifice himself for the sake of others', although we weren't quite sure what that meant at the time. In his grey flannel trousers, white shirt and V-necked sweater, he cut a pretty unassuming figure and spent most of the evening hidden away in the background. I think Mother hoped that if she introduced them, some sort of friendship might develop.

"Look," she said, guiding Frank gently by the elbow. "There's Cyril. You remember Cyril, don't you dear?"

Frank surveyed the array of people before him.

In the far corner Cyril sipped tentatively at his glass of orange and lemonade, then nodded a form of acknowledgement.

Frank's response was a weak and cynical smile. There may have been stirrings of a vague recollection, although I don't think Frank really remembered Cyril at all. In fact, at that moment I don't think Frank remembered much of anything and it had all become something of a blur. The effects of his pint and whisky chasers had begun to bite – or rather, dull – and the world as he saw it was taking on an acceptably rosy hue. He'd reached the pleasant part of his journey, a long and gentle plateau where he was still in the world but had ceased to care about it. He resembled an anaesthetised patient who'd received his injection and was floating in a permanently woozy state, i.e. he'd totally forgotten the illness from which he suffered, but hadn't yet fallen unconscious. I'm convinced that the greater part of his pleasure at that point lay in the fact that he'd succeeded in avoiding any further introductions. Above the general hubbub, you could still hear reminders of his first encounter.

"...alright until the Americans came charging in," droned Major Shuttleworth. "All bull at a gate...no sense of proportion..."

I groaned, but rather than irritate Frank, the words probably did no more than drift in and out of his alcoholic haze.

Mother finally succeeded in getting his attention. He blinked once more and attempted to focus.

"Weren't you two in the same woodwork class at college?" she said.

Cyril had actually got as far as opening his mouth to reply when a loud volley of laughter burst out from the other side of the room. Major Shuttleworth had cracked a joke and his audience was roaring with relief. In the subsequent pause, Mother took the opportunity to retreat.

"Now why don't you two have a nice chat to each other while I go and fill up some glasses," she said. "I'm sure you've got lots of catching up to do."

And she slipped away to attend to her guests.

Left alone with Cyril, this act of abandonment might have put Frank in an awkward position; but far from it, and of the two of them he was best placed to deal with it. He was now in the autumn of his intoxication, a season of mists and fellow fruit-fulness, somewhere where events took place but to which he neither felt the need nor the ability to respond. Mother was no longer there – but he was used to that, and whilst in the Army this was how he'd learnt to cope with her absence and much else. In this kind of mood he would give off nothing but silence and his weak and silly smile. His presence was consequently unnerving.

Cyril was the one who was exposed. It was his prop that had been removed, not Frank's, and with Mother gone he became perturbed and flustered. Beads of sweat formed on his troubled brow. Desperate to find a way forward, he decided on a handshake and duly extended his arm.

Frank appeared not to notice. He totally ignored the gesture and maintained his fixed and stupid look. Cyril curled up his fingers and slowly replaced his hand in his pocket. Meanwhile, Frank's inane smile grew wider and he starting grinning like a Cheshire cat.

God knows what Cyril must have felt like. Straight up and down and stone-cold sober and he hadn't a clue what to do with himself. Now he was forced onto another tack and gathering himself up as best he could, he tried the obvious line, the one comment that seemed totally inoffensive.

"Your mother tells me you've been in the Services."

Frank's response was reportedly short but not very sweet.

"Fuck off."

Cyril told me afterwards he was shocked. In his cloistered circles they didn't use the 'f' word and he was mortified to hear it. I can understand that. He *was* a bit precious and he couldn't for the life of him see how he could inspire such abuse. Had Mother been there of course, Frank might have felt more restrained although it didn't excuse him in the slightest.

But if Cyril was expecting an apology, he was in for a disappointment. Frank had no intention of hanging around to explain himself. He wasn't 'on duty' but he still had a mission for the evening – and that was yet to be accomplished. Without so much as an *Excuse me* he shoved Cyril aside and headed directly for the liquor store. Cyril could be ignored – he had far more important matters to attend to.

It was the fourth or fifth occasion Frank had returned to the kitchen. Each time he'd gone through the same routine, taking a can from the case of Tetley's and splashing two or three fingers of whisky into a tumbler. The spirit bottle was now close to empty, and with a theatrical gesture he pinched it by the neck and dropped it carefully into the waste bin, his face locked in that inane grin of his. I think he wanted to show he was still in control and capable of co-ordinating hand and eye despite how much he'd consumed. He set about garnering another round of drinks.

I'd been too busy to keep count. My remit was to supply the demands of the buffet table, and with Terry's assistance I'd despatched a continuous stream of comestibles in the direction of the living room. But my brother's repeated intrusions had not gone unnoticed, and in the brief interval between cooking the cocktail sausages and slicing up a quiche, I had time to ask Terry a question.

"What's going on?"

"Frank's getting plastered."

"Are you sure?"

"Absolutely certain."

I could rely on Terry to spot the signs. He liked a few drinks himself and from time to time I'd been known to wait up with the rolling pin. But by comparison with Frank, my husband was an amateur. I began to get worried.

"Keep an eye on him, will you."

"Alright, luv."

He adjusted his grip on his pint and shifted his backside further along the sink.

When Frank next returned, Terry took the opportunity to comment. He was reluctant to interfere (a man had a right to a few drinks if he wanted) but now he had me to contend with. He waited until the kitchen door opened and Frank's grizzled head appeared, empty glass in hand. It had been less than fifteen minutes since his last visit.

"Don't you think you've had enough?"

Frank raised himself up like a wounded animal and looked Terry disdainfully in the eye. His inane grin disappeared and was replaced by a front of defiance as he deliberately took another can from the case, ripped off the ring pull and downed half of it in one go. The whisky was gone but he could still make his point with the beer.

Don't you tell me what to do.

He shuffled off, clutching the can to his chest like a child with a comforting blanket.

Terry and I looked at each other, the same thought running through our minds.

There'll be trouble…

In the crush of the front room, Cyril was making his excuses.

"I've had a really lovely evening, Mrs Johnson. But I think I should be off now."

"Oh…" said Mother. "Must you go? It seems you've only just arrived. Are you sure you can't stay a bit longer?"

She'd rather hoped that the seed she'd planted would take root and grow into something meaningful. But if Frank and Cyril were to hit it off together, there was no evidence of it as yet.

"Well…" Cyril pulled back the cuff of his clean white shirt and inspected his watch. "Goodness me, look at the time. It's quarter past ten already and I've got a six o'clock start in the morning. We joiners are early birds you know."

He looked round the room with a sense of unease. The incident earlier in the evening had unsettled him and he appeared distinctly on edge.

"I see," said Mother. "Well, if you must, you must, I suppose. Anyway, thank you so much for making the effort to come. Frank will have been so pleased to see you. I'll just let him know that you're going…"

"No! There's no need. I'll…"

Cyril raised a hand in protest but it was too late – Mother had already turned away and was searching the room. There followed a brief moment of hesitation in which a more resolute character might have made his escape – but Cyril dithered and the chance was lost.

Frank stood in the far corner, swaying gently from side to side. With both feet rooted to the floor, he resembled a supple tree bending in the wind. Gone were the pastel shades of autumn and his state of inebriation had progressed to a dark and discontented winter in which everything seemed destined to annoy him.

I'm told it's a bleak and desolate place. Your head throbs, there's a stabbing pain in your temples and you begin to feel tired – but if you close your eyes for more than a second the room starts to rotate about you and you're forced to wrench them back open.

Whatever pain Frank was experiencing, it seemed to permeate his entire being. It was doubtless made worse by an ever-present, high-pitched drone. It came from the area surrounding Major Shuttleworth who was still regaling his audience with his tales of derring-do. It was as if Frank were trapped inside a greenhouse full of flowers where a bee buzzed incessantly from one plant to another and yet always remained infuriatingly out of sight. If only it would come close enough, he could swot it.

Mother was waving at him from the other side of the room. He blinked hard, forcing himself to concentrate and recognise who it was. There was a chance that in her company, the continual buzzing might cease. He lurched towards her, clutching the half-empty can to his chest, anxious to escape the Major's ceaseless prattling. Rebounding from one body to another, he would have fallen before he reached her had it not been for their support.

Cyril must have seen him coming. At last he took action and with thoughts of self-preservation in mind, headed smartly for the door.

"Excuse me..."

Mother, who'd turned away to wave, turned back and found her companion gone.

"Oh..."

Frank blundered heavily past, intent on causing damage. Initially attracted by Mother's signal, he completely ignored her and focused on his prey. The bee that had been buzzing to such irritating effect had manifested itself in human form and his one overwhelming desire was to silence it. But it was intent on making its escape and he had to catch it before it left the greenhouse. Lurching backwards and then stumbling forwards, he reached the door to the hallway just before it closed.

What happened once the door had shut behind them was later the subject of conjecture. There were no independent witnesses and the participants themselves gave confusing accounts. Frank was too far gone to remember anything much the following day, so the only testimony that could readily be admitted was that of the victim. Cyril claimed he was about to go out into the street when Frank fell on him from behind, though whether he thought it deliberate or accidental, he was too polite to say. All he knew was that he'd reached up to fetch his coat, then found himself face down on the floor, his nose pressed flat to the carpet, with Frank sprawled on top of him. It was his compressed cry for help that alerted everyone else – that and the resounding crash as the coat stand, heavily laden with coats, toppled over and smashed into the telephone table.

Mother had watched the both of them go out and was first to react as a noise like a felled tree spread quickly through the lounge.

"What on earth...?"

"Did you hear that?"

"Someone's fallen down the stairs if you ask me..."

Wrapped up in his private world of military combat, Major Shuttleworth was the last to cotton on. He'd gone back to 1940 and was planning his retreat to Dunkirk – but even he tailed off into silence as they waited for news.

It was Mother who provided it, her hand resting on the doorjamb as she surveyed what was in front of her.

"It's Frank. There's been an accident..."

She'd leapt to the wrong conclusion of course but that was understandable.

Out in the kitchen, Terry and I were the last to get wind of affairs. Still glued to the edge of the sink, he heard the thump, then the buzz of voices and instantly guessed what had happened.

"Damn!"

"What is it?" I was all bound up in my apron and oven gloves.

"I'll go and check. You stay here."

After Mother, he was next to arrive on the scene. The others had sensibly decided not to push through into the hallway and remained clustered together in small groups in the sitting room. Terry made his way to the front.

"Could you let me by please?" He ushered Mother's shocked and static figure gently to one side. "I'll deal with it."

The situation in the hallway was not quite as he'd thought. Half obscured beneath a pile of coats, Frank lay prostrate at the foot of the stairs, pinning the hapless Cyril underneath. The coat stand, still with one or two coats hooked to it, was skewed at an angle while next to it, the telephone table had fallen over and the telephone was dangling off the hook.

Terry reconnected it, then pulled the coats off Frank's body and rolled him to one side. He appeared to be unconscious and when Terry pulled back his eyelids, all he could see was the whites.

Meanwhile, Cyril had picked himself up. The breath had been

knocked out of him and he went to sit on the stairs.

"Are you alright?"

Unable to speak, Cyril held his head in his hands.

"I'll get you a glass of water," said Terry.

That was easy – glasses of water weren't hard to come by. It would take a lot more than that to deal with Frank and for a moment Terry avoided Mother's eye. Eventually he was forced to a conclusion.

"I think we'd better call an ambulance."

"An ambulance?" said Mother. "What on earth for? Don't tell me one of them's injured."

"Frank's passed out. And to be honest, I don't much like the look of him."

"Oh my God!" Mother's hands flew up to her face. "The poor boy!"

She was still on the wrong tack. The truth would come later.

A babble of conversation broke out amongst the guests behind her.

"Passed out? He must have had a few…"

"I didn't think he looked too good earlier on…"

Whatever had happened, it made a welcome diversion from the ramblings of Major Shuttleworth.

The inquest had hardly got started when their debate was cut short by another dramatic interruption. From the rear of the house came a second crash, this time metallic in nature. Stunned into silence once more, they froze in suspended animation. Then the kitchen door opened and I made my entrance.

I'd been oblivious to the goings-on in the hallway. The demands of my job as chef for the evening had absorbed me and I'd just extracted my latest offering from the oven when a baking tray slipped from a worktop and fell heavily to the floor. I'd decided to ignore it and quickly filled two serving dishes before making my way into the lounge. Here I found myself the centre of attention. With every face turned in my direction, uneasily

expectant, my casual enquiry was completely out of place.
"Sausage roll, anyone?" I asked.

Three

I caught up with things at the meeting that was held the following morning. It was a Saturday, I was off work and I'd gone round to help with the clearing up. Although it wasn't just the house that had to be put back into order.

Terry had taken the boys to football, but rather than stay and watch the game he'd simply dropped them off and headed straight back to Balfour Terrace. His evidence would be vital but to my annoyance his first act on returning was to go out into the back yard and light a cigarette. It had rained heavily in the night and the yellow ribbon tied around the metal clothes pole was looking bedraggled. Eventually we all sat down together at the kitchen table over a cup of coffee and our makeshift court of enquiry began.

Mother was in a state of denial.

"I can't understand how that much alcohol could have got into his system."

"He drank it, Mum," I said firmly. "Terry watched him do it."

"Well, if that's the case, why didn't you stop him? You were there – you must have known what he was up to."

"It's not as easy as that," Terry cut in. "You can't just tell a grown man he mustn't have a few drinks on a night."

I was grateful for the support. It wasn't often that Terry took my side.

In her heart, Mother must have known that we were right – although part of the problem was that she never thought of Frank as a grown man. He was still her little boy, the one she'd saved from the flood, the one she'd nurtured all those years. She shook her head.

"I still find it hard to believe…"

"You're just going to have to deal with it, Mum." I was adamant. "The facts are there for all to see."

"I suppose so…"

Frank himself was still in hospital. He'd had his stomach pumped and had been kept in overnight for observation. He was used to alternative accommodation but this was of a different kind although as yet he didn't know it, for when I phoned the ward at eleven he was still to regain consciousness.

The night before, the ambulance had taken half an hour to arrive. It was a Friday and they were in considerable demand – Frank wasn't the only case of suspected alcohol poisoning they had to deal with that evening. Terry had stayed with him in the hallway and once the coats had been cleared, he'd moved him into the recovery position. In the sitting room there was little the guests could do to help and one by one they began to slip quietly away. Although with the route to the front door blocked by Frank's prostrate form, they were obliged to sneak out of the back entrance.

Mother was in tears. The evening she'd carefully planned had been ruined and her dear boy was lying comatose in the hallway. It was as much as I could do to prevent her from joining Frank in the ambulance and going to the hospital with him.

"That's not going to do any good, Mum. Let Terry take care of it, it'll be alright. You stay here with me and I'll make you a nice cup of tea."

After a while she'd seen the sense of it and let herself be looked after. That had been last night and now we faced the problem of what to do next.

There was no question of Frank coming home. The hospital wanted tests carried out and besides, Mother found the idea of having him in the house in his current condition rather daunting. *I wouldn't know what to do...*

She was naturally in two minds about it. Her instinct was to have him back home where she could look after him and lavish the care and attention on him that she'd done when he was a child. But common sense told her this was different and it wasn't going to be cured by the likes of a sticking plaster and a dose of

TLC. This was something best left to the professionals.

The following day the decision was taken out of her hands. Frank was deemed to be suffering from long-term alcohol abuse and further treatment was required. The consultant responsible recommended a spell in a rehabilitation unit. Coming so soon after the first, this second set of news required careful consideration. Another kitchen cabinet was convened.

This time we held it on a Wednesday evening after tea while the boys were at swimming. Mother opened the debate.

"So how long do you suppose this has been going on?"

"It must have been a while," I said. "You don't develop something like that overnight."

"The Army must have known, surely. Why didn't they do anything about it?"

She'd now moved on from denial and was looking to allocate blame.

"I don't see why they should know," said Terry. "Plenty of squaddies go out and get drunk on a night. Even if the Army did know, they probably turned a blind eye. There's a lot goes on we don't get told about."

Terry often repeated stories he'd heard on the building site or down at the pub. Up until now, I hadn't always believed them.

Mother looked round at me.

"Did you know?"

"No, Mum, I can't honestly say that I did. I'd have told you if I had, you know I would."

Mother sniffed. I sensed a tear coming on.

"And when I think of all the times he was home and went out drinking and came back worse for wear. I thought it was just high spirits – you know, being on leave and off the leash a bit. Frank always did like a drink, but I thought nothing of it. If I'd known it was serious…"

"You mustn't blame yourself, Mum. There's nothing you could have done. Frank's the one at fault. Isn't that right, Terry?"

Terry nodded. But it didn't make Mother's pain any the less.

"I know. But it's so upsetting…"

Eventually the discussion moved on as to what could be done about it.

"I don't see what you can do about it," said Terry. "Frank's got himself into it, and Frank's the one who'll have to get himself out of it."

"That's not particularly helpful," I said. "I can see if it was left up to you nothing would get done at all." It was a common complaint with Terry – he was never the one to take action. "So what about this rehabilitation unit?"

"You mean The Priory?" Terry scoffed. "Where all the celebrities go? That would be something – Frank rubbing shoulders with the stars!"

"I wish you'd stop being flippant and take this seriously." His attitude was beginning to annoy me. "There must be other places he could go."

"Well, I suppose it can't do any harm if we could find him somewhere," Terry was forced to admit.

"Yes, but will it do any good?" Mother dried her eyes and prepared to be practical.

"There's nothing to lose," I said.

"What's the alternative?" asked Terry.

And when we thought about it we concluded there wasn't one – or at least, not one we could come up with. Had we been more aware of the rigours of the treatment we might not have been so casual about it. But then, it wasn't our own lives we were deciding, it was Frank's and he was in no position to argue.

The key issue was funding. Despite Terry's jokes, we soon came to realise why it was the rich and famous who went to The Priory – a week in a clinic didn't come cheap. In the end we managed to stump up enough for six. Frank had no money to speak of, although, to give him credit, he'd been a dutiful son and sent any excess pay back home to help with the upkeep of the house. So Mother was the one with the savings but they certainly weren't enough to cover the whole of the expense.

"I can't do it all myself."

After a discussion with Terry, I stepped into the breach.

"I'll go halves with you, Mum."

Despite all Frank's faults, he was still my brother and I remembered Mother's words in the caravan. *We're a family and we stick together, no matter what...*

But then, I'd done well for myself and I could afford to be generous. My studious nature at school had carried through into college where I'd won a Diploma in Personnel Management, although why I'd chosen that particular discipline had always puzzled Mother.

What do you know about people?

Quite a lot, actually. Besides, it's the management side that's important.

And it was the management side I was good at – managing others, managing myself, managing money. Over the years I'd got to manage Comet and I was earning the salary that went with it – far more in fact than my bricklaying husband. It was sometimes a bone of contention and I often thought it contributed to his offhand manner and the way he was prone to sarcasm.

So there we were, Mr and Mrs with two boys, living in a four-bed detached, and despite the mortgage, still with enough cash in the bank to say *I'll help you out* when the occasion arose. Now it was Frank who wanted assistance. And there was Terry, sitting in the corner, sipping his tea, the brick dust still on his clothes...

It's your decision. You're the one that earns the money.

I was, and as a result Frank got his six weeks; though it was as much for Mother's sake as it was for his.

Our primary concern was that he wouldn't go. Frank could be awkward at times and there was a danger he wouldn't see the sense of it and all the work we'd done would be in vain. The smart thing to do, I said, was not to let him come home first but to transfer him straight from the hospital to the clinic as though it were part of the same healing process. That way, he'd never know he was being managed. The doctor agreed. *That's a great idea*, he said. *I'll leave it entirely up to you.* And so the field was left clear for us.

Mother and I went to the ward together to present a united front. If there was going to be any resistance it would help if there were two of us, but much to our surprise Frank didn't need any persuading. He lay flat on the bed, staring up at the ceiling, and when Mother took his hand and started off with the words *Your sister and I have something to tell you...* there was barely a flicker of reaction. He either didn't care what happened to him next or he'd reached the point where he was prepared to entrust his future to someone else. But whatever the reason, he went as quiet as a lamb.

It was as though the night of the party had been the nadir of his condition, the culmination of his life in the Army and the culture of heavy drinking, and his behaviour that evening had been a cry for help. Freed from the discipline of the parade ground, he'd found himself sliding unfettered into the depths of some personal abyss. God knows what was down there, I dread to think, but whatever his mental state, the crucial thing was that on the day we shipped him out, other than water he'd not had a drink for over a week.

"Well," said Mother, once he was installed at the clinic, "I don't think that could have gone much better."

"No," I said with a wry smile. "I don't think it could."

But then, I always was the clever one.

The six-week period passed quickly. It was easy for us – we had a regular routine we could rely on to speed up the passage of time. I had the school run followed by work and then the preparation of tea. Mother was now spending two or three hours every morning working in the newsagents at the end of the street to supplement her pension. After lunch, she'd sit in front of the fire with a magazine or a book. We each had our ways to get by.

It was totally different for Frank. We could only imagine what privations he must have suffered. In Mother's spare moments (I had none – I was far too busy to spend time daydreaming about my brother) she would conjure up pictures of cross-country runs and cold showers as if he were staying in some old-fashioned boarding school. Then she'd tell herself it was no more than he was used to when he was still in the Army. It never occurred to her that it was those same impositions which had driven him to drink in the first place. If so, she might have felt less comfortable about his so-called Dry Me Out regime.

As it was, neither of us knew much of what went on at the clinic. Whatever knowledge we possessed had been gleaned from the brochure, so we were at least familiar with the Twelve Steps to Freedom programme and the terms 'abstinence', 'detox' and 'rehab'. What they meant in detail we had no real idea. All we knew was that whenever we went to visit, Frank looked tired and drawn – to the point where on one occasion Mother took one of the assistants aside and asked him directly.

"Is he alright?"

"He's doing fine, Mrs Johnson," was the confident reply. "Don't you worry, we'll have him back to you soon, right as rain."

So Frank came home for the second time. But there was no party, no welcoming committee and no yellow ribbon tied round the clothes pole in the garden. There was no alcohol in the house either – Mother had taken the precaution of removing it all. Abstinence, she'd been told, meant cutting out, not cutting back, and if the weeks Frank had spent in the clinic were to count, she knew she had to be ruthless.

The beneficiary of this clear-out was Terry who was surprised to receive the remnants of the case of Tetley's, half a decanter of sherry and a couple of bottles of wine. The whisky had gone, as we knew. He willingly accepted his prizes – a bit too willingly for my liking.

"Every cloud has a silver lining," he chortled.

"That's a terrible thing to say," I retorted. "Just think yourself lucky I don't pack *you* off to the clinic for a week or two."

He didn't find that quite so funny.

Four

Frank's room hadn't been occupied since his return from the Forces. Prior to his arrival Mother had been at pains to make it as inviting as she could. Up until then, it had just been somewhere for Frank to stay whilst he'd been home on leave, a temporary refuge from the Army; but now he was to be there on a permanent basis and some form of embellishment was thought appropriate. He was her hero and she wanted to make it a home fit for one.

She asked my advice about it. I have a penchant for soft furnishings and I like to see a house made homely. Hence my choice of peach-coloured pillows and cushions, while Mother, in a rather more sentimental mood, added cuddly toys in the form of a bear and a panda. On reflection, these adornments were unlikely to be suitable for any grown man, let alone a soldier returning from a lifetime of duty, but even so, Mother thought they might prove comforting, especially after his sojourn in the clinic. She'd already removed one source of relief and besides, she still thought of him as a child.

His reaction both surprised and disappointed her. At first he said nothing and seemed happy to be back in the house. But on the second morning after his return, when Mother came out onto the landing to get ready to go to work, she noticed that the furnishings we'd laboured over were piled up outside his door. On top of the heap of peach-coloured cushions, looking rather forlorn, sat the teddy bear and the panda. Later on, she discovered that Frank had in fact slept on the floor and had taken a blanket down from the top of the wardrobe to cover himself.

She returned from the newsagents sometime after eleven to find him sitting on the edge of the stripped-down bed with his hands clasped together in front of him, his body trembling and one leg jiggling furiously. Thinking he was cold, or that he might have contracted a fever, she picked up the blanket from the floor and spread it round his shoulders.

"Whatever's the matter?"

There was a shake of the head and a stifled sob.

"I'm doing my best, Mum, honest I am."

"Of course you are, dear." She attempted to draw him out. "You can talk to me about it if you like."

All this invoked was another shake of the head. Tears plopped on to the carpet.

"I don't want to talk about it."

"Alright... Why don't we just sit here together for a while until you feel better."

And with the outward intention of adjusting the blanket, her arm circled his shoulders and she drew him towards her. After a brief pause his head inclined to one side and rested in the crook of her neck. Soon the jiggling stopped and he was alright again.

From then on, Mother said it was like a pact between them, an unwritten agreement that would allow them each to move forward. Frank would do his utmost to stay dry while Mother would keep silent on the issue and spare him from any embarrassment. If he didn't want to talk about it, fine – just as long as he didn't renege on the deal. It was a bargain based on trust and would suit them for as long as it lasted.

The problem for Frank was that he was essentially confined to the property. Balfour Terrace had been declared an alcohol-free zone but beyond the front door lay temptation in all its guises and he knew he couldn't rely on himself if he became exposed to it. There was a salient case in point. One day, his will had obviously been broken and he'd ransacked the house in search of something to drink. Mother came home to find an empty bottle of meths lying on the floor. He'd either downed it or the smell had so disgusted him that he'd felt sick and poured it away. Fortunately it proved to be the latter – but there were no guarantees.

He'd then gone to sit at the foot of the stairs where he'd remained for an hour, body trembling, leg jiggling, daring himself to go out, knowing that if he did so his promise to Mother would be broken. That was how she found him, in crisis, much as she'd done that first time when he'd been on the edge of the bed. Only now she didn't say a word but went straight to fetch the blanket and sat with him until the moment passed.

If Mother couldn't talk to Frank about it, then at least she could confide in me. We'd fallen into the habit of meeting at the conclusion of her weekly shopping expedition. She'd take the bus to the retail park, collect her goods from Tesco and deposit them in the boot of my car for delivery later on. Afterwards, we'd meet in the restaurant for a cup of coffee or a bite of lunch so she could return the keys.

By then I'd formed a definite view.

"He'll have to get a job, Mum. I know he's got problems and all that but he can't sit around the house for the rest of his life."

"You're right, I know – but..." Mother stirred the froth on top of her cappuccino. "I worry. And I don't like the idea of letting him go. You never know what might happen."

"I understand what you're saying – but it's a risk you're going to have to take. He's what now? Forty? Forty-one? You can't keep him home for ever. At some stage he's going to have to go out there and earn a living. He's an able-bodied man for goodness sake."

"I suppose so..."

There was another reason for Mother to yield. With Frank at home, there were now two of them in the house and without his regular contribution the budget was becoming stretched. The bill for the shopping that day proved the point – she'd spent as much in a week as she'd normally have spent in a month – and with most of her savings gone, she'd little extra to draw on. The last thing she wanted was to come knocking on my door again.

"Well, alright – but it's difficult for me to talk to him about it.

I know it sounds silly but we have this kind of agreement. I don't ask him about...things...and he stays away from the drink. To be honest, I think it's the only thing that's kept him straight these last few months and I don't want to spoil it. Do you see what I mean?"

I nodded. I was beginning to get a feel for where this was going. Mother's next statement confirmed it.

"I wonder whether you could speak to him at all?"

I could have kicked myself. It was as if I'd talked myself into it, simply by being forthright and speaking my mind. Either that, or Mother was far more Machiavellian than I gave her credit for. But one way or another, I now found myself in the unenviable position of mediating between Frank and my mother. I could hardly say no – I was supposed to be good at that sort of thing. Wasn't that part of my job, keeping the peace between the parties? Only it wasn't as simple as that, especially when there was family involved.

I have to say I came out of my meeting with Frank feeling rather resentful. It seemed to me he was being cosseted and that Mother was spoon-feeding him. What irked me most was the fact that I was supposed to come along and bail him out yet again. I'd done it once before over the question of the clinic and I wondered how often I'd be expected to do it in future. Nothing had ever been handed to me on a plate – I'd had to work for it. But as Mother kept telling me: *You always were the strong one.* And that was why she looked to me now.

On account of Frank.

Frank – my little brother.

Frank – who could never quite get it together.

Frank – who, despite, or perhaps even because of, his weakness of character, made me curiously afraid that at any moment he might erupt out of his stupor and descend into violence as the temper that was stored up inside him became uncontrollable.

Actually, I needn't have worried as my brother proved as amenable to the idea of work as he had to going into the clinic. In fact, he was pleased to be released from his confinement and was happy to submit himself to the guidance of others once again. *It's not a problem, he'll do it,* I told Mother, much to her relief. The nature of his employment was far more problematic, however.

Liberated from the house and the clinic, Frank enjoyed his freedom. He craved fresh air and a life out of doors – just as he'd done in the Army. Office work was restrictive and the need to wear a shirt and tie proved too much. One placement in such surroundings lasted no more than a day. *I can't be doing with it – it would drive me insane...* or to something worse, and the implication of that alone was enough to move him on. Eventually I found him a position in a sawmill and the combination of manual labour and an outdoor existence seemed to suit his temperament. Things settled down, and for the next eighteen months there were no more problems.

Then Karen arrived on the scene and that set the cat amongst the pigeons.

It was a mystery to me as to why Karen and Frank ever got together in the first place. I knew the how of it – if Mother told me once, she told me a dozen times – but it was the motivation that lay behind it that puzzled me. While Frank had been in the Army we'd no idea of what he'd done as far as women were concerned, and in all the time he'd been at home he'd never shown the slightest interest in finding a partner. To be honest, it had never occurred to me that he might want one. But there he was, a single man, over forty, not 'going out', then suddenly he was in a relationship and an apparently serious one at that. My first thought was that he was merely gratifying his needs but it soon became clear that there was more to it than that.

It was a point that completely escaped Mother. She was so

overcome by the prospect of her boy settling down into family life that the whys and wherefores of the process totally passed her by. So when she broke the news – *Frank's met someone* – she immediately assumed I'd understand what she was talking about. Instead of which, I greeted her remark with bewilderment.

"What do you mean?"

"He's met someone," she reiterated.

"Yes, you said that – but I still don't get it."

"There's a woman in his life."

"Oh, I see…"

Though I still wasn't sure that I did.

Disclosures of this nature warranted a conference, so one was arranged at the usual time and place – Saturday morning round Mother's kitchen table. This time Terry wasn't invited and stayed at football with the boys. With Frank at the sawmill doing overtime we had the place to ourselves and so we made the most of it.

"What's this all about then?"

"Well…" Mother made herself comfortable and settled in for the long haul. "It all started with that party for Cyril's sister…"

Cyril was still around – he'd been hanging about ever since the incident with Frank. I didn't think we'd ever see him again, but a week later he'd turned up at Balfour Terrace in a particularly contrite frame of mind.

"I've come to apologise, Mrs Johnson."

"Apologise? What on earth for?"

"About what happened the other evening."

"Don't be silly. That wasn't your fault."

"I know, Mrs Johnson, but I wanted to tell you I've decided to forgive him."

"Oh…"

That changed things. Contrition was one thing – the promise of absolution quite another. Mother felt slightly offended.

"Well, that's very kind of you. I'm sure he doesn't deserve it."

"Ah, but he does," continued Cyril. "You see, we are all sinners in this world."

At this point Mother would normally have given a polite *No thank you* and closed the door. Despite all her tribulations, she'd never let God into her house. But Cyril was a friend of a friend and not someone she could easily turn away.

"Well, you'd better come in and have a cup of tea. Frank's out at the moment but he'll be back later on."

And so Cyril began his attempt at Frank's redemption, a project he pursued doggedly over the course of the following months. It was as though the Church had set him the objective of pulling a lost soul back from the brink and Frank was the obvious choice. Not surprisingly, Frank proved unresponsive, but Cyril continued undaunted and eventually his persistence paid off. Invitations to Church socials were declined, but an invitation to a party was an entirely different matter.

Mother lent him encouragement.

"You should go," she told him.

Ensconced in his favourite seat in front of the television, Frank did not reply. She took his silence to mean he'd no objection and pressed on.

"I'm sure Cyril's sister is lovely..."

No doubt she was. Cyril's family were 'safe' and there were no worries to be had on that score. And if Frank couldn't go out in their company, whose company could he go out in? Although as things turned out, Cyril's revenge couldn't have been more comprehensive than if he'd planned it in detail himself.

Karen was a friend of Cyril's sister. Probably in her early thirties, she was single and had a child of eighteen months called Melanie. Karen was on the short side, slim, and with straight blonde hair that was always gathered up behind her head with an elasticated tie. Except when she was at parties (which, to be fair, wasn't often), she wore an old pair of jeans, trainers and a grey tracksuit top with a hood and carried Melanie permanently on her hip. I never understood what Frank saw in her. He must have found her attractive although to me she looked as if she'd had a hard life.

Her previous partner had absconded and left her in the lurch so she survived on a combination of benefits and whatever money the authorities could wring out of her ex. That was never enough of course and she lived in a state of continual want. To hear all this, you'd think she was common, but she wasn't. Beneath her deprived appearance, she was actually quite a pleasant person. But the world had wearied her and she invariably looked saddened by its burdens.

I think what Karen wanted was a man, any man, someone to fill the void in her life, and at times she was desperate to secure one. She needed to be looked after, and if not loved then at least respected and to have Melanie provided with the father figure her daughter required. What she got, however, was Frank, and although he may have tried to fulfil those roles he was fundamentally ill-equipped to carry them out, and in that respect he fared no better than his predecessor. You'd have to say Karen's actions in this field were not exactly inspired. She was unfortunate in her choice of men, and consequently unfortunate in life.

Karen's motives were at least transparent. From Frank's perspective things were much more opaque. Had he fallen in love? I thought it improbable. Had he become bored with sitting at home? Or, on a much deeper level, had he concluded that in order to live a normal and productive life he needed to have a relationship with a woman other than his mother? That too seemed doubtful – Frank didn't do self-analysis. What was more likely was that he hadn't thought about it at all and had simply allowed himself to be taken in.

The facts of the affair were well documented. He and Karen had met at the party. Cyril had introduced them – or so he told

Mother. Some chance comment had been made and it had served as a hook from which to suspend further conversation. It may have concerned Frank's former membership of the Armed Forces or some other equally trite subject, but whatever it was it had allowed them to continue talking. Although just to have known he was male and single would have been enough for Karen to have gone on with the discussion. The rest, as they say, is history.

Frank seemed unaffected and no one would have guessed at the transformation which was about to take place. It wasn't as if he came home from the party a changed man. Mother's polite *Have you had a nice time?* was met with a straightforward *Yes thank you* and a frustrating lack of detail. It was only a few days later when he announced he was going out for the evening and declined to say where or with whom that Mother's suspicions were aroused. Other such evenings followed and the mystery gradually deepened.

On the night Frank didn't come home at all, my telephone started ringing in the middle of the night. I ran downstairs to answer it – calls at that time of day always make me nervous. When I discovered it was Mother, I was none too pleased.

"For God's sake, Mum, have you any idea what time it is?"

"Don't be silly, of course I have. It's half past two and I can't sleep. Frank's not back and I'm worried."

My first reaction was one of relief. Of all the things the phone call could have been about, that was of least concern.

"So what are you worried about?"

"I'm worried that he might have... Well, you know..."

"Gone back to his old habits?"

"Yes, that's it."

"Have you phoned the police?"

"No, not yet." Mother hesitated. "I didn't want to get him into trouble."

"You won't get him into trouble, Mum, unless he's done

something wrong. That's what the police are there for."

I was now wide awake and it was clear I wouldn't be going back to sleep until the matter was cleared up. I had a quick think about what we should do.

"I suppose I'd better come over."

"Thank you, dear. I'd be so glad if you would."

I went back upstairs to get dressed. Terry had woken up and was looking out from under the duvet, half conscious.

"What's going on?"

"Frank's gone missing."

"Oh really?"

He might just as well have added *Good riddance*. He turned over and buried his head beneath the covers.

I reached Balfour Terrace to find the lights full on and Mother putting on her street clothes ready to go out.

"Where do you think you're going?" I said.

"We're going out, aren't we?"

"Whatever for?"

"To look for him."

"Don't be ridiculous. Where do you think we're going to find him at this time of night?"

"I don't know, I thought…"

"You thought what? That he'd be sleeping on a park bench like some tramp? Or maybe he's jumped into one of those skips at the back of Sainsbury's for a kip? You've been watching too many American movies, Mum. If he's out there, the police would have found him by now. Have you rung them yet?"

"Well… no." Mother shook her head. "I was waiting for you."

"I'll do it," I snapped and went out into the hallway to make the call.

Compared to Mother's diffidence, I'm afraid I was rather brusque. Yes, I was wide awake but I was tired and irritable and conscious of the fact that at eight o' clock in the morning I'd have to look smart and presentable and ready for whatever the day had in store. I really should have been home asleep, instead of which it was just after three and here I was at Mother's house engaged on some wild goose chase. And all because of Frank – my little brother.

Frank – who could never quite get it together...

The ring tone ceased and someone was on the line. The night-duty sergeant who answered was having a bad evening too and was equally as sharp as I was. No one fitting the description had been found – was there anything else?

"No, there isn't," I said and slammed the phone down.

I reported back to Mother.

"And I've left my mobile number just in case..."

But Mother was still standing there with her coat on, looking as though she expected something more. She had that pleading expression on her face so there was nothing else for it but relent.

"I suppose we could drive to A&E and see if he's checked himself in."

I didn't hold out much hope – but it was better than sitting about waiting.

A&E was empty and we drew the expected blank. Coming out into the grey morning there was nothing else to do but tour the streets, and for a couple of hours we cruised around poking our noses into every nook and cranny. Eventually, I rebelled.

"This is ridiculous..."

Back at Balfour Terrace I gave the police another ring while Mother made some tea. There'd been a change of shift and the duty sergeant was far more obliging than his colleague.

"Would you like to report him missing?"

"No, not yet. I'm sure he'll turn up."

"Have you thought about contacting his friends?"

It was a good suggestion. But of course Frank didn't have any friends. Mother was more positive however.

"We could always ask Cyril…"

I raised an eyebrow. It seemed like the last resort, but it was always worth a try. We waited until what we thought was a reasonable hour, then made the call.

Cyril was more helpful than we could ever have imagined.

"Perhaps he stayed over at Karen's."

Mother and I looked at each other and chorused the same question.

"Who's Karen?"

And that's when the story came out.

Five

So Frank was having an affair. Or was he? 'Affair' implies some element of passion and as far as I could see there was nothing like that about it. It was more of an agreement than an affair – a mutually satisfactory arrangement between two consenting adults who'd decided to live together. There's nothing wrong with that by the way. That's what marriage is at the end of the day – an agreement between two consenting adults to live together. I can testify to that. Although in Frank's case, whether it was satisfactory or not was an entirely different matter.

As you might imagine, Mother took a romantic view of things. Perhaps Frank had fallen in love, perhaps he'd met his soul mate, perhaps he might settle down and lead that normal family life she so wanted for him. Wedding bells rang unwarrantedly loud in her head. It was only when this early rush of thought had run its course that she became more practical. Who was this Karen? What was she like? When would she be able to meet her? I had to try and stem the flood of questions. If we weren't careful, Frank would feel overwhelmed and be put off altogether. As it was, even when given time and space he was not particularly forthcoming and confined himself to his usual monosyllabic replies. So for a while, *Yes, No* and *Maybe* were as much as we could get out of him.

In the end we resorted to another pact. He might be forty-two but he still lived at home and Mother insisted that she shouldn't be put to the worry of not knowing where he was (the night we'd spent trawling the streets had been traumatic) while he added Karen to the list of things he didn't want to talk about. So as long as he told her his whereabouts – *I might not be coming back tonight* – she wouldn't press him on the details of his relationship. *All in good time, Mum, all in good time.* And like their accord on the matter of alcohol this worked well for a good six months – until one evening he neglected to mention that he might not be coming back at all.

And so the first opportunity we had of meeting Karen was the day she turned up on the doorstep at Balfour Terrace to collect Frank's things. It was just after eleven and Mother was not long back from the newsagents when the doorbell rang. The night before, Frank had announced his intention of staying over and she naturally thought that this was him returning. But when she opened up she found herself confronted by a slight female form in trainers, jeans and a hooded top, the child Melanie balanced on her hip with her head resting on her mother's shoulder, sucking a thumb.

"Mrs Johnson? Hello, I'm Karen." A wisp of blonde hair had escaped the elasticated tie and she paused to brush it from her face. "I've come to pick up Frank's stuff."

There was no *May I?* about it. It was a statement of intent and although delivered calmly and without aggression, there was a quiet determination behind it that was not to be denied. At other times determination, and possibly some aggression, had clearly been called for – Karen was used to standing her ground. She looked Mother straight in the eye.

Mother was taken by surprise and offered no objection. "I suppose you'd better come in then…"

She was completely unprepared for what was to follow. Hidden behind his wall of silence, Frank had given no indication, while Mother had adhered strictly to their pact and had asked no questions. She'd have loved to extend an invitation: *Why don't you invite Karen round for tea? We could all have a nice meal together. It would be good to get to know her.* But there'd been no such introduction, no smoothing of the way.

Even now, she was unsure as to the purpose of Karen's coming. At first, she thought Frank had forgotten some small item, a toothbrush, or his razor for instance. But when Karen emerged from Frank's room carrying the holdall he'd brought back from the Army, crammed with all his belongings, she realised it was something permanent. He was leaving home and he hadn't told her.

A sense of deep disappointment touched her heart. It wasn't so much that he was going – she couldn't expect to keep him there for ever – but rather that he should feel so distanced from her that he couldn't come and break the news himself. Was he afraid that she'd be angry? Or was he so ashamed of his liaison that he couldn't face her with it and had sent Karen to do his dirty work instead? She looked brazen enough.

And so Mother was forced to stand by powerless and look on as Karen loaded the holdall into the boot of her battered green estate, swinging the bag with one hand while juggling her child with the other. There was an ease about it that suggested she was accustomed to it, gathering up a man and his belongings into her life with a casual sweep of her arm.

Mother dared to ask if there was any message.

"Frank said he'd be in touch…"

Then the car disappeared and Mother's heart went with it. She'd tried to exact an assurance, but had failed. Karen had not only taken Frank's belongings, she'd gained possession of her boy into the bargain, and he wasn't ever coming back.

The next few months were amongst the hardest Mother had to endure. Suddenly she was alone again and this time she found it particularly difficult to bear. She'd been alone before, when Dad had abandoned her, but the separation from her husband had been a gradual process as week by week, month by month, she saw less and less of him until finally she'd realised their relationship was over.

Frank's leaving was altogether different. It had come without warning and was thereby more of a jolt. True, while he'd been in the Army they'd spent long periods apart, but in all that time she'd felt he was living at home and his absence was purely temporary. The thought that at any moment he might return had always been enough, but over the last two years she'd grown used to his being about the place and despite his silent and reserved nature it had been a comfort to her. Now, another woman had snatched her boy away and she was plunged into a state of solitude from which it was difficult to extricate herself. Although, in an emergency, I was always there to fall back on.

"Perhaps we were too hard on him."

Mother was prone to putting her own failings before those of others.

"What do you mean?" I said.

"Perhaps we should never have sent him to that clinic."

"Nonsense. That was the best thing that could have happened."

"You think so?"

"I know so. Frank was desperate to go. You could see it in his eyes."

I could tell a lot about people by looking at their eyes. Sometimes, when I looked into Frank's, they were full of fear.

"All he needed was for someone to tell him to do it. Trust me, Mum; sometimes I know him better than you do. Anyway, he was sick and we couldn't have allowed that sort of thing to go untreated. Think what might have happened if we had."

"You're right, I suppose. But perhaps he wouldn't have left so readily..."

"What? You think you've driven him out?"

"Well, maybe."

"I doubt it! You shouldn't be so hard on yourself, Mum. We both know where the fault lies – you've seen her. From what you've told me it's obvious she's got her claws into him. I know the type. A pound to a penny she came round here instead of him so there was no chance of you talking him out of it. She's not stupid."

"Really? I hadn't thought of that."

And in her innocence, Mother hadn't.

"Well, I suggest you do start thinking about it. Because that's the sort of thing you're up against if you want to get him back."

Although I'm not sure Mother did want him back. Twenty odd years ago, Frank had left to join the Army. Now he was nearly forty-three and he was leaving to set up a home of his own. Things had changed and perhaps it was time for her to sacrifice her desires for the future so as to give Frank the chance of realising his. If that's what it took to make him happy...

"Do you think he was forced into it then?"

"Maybe. Perhaps she twisted his arm. It wouldn't surprise me. You never know with Frank."

And you didn't. Perhaps Karen had caught him on a good day.

"Anyway, it won't last."

"It won't?" Mother grasped at the straw.

"Of course it won't. I can't imagine for one moment that life with Karen is a bed of roses. Give him a couple of weeks and he'll come to his senses – if he's got any, that is. You mark my words, Mum, he'll be back here by the end of the month with his tail between his legs."

But he wasn't. And just for once, my judgement in the matter of human relations was shown not to be infallible.

News of the fugitive proved hard to come by. We knew where he was (Cyril's sister provided an address) but not what he was doing or how he was coping. That was no surprise – Frank was no more communicative now than he was when in the Army. Then, we'd put up with his long periods of silence. There'd been the occasional card or letter, often postmarked from some outlandish location as a way of showing off, but there'd been no regularity about it. I'd no reason to believe he'd changed his nature, and after several weeks of nothing I wouldn't have put it past him to drop us a note and make some startling announcement. *I thought I'd let you know I'm doing fine. And by the way, Karen and I are getting married...*

Mother was disappointed by these shortcomings. *Frank said he'd be in touch*. But he wasn't, and either Karen had been fobbing her off or Frank had forgotten his promise – if indeed he'd ever made one.

So we were forced to seek out other sources of intelligence. Cyril was an obvious target and for a while he was regularly invited to tea at Mother's. That too proved disappointing as he supplied annoyingly little in the way of hard information. Karen, it seemed, kept her news as well as her men under strict lock and key and nothing was allowed out. Even Cyril had to confess he'd been denied access and his attempts at saving Frank had stalled – there'd been more chance of securing Frank's redemption while he'd been under Mother's auspices than there was under Karen's.

A month went by, then two, then three. There was still no word, and as the year progressed our expectations dwindled. Then we made a breakthrough. An old acquaintance of Terry's in the building trade had visited the sawmill and was able to give us an account. Frank was no longer there. He'd not been seen for weeks and as was the practice with an itinerant workforce, his employer had struck him off his list.

At the same time, news began to filter through from Cyril's connections. There were reports of arguments, raised voices and disturbances in the neighbourhood. Late at night, the sound of squabbling spilled out into the street. A child could be heard crying, and at one point, fearing for its safety and angered by the continual bickering, the people next door called the police. Nothing had come of it, but whatever the nature of Frank's relationship with Karen, it was clearly not all harmony and light.

We sent messages to be passed on via Cyril's sister but there was no response. Finally, becoming desperate and with the address she'd been given to hand, Mother wrote a note. She wished Frank well and hoped that he was in good health and that he was happy. She missed him and asked that he might take a few moments to let her know he was alright. When he'd been in the Army she'd signed her letters *With all my love, Mum,* and she saw no reason to change that now. She *did* love him and whatever had happened in the past, she'd always been a mother to him and she always would be.

But even this heartfelt plea failed to exact a reply, and after almost a year of trying, we became reconciled to the fact that Frank had been lost to us and there was nothing we could do to get him back.

Six

It was about now that Dad got in touch for the first time. Well, it was the first time for me as it appeared he'd already been in contact with Mother.

Why didn't it surprise me? Perhaps it was because after all the goings-on with Frank my mind had been opened up to the idea that anything could happen. You know, one door opens, another one closes, that sort of thing (or is it the other way round?). Anyway, I may even have been expecting it, as if the thought of his appearance had been subconsciously working its way forward over the years until it arrived at the same time as he did. I'd often wondered about him – who he was, what he was like – and the thought of eventually meeting him had crossed my mind. It never seemed to be a question of whether he'd show up, but rather a question of when.

What puzzled me was why, after forty years of silence, he'd chosen that particular moment. It was some time before he became ill, so his state of health wasn't a factor. Did he know that Frank was temporarily out of the picture? Or was that purely coincidental? Because had it been otherwise, it could have made things extraordinarily difficult.

I've always answered the phone. It's an integral part of my job and I do it instinctively and without consideration of who might be calling. It's the same at home – although at eight o'clock in the evening my automatic assumption is that it's Mother, probably with some worry about Frank. I was on the point of responding *I'm just in the middle of something, Mum – can I call you back?* when I realised it must be someone else. A strange voice was on the line calling me by a strange name.

"Patricia, is that you?"

I hadn't heard that in years.

"Who is this?" I asked.

There was a pause for dramatic effect, then, in that self-important tone I was to hear so often, "It's your father…"

My dilemma was whether to tell Mother. Would it upset her to know that Geoffrey had resurfaced? In the first instance I decided to consult Terry.

"I can't see the harm in it," he said. "I mean, what can he do now, after all this time?"

But as I say, Terry never saw the harm in anything.

In the end, I opted to confide. Mother and I didn't keep secrets (or so I thought) and I resolved to tell her at our next meeting in Tesco.

"Mum, I've had a strange phone call…"

"From your father?"

Now that *did* surprise me – she spoke as if it were common knowledge.

"Yes," I said. "How did you know?"

"We've kept in touch."

"So, what, you've been talking to him, seeing him?"

"Don't be silly, of course I haven't seen him – but we've spoken." She sat fiddling with her fingers in her lap like a nun with a rosary. "A few years ago he wrote me a letter."

"Let me understand this," I said slowly. "He wrote you a letter…"

"Yes, do you want to see it? I can show it to you if you like."

Perhaps she thought this would make up for her lack of candour, but I was not that easily appeased.

"No, Mum, I don't want to see your letters. What you and Geoffrey get up to behind my back is no concern of mine."

"Don't be cross with me." She laid a hand on my arm. "We haven't got up to anything. I didn't reply to it of course, but somehow he got hold of my number and rang me, and we've spoken to each other ever since. We do have things to talk about, you know."

"What things?"

"Well, naturally, he wanted to know about you and how you

were." There was a hint of diplomacy in her statement I did not find entirely convincing. "And he wanted to know about Frank. In fact, he was particularly interested in Frank…"

Mother tailed off.

I was still incensed and went charging on like a bull at a gate.

"So what did you tell him?"

"Not a lot really. Just that you were married – and about Terry and the boys. And that Frank was… Well, just Frank, really."

For the second time in as many minutes I ignored the hint about Frank. Instead, I focused in on the part about my family as my maternal instincts took hold.

"You told him about the boys?"

"Oh dear, shouldn't I have done?"

"Well, I wish you'd spoken to me about it first."

"I didn't see the need. You see, it's complicated and I didn't want to get you involved."

"No, but you obviously saw fit to give him my number."

"Yes… Perhaps that was a mistake." She began to relent a little. "Maybe I shouldn't have done that, I'm sorry. But he asked me for it and there seemed no harm in it at the time." She was starting to sound like Terry. "Look, I can see you're angry with me, but after a while I thought it best that you spoke to him yourself. After all, he is your father – and it's not as though you're still a child. You're old enough to deal with that sort of thing yourself now. And anyway, I've reached a point where I don't want to carry the burden of it all anymore."

"Burden?" I said. "What burden?"

What was Mother talking about? Had I missed a trick somewhere in the conversation?

"So what did he say to you?" Now it was Mother's turn to ignore *my* remark.

"Well, that's the strange part," I replied, momentarily diverted. "He didn't really say very much at all. He just intro-duced himself, hoped I didn't mind him calling and then started asking me questions."

"What about?"

"Well, the same he asked you, I suppose. Firstly about me, and then about Frank."

"And did you tell him anything?"

"No, I don't think so… Nothing of any consequence." I tried to recall the details but it had all happened so quickly. "To be honest I was too flustered to say anything particularly sensible. And anyway, you know what Frank would have to say about it."

"Yes…" Mother thought for a moment. "He's clearly after something. He didn't get it from me and now he's decided to tackle you instead. I'm sorry to have to say it, but I know your father – he wouldn't do something like this unless there was a purpose. I suspect he'll try and contact you again. At least next time you'll be prepared."

Prepared for what? I wondered. Mother wasn't giving me any clues and it was clear I'd have to find out for myself.

So that was what kept me going – the thought of getting to know my father and my ingrained sense of curiosity. I had no issues with Dad. Why should I? There I was, a happily married woman (well, most of the time) and I'd two fine boys to delight in. What was there for me to carp about?

Ok, so we'd had some hard times. A caravan isn't the most inspiring of places to grow up in, but on balance I felt I'd enjoyed it. I tended to remember the summers rather than the winters, the sunshine rather than the rain. For Frank, of course, it was different and he had an axe to grind.

What then, was *my* interest in Geoffrey? And why was I suddenly involved? He'd shown no interest in me for over forty years and neither me in him. I'd never felt the need for a father figure – and yet, now that he'd made himself known…

Besides, Mother was hiding something. I'd known her too long not to recognise the signs – the way she fiddled with her fingers, the furtive glances to one side, the skill she used to evade my questions – they all proved the point. I began to wish I'd taken up her offer and looked at the letter. It might have thrown some light on the subject and saved us an awful lot of trouble, but I'd left it too late and the damage had already been done. Mother and Geoffrey were talking to each other – and now my father was talking to me. My mother was leading me to believe he wanted something. If she was correct, what could it be?

She was right in as much that Geoffrey continued to contact me, although not in the way I'd imagined. I assumed that once it started, it would become part of an established routine. Once a month, or even once a fortnight, I thought he'd call me and gradually, as time went by, we'd begin to form some kind of relationship. Eventually, if things went well enough, we might even arrange a meeting.

I was being naïve of course, but I guess what was lying behind it was a subconscious desire for unification. Here was the opportunity for family reconciliation, a chance for a wayward relative to be coaxed back into the fold. In fact, I almost felt it was my duty to do it. Perhaps this was the 'burden' that Mother had mentioned and she was passing it on to me. For a start, the boys had never known a grandfather (Terry's parents had both died young) and there was a gap there to be filled. How foolish I was to think I could bring it about!

Geoffrey proved obdurate and unmanageable. He was a most irregular caller. Sometimes months would go by and I'd not hear a word. Then just when all thought of him had vanished, he was on to me two or three times a week. There was nothing I could do about it and just like my mother before me, I realised I'd have to live with his capricious habits.

One thing remained constant throughout his enquiries – he wanted Frank. After we'd been through the usual preliminaries – *How's your mother these days?* – he'd begin to press me for infor-mation, just as we had pressed Cyril. Where was he? What was he doing with himself? Would it be possible to speak to him? At first, I was motivated by family loyalty and declined to reveal much detail. What was I supposed to tell him? That Frank had become an alcoholic, that he'd had to spend time in a clinic and now he'd run off with a controlling divorcee? I even managed to hide the fact that we weren't in touch with him, saying things like *I'll pass your message on* or *I'll let him know you rang*. But after what felt like the hundredth time of asking, I was forced to confess we weren't speaking.

This disclosure initially gave me some respite, but Geoffrey soon returned, although now on a different tack. Did I have an address I could give him? If not, would I write to Frank on his behalf? When did we expect him back? I'd hoped for a family reunion – instead of which all I heard from Dad was Frank this, Frank that and Frank the other. It was gradually becoming clear where his true interest lay.

Frank – my little brother.

Frank – who could never quite get it together.

Frank – the very mention of whose name now drove me to distraction every time I picked up the phone to answer my father's calls. And the irony of it was, Frank wasn't even there. But just as he'd always done, his presence – and now the very lack of it – continued to dominate our lives. It meant I'd now assumed the burden and I began to wonder when I'd ever be free of it.

Seven

Two years went by before I decided to pay my brother a visit. It was a drastic measure but I'd come to the conclusion it was the only way I was going to resolve things.

I was under pressure from two sides. Mother was living alone and becoming ever more fretful. Not a day passed without some heavy hint or another being dropped into the conversation. *I wonder how Frank is.* She began to age dramatically, her mind became feeble and she was forced to give up her job at the newsagents. She seemed to spend all her time sitting at home, worrying.

Meanwhile, Dad's erratic but persistent pleas for intervention continued. I began to feel obliged to respond, if only it meant I could put a stop to them. I eventually wrote the letter to Frank he'd been asking for, but as expected, there was no reply. And so, in the words of the prophet, if the mountain wouldn't go to Mohammed, then Mohammed would have to go to the mountain.

The address we'd been given corresponded to a block of flats in a run-down area of town. I'd driven through it on a couple of occasions, partly out of curiosity and partly in the hope of catching sight of my brother. In the middle of an estate dominated by concrete and devoid of trees, it struck me as rather desolate and unloved. Sheets of discarded newspaper blew about in the wind, haunting the streets. It was not the kind of place you'd want to leave your car unattended, so to be on the safe side, I chose a Saturday afternoon. Previous observations had revealed that Karen's battered green estate was often absent then.

The flat was on the second floor. There was a vaguely unpleasant smell in the hallway and I held my breath as I ascended the stairs. I checked the number and pressed the bell, although the chances of it being answered seemed minimal as it could hardly be heard above the blare of a television set. I pressed again and after what seemed like an age the door cracked open and the outline of a face appeared.

"Frank?"

The door immediately slammed shut.

"Frank, don't be stupid – it's only me."

I rapped on one of the panels.

"Frank, open the door for goodness sake."

I waited a moment, then the door reopened and the face reappeared.

"What do you want?"

"It's me – Pat. I just want to talk to you."

"Talk to me? What on earth for? There's nothing to talk about."

"Mother's worried about you and I just want a few words, that's all."

There was a scraping sound as the door chain slid back. Mention of Mother usually did the trick. Frank had decided to admit me, but not before leaning out and furtively checking the hallway.

"You can't stay long – she'll be back soon..."

He ushered me inside.

Standing in the glare of the hall light, I found myself shocked by his appearance. He'd aged still further since I'd last seen him and he'd evidently put on weight as slabs of puffy flesh sagged from his cheekbones, giving his face a careworn look. Life with Karen clearly hadn't treated him too well.

My fixed stare made him self-conscious and from beneath the folds of skin he stuck out a defiant chin.

"Come to spy on me, have you? Well, here I am – this is it."

He gestured loosely behind him as if inviting an inspection.

I looked about me. We were standing in the living room of a small, cramped flat. What comfort Frank might draw from these surroundings, I found it hard to tell. Against one wall was a black mock-leather sofa, while next to it stood a clotheshorse draped with damp washing. On the other side of the room a large TV set continued to blare out. Sitting on the floor in front of it, watching cartoons and utterly oblivious to our presence, was the child Melanie, who must now be aged three or four.

"Karen's out shopping," explained Frank.

"And you've been left holding..." I stopped myself from completing the sentence and changed what I was about to say. "...the fort."

"You could say that."

We gathered ourselves for what might come next. I got in first.

"Frank, there's something..." *I have to tell you,* but I was cut off by my brother's simultaneous and predictable interruption.

"So, how's Mum?"

"Oh, she's fine."

This was a lie, of course. Mother was not fine, but this wasn't the time to begin that conversation – the visit had been intended for an entirely different purpose.

"Good. So now you can go and tell her all about it, can't you?"

"What do you mean?"

"Oh, don't think I don't know why you've come here." He curled his lip. "Let's go and check Frank out. Let's go and see what a shitty mess Frank's got himself into. You can't deny it."

"Frank, that's not the reason I've come here at all. And anyway, that's hardly fair. You know Mum would never say anything like that."

"Fair? Don't talk to me about fair! Why should I be fair? No bastard's ever been fair to me!" He was starting to get animated. It was as if I'd set light to a touchpaper and at any moment the firework itself might go off. "As for that sod down at the sawmill. If I ever get my hands on the bastard who shopped me..."

"Why? What happened at the sawmill? I thought you were settled there."

"I was, but…" He waved it away and seemed to calm down a little. "Anyway, I don't want to talk about it."

I thought it best to move on, but apparently I didn't move far enough and merely reignited the flames.

"So, are you working now? Did you manage to find something else?"

"Working? Does it look as though I'm working?" Based on what I could see around me and his unshaven, dishevelled appearance, I had to confess it did not. "Of course I'm not bloody working. Do you think I'd still be in this shithole if I was? All these bloody questions! I can't be doing with it. Why don't you leave me alone?"

He lowered his head into his hands. The fuse which had earlier been lit had burnt to an end and sparked the inevitable reaction. Turning his back, he disappeared into what I assumed was the kitchen. There was the brief sound of rummaging, then the soft click of a ring pull and the hiss of escaping foam. Frank reappeared, a beer can clasped in one hand while he wiped his lips with the other.

Away from Mother's influence, under pressure from Karen and whatever else ailed him, he'd reverted to his old ways. Inwardly I grimaced. In my anxiety to convey my message, it was an aspect of my brother's character I'd forgotten and I regretted pressing him so hard. Although, in my defence, it didn't look as if it was the first time that day he'd resorted to alcohol.

"I'm sorry, Frank, I didn't mean to pry. Mother's worried about you and we don't get any news. Cyril doesn't tell us much."

"Cyril? That little poof! If he tries to come round here again I'll knock his teeth back down his bloody throat. I'm sick of him and his God squad. They think they're going to recruit me. There's no chance of that!"

He took another swig from his can.

I hesitated before replying. It seemed that whatever subject I raised was bound to get his back up. The chances of mentioning

Geoffrey without causing a major explosion were becoming ever more remote, but I felt I had to make one more attempt.

"Did you get my letter?"

"What letter?"

"The one I wrote to you about a year ago."

"I don't get any letters. She keeps them all."

By 'she' I assumed he meant Karen. No wonder it wasn't a happy household.

"What about the one Mum sent you?"

"I didn't get that one either. I told you, she keeps them."

"I see…"

We fell silent and let the sound of a *Tom and Jerry* chase fill the void between us.

Frank consulted his watch. "Look, you'd better be going…"

But I wasn't quite ready to leave. I'd gone to too much effort to come away empty-handed, although yet again I was thwarted because just as I was about to begin my speech for the final time – *Frank, I have to talk to you* – the noise of the television ceased and was replaced by a wail of anguish from the seated child. The tape providing Melanie's entertainment had either jammed or come to an end and Uncle Frank was required to attend to it. It was the last straw, a sure sign that I wasn't going to succeed, however hard I tried.

After he'd fixed the tape, Frank escorted me out and softened his tone.

"You won't tell Mum, will you?"

"I won't tell her what?"

"About this."

He jiggled the empty can in front of me.

"No, I won't."

"Promise?"

"Promise."

I'd already decided that – but was more for Mother's sake than Frank's. She had enough problems already.

From the safety of my parked car, I looked out at the sterile concrete and contemplated the failure of my mission. I'd come equipped with an axe but I'd been unable to break the ice. I'd intended to tell Frank about his father and I was leaving in the knowledge that I hadn't. Now there were things about Mother I couldn't tell Frank, and there were things about Frank I couldn't tell Mother. This whole business of reconciliation and of binding families together was proving far harder than I'd thought. I was privy to too many secrets and they weighed on me. This was *my* burden and at the back of it all lay the certainty that one day, Frank would *have* to be told. It was not a welcome prospect.

I divulged as much as I could at my next meeting with Mother. Our customary Saturday conference was held over until the Sunday so I could present a full report.

"Well, how is he?" she was eager to ask.

"He's fine."

Another of my little white lies. In my newfound position as arbiter, the demands of family life were making me devious.

"And was *she* there?"

"No, Mum, she wasn't. I planned it when she'd be out so I could get Frank on his own."

"So what did he say then?"

"Nothing much really. You know Frank – it's difficult getting him to talk at the best of times."

Desperate for news, Mother pressed on. I could see how frustrating this was for her.

"Did you tell him about Geoffrey?"

"Not exactly."

"Well, did you or didn't you?"

Feeble-minded or not, she wasn't going to be put off.

"To be honest, Mum, no I didn't. There wasn't the opportunity. It's been over two years and you can't just go charging in with something like that at the first time of asking. It's going to take a while."

"You'll be going back then?"

"I hadn't planned to."

"But I thought that was the whole point..."

For a woman in her condition, Mother could show inexorable logic. It *had* been the point, but once I'd seen things for myself, it didn't seem to matter any more. In a few days' time, Dad would be back on the phone wanting information, but I could always fob him off, just as I'd done in the past. And if my secondary objective was to try and reunite Frank with my mother, perhaps it was best they be kept apart until certain issues had been resolved. Although as yet, I couldn't see how that was to come about.

The solution came a week later by way of a telephone call – only it wasn't Geoffrey who rang, it was Cyril. He was passing on a message from Karen and he did so with some degree of relish, as if gloating at an enemy's misfortune. Frank had gone out on a bender for the weekend, and rather than face going back to the flat had chosen to admit himself to hospital in the early hours of the Monday morning. At the same time, Mother (still clad in her dressing gown) opened her front door to retrieve the milk and discovered it was accompanied by the holdall that Karen had packed and taken on her first and only visit. Frank's belongings were stuffed inside. They'd changed little since his departure.

I'd not yet left for work. Terry was on his way to school with the boys, so I cited an urgent domestic situation and cancelled my meetings for the day. My first duty was to ring Mother.

"Apparently he's in the District..."

Visiting hours began at 10am. The wait felt interminable, but once we arrived on the ward there was a distinct sense of déjà vu about it. By the strangest of coincidences, Frank lay in exactly the same bed as he'd done four years previously. It was as if he'd deliberately sought it out, knowing that from this point on his journey would lead him back to safety and salvation. This time there was no coma, only the deep and blessed sleep he'd been denied whilst at the flat. He appeared completely peaceful and for all the flesh his face had acquired, he still had the underlying image of a child.

Seated at his bedside, Mother took his hand. Half awake, he stirred and turned towards her. As recognition dawned, I watched as the fear which had once filled his eyes was replaced with remorse. His speech was a barely audible croak.

"I'm sorry, Mum. I'm so, so sorry..."

"Hush now, it's alright..."

She squeezed his fingers tight. It was not that she'd forgiven him – in her eyes there was nothing to forgive. He'd done nothing wrong, he was her special boy and she was pleased to have him back.

A second stay at the clinic followed. On this occasion, Mother insisted on paying for every penny of it. Her savings were exhausted and she was forced to take out a loan which she struggled to service out of her meagre income, but it meant the world to her.

After three weeks of rest and recuperation, Frank came home for the third and final time. Once again there was no celebration, but in my mother's heart there was immense relief. For a long while, things settled down. Eventually, I found Frank a job at Do It All and we were happy – then Dad fell ill and started calling me again.

Part Five

Geoffrey

One

Sometimes, if he was woken suddenly, startled by the crash of a trolley or the shrill ring of the telephone on the ward-sister's desk, his eyes would shoot open and he would find himself staring wildly into space. At first he would see nothing and it would all be a blank grey mass, then one by one the cracks in the ceiling would gradually appear and he would recognise where he was.

But waking was usually a gentle process. He would feel as if he were swimming unhurriedly upwards from a great depth, encouraged by the low murmurings of a nurse or a soft light from above. When he broke the surface, his surroundings no longer came as a surprise and the ward would be there exactly as he was expecting it. The inmates would each appear in their appointed place: the bald man with the crooked nose in the bed opposite; the lady in the corner with the arthritic hands; even the cleaner, rearranging the dirt on the linoleum floor.

At moments like these, trapped in the no-man's-land between sleep and wakefulness, he would remember what he thought were his dreams. Or perhaps it was then that his imaginings took place, for being half asleep, the distinction between memory and what was real was hard to discern. All he knew was that he was experiencing a series of vivid recollections – Bristol, London, Weston-super-Mare – sections of his life were being paraded before him. The curious thing was that the further he went back in time, the clearer these pictures became. He could barely recall the events of the past fortnight, but what had taken place over fifty years before was now as clear as if it had been yesterday.

He was tempted to blame it on the morphine. The same drug which suppressed his physical senses almost certainly excited his mental ones, although now his dosage had been increased, he seemed to spend more time drowsy than alert.

Whenever he was awake, he had difficulty in telling the time.

It might be day or night (that much was obvious) but he was never sure of the hour. The clock over the ward-sister's desk faced away from him, and besides, if his curtains were drawn for some reason such as a blood test or to remove his waste sack, he could see nothing anyway. He had a watch, a present from an uncle who'd once owned a pawnshop in Totterdown, but it had been removed and put out of reach in the drawer of his bedside table.

Someone had replaced it with a narrow plastic strip around his wrist. It bore his name and date of birth, *Geoffrey Jones 20.9.1922*, presumably so that in the event of anything untoward, he might readily be identified.

This 'un's gone, Jim, better get 'im downstairs.

Who is it?

'Ang on a minute an' us'll 'ave a look at 'is tag.

The irony was that if anyone took the trouble to turn it over, the self-same information was inscribed on the back of his timepiece.

So he was forced to gauge the hour by simple observation. He would occasionally entertain himself by attempting to work it out from the angle at which the shadow of the window fell across the floor, or whether there were visitors on the ward and so on. Mealtimes were a helpful clue, although because of his near-liquid diet they were not infallible. Breakfast was easy enough, it was always a thin porridge, but lunch and dinner could be difficult to tell apart. They usually consisted of soup and semolina which, if he was lucky, was accompanied by a dollop of jam. Then, as soon as he'd got through the effort of eating and of emptying his bowels, he would invariably fall back to sleep and the dreams he'd been encountering would begin again.

Today they were all about Mrs Beazley. She was standing at the top of the steps leading up to the door of the guest house, her hands on her hips, the inevitable cigarette dangling precariously from her bottom lip. He noticed it had burnt down to the point where there was now as much ash as there was remaining tobacco, although it stubbornly refused to fall away even when she opened the corners of her mouth to speak.

What, you again, Mr Jones?

She turned toward the door, still in an attitude of rebuke, mumbling so he had to strain to catch her words.

I don't know where you find 'em, Mr Jones. Honest to God, I don't.

He'd wondered why she chided him and it crossed his mind that her stance arose out of jealousy. In the first flowering of youth she must have been an attractive woman, but the years had taken their toll. She'd aged into an overblown rose and with no Mr Beazley to comfort her she'd been left to wither away in an unfashionable seaside town. At first she'd been welcoming, but over the years she grew contemptuous and when Elisabeth arrived on the scene, she lapsed into silent acceptance. She was not, and never had been, on his agenda.

At the time, he'd thought her remark rather comical and had laughed at her in his carefree, devil-may-care kind of way. It sounded brash, but it was really to cover his embarrassment in case the girl he'd brought with him had overheard. It wasn't Elisabeth – of that he was certain. She'd come later, much later, and was the last in his string of successes.

They'd met purely by chance. On the way home from the office he'd dropped in at Freddy's to pass away an hour before dinner. You could hardly have called it a party, more of an informal gathering, and he'd expected nothing from it. But life was full of surprises and Elisabeth's presence had been one of them. Even then, it hadn't been easy. She'd come with a friend, and he'd had to peel them gently apart like the pages of a dampened book, discarding one and eventually keeping the other. It was a skill he'd grown to admire in himself and confirmed how practised he'd become in the art of seduction.

In the beginning she was no different from the others. She couldn't resist the appeal of his sports car and her hair blew in the wind just like those who'd gone before her. But when the thrill of the chase had died away and he'd made his conquest, there'd grown up between them a kind of tenderness and companionship he'd not experienced before. He'd found it touching the way she clung to him as if he were her only hope in the world. He'd not moved on but had stuck with her throughout the summer, and under the watchful eye of Mrs Beazley had conducted a full-blown relationship. How he'd enjoyed those balmy days in Weston-super-Mare: the slow walks along the promenade; the visits to the theatre; the quiet cups of afternoon tea! There'd been sun, there'd been sand, and yes, there'd been sex – but for him it was of a different kind, unhurried, and without the need to prove himself. He thought the girl had responded but perhaps he'd been mistaken. What on earth had gone wrong?

Georgina had tried to warn him.

One day you'll come a cropper. One day you'll meet someone and then you'll wish you hadn't.

She'd not even been referring to Elisabeth. She'd been speaking in general terms and her remarks could have applied to any one of dozen different girls. His reaction was the same as when he'd been chided by Mrs Beazley and he'd laughed it off as if it were of no consequence. That too was a front. If it were of no consequence, there was no danger. If there was no danger, there was no excitement – and it was the excitement he so desperately craved.

If you play with fire, like as not you'll get your fingers burnt.

And yes, he had got burnt. Things had turned sour, but not as a result of romance.

Elisabeth wasn't the first girl he'd 'knocked up'. But he'd always managed to get things taken care of – Georgina had seen to that, although it became progressively more difficult on each occasion.

I don't know how long you think I can go on doing this, Geoffrey.

But she *had* gone on doing it, either out of loyalty or whatever love she bore him, until finally she'd foundered on the rock that was Elisabeth.

She won't be moved. She's not like the others. She's stronger than you think.

Elisabeth was strong alright, stronger than he was himself, he knew that now. He'd given in under the pressure and had walked down the aisle after years of trying to avoid it. What had seemed so promising in Weston-super-Mare had soon turned into a sorry mess – Elisabeth pregnant, nowhere to live, his freedom curtailed – the future had looked irredeemably bleak. Then, just when he'd reached the point of despair, he had a stroke of luck. His promotion arrived – and that had changed everything.

He suddenly found himself in darkness, staring up at the ceiling. He'd been jolted wide awake but this time he knew exactly where he was. There'd been a disturbance on the ward, a voice had cried out in pain and then, almost immediately, the night light over the ward-sister's desk had come on and the nurse with the calming voice was amongst them.

"Now, now, Mrs Walker. What is it?"

The curtains were drawn tight around her bed, but in the far corner the woman with the arthritic hands could clearly be heard.

"My daughter! My daughter! I must see my daughter!"

Did her cries arise from a mental or a physical pain? Or perhaps a combination of the two? Whatever the answer, her bent and crooked fingers presaged no relief.

"Your daughter will be here in the morning, Mrs Walker. You'll be able to see her then."

"But I want to see her now!"

"I'm afraid you can't see her now, Mrs Walker. It's two o'clock in the morning and I expect she's tucked up in bed asleep like everyone else. And so should you be. You need your rest too, you know."

The quiet voice of reason gently soothed, as though it were a child she were comforting.

Geoffrey ceased scrabbling in the drawer of the bedside table and drew himself up into a sitting position. Why did it take so much effort? He sank back onto his pillows, exhausted. *Two o'clock.* The few scraps of conversation he'd caught had at least saved him the trouble of finding his watch.

What a foolish old woman – fancy calling out like that in the middle of the night! He was living in a madhouse; it must have been like this in Bedlam. It would be hell's own job getting back to sleep and he'd probably still be awake at daylight. If only he didn't feel quite so tired…

So you see, Mr Jones, I'm afraid that's the best I can do.

His prospective landlord was a rat-faced, plump little man with sharp features and a check jacket. He looked as if he belonged on a racecourse, touting as a bookie's mate, rather than in property. Seemingly unconcerned as to an answer he lit a cigarette, then blew away the smoke and inspected his fingernails while he waited. Apparently, he could let the place to anyone he chose.

Take it or leave it.

I'll take it.

It wasn't ideal but it would do. It was the third one he'd looked at that day. The other two had been snapped up within hours of becoming available and he was learning he had to move quickly if he wanted something decent.

He could remember more about the landlord than he could about the house. Even if he focused hard he struggled to recall the details, particularly of the upstairs rooms. But then, it was over fifty years ago and sometimes the memory dimmed. He could at least remember the exterior. There was a photograph somewhere of the three of them taken by a kindly neighbour – himself, Elisabeth and Pat as a baby. They'd just come out of maternity hospital and were standing on the doorstep. The wooden porch, the rickety little green gate, it all came flooding back to him.

Elisabeth had said it was too small. And by comparison to what he'd been used to in Bristol, she had a point. But this was London and he'd had to take what he could get. In Bristol he'd been a big fish in a small pond and could command what he liked – now the pond was vast and it was he who was correspondingly small.

There were some compensations. For example, his new job far exceeded his expectations. At first he'd thought of it purely as a way out of his difficulties, a means of escape from the cloistered society that his marriage had brought about, a society overseen by his sister. He could no longer play the field, so he'd abandoned it altogether and had retreated into a sullen seclusion. This new posting would take him away from all that and provide him with fresh opportunities. That, at least, was the theory.

In fact, it did much more than that. It gave him a new social context and also reinvigorated his enthusiasm for sport. He'd become bored and rather stale in the South West. After covering the same events for three years in a row he'd found himself disinterested and slack in his approach – it was easier to pull out the file and reiterate the words he'd used before instead of composing something new. Things in that part of the world didn't change a lot.

But London was the hub of so much that excited him. Twickenham, Wimbledon, the White City Stadium, these and other venues beckoned. Only two years before it had hosted the Olympic Games and he regretted the fact that he'd missed out on it. He'd been deemed inexperienced but now, if he could get in a good couple of years at some major events, there was always Helsinki to look forward to.

Meanwhile, Elisabeth was steadily increasing in size. It

shocked him to see how quickly her physical appearance could change. Before they'd left Bristol, she'd thankfully not shown much, but as soon as they reached New Malden she began to swell up like new bread. Sometimes he had to look at her twice to recognise her and he found it hard to believe that this was the thin slip of a girl he'd picked up from the corner near her parents' house in Brislington, nervously clutching her suitcase. She was still attractive and the radiant bloom of pregnancy made her skin glow – but she'd blown up like a balloon and he felt she might burst at any moment. Her bulk repelled him. Sometimes it was as much as he could do to glance at her, never mind make contact. He could not inwardly admit to being the cause – everything had conspired against him and he was filled with a continual sense of resentment. He was simply not ready to be a father.

He started to spend more time away from the house. It wasn't hard to find a reason. In London there was always some sporting event to attend and in his drive to achieve the recognition he craved, he was always able to convince himself of the necessity of being at it.

The appearance of a baby in the house did nothing to alter his attitude. In fact, it strengthened it. What had once been a haven of peace was now filled with the howling cries of a young child and every time he returned home it was to the acrid smell of vomit and soiled nappies. The process of rearing offspring disgusted him.

Added to this feeling of antipathy there was also one of disappointment – the child had been born a girl. He'd not consciously considered it before but he began to realise that he'd secretly been hoping for a boy. After all, of what use were women in the world? They could cook, and as Elisabeth had shown, they could have babies, but it was men who were in charge of affairs and what a man wanted was someone to follow in his footsteps. So if there *were* to be children, for God's sake let them be boys. And if he took nothing else from the experience, for all his ambition, for all that he was desperate to go to Helsinki, the birth of his firstborn made him realise that when it came to the question of progeny, what he wanted above all things was a son.

Two

He was awake again and it was broad daylight. A shaft of sunlight had fallen across the ward and the shadow from the window frame was already well advanced. Dust motes danced in the beam.

He must have missed breakfast. On his bedside table someone had placed a tray on which stood a bowl of congealed porridge. Not that it mattered anymore. He'd long since lost his appetite for food, and although there was a gnawing sensation in his gut, it wasn't pangs of hunger but a growling feeling of discomfort. The effects of the last dose of morphine had already started to wear off.

He'd decided not to ask for any more and had resolved to bear as much of the pain as he could. The easy course would be to take the needle and dissolve back into the woozy state from which he'd emerged, but the events of the previous night had convinced him otherwise. Mrs Walker's incoherent ramblings were still fresh in his mind. They'd no doubt been brought on by whatever narcotic she'd been administered, and whatever else might happen, he was determined not to cry out as she had done. He'd no intention of making a fool of himself by publicly admitting his problems.

Mrs Walker herself seemed to have fully succumbed to the drugs. She lay on her back, comatose, her elbows bent, her stick-thin arms pointing upwards and her crooked fingers splayed out like the stumps of a pollarded tree. As for her daughter, whose presence had been so fervently desired the night before, if she were to arrive now as requested, she would find her mother unconscious and unable to respond.

There was a bustle around the ward-sister's desk at the nurses' station. Soon they would see he was awake and someone would come across to him, push back his curtains, plump up his pillows and like a waft of warm honey, the quiet voice of reason would breathe its sweet amalgam.

Good morning, Mr Jones. And how are we today?

His response would be to manfully clench his stomach, grit his teeth and smile as best he could.

During his waking hours he continued to conjure up old images. He'd discovered that memory was the best antidote to pain. It gave him something on which he could focus, something to distract him, a lifebelt to cling to in this sea of wreckage. Instead of trying to banish whatever thoughts had come to him whilst asleep, he'd take what his subconscious mind had given him and attempt to expand on it. And if he concentrated on the past, there was a chance he could ignore what his stomach was telling him about the future...

If Weston had been about Elisabeth and Mrs Beazley, then London was all about Marion. London – he could never think of the place without her name springing instantly to mind. But it was not just Marion's name – her face, her clothes, her smell, her touch; it would all come back to him in an overwhelming rush, a rush he felt as keenly now as he had done then. He'd been obsessed by her, he knew that, but even if he'd realised it at the time it was doubtful he could have done anything about it, such was her power over him. He must have her, he wanted no other, and the mere thought that she should be possessed by another man was enough to drive him wild with jealousy. He'd been infatuated with her and it had cost him his marriage, his happiness, and almost his job into the bargain.

It was ironic that it had come at a time when he wasn't looking. Things had changed since his arrival in the capital. The fact of being married, of having a child, and the requirements of his new position had consumed him and he'd given no thought to philandering. As yet he'd made no friends beyond his immediate working colleagues, there was no society in which to operate and hence no opportunities, so he'd given himself to observing sport rather than women. Marion's advances therefore came as a complete surprise and left him totally unprepared.

Later on he would curse himself for being so unworldly – he of all people should have known what was happening. It was obvious to everyone else in the office that Marion was a vamp. Everything about her said *Stay away from me, I'm trouble, approach at your peril.* But he'd failed to read the warning signs and fell straight into her trap. What made it even more galling was that for all his supposed experiences with women, he came across as excessively naive. He could imagine what they said about him behind his back.

Geoffrey Jones? That hick from the West Country? Hardly a day in the jungle of big city life and he's eaten by a tiger!

The BBC World Service was based at Bush House in Aldwych. Most mornings he'd go into the office to file his report on whatever event he'd covered the day before, conduct his research, prepare for his next assignment and, most importantly, record his output ready for transmission. At around 8.30am he'd emerge from the Tube across the road or if it was fine and he'd time, he'd appear on the steps having walked the mile or so from the station and go up to the Sports Department on the third floor. Being a new recruit, his desk was positioned at the back of a large open-plan area. Toward the front was the boss's office, and immediately adjacent, that of his secretary. It was here that he handed his reports in for typing – and it was here that he first met Marion.

He'd opened the door and there she was, sitting behind a desk with a typewriter in front of her. She was hunched over her machine, a light cardigan draped around her shoulders and a pair of thick-framed black glasses perched on the end of her nose. He hadn't given her a second glance. She barely looked up at him when he entered but simply motioned toward the in-tray on one side.

"In there," was her only comment.

There was a saying about women in spectacles. *Men don't make passes at girls who wear glasses.* But even that didn't occur to him at the time.

It wasn't until she came down to the back of the office to return his work that he really began to take notice. He'd expected to have to go and fetch it himself, so the fact that she took the trouble to walk the length of the room to deliver it struck him as unusual. Once she'd arrived, she tossed the file onto his desk and retreated a yard or so to rest against a nearby table, facing half towards him. Without her glasses and now in full profile, she reminded him of Ava Gardner.

She had a sultry, smouldering presence, an impression accentuated by her habit of pushing her mass of auburn hair back from her forehead, then arching her head and smoothing it down the back of her neck. When her legs moved, which he noticed they often did, there was a rustle as the stocking on one thigh stroked gently against the stocking on the other. Whether these ploys were deliberate or not was neither here nor there – they secured his attention regardless.

"You must be the new boy."

She spoke without looking directly at him, as if by partly ignoring him he might be further engaged.

Boy? Was that how she thought of him? Here he was, twenty-eight, pushing twenty-nine, and she could hardly be a year or so older, yet in her eyes he was the junior partner.

He struggled for a reply, searching for something clever and witty to say that would show how debonair he was rather than the country bumpkin he appeared. But he failed, and was forced to settle for a simple admission.

"Yes, I suppose I am."

He must have sounded as green as grass.

But if so she ignored it and pressed on.

"Well, I'm Marion. I'm sure we'll get to know each other soon." There was a sense that she'd gained the upper hand and now she looked him straight in the eye. "You know where to find me."

It was a provocative statement and he knew it – he might seem like an amateur but he wasn't that stupid.

She pushed herself decorously off the table and began to walk calmly back to her office. She'd deliberately travelled the length of the room to check him out and now that she'd succeeded she could safely return to her lair.

His eyes felt compelled to follow her, noting the tightness of her skirt.

The encounter left him deeply unsettled and he found it difficult to work for the rest of the morning. It was not as though she'd left him in doubt. There was no teasing with Marion, she'd made her intentions clear. She needed a man and after a short but adequate investigation, Geoffrey had ticked the box. On reflection, it was doubtful she'd even read his work.

He was tall, athletic and extremely presentable – all of which came as an added bonus. That he was married was a minor inconvenience but fundamentally irrelevant. If two adult people had decided they wanted each other, then that was the end of it – the small matter of marital infidelity wasn't going to stand in their way. She must have recognised something of herself in him, a like spirit, ready to flout propriety and abandon convention for the sake of a relationship, gambling that wherever she led, he would follow.

In fact, she came close to making a big miscalculation. Geoffrey was not a fan of office romances. He'd made that mistake once too often and had no desire to tread in the dirt on his own doorstep. But on this occasion he blindly ignored what his common sense told him and blundered on irrespective. In truth, she had only to shake her tail at him and he would run after her. Like a stag chasing a hind in season, he acted heedlessly with only one thought in mind.

Despite her initial approach, Marion proved surprisingly patient. If she *was* a tiger then like any big cat she had the ability to lie in wait until the moment to pounce was right. It was true that instead of 'Mr Jones' she began addressing him by his first name straight away, a stage it had taken her several years to reach with her boss (a short and rotund man in whom she had no interest), so there was to be no standing on ceremony, no unnecessary preliminaries – Marion didn't bother with small talk. But she wasn't unaccomplished either and when the time came to move in for the kill it would be final – there would be no juvenile fumbling in the stationery cupboard as far as she was concerned.

Her moment arrived the first time he brought his sports car to the office. For the most part he used public transport to move around but once in a while an event would crop up which was out of town and difficult to reach and he needed the use of a vehicle. He'd come close to selling it after the move, seeing it stand idle outside the house for days on end, but had decided to keep it for sentimental reasons. Besides, it still gave him a certain cachet.

Marion must have found out about it when he applied for a parking permit for the day. Within an hour of it being issued, she'd made the long trip down to his desk at the back of the open area.

"I need a lift," she announced, smoothing her hair down the back of her neck. "Tonight, after work."

That he might have other plans was of no consequence. They could be changed at a moment's notice and she knew she'd take priority.

Her message disturbed him and he was once more unable to work. He sat for an hour at his desk with a vacant expression until one of his colleagues reminded him of the time by tapping at his watch.

"I say, old boy, you're cutting it a bit fine aren't you? You'll miss the off if you're not careful."

He immediately came to and cleared his papers, then collected his car from the compound and drove off as if he were leaving. Instead of which he found a spot around the corner, directly opposite the door from which he knew she would later emerge and waited there, chain smoking. All thought of the event he was supposed to be covering had evaporated. In fact, he'd have been pushed to remember what it was.

It was just after five-thirty when Marion appeared, crossing the road and getting in beside him. She brought with her a faint musk-like scent which despite its lack of power, filled both the car and his senses straight away.

"Here."

She handed him a slip of paper with an address scrawled on it, a flat somewhere near Hampstead Heath.

He gave her a quizzical look.

"It's my sister's place," she explained. "She lets me use it when she's not in town." And, when he still seemed questioning, "She's *not* in town by the way..."

He'd already gained a little knowledge of London and headed straight for the Finchley Road. When they got closer he imagined she'd give him directions. It would have been simpler to have taken the Tube and he thought of asking her why not, but he already knew the reason. They travelled the rest of the way in silence.

The flat itself impressed him. He'd expected a seedy bedsit in Neasden, but Marion had chosen far more sumptuous surroundings in which to conduct their affair. The apartment was on the ground floor overlooking the Heath, and as soon as he went inside it brought to mind Georgina's place in Bristol, spacious and with a tasteful décor that lacked ostentation. He immediately felt drawn to the window where a small table lamp gave off a pale yellow glow next to the net curtain. In the street outside, someone was blithely walking their dog. It all felt rather homely and familiar, although he couldn't escape the thought that he wasn't the first man she'd brought there for the purpose.

How the tables had been turned...

"Can I get you a drink?"

Marion was already in the kitchen, breaking ice cubes from a box, the door of the refrigerator wide open. On the side, two large measures of gin stood waiting.

"Thanks."

"Why don't you put some music on?"

She gestured toward a wooden cabinet containing a turntable and a selection of 78s.

He leafed through them, attempting to appear as casual as possible. Parker, Bechet, Sinatra – it was an eclectic collection. Rather than anything brash, he picked something orchestral by Dorsey thinking it smooth and seductive and more suited to the occasion.

Marion came through with the drinks, accompanied by the heady smell of her perfume. She was in no hurry. If he'd imagined she was going to tear at his clothes the moment they walked in the door he was mistaken, and just as she'd waited for her opportunity at the office, she was prepared to be patient now, kicking her shoes off before sinking onto the sofa and curling her legs up beneath her. Whatever her needs, she was not going to rush into it and her approach was almost matter of fact.

"We'd better draw the curtains first..."

Later, in the bedroom, she proved passionate enough and at times the intensity of her lovemaking surprised him, although he was only too happy to oblige her. Afterwards, as they lay there, exhausted, smoking their cigarettes, she seemed distant and he felt a curious need to confide in her as if wanting to bridge the gap between them. A question lingered on the tip of his tongue. Was their liaison to be purely physical, or was there to be more to it? The fact that he invited himself to stay over suggested there might – although the offhanded manner in which Marion assented suggested there might not. Either way, he didn't go home that night.

Three

He was suddenly aware of his surroundings again. He'd reached the natural conclusion of the section of the story he'd been telling himself and realised he'd been staring at the bald man with the crooked nose in the bed opposite. For how long he wasn't sure. Denied the use of his watch it was difficult to tell, but at a guess he'd have said ten minutes. And in all this time, he hadn't moved.

Nor had he spoken and now his attention had been drawn to it, Geoffrey couldn't ever recall him doing so. Unlike Mrs Walker who seemed to cry out at the slightest opportunity, the bald man had maintained a stoic and dignified silence from the moment he'd been admitted. He was lying on his back, motionless, the recipient of the contents of an intravenous drip that stood at the side of his bed, inhibiting movement. And that Geoffrey should be staring at him was not an embarrassment to either party as all the bald man could see at present was the ceiling – and all that could be seen of the bald man was his crooked nose protruding above the bedclothes like the fin of a partly submerged fish. His position never seemed to change. It puzzled Geoffrey as to how he knew he was bald.

Meanwhile, the shadow from the window had advanced halfway across the floor and would shortly reach the end of his bed. In the far corner Mrs Walker remained peacefully asleep, saving her energy for another night-time adventure. All was quiet on the western front and Geoffrey settled back into his thoughts.

Following his night of passion with Marion he was consumed with a feeling of anxiety. It wasn't guilt – the fact that he'd cheated on his wife was of no concern to him, he had no moral conscience. The worry was how to get away with it. His first concern was to explain his whereabouts to his boss and cover up the fact that he'd not been at the event to which he'd been assigned.

Partly through fear of discovery and partly through the fact of sleeping in a strange bed, he woke early. He dressed quickly then slipped on a coat and went out to walk on the Heath to compose his thoughts. He strode back and forth for an hour, smoking nervously and biting his nails. Eventually, when he thought they might be open, he found a newsagent and bought one of the more reputable papers. Much to his relief, the event he'd been supposed to cover had been well reported and based on this account he felt sure he could cobble something together. He returned to the flat in a much more confident mood.

By now, Marion was up and dressed for work and emerged from the bathroom fixing her lipstick. Even at half past seven in the morning she still had that come-to-bed look about her.

"Drop me off at the Tube – I'll show you where."

With his thoughts fixed firmly on compiling his article, he didn't argue. What was to be gained by them being seen together now?

He determined to tell Elisabeth it had been an evening assignment. He'd say it had been out of town, it had finished late and not wanting to travel back that distance at night, he'd found a B&B to put up in. In some respects, it wasn't that far from the truth. Besides, she'd have no choice but swallow it – her hands were too full with the child to check things out. Frankly, he didn't care whether she believed him or not – that was his story and he was sticking to it. If nothing else it had given him a night away from the howling cries of his daughter and the smell of her soiled nappies. That was always worth a lie or two.

Luckily, both of his strategies proved successful and he survived the experience undamaged. His boss accepted his article, Elisabeth accepted his story and neither pried for details. Encouraged by these reactions, it then became a question of whether Marion was willing to continue the liaison or whether it had simply been a one-night stand. The answer came a week or so later when she walked down the office to return one of his reports.

"My sister's gone away for a while – we can use the flat whenever."

'Whenever' turned out to mean whenever she needed a lift and he soon started using the car as much as the train. They met as often as they could and it wasn't long before the flat began to feel like a second home. He was more comfortable there than he was in New Malden – the soft lights, the tasteful décor, the smooth sounds of Tommy Dorsey, the promise of Marion and a warm bed – it was where he felt he belonged.

This pattern continued for upwards of a year and he went to the flat as often as he dared. He came to view it as a refuge from his daily routine and just as he'd gone to Weston-super-Mare to escape the pressures of Bristol, now he went to Hampstead to escape those of New Malden. The little house had become hateful to him; it was small and cluttered and he found nothing of any quality to keep him there. Not even the sight of his one-year-old daughter attempting her first uncertain steps could tug at his heartstrings. It seemed he was losing touch.

The arrangement appeared ideal, but after a while a dark cloud began to form in his mind. Marion's sexual appetite exceeded his own and they could spend days on end at the flat doing little else but making love. But he wasn't there all the time, and now that Marion had secured permanent possession of the place, it worried him that he might not be the only one she was entertaining. When he wasn't there himself, other men might be, and whenever Marion went out he started looking for evidence of their presence, checking for shoes under the bed, strange coats in the wardrobe or different-coloured hairs in the sink. He discovered nothing, but remained deeply suspicious and began to harbour an irrational jealousy until he could no longer look at another man without somehow thinking he might be Marion's lover. This unhappy thought grew as the months wore on, and gradually came to dominate his actions so he eventually became obsessed.

1952 arrived and the Olympic Games were looming on the horizon. The prospect of going to Helsinki excited him, but he could not think of it now without giving a shudder. Despite his enthusiasm, the project turned into disaster.

The incident of the missed event had worried him. If repeated and he were discovered, his chances of being selected for the Games would be ruined. He was determined not to reoffend and consequently upped his game. He was scrupulous in his attendance at matches, his reports were filed on time, his presentations had an added edge – everything was done to impress and ensure there were no mistakes. To boost his case, he started to create a card index of every athlete likely to take part, often staying up late into the night to work on it either in New Malden or Hampstead. These nocturnal shifts attracted the attention of his respective partners and at one or two in the morning, depending where he was, Elisabeth or Marion would poke their head around the door clad in their nightwear and complain.

What on earth are you doing up at this hour? Why don't you come to bed?

But he persisted. In his mind, women didn't understand ambition. They were either homemakers like Elisabeth or, as in Marion's case, providers of sensual pleasure. What else could he expect?

His efforts paid off, and when the list went up in the office his name was on it. His colleagues paid him grudging respect.

I see you've been chosen, old boy. You lucky bugger!

Lucky? There was nothing lucky about it! He'd worked hard to earn it and he intended to enjoy every moment. But as it turned out, things proved quite the opposite.

He planned to be away for a period of almost three weeks. As the day of departure grew closer, the realisation of what this meant slowly began to dawn on him. He'd no compunction in quitting New Malden but the notion of leaving Hampstead, and more specifically, Marion, filled him with dread. He couldn't trust her on her own for a few days – let alone a fortnight. The thought of what she might get up to gnawed at him until he found himself thinking more about Hampstead than he did of Helsinki. He lost concentration and in the days leading up to his flight he couldn't sleep for worry – and it wasn't about his job.

On the day he was due to leave he arrived at the airport flustered and agonising over what he should do. He joined his colleagues in the departure lounge but was unable to settle and paced up and down, his face twisted into a grimace of pain. Someone eventually asked if he was feeling alright. His emphatic *No!* was followed by a mumbled *I think I'm unwell.*

When the flight was called, he was unable to force himself onto the plane and locked himself into a toilet cubicle, where he sat wringing his hands. After a brief search, his colleagues continued without him.

Where's Jones got to?

Taken ill apparently. Got himself into an awful state. If you ask me, I think the blighter's bottled it. Couldn't handle the thought of flying, I shouldn't wonder...

He managed to compose himself and retreated to the flat in Hampstead with all his kit. Marion was in and thankfully alone.

"Aren't you supposed to be in Helsinki?"

What was he supposed to tell her? Was it time to make some grandiloquent gesture and say he was in love with her? In other less trying circumstances he might have done so, but it wasn't love that moved him, it was lust, and it was therefore inappropriate. And anyway, Marion's reaction would have been entirely predictable.

Don't be ridiculous...

As it was, she merely shrugged her shoulders and let him in.

He remained at the flat for the whole of the time the Games

were on. He couldn't face going back to New Malden or the office and publicly admit his failure. Instead, he went 'on the sick' and to cover his absence succeeded in persuading a doctor to write him a note with a performance that would have graced a West End stage. The problem then was what to do with himself.

Sworn to silence, Marion went in to work while he was left to roam the Heath. He lost count of the aimless miles he covered, back and forth in the summer sun, worrying. The alternative was to sit in the flat with the newspapers and torment himself by reading the accounts of proceedings in Finland. The one thing he dare not do was listen to it on the radio, as to discover who had taken his place was more than he could bear. In the evenings when Marion came home they lived like an ordinary couple, barely speaking, each consumed with their own interests. Despite the initial embarrassment it was a relief to get back to work, although he was forced to endure the inevitable comments.

Bloody shame that, old boy. You missed a corker of a show. Still, better luck next time.

Next time? He wasn't convinced there'd be a next time. The management were not amused. They accepted his story but made it very clear they thought he'd sailed close to the wind. Notes were added to his file, but after the appropriate disciplinary action they returned him to duty. He'd ridden his luck yet again and somehow he'd got away with it. After that, it was back to the old routine.

But the old routine wasn't quite the same any more. Things had changed and the events surrounding Helsinki had taught him a formative lesson. He'd thought himself ambitious and his failure to carry through on it had come as a shock to him. What made it all the more galling was the realisation that he'd no one to blame but himself. He'd stood in his own way and somewhere, deep inside, there were inhibitions he'd been unaware of. His ambition was now tempered, his work lost that cutting edge and

he became withdrawn, sullen and resentful.
He started taking it out on his wife.

Four

His relationship with Elisabeth was already under strain but he'd maintained their pretence of a marriage purely as a matter of convenience. They continued to live in the same house and sleep in the same bed, although there was no real warmth in either. If he gave her any credit it was for the fact that she'd recognised his aversion to the messy details of raising children and was at pains to keep this subject out of her conversation. For his part he was reluctant to discuss his work, so there was little common ground between them. There were long, and at times embarrassing, silences, punctuated occasionally by her forlorn attempts to get him to talk. On his supposed return from Helsinki she'd naturally asked him "How was it?"

Only to be met by his gruff and dismissive, "Alright…"

After weeks of desperation she resorted to questions of pure practical necessity such as *Will you be here at the weekend?* and although he felt she was testing him, she gave no clue as to whether she suspected the truth. There were often tears accompanied by the phrase *Sometimes I think you don't love me any more.* Then, for the sake of preserving the status quo, he would allow her into his arms and subsequently make love to her as if to prove he still cared for her. It was a cruel deception, but not one that caused him to feel guilt. He was too concerned with himself to worry about anyone else.

Things with Marion were not altogether rosy either. Their affair had definitely cooled, although that was only to be expected as they could never hope to sustain the heights of passion they'd reached in the early days of their relationship. Rather than being exciting, sex was now a necessity and the familiarity that had grown up between them meant there were no longer any surprises. Since Helsinki he'd turned in on himself and become introspective and his lovemaking lacked its former intuition and grew stale. And to tell the truth, once he'd got into his new frame of mind, he didn't always feel in the mood.

At the same time, the jealousy that had been the cause of his problems subsided and he felt much less inclined to look accusingly at other men. His periodic searches of the flat continued but it was more out of habit than conviction and he still found nothing to alarm him. Two months after his fortnight's stay however, his suspicions were aroused in another connection when there was a distinct change in Marion's habits.

It began one Saturday evening in early October. He was allegedly staying in Northampton whereas he was in fact in Hampstead. Marion had uncharacteristically got up in the middle of the night to go to the bathroom and when she failed to return, he got out of bed himself to find her in the kitchen crouched in front of the open refrigerator.

"What on earth are you doing?"

"I'm hungry…"

He'd left her to it but in the morning he discovered she'd consumed an odd assortment of the contents. Later that day she was violently sick and when the incident was repeated and the sickness continued he immediately grew alarmed. Proof arrived when she confirmed that she'd missed not just one but two of her periods. If there'd been any doubt, this dispelled it – now it was Marion who was pregnant.

Next day he woke with it fixed in his mind and lay there staring blankly at the wall. He resolved to tackle her on the subject straight away, and after she'd got up he lay in wait for her outside the bathroom. If he bided his time the right moment might never arrive, and in the meanwhile she could do something he might regret. It was damnably inconvenient, he had to admit, but still an opportunity nonetheless.

She immediately got the wrong impression.

"It's nothing for you to worry about, Geoffrey. I'll take care of it."

But that was precisely the point. His concern was that she *would* take care of it.

She still failed to understand.

"Look, you really don't need to get involved. It's not your business."

But it *was* his business. He'd every reason to suppose he was the father – and there was a chance that it might be a boy…

He was woken by a clattering of cups as the late-afternoon hush of the ward was broken by the rattle of the trolleys. Like the tolling of a bell, it signalled the end of the interval between the departure of visitors and the arrival of tea. Mrs Walker's daughter had been and gone, filling the corner space with her empty chatter, her restless energy swirling the dust motes next to the window. Her mother had been awake for once but had become exhausted by the contact and now lay silent, her crooked hands raised as if in supplication. Directly opposite, the bald man was completely immobile, his fish-fin nose stationary amongst the wave-like folds of blanket and pillow. There, all had been quiet – he'd had no such visitation.

Neither as yet had Geoffrey, though he continued to wait in hope. When the moment came, he did not want to be found asleep. Why else would he resist the attractions of the morphine if it were not to remain conscious in the event of being called on? There was nothing else to live for. He was eighty-three, for God's sake, and there was little time left. He was riddled with cancer – besides being diagnosed diabetic – and the prognosis was undeniably terminal. And yet, if only Frank would come, if only he would heed his message, there might still be some point.

He heaved himself up onto his pillows and a stabbing shaft of pain shot through his side, causing him to grimace. In a moment, tea would arrive and with it the quiet voice of reason with its soothing tones and honeyed balm.

Is everything alright, Mr Jones? And what would you like to eat today?

What a fatuous question that was! What he would like to eat and what he could manage were two entirely different things. He would doubtless do what he usually did – pass on the main course and settle for a helping of the semolina, slopped into a bowl, consoling himself with the meagre portion of jam. Once the food had taken effect, he would slump downwards and doze off again as if after a heavy meal. And for a while at least, the morphine could wait.

You bastard!

It was one of those occasions he was jolted awake because he found himself staring straight at the cracks in the ceiling. It was dark (so it must be night-time) and he could just make them out in the glow from the light on the ward-sister's desk. His heart was thumping and his breath came in short, shallow spurts. But it wasn't pain that had roused him, rather the force of the words. His dream had been verbally violent and it had disturbed him, involving, as it did, a fearful row with Marion.

"No! I won't have the child."

"Why not?"

"Why not? Have you any idea what you're talking about?"

He opened his mouth to reply, but then thought better of it. His experience of parenting was not a good example as his involvement with Pat had been minimal. His lack of response only encouraged Marion to continue.

"No, you haven't, have you? Well, I'll tell you why not. Because it's absolute bloody hell, that's why not. Can you imagine what it's like when your body blows up to twice its normal size and you can hardly walk? Not to mention the pain and the bleeding." She gripped herself by the elbows and shuddered. "It's awful – and I'm not going through that for you or any man."

She spoke as though the thought of childbirth frightened her – or perhaps she'd been through it before and had vowed not to do so again. He would never know. Whatever the reason, she was set in her resolve.

"Anyway. I've told you once already – I'll get it taken care of."

With Georgina, he'd studiously avoided involvement with women's issues. This time he was not to be put off that easily.

"Look…" He began preparing his counter-argument. He'd have to concede the point on childbirth but if it was really a question of the longer term, he was prepared to make sacrifices. "It'll be alright, I'll look after you."

Marion laughed. She was the kind of woman who looked after herself – she didn't need a man to do it for her.

"You? Look after me? That'll be the day!"

You've already got one wife and child and you can't even look after them.

The unspoken implication stung him into desperate and unprecedented action.

"I'll marry you then, for God's sake, if that's what it takes."

"Marry me? How the hell can you marry me? You're married already."

"I'll get a divorce. I'll plead adultery. It won't be difficult to prove. For God's sake, Marion, be reasonable."

But Marion was not to be moved.

"Forget it, Geoffrey. It's not going to happen and you know it."

And for the time being, those were her last words on the subject.

The real trouble began a week later when he showed up at the flat carrying a small blue box containing a ring. He'd hardly set foot inside the door before he presented it to her.

"I've persuaded Elisabeth to sue for divorce. I've been to see the solicitor this afternoon and filed the papers. He says it'll take about six weeks. In the meantime, I've brought something for you."

It wasn't the most amorous of declarations, but it showed the sincerity of his intent. Even then Marion remained ignorant.

"What is it?"

She took the box and opened it, but as soon as she'd looked inside she snapped it shut and flung it across the room at him as hard as she could. It missed and clattered harmlessly onto the sideboard, knocking over a framed photograph of her sister. That was when she screamed out the phrase that had stuck so vividly in his memory: "You bastard!" and added "You can't do this to me!"

And before he could respond, she'd burst into tears and run into the bedroom, slamming the door behind her.

Geoffrey retrieved the box from where it had fallen. He imagined she must find the thought of marriage overwhelming. Men had used her for bedding, not wedding, and she was unaccustomed to being made a proposal, even one delivered in such an offhand manner as his. In the past, her body had been wanted for a particular purpose – now it seemed it was required for another.

Later on, when she'd calmed down and Geoffrey had persuaded her to come out of the bedroom, she emerged with a sodden handkerchief pressed to her nose, snivelling and tearful. For someone so supposedly self-reliant it was strange to see her reduced in this way. Once her emotion had subsided, her first question was typically practical. "And where did you think we would live?"

He'd already thought that out. "Your sister's never here – we could rent the place from her permanently."

It seemed as good a place to bring up a child as any.

"You can't be serious..."

But he could – he most definitely could.

Over the course of the next few weeks he kept a close eye on Marion. He felt that they'd come to a tacit agreement but her outburst had shown her to be volatile and he was fearful she might thwart him with a visit to some backstreet clinic. He made the task easier for himself by moving into the flat. After the concession he'd wrung from Elisabeth he could hardly stay in New Malden. He'd burnt his boats in that regard and there was no going back.

When this crucial period had passed he began to feel more relaxed and afforded himself the luxury of watching Marion grow. To his disappointment it was not an edifying experience. He thought she might bloom as Elisabeth had done, but as she advanced in size she became increasingly broody – although not in the sense that befitted her condition, but introspective, sullen and resentful of the load she was carrying. As her time approached, she became silently resigned and they barely spoke to each other on the matter, other than for her to make him aware of her basic requirements. The principal one was outstandingly simple.

Let's just get through this, shall we?

For the delivery they went to the same hospital he'd used for Elisabeth two years before. This time he booked a private room – Marion had no intention of bearing her pain in public. And instead of absenting himself at some sporting event, on the day in question Geoffrey properly enacted the role of the expectant father and sat fidgeting nervously in the waiting room, or paced up and down the long corridor outside the maternity suite, smoking. He was kept in touch with progress by the strength of Marion's cries, her shouts of *Oh God!* and *Jesus Christ that hurts!* growing louder through the night. At last they reached a crescendo and in the early hours of an April morning, Frank entered the world. He arrived peacefully enough, gurgling and bawling no more than any baby should – it was Marion who did the kicking and screaming.

Afterwards, when her torn skin had been sewn up, the room had been tidied and Geoffrey was allowed in to see her, he found her lying exhausted on the bed, propped up by a mound of pillows. Her face was pale and she seemed drained by the effort. He looked around for the child, which instead of being placed on its mother's belly or clasped to her breast lay in a cot on the far side of the room, quietly snuffling. Marion raised her hand weakly toward it.

"Here. Take it. It's a boy. That's what you wanted, isn't it?" She sank back down for a moment, briefly closing her eyes before they flashed open again and with a sudden burst of energy, she turned on him like a cornered wildcat. "And as for you, you bastard, don't you ever come near me again! You hear me? Never!"

Geoffrey recoiled in shock. So here was the real Marion, the Marion that lay underneath. This was the tiger he'd been promised. It was as if she were possessed by a malevolent spirit that had previously lain dormant but which the experience of pregnancy and childbirth had brought to the surface. What kind of woman was she?

Meanwhile, in the cot on the other side of the room, the boy lay waiting to be loved…

It had already occurred to him that Marion might not make an ideal parent. She was not going to be a stereotypical young mother, proudly steering her pram through the park, feeding the ducks and showing off to the neighbours. Just like Geoffrey, Marion was the wrong side of thirty, tending towards thirty-five, and life had formed in her habits that were hard to change. On her first day out of hospital, her initial act on returning to the flat was to throw down her coat and pour herself a large gin and tonic before slumping onto the sofa and lighting a cigarette. It was Geoffrey who carried in the baby, swaddled in a white shawl, and then stood by the open door wondering what to do. Marion waved dismissively toward an empty armchair, the smoke from her cigarette curling up her fingers.

"Oh, for God's sake, Geoffrey, stop looking so pathetic. Stick him over there. He'll be alright for five minutes."

He laid the boy down, doubtful of the instruction but ignorant of an alternative. An anxious half hour passed before she finished her drink and paid the boy any attention. Even then her check seemed cursory to say the least. Geoffrey remained dubious. Marion might be inexperienced but he had the advantage of having seen it done before, albeit from a distance. Elisabeth would have acted differently. When Pat had been born it was as much as she could do to put the baby down. It was for this reason – and also perhaps out of instinct – that he began to suspect something wasn't right.

A week or so later he was proved correct. Partly in anticipation, and partly because he'd had no meaningful break since Helsinki, he decided to take a few days' leave. He'd promised to help Marion with the baby – *You can't leave it all up to me, Geoffrey* – and it gave him the opportunity to keep an eye on her. Even now he wasn't entirely sure what she might do.

They fell into a routine, taking it in turns to do the chores, although it was always he who got up in the middle of the night while Marion slept soundly on, impervious to the boy's cries. After he'd given the child its bottle he would sit on the edge of the bed, staring through the bars of the cot as the little lad repeatedly balled and unfurled his tiny fists, gurgling softly. When the boy had settled back to sleep, Geoffrey, now wide awake, would crawl back under the covers and lie there listening for any sounds. Sometimes it was an hour or more before he could comfortably doze off.

The arrival of the health visitor was cause for hope. Her very appearance inspired confidence. In contrast to Marion's slim, lithe figure, Mrs Brodie was Scottish and of a motherly build with good stout legs and thick ankles. She wore no formal uniform but her tweed suit and brogues told a compelling story.

"I'm Academy trained, Mrs Jones," she announced on arrival.

"And I don't stand any nonsense." She had a booming voice, designed to let the neighbours know their business. "So if we want a good, healthy baby, we'll be doing things my way, if you don't mind." She removed her jacket and rolled up her sleeves in readiness. "It's a boy I believe. Now what's the little man's name?"

The remark was directed at Marion but it was Geoffrey who responded. "It's Frank."

It had been solely his choice. Marion had shown no interest.

I couldn't care less what you call him – it's of no concern to me.

The only names he'd been able to conjure up came from the record collection in the lounge – Glen, Tommy, Dizzy, they'd all come to mind. For a while he'd considered Benny (after Goodman) but it wasn't solid enough for his liking and in the end, although he'd rejected Sinatra musically, Frank seemed to fit the bill.

"Well, fetch him in then," said Mrs Brodie, "and let's have a look at the wee lad."

Geoffrey did the honours, lifting Frank out of the cot and presenting him to the nurse, who duly weighed and inspected him. Much to his father's relief, she pronounced the boy fit.

"He doesn't look so bad. What are you feeding him on?"

Geoffrey was about to reply when Marion cut in and gave out the formula. Up until this point she'd taken no part in proceedings but had remained leaning up against the doorjamb at the entrance to the kitchen, observing affairs and quietly smoking. Now she pointedly extinguished her cigarette and walked forward into the room, her arms folded in front of her. She'd realised that if she didn't join in soon she'd forever be excluded but her intervention worked out badly and she was forced onto the defensive.

"That's all very well," said Mrs Brodie. "But breast is best, Mrs Jones, as I'm sure you're aware."

"Not for me it isn't," Marion was quick to respond.

"Well, we'll have to see about that," said Mrs Brodie, in a lecturing tone.

After she'd gone, Marion returned to the subject. "If that bitch imagines I'm breast feeding after all that I've been through she's got another think coming."

Geoffrey kept his counsel and stayed silent. Whatever his feelings on the matter, he knew it was a battle he wasn't going to win.

Five

He returned to work on the Monday with some trepidation. The thought of leaving Marion alone with the child filled him with unease. Who knew what she might get up to? Nurse Brodie would be back on the Wednesday, but in the meantime there were two long and arduous days to get through.

He arrived back at the flat around six-thirty. It was still daylight but it had been raining and the sky was overcast. The curtains had not yet been drawn and the downstairs lights blazed out into the street. As he opened the front door and entered the hallway, he could hear music coming from one of the rooms on the ground floor. Someone was playing an old and cracked version of 'Dancing The Blues Away'. The song floated lazily down the corridor. He could readily recall the words.

Dancing the blues away
Romancing the blues away
Kick off your shoes, shake off the blues
Dance them away!

And the reason he knew this was because it formed part of Marion's record collection.

He was seized by a sudden feeling of panic and hastily flung open the door to the flat. He was immediately assaulted by the noise of the phonograph at full blast. In the lounge, scattered around the base of the record cabinet, a pile of 78s had spewed out across the floor. A party was in full swing – but one at which there was only one guest.

Marion was pirouetting round the end of the sofa. In accordance with the instructions of the song, she'd removed her footwear and stood in her stockinged feet, a cigarette in one hand and a half-empty bottle of gin in the other. Her mass of auburn hair, normally brushed and tidy, hung waywardly across her face. She seemed utterly oblivious to his presence – until he announced himself in no uncertain terms.

"What the hell d'you think you're doing?"

"I'm having fun. What are you doing?"

She replied without looking up and for a moment continued dancing as if trying to provoke a reaction. When there was none, she stopped abruptly and offered the bottle in his direction.

"Want some?"

"No thank you. You're drunk, by the way."

"You could be right there." Marion closed one eye and cocked a pair of cigarette-loaded fingers at him. She'd have been hard pushed to deny the accusation as her speech was slightly slurred. "So what if I am? It's not a crime is it, being drunk in your own house? You should try it sometime."

In the background, the music continued unabated.

Kick off your shoes, shake off the blues
Dance them away!

It was an invitation Geoffrey couldn't possibly accept. He chose to confront Marion with the reality instead.

"Do you realise how irresponsibly you're behaving? You're supposed to be looking after the baby."

Marion's reaction was to sneer and go on dancing.

But Geoffrey was determined. He strode across to the phonograph and lifted the needle, cutting the artist off in his prime.

"Oh, for God's sake! I'm putting a stop to this nonsense!"

"Hey!" Marion protested and began stumbling toward the cabinet, treading clumsily on one of the 78s, shattering it to pieces. "Now look what you've done!"

Geoffrey refused to be distracted. "Where's Frank?"

"Where's Frank?" mimicked Marion, haughtily inclining her head. "If he's got any sense, your precious little Frank is fast asleep in there, keeping quiet."

She waved in the direction of the bedroom.

Her offhand manner aroused Geoffrey's suspicions. Perhaps she'd given the child some drug to induce his silence.

"What have you done to him?"

"I haven't 'done' anything to him," said Marion. "Why should I have 'done' anything to him? Just because there's a baby in the house it doesn't mean to say I can't play a few records for christsake."

Geoffrey had got as far as the bedroom door before she could finish her sentence. Marion called after him. "You don't believe me, do you? Look at him! He can't wait to rush off and check on his bloody kid! Hah! You should have let me get rid of him while you still had the chance. Now you're stuck with the little bugger!"

Her words failed to halt his retreating figure, but with him gone she could now resume control of the record player. A series of scratching sounds followed as she struggled to replace the needle before the record started up once more, filling the lounge with its carefree message.

Dancing the blues away...

Geoffrey shut the bedroom door to reduce the noise, then sat on the edge of the bed, staring at the cot. Frank was couched peacefully amongst his bedclothes, seemingly fast asleep. On the floor at Geoffrey's feet, a part-finished feeding bottle lay where it had been discarded. Whatever had transpired prior to Geoffrey's arrival, at least the child had come to no harm and with his fears momentarily quelled, he could afford to take a few minute's rest. He closed his eyes and let his head fall forward.

It was a tiring business, this raising of children, the continual anxiety, the constant demands. He'd never known the extent of it with Pat. But then, he'd never been there – it was Elisabeth who'd done all the work. And of the three of them, she seemed best cut out for it.

His thoughts were interrupted as Frank stirred in his cot. Rather than let him cry out Geoffrey bent and picked him up. He was damp and needed changing. It was a task Geoffrey despised but one which he was forced to undertake. He'd learnt a lot under the watchful eye of Nurse Brodie. He'd felt he had to.

Afterwards, he nestled the boy in his lap and coaxed him into downing the rest of the bottle. When it was gone and the lad's eyes began to droop he finished him off and laid him carefully back in the cot. It had taken him half an hour, by which time both the lounge and its occupant had fallen silent. Switching off the light, he tentatively pushed open the bedroom door and walked through.

Marion lay face down on the sofa, breathing heavily and unconscious. Her skirt and hair were rumpled and one arm dangled toward the floor still clutching the now-empty bottle of gin. On the phonograph, the abandoned 78 continued to rotate to no effect, the needle flicking repeatedly over the last few revolutions with an eerie hiss. Geoffrey elected to put it out of its misery, moving carefully to avoid its companions on the floor, several of which were in pieces. Outside it had grown dark. He drew the curtains and turned down the lights.

There was no point in waking Marion. She was dead to the world and no amount of shaking or shouting would rouse her. But that was what he wanted to do – he could not deny it. He wanted to take her by the shoulders and jolt her into consciousness, backwards and forwards until her eyes were wide with fear. Then he could roar at her and call her a stupid bitch and all the names under the sun so she truly understood the extent of his anger. Yes, at that moment that was what he wanted above all things.

Oh, how he hated her now! How he despised her! The very idea of her filled him with loathing and contempt. She'd seduced him and taken him away from his home, his family and all that was good and had led him into this wilderness, this desolate isolation in which he now found himself. At first he'd been a willing participant, but it was she who'd started it all, she'd been the leader. Looking at her now, lying there, comatose, he realised it had all been a great mistake and he was filled with a sense of regret.

He'd never hated Elisabeth. He'd never loved her either, although there'd been moments of fondness and a general acceptance of her presence. There'd been no great passion and his feelings toward her had generally been those of indifference. But he was beginning to feel that indifference might be an altogether better basis for long-term stability rather than the violent emotions that Marion induced. From the very beginning, life in Hampstead had been a rollercoaster ride, and yet what he yearned for now was the unexciting contours of New Malden. How strange! Sometimes you didn't know what was best for you until it was taken away.

It was too late for that now. For better or for worse, he and Elisabeth had parted company and there could be no going back. New Malden might just as well be New Mexico for all the distance he'd have to travel to return there. It wasn't an option.

All this seemed clear. But things were never as simple as they appeared. If he only had himself to think about he might have been inclined to draw a line under the whole sordid affair and move on, but now he had the welfare of another to take into account. For his own petty and selfish reasons, he'd deliberately caused a child to be brought into the world and for the first time in his life he felt the weight of responsibility. Someone had to look after Frank, someone had to take care of the boy, and if he could at least salvage him from the wreckage then there was a chance he might redeem himself. He couldn't do it alone – and Marion couldn't do it at all. What choice was there, other than the obvious? The only doubt in his mind was what he should say to Nurse Brodie on the Wednesday.

It was really not long since he'd been in New Malden – six months perhaps, a year at the most – but it felt like an awful lot longer. As he stood on the street corner opposite, the collar of his raincoat turned up and his hat pulled down over his eyes, it was as if the house were part of another life, something dug up from a deep and distant memory. The low green fence, the rickety gate, the wooden porch above the front door, nothing had changed and yet their appearance seemed to stun him as though they carried the instant reminder of what had once been.

I used to live here, years ago. It was different then.

Later, on the drive back to Hampstead, he put it down to the fact that so much had altered in his life in such a short space of time that he'd not yet had the chance to adjust. And now, before he could stop and do so, it was about to change all over again.

But this had been the last thing on his mind when he'd set off that morning. His primary concern had been to get the boy out of the flat without waking Marion. It was paramount that she didn't discover his plan and raise some spurious objection. It should have been an easy task. Marion was a heavy sleeper and there was a bottle of gin to take into account. But he'd not wanted to take the risk, and the night before he'd lifted her from where she'd collapsed on the sofa and tucked her safely into bed. Once she was settled, he'd moved the cot containing the boy into the lounge, closed the bedroom door, and taken up her former position on the settee.

He didn't get much sleep that night. He didn't expect to. Unaided by alcohol, the sofa was not the most comfortable of beds and besides, his mind was awash with thoughts of what was to come. As he'd foreseen, the alarm clock that was Frank ensured he was awake at half past two, and by half past three both he and the boy were fully fed and clothed, Geoffrey in his raincoat and trilby, the boy wrapped in the white shawl in which he'd left hospital no more than ten days before. Marion slumbered on. Or at least he assumed so as there was no sound from the bedroom and he'd no intention of trying the door for fear of rousing her.

It was dark outside as he left the flat, closing the front entrance quietly behind him and treading carefully down the steps, clutching his precious bundle. Beneath the yellow glow of the street lights the pavement glistened with the sweat of overnight rain. In front of him lay the Heath, black, empty and silent.

The journey to New Malden took far less time than usual. At that hour there was virtually no traffic, just a few delivery lorries with their loads of milk cans or coal and the occasional bicyclist or bus. At one point, a rag-and-bone cart, its owner keen to be out on his rounds, shot out in front of him, the horse rearing awkwardly, and he had to swerve to avoid it. His first instinct was to reach down beside him and protect the cargo he'd placed on the floor. Prior to setting off he'd emptied the tools out of a wooden box he kept in the boot of the car, removed the lid, and stowed the boy carefully inside. It was this arrangement that now lay in the well of the passenger seat. As makeshift as it appeared, it was the only safe means of carriage that had presented itself.

He arrived at the house at twenty past four. It was still not yet light.

His intention was to leave the box on the doorstep under the shelter of the porch. He could then retreat to a safe distance and watch for what transpired. He would wait for as long as necessary. He would not leave the box unattended – Elisabeth might not be at home; someone might make off with it; and anyway, he wanted to see it taken in.

The idea of calling on her and explaining had obviously crossed his mind, and it had been the thought of this as much as anything else that had prevented him from sleeping. In the end he'd dismissed it. However small, there was always the risk she might decline. But presented with a fait accompli, his calculation was that he could rely on her sense of compassion. What mother could turn her back on the plight of an abandoned child?

To assist his case he'd hastily written a letter and had pushed it into an envelope together with a ten-pound note he left at the boy's feet.

This is Frank. Please take care of him. I'll send some more money soon. I'm sorry. Geoffrey.

It was his profession to express things in words but these bare statements of fact sounded feeble. What else was there to say? He *was* sorry, sorry to have burdened her, sorry to have caused so much hurt, sorry to ever have left. Although whether she would glean all this from such a short message was hard to imagine. In the short time available between the inception and execution of his plan it had been the best he could come up with. Even if he'd had longer it was doubtful he could improve on it. To describe a sporting event was one thing – to describe his emotions, entirely another.

He positioned the box beneath the porch and retreated to his observation point across the road. It was approaching half past four and he'd no idea how long he might have to wait. At some point during his vigil he presumed the birds would start singing and the place would come alive, but in the meantime, in the half-light, all was eerily quiet.

It was during this period of uninterrupted calm that doubts began to form. Up until then there'd been no time for reflection. Now there was too much, and his mind began to swim with contradictions. Was this an act of responsibility? Or was it precisely the opposite? He didn't know – he was unused to such calculations. Was he being selfless or selfish? Again, he was unsure as prior to this moment he'd only ever thought of himself. Was he doing the right thing? What, in fact, *was* the right thing? How could he tell? He'd nothing to go on.

After half an hour of deliberation he was overcome by a feeling of panic and almost abandoned the whole scheme. His gloomy train of thought was broken by the rattle of a milk crate and the realisation that the boy was about to be discovered in a way he'd not anticipated. His misgivings instantly got the better of him and he hurriedly retrieved the box and its contents from the doorstep and tucked it under his arm. When the milk had been delivered, his anxiety subsided and he replaced it. Thankfully, the boy had not been disturbed, but it had been a close call. Soon, the dawn chorus began and he was grateful for the distraction.

At six-fifteen a light came on in the hallway, causing him to extinguish his latest cigarette and draw back into the shadows. The door cracked open and a hand appeared to withdraw the milk. At first he feared the box would be missed, but instead of closing, the door swung back and Elisabeth emerged in her housecoat and slippers. From his hiding place across the road Geoffrey watched as she inspected the package, found the envelope and took out the note, hastily reading it before running to the rickety gate and looking up and down the road. Finding the street empty, she returned to the porch and for a moment his heart was in his mouth until at last she picked up the bundle in the white shawl and took it inside.

He knew he could rely on her! He felt overcome with relief and had to physically prevent himself from dashing the thirty yards or so to her door and thanking her. That would have been a mistake. Right or wrong, selfish or not, the deed was done and he was not going to endanger it now.

He barely remembered the drive back to Hampstead. When he arrived, Marion was still asleep and the hush of the place was so at odds with the turmoil in his head that he felt the need to pour himself a scotch and sit on the sofa gulping at it in an attempt to calm down. When she eventually appeared around half past nine, it did not escape Marion's notice.

"You've started early..."

He immediately told her the reason. There was a chance she might protest and feel affronted by this slight to her mothering ability but her reaction to his news was quite the opposite.

"Thank God for that!"

And with that out of the way, he could spend the rest of the morning thinking through his words for Nurse Brodie.

I wanted a son. I had one, but I couldn't keep him.

That was all there was to it. It seemed so brief – but it was as close as he could get to the truth.

Six

Then he was back on the ward again. As usual, he was deprived of the assistance of his watch but he guessed it was early morning, just as it had been in his dream. The evidence appeared conclusive. The ward was bathed in a half-light and through the window to his right came the glimmer of dawn. A thick layer of air hung between the beds like a heavy blanket, muffling any sound. Had it been evening the place would have been full of visitors.

Over at the ward-sister's desk, the night light shone with a dull glow. At present the radio was off, but later, when the clock had crawled past seven, porridge would be served to the accompaniment of Wogan's breakfast banter. Fifty-odd years ago he'd been standing outside a house in New Malden – today he was in a hospital bed, waiting for the day to begin.

Last time it had been the violence of Marion's words that had woken him. Now it was the pain in his side. It had worsened during the night and he could tell it would take more than gritted teeth and the desire to remain conscious to get through it. Before long, medicine would be required. It was so severe that he wondered whether he'd actually slept at all and to alleviate the effects, he rolled over onto his side and drew his knees up towards his stomach.

In the opposite corner, the gnarled and pollarded tree that was Mrs Walker's hands thrust upwards against the grey. Across the aisle, the bald man with the crooked nose was barely discernible amongst the shadows, but his presence was confirmed by the gentle rise and fall of his chest beneath the sheets. There was comfort to be gained from these sights. They were his constant companions and it was good to know they'd all outlived the night – he with his cancer, the others with their respective ailments, whatever they might be. He'd no idea what they suffered from. They didn't talk, despite the fact that they were neighbours.

Could they survive? They surely couldn't all get out in one piece – sooner or later one of them would have to go. Who would be first? he wondered.

Another day was beginning, another day to endure, another day of hope. If only Frank would come! If only the boy might spare himself and make the effort. Then he could let go and slide into the welcoming arms of darkness. Then he wouldn't mind being first. To tell the truth, he might even volunteer...

He'd always meant to go back. He said he would a number of times and yet, like so many promises he'd make to himself and to others, the strength of it gradually faded until in the end it came to nothing. On the day he'd driven back from New Malden it was certainly in the back of his mind, although for the most part his thoughts were focused on the fact that the boy had been taken in. Then, as he crossed the river, his attention turned to Marion and to Hampstead and to what he might find when he got there and the further he travelled from New Malden, the more his motivation to return diminished. Thereafter, that was the way of it. North of the river he had one set of concerns, south of the river another. And to move from one to the next meant crossing a bridge, both physically and mentally, a task which was more often than not beyond him.

He'd meant to send money too. He'd said as much in the note he'd left in the box along with the child. That was a written promise, but it too fell by the wayside. It would have been easier to keep as he didn't need to cross the bridge to do it. All that was required was a cheque, an envelope and a stamp, followed by a short walk over the Heath to a post box, but there was always something to prevent it. Finances were tight, the flat wasn't cheap and besides, he was already paying maintenance. Wasn't that enough? Did she really need more? Possibly not – surely it was as easy to keep two children as it was to keep one. Finally, when he broke up with Marion and was forced to find a place of his own, the idea was out of the question.

Their separation was inevitable. With the boy gone, there was nothing to bind them together any more. They were not going to revert to their former relationship. Marion was true to her word and Geoffrey was not allowed near her. Matters came to a head during the course of the Commonwealth Games a year later.

After the debacle of Helsinki, he'd worked hard to redeem himself in the eyes of his employers and had been awarded the trip to Vancouver. This time he managed to board the plane without worry and his problems began on his return. On arriving back at the flat, he discovered that the locks had been changed and at half past ten in the evening he found himself standing on the doorstep with a fortnight's luggage watching the taxi he'd taken from the airport driving off into the night. Marion had shut him out. So when he finally turned up at the house in New Malden a month later, hoping for some form of reconciliation, it was hardly the selfless act he'd originally intended.

But by then it was too late and Elisabeth had already gone. The new tenant was a widow with a teenage daughter and they knew nothing of the previous occupants' whereabouts. *'Aven't a clue, mate. We don't come from round 'ere.* To make matters worse, he'd even taken some flowers. He thanked them for their trouble and left them the bouquet – he'd no further use for it.

And so his years in the wilderness began, his odyssey through middle age. Shunned by Marion, the boy given away and Elisabeth disappeared, there was nothing for him to cling to. He could not go back to Bristol. He was, on the face of it, lost.

There was always work of course, and with no other refuge he became driven by it, seeking to improve himself at every available opportunity. Vancouver was followed by Melbourne, then came Rome and Tokyo, and soon he'd been to every continent on earth. Eventually, he grew weary of it.

He had occasional affairs, although none of them endured. And none of them ended in pregnancy – a fact for which he was grateful; he'd had enough of children.

But if there was one continual thread, it was his desire to find Elisabeth and thereby meet his son. For the most part he was occupied, but at times of inactivity or boredom his thoughts would revert in that direction and he would determine to do something about it. It was usually no more than a daydream, but there were sporadic attempts at action. He tried the solicitors she'd used for the divorce, but they declined to divulge any details. On a trip to Bristol to visit Georgina, he took time out to go to the house in Brislington where he received short shrift from an irate father.

You! You're the scoundrel that ruined my daughter. I don't know how you've got the gall to turn up here. I'm damned if I'll tell you a thing.

Crouched behind him, the mother looked far more contrite – a fact which gave him hope – but nothing immediately came from it.

Despite these setbacks, the flame that burned within him continued to flicker and would occasionally burst into life. And rather than diminishing, its power got stronger as he grew older. He came to realise that if something didn't happen soon, it might never happen at all and so as time went by he became ever more determined until eventually it became a crusade.

Many years later he finally received his reward when he went back to the house in Brislington for a second visit. Arthur had passed on, leaving Dorothy to continue alone. Desperate for company and conversation, she'd let him in and they'd talked for over an hour. Yes, of course she knew the whereabouts of her daughter – and those of her grandchildren. At last, after some cajoling on his part, she came up with an address. Elisabeth had gone north and was now living in York.

By then he'd retired and had bought a bungalow in the country. Having given it a couple of days' thought, he cleared some space on the kitchen table, sat down and penned the following letter.

East Dereham, 14th July 1990

My dearest Elisabeth,

I'm sure it will come as a surprise for you to receive a letter from me after all these years. It's taken me so long to find you! Dorothy gave me your address – I hope you don't mind.

Well, here I am, on my own, and living in the middle of nowhere. I've stopped working now and I've retreated into the depths of East Anglia. God knows why! There's nothing here. It's so different from the hustle and bustle of London. Do you remember those days? Perhaps not. Anyway, somehow I've managed to survive, although the last few years have not been at all easy.

So how are you? Your mother tells me that you're on your own too. That must be dreadful, I know how hard it can be. Did you never remarry?

(Dorothy had said not but she'd not been entirely lucid on the point and he hadn't been sure whether to believe her.)

Whatever made you move up north? Did you find someone and did he take you away? Not that I need to know of course, all I want to hear is that you're alright.

And what about the boy? How is he? Dorothy says he's in the Army. I daresay he's a fine young man to be serving his country like that and I expect you're terribly proud. Some news of him would be good. It's been a long time and I've heard nothing. Does he ever ask about me? A letter would be fine, although better still get him to ring me and then we can speak direct. I'll put the number overleaf. One day we might all meet up again, you never know.

Elisabeth, I'm truly sorry, I really am. I know I've behaved badly in the past, but if I know you at all I'm sure you have it in you to forgive me. Can we not at least be friends again like we were before? Here we are approaching the ends of our lives and it seems silly not to make some effort at reconciliation before it's too late. Will you at least write to me? It would give me some hope. I should really like to

hear from you.
  Yours, in expectation,
  Your ever-loving Geoffrey.

When he read it over he thought the final passage might be a little overdone. But he hadn't waited almost forty years just to be diffident and he wasn't going to hold back on it now. Besides, he wasn't minded to do much in the way of revision. He was used to the immediacy of broadcasting live – a fact which had made him lazy in this regard – and anyway, he thought it better to express what he truly felt rather than run the risk of diluting his message through constant refinement. The trick was then to post it as soon as possible so as not to give time for reflection. And whether it was his zeal to make contact or the excess of emotion he displayed that betrayed him, there never was a reply.

He'd continued his efforts nonetheless. A thorough search of the telephone directory for the area yielded a number and at last a conversation began. But Elisabeth would no more give him access to Frank than she would agree to meet and the best he could come up with was another number and Pat. His daughter seemed more willing to talk but it all took so much time and there was still no contact with the boy. At times he pressed too hard – at which point Pat would become exasperated with him so he was forced to leave off until things had calmed down.

And so it had gone on, with no prospect of resolution.

He let go for a moment and the pain surged through his side. Somewhere deep within him a process that had begun a few months ago, a few years ago, perhaps even from birth, was finally taking its toll. To try and evade it and distract from his fears, he'd been telling himself a story. But now he had run out of words and there was no more story to tell.

He clenched his teeth, sucked in his aching stomach and hauled himself up the bed. Beneath the heavy blanket his bones creaked in protest. What, if anything, had this life of his taught him? What had he learnt that was of any use? Elisabeth and the boy – he'd made so many mistakes. If only he could have his time over again. But that was all in the past and there was no point dwelling on it now. He'd transgressed and the punishment meted out to him was to lie in a hospital bed in some neglected corner of the world and suffer the pain that was his.

If only Frank would come! Then he might redeem himself. Why, at this last time of asking, did the boy continue to deny him?

"Frank!"

Suddenly, the name that was in his mind was the sound on his lips and he realised he may have spoken it out loud. He searched the ward for clues. Across the aisle the bald man with the crooked nose remained obstinately unmoved. In the far corner, Mrs Walker's stumps swayed gently back and forth. A day or so before, she'd cried out for her daughter and he'd despised her for it. Had he just cried out for his son?

Over at the ward-sister's desk he caught sight of a brief movement beneath the night light. Flickering neon tubes burst into life and the ward became fully lit. Was this the normal break of day or had he triggered some disturbance? Somewhere hidden from view, the clock hand moved past seven, the ward radio clicked on and the smooth, urbane voice of Jim Reeves broke out amongst the beds.

In a moment, the quiet voice of reason with her honeyed tones would emerge out of the shadows and plump up his pillows.

Why don't you let me make you a little bit more comfortable, Mr Jones?

But he didn't want comfort – at least, not of that kind. What he wanted was his son! The comfort *she* offered was the painless oblivion that came out of a syringe. He feared the silent prick of the needle and instead of breakfast, the insidious ingestion of drugs. His stomach pleaded for relief – but he wasn't ready, he needed more time.

Too late, too late! His guts ground within him like broken glass. Soon he'd be forced to take his morphine...

Part Six

Saturday 8th October

One

Frank was sitting at their usual table in the coffee shop. As Pat walked across from the till, he turned to face her. "You're late."

It was true, she'd been held up in a meeting and had almost run across the access road to get there. Funny how he could always find a way of placing her at a disadvantage. Although today, she was not to be put off.

"Some of us have work to do, you know."

"Tell me about it."

She set her tray down and stowed her purse away in her handbag before taking her seat. "So, how is she?"

She already knew the answer, or could at least guess at it, but had posed the question to initiate some form of conversation. Her intention was to coax Frank out of the sullen and laconic state he'd fallen into and it seemed the best way to try and engage him. The subject of their mother's wellbeing was the one topic she could rely on to provoke a response and although Elisabeth's condition was hardly likely to have changed, there was something important she wanted to tell her brother and she needed to prepare the ground in advance.

Frank shuffled in his seat.

"She's fine. Another couple of weeks and she'll be ready to come home."

Another couple of weeks? What was he talking about? Why did he persist in deluding himself? Elisabeth was never coming home – not now, not soon, not ever. When was he going to admit to it and face the facts? Not that he ever had about anything.

She's not coming back, Frank. You may as well get used to that now. I don't know why you can't see it.

The words stuck in her throat, held back by his stifling presence. In the silences that invariably followed, the silences he so cultivated and enjoyed, she thought she could hear herself breathing. It was not a comfortable feeling.

293

"So what is it this time?" he demanded.

She'd come on an important mission, this was her last chance, the last throw of the dice, but he made it all sound so dull.

The last time they'd got together he'd caught her on the hop but today she'd come prepared. When she and Elisabeth had been discussing Frank, they'd sat at the kitchen table in her mother's house. Now she and Frank were discussing Elisabeth, they'd reverted to the coffee shop. Ever since their mother had gone into the nursing home, Pat had been denied access to Balfour Terrace. Frank did not allow her to enter the sanctuary. It had to be protected, preserved in his mother's memory. To tell the truth, she'd found it rather tiresome and had grown weary of his antics. Perhaps that was why she'd chosen this particular moment to give him a wake-up call. Steeling herself against his wrath, she pushed the letter across the green vinyl surface that lay between them.

"I thought you should see this."

Frank gave a sigh of exasperation and drew the letter toward him. He'd already decided on the nature of its contents before he'd even opened it. It was obviously a last-gasp plea from Geoffrey for him to go to the hospital so the old man could ingratiate himself before he said his final goodbyes. If so, it would go straight in the bin. There would be no such visit, he'd made that clear from the start. It had been his steadfast response to everything Pat had thrown at him. Over the last three weeks she'd subjected him to a constant stream of pleas, delivered with an increasing sense of urgency over the telephone. So much so that he'd grown wary of answering it but had felt it necessary in case it related to Elisabeth. The awkwardness of taking calls in the corridor at work was always an embarrassment.

Look, I've told you not to ring me here.

But he's dying, Frank. The nurses say he won't last much longer.

What's that got to do with me?

He's your father, for God's sake!

He'd only agreed to this further get-together with great reluctance. His every instinct told him to say no, but there'd been something in Pat's voice that had suggested a higher importance, and in the end he'd given in. It was a decision he was beginning to regret and the letter would be nothing more than the latest ploy in her long campaign. He fingered it carelessly as if it were of no consequence.

"So?"

"Aren't you going to read it?"

"No."

"Aren't you even going to look at it?"

"Why should I?"

"If you could just bring yourself to try, you might find out."

Frank gave another long sigh of boredom. If he must...

He turned the letter over to inspect the envelope and noticed it wasn't addressed to him as he'd expected, but rather to his mother. His air of apathy immediately evaporated and scrabbling to pull out the enclosure, he folded open the letter and began to read.

My dearest Elisabeth...

The address at the top of the page told him its origin but his eyes still shot to the bottom for confirmation.

Your ever-loving Geoffrey.

The words in-between he could guess at, and as much as he told himself to read it carefully and take in every line, in the panic that had now set in he found himself skimming through it so as to reach the conclusion more quickly. Certain words inevitably jumped out at him, such as *one day we might all meet up again* and *reconciliation*, and by the time he reached the end he felt quite sick with disgust. Beneath the table, resting against his thigh, he found his hand had started shaking.

How could this have happened? He'd been so vigilant – or so he thought. For the last two years he'd taken a leaf out of Karen's book and had intercepted every item of mail intended for his mother in order to prevent just such an eventuality. How could this have slipped through his defences? The bile of failure rose inside him and growing ever more angry at his own imagined shortcomings, he was bound to turn on Pat.

"Where did this come from?"

"I found it in her purse."

"In her purse? What the hell were you doing looking in her purse?"

These were the kind of privileges Frank reserved for himself.

"It was on the floor by her chair. She must have dropped it. The letter fell out when I picked it up."

This was another of Pat's lies. The letter had actually been in her possession for some time but it was not a fact she wanted to admit to. When Elisabeth had finally shown it to her, she'd also extracted a promise. *Whatever you do, don't let Frank know about it – it'll only upset him.* She was breaking that promise now, but the circumstances were extreme and in her current state of mind her mother would be none the wiser. Once it came out, Frank was sure to subject her to extensive questioning and so she'd carefully prepared her story. She'd concluded that it would be easier if things were seen to come directly from Elisabeth – Frank would never castigate his mother. But if he ever thought that Pat was responsible...

There was more to come.

"I also found a photograph."

"Photograph? What photograph?"

"It's a picture of the two of them walking along the front at Weston-super-Mare. Before they got married, I suppose."

"And?"

"I left it in her purse. I didn't take it as I thought she might miss it."

This was also a lie. The real reason was that she was sure the sight of it would only incense Frank still further. That was something she was keen to avoid. He was growing hotter by the minute and as like to put two and two together and make five. For the time being, four would do just fine and the mere mention of it was enough.

"I knew it!" His fist thumped the table, causing Pat's cup to rattle in its saucer. "I knew the old bastard would get to her one way or the other."

"Keep your voice down, Frank, for goodness sake. People will hear you." Pat looked round and rearranged the components of her tea tray in an attempt to restore calm.

At the next-door table, a family of four had arrived and were tucking into jacket potato with assorted fillings. The sound of his voice caused their heads to turn, their mouths hung open to reveal their half-chewed contents.

Frank was oblivious. He didn't care. He didn't care about his father and he didn't care what people thought of him. All he cared about was his mother.

Somewhere in the tangled darkness of it all he began to suspect a plot. "Something's been going on."

"No it hasn't. Nothing's been 'going on', Frank, I assure you," Pat was quick to respond.

"Yes it has. Don't lie to me." He snarled defiantly like a cornered animal. "Something's been going on behind my back and I haven't been told about it."

"Nothing's going on. Look, the letter's fifteen years old for a start, how can anything be going on?"

He snatched the letter up and looked at it again, more carefully this time. It was true, and in his haste to get to the bottom of the affair he'd failed to notice the date. But in some ways that was worse. Not only had something been going on without his knowledge, but it had been going on for years. All the more reason for him to get angry.

"This is your doing." He pointed accusingly at his sister.

"No, honestly, I swear I had nothing to do with it."

"Yes you did, of course you did. You're the one that's been

talking to him. You and your bloody interfering ways."

"I never meant any harm."

"Well, never mind what you meant. I warned you to stay out of it and now look what's happened."

"Nothing's 'happened', Frank," Pat protested.

"Yes it has. He's wormed his way back in, just like I knew he would. Can't you see? Next thing you know he'll be up here knocking on her door."

"Don't be ridiculous. He can't – he's dying for goodness sake. He's not going anywhere."

"Don't you believe it. I don't trust him further than I could throw him. Jesus Christ!" Frank buried his head in his hands, his elbows resting on the vinyl. "You stupid bitch – you stupid, stupid bitch!"

At the adjacent table, the family of four had resumed their meal but their ears remained pricked, waiting for the next revelation.

"I should have known! He'll be up here any minute, you'll see. He'll ruin everything."

"You're over-reacting." Pat took a firm grip on her tray, just in case.

"I'm over-reacting, am I?" Frank straightened up and wagged a censoring finger. "Well, let me tell you something. Someone's got to react. Someone's got to *do* something. Someone's got to look out for her. And it's not going to be you, is it?"

It was the same old taunt he'd levelled at her for years. Pat declined to respond, staring deep into the cup she'd succeeded in rescuing.

Suddenly, he was standing up from the table as if something inside him had snapped.

"Right, that's it. I'm going."

"Going? Going where?"

"Where the bloody hell do you think? I'm going to sort this out once and for all."

For a moment she'd thought he meant home.

"What, now?"

"Now, tomorrow, as soon as I can. I'll get some time off."

She gave him a quizzical look.

"Well, it's hardly going to wait, is it?" he continued. Then, with a sarcastic sneer, "Not if he's *dying*, that is."

Pat pursed her lips and bore the shaft in silence. Even if she'd felt like it, there was no point in arguing. Frank would do whatever Frank would do, never mind what she said. Once he'd made up his mind...

He was already on his way out. Halfway through the exit door, his carrier bag swinging against the glass, a final sisterly thought occurred and she too stood up to deliver it, calling out as he left.

"Frank?"

But the door had closed behind him before he could hear her and the intended remark remained buried.

Don't do anything you might regret...

At the nearby table, the family of four conferred hurriedly amongst themselves, then turned to face her, seeking an explanation.

Pat smiled politely back. She'd grown used to excusing her brother's unpredictable behaviour. He was usually rude and comparatively wordless, but occasionally, when pushed to the limit, a violent temper would explode from within and spill out into the world. It was as if the peace of a sleeping giant had been disturbed. Once awake, it would roar with anger and somewhere deep inside lay a capacity to cause damage. If it were ever released, who could tell what might happen? You never knew with Frank...

Meanwhile, a subdued calm had returned to the coffee shop. Pat stared blankly out of the window as her brother made his laboured way across the car park and back to Do It All. From the checkout till behind her came the reassuring sound of coinage dropping into a tray. She took a sip from her steadied cup and sighed. She'd succeeded in rousing the giant – but would it be enough?

He's your father, for God's sake...

Pat's words were still ringing in his ears a day and a half later as he sat staring fixatedly at the road ahead. In the outside lane cars sped past while he motored on at a steady sixty, searching for the exit sign. He was anxious not to make a mistake and his hands tightened on the wheel.

After their rendezvous in the coffee shop, he'd spent the whole of the following day brooding amongst the copper pipes and fittings at work while he tried to come to terms with his decision. His sullen mood, although not unusual, had not gone unnoticed.

"Wakey, wakey! There's a war on, you know," his supervisor had quipped. But the joke had failed to have the desired effect and he'd continued to appear depressed. "So, is there a problem you'd like to share with us, Frank? Or are you going to keep it all to yourself?"

"I want a day off."

"Don't we all, pal, don't we all. And what makes you think you're so special?"

"As a matter of fact, my father's dying. I need to go and see him."

"Ah." His supervisor moderated his tone. "Well that's a different matter. I'm sorry to hear it. You should have told us before. We'll make it compassionate leave. Take as long as you want."

"Just a day – that'll be enough."

Or so he hoped.

And now, here he was, halfway down the A1 and looking for the A17.

The night before he'd almost relented and had rung Pat up late in the evening.

"If you're so bloody keen about this, why aren't you going?"

It irked him to think that she was the one who'd made all the running, and yet it was he who was taking the action.

"I thought we'd discussed that. I thought you said you were going."

He had, and at the time he'd meant it, but in the cold light of day it didn't seem like such a good idea.

"Anyway," she continued, "I've rung the hospital now and told them to expect you."

"So? That doesn't mean you couldn't go instead."

"Look." His sister sounded tired and there was an edge to her voice. "I've told them you're going and that's that. I couldn't go tomorrow in any event. I'm busy, I've got a day full of meetings and it's my turn to do the shopping."

Meetings? The whole bloody world had meetings! Why was it that when you wanted something done, everyone was in a meeting? And as for the shopping, that seemed a pretty trivial excuse.

"Can't Terry take care of it?"

"Terry's got his own issues." It was a subject on which Pat had seemed rather touchy lately. "Anyway, that's not the point. Geoffrey doesn't want me, I've known that for years. He's never shown the slightest bit of interest in me. It would be a complete waste of time my going. I'm just a point of contact as far as he's concerned, it's you he really wants to see."

And from the little he knew about her dealings with him, Frank couldn't deny it was the truth. An uncomfortable truth, all the same.

Besides, Pat couldn't be trusted on such matters. He feared that if she were confronted, she would meekly acquiesce to anything that Geoffrey might ask of her. And given the nature of his mission, i.e. to warn the man off, something much firmer was required. And yet he still equivocated, protesting right down to the last until she finally lost patience with him.

"Why can't you just go, for God's sake? It's not going to kill you, is it?" In the coffee shop there'd been the restraint imposed by a public place, but now it seemed she could lash out all the more easily. "All he's asking is a day of your time. Can't you at least give him that? It's not the end of the world, for christsake."

And yet, for all he knew, it might be...

The day itself was bright but cold. A stiff easterly breeze had sprung up and a line of white cotton-wool clouds scudded across the landscape. In the country beyond Sleaford the harvest had begun, the flat fields ripped of their crop, turning from the green and gold of summer to an amorphous winter brown. Here and there, giant tractors clawed the soil. The ritual movement of the earth, the ever-changing kaleidoscope of sky and cloud, all this he sensed would take place whether he was there or not. What effect he might have remained in doubt.

It wasn't that Pat had pricked his conscience. He'd no conscience to prick in that regard, he owed his father nothing. But her continual goading seemed to have struck a chord within him.

The ball went over the gate and into the cow field again.

Your turn! said Paul, pointing.

Frank looked into the field. There was the ball, lying in much the same place as it had before. And there were the cows, munching.

I'm not going, he said.

But it's your turn, said Paul, you have to go.

No I don't, said Frank. His feet remained glued to the gravel path.

Paul stood with his hands on his hips.

I reckon you're frit, he said.

Frit? Here was another word, a short one this time but just as strange.

What does that mean? asked Frank, although he'd already guessed.

It means you're frightened, said Paul. You're frightened of cows! Ha, ha, ha! Frit, frit, frit!

And he danced up and down, pointing.

Shut up, said Frank. Just shut up will you. I'm not listening.

He put his hands over his ears and ran back to the van. He didn't always like Paul's new words.

Was that why he'd joined the Army? To prove he wasn't afraid? If so, then that had been a failure too for he'd no more faced up to the demands of a military existence then he had to cows, or Karen, or alcohol, or anything at all for that matter. In his struggle to come to terms with life, it had all slipped by like some ethereal mist that he could never quite grasp hold of.

Mr Johnson, said the sergeant major.

Yes, said Frank.

Yes SIR, said the sergeant major.

Yes SIR, said Frank.

The sergeant major cleared his throat.

I'm not sure I like you, Mr Johnson. I'm not sure I like you at all. In fact, I think you're a bloody disgrace.

He waited for a response. When it failed to arrive he decided to prompt one instead.

What are you, Mr Johnson?

I'm a bloody disgrace, Sergeant Major, said Frank.

I'm a bloody disgrace, Sergeant Major SIR, said the sergeant major.

I'm a bloody disgrace, Sergeant Major SIR, repeated Frank.

That's better, said the sergeant major.

He paced up and down the room, then came and stood in front of Frank, twitching his swagger stick underneath his nose.

You don't get it, do you? he said.

I don't get what? said Frank.

About being in the Army, said the sergeant major. You see, you think you've come here to be brave and take a few pot shots at some foreign Johnny. You think the Army's going to look after you and put a rifle in your hands and say 'Go on son, there you go. Have a go at him, knock him over if you can.' Then you can go home and tell your mother all about it and she'll say how bloody wonderful you are and she'll pat you on the head and give you tea and cakes. Well, it's not like that.

It's not? said Frank, puzzled.

No, it bloody well isn't, said the sergeant major. I'll tell you what it's like. You haven't come here to be a hero, Mr Johnson, you've come here to do whatever I bloody well tell you, that's what. And the sooner you realise that, the better. Do you understand me?

Yes, Sergeant Major.

Yes, Sergeant Major SIR.

Yes, Sergeant Major SIR.

Good, said the sergeant major. You see, I don't want there to be any trouble. I don't like it when there's trouble. You're not going to give me any trouble are you, Mr Johnson?

No sir, said Frank.

Well I'm really glad about that, said the sergeant major. Because I'd hate to think what would happen if you did.

But here at last was a chance to be brave, here was a chance to do something truly heroic. Two hundred miles away (a safe enough distance in his mind) an old man lay dying, unloved and unwanted. Surely now he could say what he liked and speak the truth without fearing the consequences?

I'll tell him. I'll show him who's boss.

What did it matter that it was his father? Anyone in like circumstances would do. And what did it matter what was said? In a few weeks' time (less, if Pat were to be believed) the old man would be gone and whatever had passed between them would have gone with him. And if things didn't work out that way he could always walk away, get back into the car and escape back to Yorkshire and no one would be any the wiser. He didn't see how he could lose. And all this to protect Elisabeth, to prevent her from enduring what he imagined she must dread, contact with Geoffrey.

Contact with Geoffrey...

His mouth parched at the thought and the old familiar dryness returned to his throat. Despite his apparent confidence, ancient anxieties remained. He could really do with a drink, just to steady himself down. In the glove box of the car he'd kept a hip flask, purely for emergencies...

He began to feel a rising sense of panic. To try and overcome it, he convinced himself it was hunger rather than the desire for alcohol that moved him and he stopped for breakfast at a wayside café.

He'd left the house first thing that morning and had been on the road for two and a half hours, driven initially by the same resolve that he'd shown in the coffee shop two days earlier. But the further from home he travelled, the more his determination waned as if he were gradually changing his mind in line with the gradual change in the scenery. Compared to the night before last, he now felt as flat as the fields and as he left the café and stood alone with the busy companionship of the A1 far behind him, staring out at the vast expanse of Norfolk, he began to experience a nervousness that progressively undermined his intent.

For the last twenty-four hours, ever since his request for the day off had been granted, he'd inwardly been planning a speech. He'd rehearsed it several times at home and then in the car that morning. He imagined himself standing at his father's bedside, delivering it in a confident tone. He might even raise an accusatory finger, or his voice, or in extreme circumstances, both.

Don't imagine for one moment that I've come here for your sake. After all you've done you can't expect me to turn up just to listen to you say you're sorry. I'm warning you – stay away from her.

In front of the mirror in his mother's bedroom it had sounded impressive. But in the space of the great outdoors it suddenly seemed hollow and ineffectual. And it was no coincidence that although he'd eaten tolerably well and his stomach no longer felt empty, his hand had once again started to shake.

Soon his resolve would be tested further. Beyond Kings Lynn the road grew slow and tortuous, winding its way across unbroken countryside. Gaggles of traffic slackened to a crawl behind the inevitable farm vehicles, and even this late in the season the occasional caravan blocked the route. And all the while, his unease gnawed at him and he sensed his courage ebbing away.

He gripped the wheel still harder and told himself he must resist these fears. He must not weaken now, not at this the crucial moment. It all depended on this one thing. The health and safety of his mother and his promise of abstinence would all be washed away if he failed to stay strong. A phrase ran through his mind, and like some sacred mantra he began to repeat it to himself, over and over.

I'm going to finish it today, one way or the other.

Two

He arrived at the hospital feeling creased and somewhat jaded from his journey. It was now four hours since he'd left York – long enough to ready himself he'd have thought, but suddenly here he was, somewhere on the outskirts of Norwich feeling horribly unprepared. To add to his sense of uncertainty, a few spots of rain had begun to appear on his windscreen. Dithering as to whether to use his wipers, he'd almost missed the entrance to the car park.

The building he'd come to call on was located on the outskirts of the city. Brand new and of modern construction, it was built predominantly of brick, although the entrance was formed exclusively from glass and steel. Once inside, it opened out into a wide foyer beneath an atrium that towered up to the sky. This, it seemed, was the hub from which all things were reached. Around the edges, a succession of corridors led off to the various departments. Up above, if all else failed, was a route to a higher place...

It was eleven o'clock on a Saturday morning, peak visiting time, and the foyer was thronged with friends and relatives seeking their loved ones. A queue had formed at the reception desk and immediately in front of him a large lady in a red dress was manoeuvring a buggy with child.

"Coronary Care Unit?" she enquired, languidly shifting her chewing gum from one side of her mouth to the other.

The desk clerk, a young woman with wayward hair, smoothed a strand behind her ear and pointed.

"Through the double doors. It's on the second floor. Turn right at the top of the stairs." Then, eyeing the pushchair and its contents, "You could always take the lift..."

Out on the fringes, a steady flow of bodies moved up and down the long corridors, looking for the places where the other bodies lay. Like ants in an anthill, the black dots scurried backwards and forwards. To Frank, it seemed more like a shopping mall than a hospital.

Now then, said Mr Thorpe, the neon light dancing on his bald patch. I want you to run me an errand.

An errand? Frank hadn't come to school to run errands, he ran enough of those at home.

Take this note (Mr Thorpe reached into his jacket pocket and fished out a grubby piece of paper) and give it to Mrs Clark in 4B. You know Mrs Clark, don't you?

Frank shook his head. He didn't know Mrs Clark and he didn't know 4B. And even if he had, he'd have shaken his head anyway, it was his habitual reaction to everything.

Ha, ha, ha! laughed Mr Thorpe, the neon light bouncing up and down like a circus clown. You will have your little jokes, won't you, Frank? Now run along, there's a good boy. I haven't got time to argue.

He put his hand on the small of Frank's back and propelled him firmly toward the set of flappy doors.

Frank inwardly resisted. Why him? Why did he have to go? What had happened to Jonathon? Wasn't he supposed to be the favourite when it came to the running of errands? He reluctantly pushed the door open and entered the long passageway. Somewhere down there, a long way from safety, Mrs Clark lurked in a strange room, waiting for her note...

"Hello? Can I help you?"

He'd reached the front of the queue and the desk clerk was calling. Caught unawares, he blurted out a name.

"Mr Jones..."

"Yes, Mr Jones. What can I do for you?"

No! Anything but that! The misunderstanding brought him quickly back to the present and he hurried to correct her.

"No, *my* name is Johnson. I've come to *see* Mr Jones."

"Of course." She gave a busy smile of condescension, the wayward strand of hair flopping forward. "First name?"

It seemed an unnecessary question, but for all the desk clerk knew there could be a dozen Mr Joneses in the building. There was a moment of difficulty as Frank struggled with the word.

"Geoffrey…"

"Thank you." She consulted her screen, then gave directions. "Mason Ward. First floor. Through the double doors," (she pointed, but he already knew where they were) "go to the end of the corridor, up the stairs in front of you and it's on your left. You can't miss it."

Perhaps not – but he could always try…

"Next!"

He moved away from the desk and out into the middle of the foyer, letting the crowd flow past him like an ebbing tide. He could feel them sucking him forward and just as on a beach where he would dig his toes into the sand as a child to resist the pull of the water, so now he pushed his feet against the floor. He wasn't ready. He'd had fifty-two years to prepare for this moment and yet still he wasn't ready! A sweat had broken out on his brow and his hand was shaking again.

He needed to compose himself. A sign for the café hovered above his head, but he'd had enough coffee for one day already and rather than set off in that direction he followed the indicator for the gents. He thought to award himself a wash and brush-up prior to his ordeal but he found he couldn't face himself in the mirror and instead sought an empty cubicle where he slumped down onto the seat and held his head in his hands.

What was he doing? Why on earth had he allowed himself to be talked into this? His leg had started jiggling and he stretched his hand out toward his pocket where he'd stowed the flask from the glove compartment. If push came to shove…

It was all Pat's fault, damn her. If it hadn't been for her constant nagging…

It was too late now of course, but he realised he should have persuaded her to come with him – that would have settled her hash. Then she'd have had to face up to what she'd been going on about for all these years instead of hiding behind that bloody job of hers. *I can't. I've got an important meeting.* How many times had he heard that excuse? She was more likely swanning around Tesco while Terry was off taking the boys to football, or whatever else it was they did on Saturday mornings. So once again, it was left up to him, just as it was with his mother.

My dearest Elisabeth...

He fetched out the letter and read it through again in an attempt to bolster his strength. How could the old man say such things? How could he, after all these years, suddenly turn up out of the blue and expect to be taken back in? What sort of fools did he think they were? And then, to arrogantly presume as to his standing.

Your ever-loving Geoffrey.

Frank felt the bile returning. It was all becoming clear to him again. This was the reason he'd come all this way – to give out the answer the letter so richly deserved and to tell the old man to sod off.

I'll show him who's boss.

Something stirred in the recesses of his mind and his brain fumbled round to locate it. He forced himself to remember until, in the echoing hush of the toilet cubicle, the opening words of the speech he'd been preparing returned to him.

Don't imagine for one moment...

That he should be able to recall it now gave rise to a sudden surge of confidence. The hand which had been hovering danger-ously close to his pocket returned to his thigh and although he could still feel the tremors, it remained under control. All it wanted was one supreme effort and it would all be over. He pressed himself upward, took a deep breath and pushed open the door of the cubicle.

Mason Ward was as easy to find as the desk clerk had suggested. She was right, he couldn't miss it. In fact, it was so simple that he found himself feeling disappointed. It would have been better had it been harder as the more difficult the task he was undertaking, the greater his sense of self-righteousness would be in achieving it. He'd already given up a day off work, a precious day, a Saturday, and they didn't come round that often. But that in itself was not enough. To justify what he was doing, there needed to be other, important, sacrifices.

It was not a big ward, half a dozen beds at most, laid out in two neat rows facing each other. At the far end, a large window looked out onto a small area of garden. Not that the patients could see anything of it as they all reclined in prone positions staring at the wall or the ceiling, although here and there one or two had attempted to haul themselves up in order to greet the day. There was a lingering smell of linoleum, mixed with disinfectant. It brought back memories of a barrack room on the day of inspection.

At the entrance, he presented himself at the ward-sister's desk. It was currently unoccupied. Scattered papers lay bathed in a pale glow beneath a desk light and from one side, a pair of radio speakers emitted the mellow strains of some country and western favourite.

He waited for a moment then pressed the bell.

A door swung open and a nurse appeared from the private office at the back. She was black, the colour of her skin as deep as polished mahogany and contrasting sharply with the whiteness of her uniform. When she spoke her voice was as smooth as silk. "Is there someone you've come to see?"

There was a warmth in her welcome that meant Frank had no choice but own up. "Geoffrey Jones..."

"Ah," breathed the voice. "You'll be Mr Johnson. We've been expecting you. Your father's very ill you know."

Of course he knew – had it been otherwise he wouldn't have considered coming.

"I think he's asleep at the moment. You can always wait. Let's go and see."

She led him out onto the ward. Her walk was as smooth as her voice and her feet seemed to slide silently across the polished floor.

They passed between the rows of beds. In the far left corner an elderly woman mumbled to herself as she lay crumpled between her sheets, the gnarled fingers of her arthritic hands tied together in an inextricable knot. In the bed next to her an elderly man with a bald head sprawled on his back, snoring gently, his thin beak-like nose pointing upward to the ceiling. A pair of naked feet protruded beyond the end of his blanket. Could this unlikely figure be his father? Was this who he'd come all this way to see?

Apparently not. The nurse was guiding him to the opposite side.

"Here..." She stopped at the last bed but one on the right. It had recently been curtained off and she began to draw back the hangings. "He had a shot of morphine about half past nine this morning and went straight off," she explained. "It usually lasts around two hours so he should come round at any minute. He'll be a bit groggy at first so you may have to be patient. I'll fetch you a chair." She arranged somewhere for him to sit and made him feel comfortable. "I'll leave you two together then. I expect you've got a lot to talk about. You know where to find me if you need me."

Her duty done, she glided effortlessly back to her desk.

Suddenly Frank felt rather alone, abandoned in the middle of a room filled with dying people. Round and about the beds, loved ones comforted their sick relatives while from the speakers at the front desk, the country and western singer continued to bemoan her fate. In time to her measured crooning, he imagined he could hear the shuffle of slippered feet leading their wearers gently toward their graves. She soon reached her crescendo and he could allow himself to focus on the scene immediately in front of him.

He was confronted by a metal-framed hospital bed covered

with a plain mattress. To his right, a bank of electronic cabinets blinked steadily on and off. An array of wires and tubes lay draped across the floor and at the other end of them rested the body of a man dressed in a surgical gown, lying on his side and facing in the opposite direction, his knees drawn up to his stomach. Untidy strands of lank, greying hair were plastered round his head while below them his cheeks sprouted a scraggly beard. It appeared to have grown out of neglect rather than purpose and obscured a face that was grimaced with pain. Beneath the gown, instead of the fullness of flesh, Frank could sense bare ribs and an emaciated skin stretched over a wasted frame. The general impression was one of great suffering – perhaps Christ had looked like this when taken down from the cross.

It should have inspired his compassion, but Frank had no pity that could be evoked by this sight. His reaction was initially one of shock – he'd not expected anything so frail. The picture he had of his father was of someone far more robust, a tall good-looking man with blond, floppy hair and of strong and muscular appearance. He'd not admitted it to Pat, but his mother had once shown him the photograph she kept in her purse of the two of them, her and Geoffrey, walking arm in arm along the front at Weston-super-Mare.

This is your father. You never met him but I believe he was fond of you...

What nonsense! He'd never shown the slightest interest, not until it suited him, not until he wanted something, not until now when it was too late. His mother was mistaken. Her remark had been made at a time when she was barely in command of her senses, and although her powers of recollection were extensive, they were not always to be relied on. Besides, she'd always deferred to his memory – even in the photograph he towered dominantly over her and the length of his stride suggested the confidence with which he approached the world, taking it head on. You had to admit he'd been a fine figure of a man – any other son would have been proud.

But Geoffrey had become decrepit. Age and sickness had taken their toll and instead of a bright and healthy youth, the body that Frank now contemplated was that of an aged and exhausted man. The sight actually exalted him and rather than the pity most would have felt, the feeling it gave rise to was one of contempt. There was no battle to be had here, surely? There could be nothing to fear from this weak and dispirited creature. Where would the challenge come from? Any apprehension he'd been feeling began to melt away and was replaced by a growing sense of courage. He'd steeled himself to expect resistance, but now, if there was, he knew that all he had to do was to reach out and he could crush it.

But what of the old man's mental powers? His body may have decayed but perhaps he'd managed to retain some sharpness of mind. Or had that too withered away, just as it had with Elisabeth? Frank had no idea, they'd never spoken and the prostrate form that lay in front of him gave no clue. Although in the light of so much physical weakness, why should this concern him? If it came to the point and there *was* an argument, he knew he could shout his father down. And anyway, hadn't he prepared himself? Wasn't that what his speech was all about?

Don't imagine…

At this point the ward music changed and disturbed his concentration. He looked at his watch. He'd been sitting there for at least twenty minutes and as yet there'd been no meaningful movement. Now he came to think of it, in the last five minutes there'd been no discernible movement at all. Geoffrey's eyes were shut tight as if in sleep, his face still locked in the grimace with which Frank had found him. There was no semblance of peace here.

Across the way, two fleshy feet and the outline of a fish-fin nose stuck out while in the far corner, the woman with arthritic hands lay prone. Dust motes floated like tiny snowflakes in the light from the window and there was blessed quiet save for the muzak and the distant hum of visiting relatives. Next to him, an arm's length away, the cabinets pinged like radar, plumbing the hidden depths. Between them, Geoffrey's lifelines curved toward the bed.

What if the old man were in a coma? It looked as though he could be. There were cases on record where this sort of thing went on for months, if not years. How ironic would it be if at these, his final moments, it was Geoffrey who refused to talk while he, always the silent one, was bursting with words? So even now the old goat might thwart him and deny him his few seconds of glory. He could not let that happen. It must be resolved – he'd travelled too far to be foiled at the last.

I'm going to finish it today, one way or the other...

He began to feel angered by his father's refusal to wake and his anxiety was replaced by frustration. What he wanted now was to take his supine form by the shoulders and shake him into consciousness – then he could tell him what he thought. He'd even prepared a speech for christsake.

He leant forward and reached out a hand. But it was more than he dare. Like some Egyptian mummy, surely that fragile frame would break and crumble to dust beneath his fingers if he so much as touched it. So what if he wouldn't come round? There had to be a way...

But there was not and Frank's blood began to boil. Then all at once he was on his feet and lashing out, and the same boot which had sent a bay of copper pipes and fittings crashing to the floor in Do It All now connected with the leg of the bed. The metal frame jumped, the shock of it causing his standing foot to slip. His sudden rise made him feel giddy and he overbalanced, falling backwards into the cabinets. Screens and radar crashed to the ground, ripping the lifelines free. The peace of the ward was shattered as relatives looked up from their loved ones and stared in disbelief. The dust motes swirled in confusion.

Lying prostrate on the floor, Frank watched as the display screens relit – but the radar flat-lined, each ping echoing into an empty abyss, unreturned. A surge of adrenalin swept through him, beginning in the pit of his stomach and ending at the tips of his fingers. His hand was shaking again but this time it was not from the want of alcohol.

Something had happened, something terrible he was yet to understand. On the bed in front of him lay the body of a man. That hadn't changed – there was the same frail form, the same grimaced face – but where before he might have imagined a slight rise and fall in the surgical gown, now there was definitely none.

There was a short pause into which the muzak briefly intruded, then someone had the presence of mind to call out.

"Nurse? Nurse! Come quick! There's been an accident..."

Frank levered himself up. The chair on which he'd been sitting had toppled over and lay half across his chest. He pushed it to one side and got unsteadily to his feet.

Behind the reception desk, the door to the office flew open and the nurse rushed out, betraying her anxiety by running down the ward. These were unprecedented times, although her voice remained smooth as silk.

"Mr Johnson? Are you alright?"

Her broad black arm reached out to rescue his, but he brushed her aside.

"Yes, yes. I'm fine."

He didn't want comfort – or questions – he wanted out. His first reaction was to run – an old priority was asserting itself.

I must tell Mother...

The nurse was bending over his father's body. She turned to give him the news but he'd already broken free and was stumbling toward the exit, passing the vacant desk. Behind him all was commotion as the babbling commenced and the unofficial inquest began. *Did you see what happened?* It was at times like these, unscheduled moments in the course of local history, that communities drew together...

The nurse started after him and raised a hand to call him back, but she'd gone no distance at all before halting in her tracks. There were other, more important, matters for her to deal with – one of her patients required urgent attention. Around the bed Frank had so swiftly abandoned, they were already drawing the curtains.

He thought about taking the lift but abandoned the idea in view of the wait and took the stairs, two at a time. Within seconds he was bolting through the foyer where the girl with the wayward hair called out from the reception desk.

"Mr Johnson? We need to speak to you..."

But he'd gone, running on out into the car park and the wide open spaces of freedom. He reached the safety of his car and stopped to catch his breath, flinging himself against the bonnet.

Geoffrey was dead! Quite how it had happened, or why, he wasn't exactly sure – but here at last was an end to it. And the thing was, it had all taken so little...

He sensed that something had happened to his hands and he looked down to check. The tremors had ceased – added to which his stomach had stopped complaining and that hollow feeling that had followed him all the way from York had been replaced by an inner glow. He felt in his pocket, took out the hip flask and looked at it for a moment, then heaved it into the bushes.

I won't be needing that any more...

He stood upright and looked toward the heavens. Out here, the sky seemed a bolder shade of blue, the cotton-wool clouds whiter than before. It had stopped raining and in the fields beyond Sleaford the tractors would be turning the soil. The cyclical movement of earth and sky and cloud would continue, whether he was there or not, but in the bright afternoon sunshine of an autumn day, the world felt like a different place.

He took in a breath of fresh country air, drew his car keys from his pocket and prepared for the long journey home.

Three

They think I'm crazy.

How many times had she said that to herself? Today, probably five or six. This week, maybe dozens. And altogether since her arrival at the nursing home, possibly thousands. Far too many to count, in any event. It would all depend on how long she'd been there. So how long exactly *had* she been there? Despite her best intentions, Elisabeth struggled to remember. Like sand slipping between her fingers, it was facts like these that eluded her. She felt she'd been there all her life. Although once upon a time she thought she'd lived in a house – and before that, a caravan...

She was sitting in her accustomed place, the armchair, looking out of the window in what she thought of as her horrid, pokey little room. Out in the garden, blackbirds scuttled across the lawn, searching for their evening meal. They at least were real, but whatever existence she might have had beforehand seemed no more than her imagination, or perhaps the by-product of a dream. To her, reality was whether her feet were cold or what she'd eaten for tea (today it had been fish and she could still feel the presence of a bone that had lodged beneath her dentures). Reality was now, not in the past, and however much Frank tried to encourage her to tell him stories, that's all they were, stories, no more than the inventions of a febrile mind, things that came involuntarily into her head. As far as she was concerned they had no basis in fact – and they certainly bore no relevance to life in the nursing home, the life she led now, the life she felt she'd always led. And yet she was aware that in one of the compartments at the back of her purse, there was a photograph...

Her hands fidgeted in her lap. While they stayed empty there was always a sense of unease. She kept her purse stuffed down the side of her chair but she felt better if she could cling on to it, her fingers clasping it tight. Her great concern was that Danny would find it and take it away from her. He was always stealing her things. Who knew what he might fancy next?

Danny was a rogue, she was convinced of it. He was real enough. He was certainly not a figment of her past imagination – he was a solid part of her present. At any moment he would come sidling into her room, sizing her up with a furtive sideways glance.

I've come to do a bit of tidying up, Mrs Johnson. Or even, *Hello dear! Sheila thinks I should cut your toenails.*

She'd never asked for her toenails to be cut. But he could always find an excuse, that one. She'd complained to Sheila about him on more than one occasion.

I don't like him.

You don't like who?

That boy.

Which boy?

The boy that keeps coming into my room.

You mean Danny.

If that's what his name is.

Yes.

Well I don't like him.

I'm sorry about that, Mrs Johnson, but we need to have someone look after you. That's what we're here for.

Yes, but can't you find someone else?

Staff are very hard to come by these days, Mrs Johnson. I'll see what I can do.

But however much she went on about it, nothing ever changed. He still came in, snooping around.

And as to what style or shade his hair would be, that was anybody's guess. Sometimes he wore it in the shape of a quiff and dyed it lurid colours. Tomorrow he'd probably have shaved it all off and gone bald. It was all part of a plot to continually disguise himself and confuse her. He pretended to be her friend but she knew different, he was just out for what he could get. Why, only the other day he'd stolen her slippers! If it hadn't been for Frank...

She reached for the purse and looked for the photograph. It was still there, buried safely at the back. She fetched it out and there she was, aged twenty, walking along the seafront at Weston-super-Mare, arm in arm with a man. He was tall and tanned and handsome and a mop of long blond hair flopped across his forehead. She'd known him once, his name was Geoffrey. They'd been in love, or so she'd thought, but then he went away. He'd said that he'd come back, although he never did. He'd even written a letter asking if he could, but Frank would never have allowed it. He'd asked her for forgiveness, but what was there to forgive? Yes, he'd abandoned her and left her wanting, but look at what he'd given her – a memory, a child (two if she counted the boy). No need to forgive him for that. And of course he'd loved her! How could she think any different? There must be something to cling to amongst all this decay. That, and Frank – and Pat of course...

Soon, Frank would be here and they could begin their nightly custom. For a while she could sit and shade her eyes against the glare of the early-evening sunshine, watching the blackbirds (there was one now, underneath the bushes at the edge of the flowerbed). Shortly, after the clock had reached seven, she would hear his footsteps in the corridor next to her room and the door would click open. Then he would be with her, his hand on her shoulder, the touch of his lips on the top of her head.

Hello, Mum.

And after he'd checked around the room and made sure everything was alright, he'd draw the curtains, light the fire, switch on one of the table lamps and settle down for the evening and her trip down memory lane.

Do you remember...?

How she looked forward to those moments! They were the reward she reaped for enduring each day in this horrid place. If only he knew what she had to put up with.

When he was little, four or five at the most, and not long after they'd moved into the caravan, they'd been through a similar routine. Each night after tea had been cleared away and while Pat completed her homework, they'd sit together on the settee for half an hour before making it up into a bed. At first she'd thought of reading to him, but when the nights drew in, the winter came and it grew too dark to see the letters beneath the dull glow of the gas mantle, rather than reciting from a book she resorted to making up stories, or at least, relating the ones she'd heard in her own childhood. It was then she discovered, after the fabric volume of farmyard animals had been tossed to one side, that he preferred to hear about soldiers and their exploits and somehow she'd always known how things would turn out. So it came as no hardship to her now to repeat the process, and in fact there was some element of pleasure in it, going through the archive of their lives, recalling what she could and inventing what she could not, the real and the imaginary. She'd been happy to do it for his sake then, and she was happy to do it now. One day she might tell him the truth – there was still time.

Elisabeth clasped her purse still closer to her chest. Even Danny, with all his silly haircuts and his clever ways couldn't take it from her now. Beyond her picture window it had grown dark and for the moment the birds had fallen silent. A gentle hush had come over the place and all she could hear was the steady drone of distant traffic on the main road.

Soon, Frank would be here...

Pat let go of the last of her shopping bags and collapsed onto a kitchen chair. She was exhausted. Tesco late on a Saturday afternoon was not the quietest of places and she'd had to battle to find what she wanted. All in all it had been a stressful day. Her meetings that morning had been long and protracted (Trade Unions, she found, always took things to the wire) and she'd been unavoidably delayed. No wonder she felt tired.

Through the door to the living room she could hear the noise of the television. Terry would no doubt be lounging on the settee in front of it. At that moment she wanted nothing more than to kick off her shoes and join him, even if it was only to watch the football results.

"Any chance of a cup of tea?" she called. There was no reply and so she continued. "I could do with a hand putting the shopping away you know – if you're not too busy."

Terry obviously couldn't hear her – or perhaps he was pretending not to. She hauled herself to her feet and started to fill the kettle.

She was on the point of taking her coat off when the phone rang. It was Frank. He sounded distant and uncharacteristically excited. "I've called twice already but there was no answer."

Pat gave a wry smile and pushed the living room door to. "I've only just got in. You could have left a message."

But then she remembered – Frank didn't do messages. And neither did he have a mobile phone so she assumed he must be in a call box.

"Where are you?" she asked.

"In a Little Chef somewhere north of Doncaster." It was as though his dislocated voice was coming from another planet.

"What on earth are you doing there?"

"I stopped off for something to eat. Look, I need to speak to you."

"You sound stressed. Is everything alright? How was...?"

She'd meant to enquire about Geoffrey but he cut her off.

"Can't talk now – short of change. Meet me at Mother's in an hour. There's something..."

Then there was a click and the phone went dead.

Pat sighed and replaced the receiver. Typical. Frank, her little brother, expecting her to jump about whenever it suited him. *I'll be on the Plymouth train...* At least she wouldn't have to take an hour off work today – this would be in her own time.

The noise from the living room ceased and Terry came through, his plump bricklayer's hands shoved deep in his pockets.

"Hello, luv. Who was that on the phone?"

"Oh, so you can hear it now, can you? It wouldn't have done you any harm to have answered it the first time."

"Sorry..."

"It was Frank, if you must know."

"Oh yeah, soldier boy. What did he want?"

"He wants me to meet him at the nursing home."

"What, now?"

"Pretty much. It sounded urgent."

Terry looked crestfallen.

"So what's going to happen about dinner?"

Pat surveyed the pile of shopping bags on the kitchen floor, then glanced at her watch.

"There's a pizza in the freezer..."

Given how long it would take to get to her mother's, it was hardly worth taking her coat off.

She was actually the first to arrive. It had just turned seven and the car park was empty. She stopped in her usual spot next to the beech hedge on the far side, then got out and leant against the curve of the boot to wait.

Frank arrived not long after, the beam of his headlights sweeping wildly along the hedge as he roared across the tarmac. His car jerked to a halt and he leapt out, then slammed the door shut. From somewhere across the city came the prolonged wail of a police-car siren. He looked nervously over his shoulder, as if it might have something to do with him.

Pat was instantly suspicious.

"Do you want to tell me what's going on?"

"You'll find out soon enough."

She thought he looked flushed. Perhaps the shock of meeting Geoffrey had all been too much and her brother had resorted to his old ways. She tried to catch the smell of his breath and she searched for the sweet heavy scent that had filled her car on the day she'd last fetched him from the station. But there was no trace and she was forced to ask instead.

"Have you been drinking?"

"Nope." Frank shook his head. "Not so as you'd notice. Now come on, we haven't got much time."

He set off at a determined pace toward the entrance.

Pat fell in with him, half walking, half running to keep up alongside.

"So what's this all about?"

Frank stopped abruptly and turned in her direction. They were now standing face to face in the middle of the car park and the outdoor light over the front door of the nursing home fell straight across one puffy cheek making him look slightly demonic.

"I've fixed it."

"What do you mean, you've 'fixed it'?"

"You wouldn't do it, so I've had to."

"I have no idea what you're talking about."

"No, you never have, have you? And d'you know what? I'm not sure you ever will."

He turned back toward the home and resumed his rapid march. The speed he was going, thought Pat, he might have been doubling up on the parade ground.

The foyer was deserted, although the door to the office was slightly ajar. Sheila must either have seen, or more likely heard them as they sped past, heading toward the corridor that led to Elisabeth's room. Curious as to what was happening, she came out to join them.

Frank raced on, eager to reach his destination, dragging the two women along in his wake. His turbulence disturbed them.

"For God's sake, Frank, slow down," his sister cried. "It's not a race. She's not going anywhere you know. Whatever it is, we've got all night if we need it."

"We won't…"

Sheila's harassed tones pursued him down the corridor. "Mr Johnson, I must ask you to show a bit more respect. We have other residents to consider."

But Frank was in no mood to stop now.

Then there were four of them as Danny emerged from a side door and tagged along behind, his stiff blond hair waxed into a quiff.

Elisabeth sat patiently waiting, her hands surrounding her purse. The wall clock above her chest of drawers told her it was already seven-fifteen. Frank was late. Perhaps he'd been held up.

Her peace was broken by the noise of a crowd in the corridor outside. She was surprised to find that the first voice she recognised was that of her daughter. She hadn't been expecting Pat.

"Frank! You can't do this!"

There was a flurry beyond her door, then it burst open and suddenly they were all in her room, filling the space along the wall – Frank, Pat, Sheila, and that boy, all come to see the show.

Frank seemed agitated, his face burned with colour and for a moment she too thought he might have broken his pledge. But he was steady enough, if just a little breathless, and she put it down to exertion. Beneath the ceiling light, a patch of sweat glistened on his brow.

Meanwhile, Pat's mouth was in motion, her words rolling out into the silence of the room.

"Frank's got something to tell you," she was saying. "There's been…"

But before she could complete her prologue, Frank had moved in advance of his cue. Without waiting for his sister to finish, he rushed across the room and flung himself at Elisabeth's feet, clasping his arms about her legs and burying his head in her lap.

Even there, rather than around her neck, he could still register the familiar scent of her, the smell of hair and flaky skin like dusted flour, the scent which ever since he'd been a child had been the hallmark of his mother.

He was desperate to tell her his news. He took her hand and pressed it gently, then whispered the words that had been in his head from the moment he'd left Norwich.

"He's gone, Mum. It's over. Everything's going to be alright."

Elisabeth looked down at him, his head resting on her knees, and began to stroke the strands of hair behind his ear. This was Frank, her dear little boy! Something had happened, something else had gone wrong, there'd been another crisis, she didn't know what. What was he talking about? She didn't understand. But no matter, she would take care of him, just as she'd always done.

She looked up and in front of her, paraded against the wall, a row of faces stared out at her, waiting for her reaction. There was an expression in their eyes that told her she should say something and not for the first time in recent months she felt slightly bewildered. What could someone like her give them? She had so little left. In the end she resorted to one of her stock phrases as a means of expressing herself.

"He's not my son, you know…"

The faces paused, deciding whether to believe. Was that enough she wondered, or had she already said too much?

There was silence for a moment and then, out in the garden, a blackbird began singing its goodnight.

Author's Note

The characters in this book are entirely fictional and are not intended to be a representation of any real person, alive or dead.

Biography

N.E. David is the pen name of York author Nick David. Nick began writing at the age of 21 but like so many things in life, it did not work out first time round. Following this disappointment he was obliged to work for a living, firstly in industry and latterly in personal finance. 30 years later, with a lifetime of normal experiences behind him, he was able to approach things from a different perspective.

In 2005, Nick started writing again and was successful in producing a series of short novellas. His debut novel, *Birds of the Nile*, was published by Roundfire in 2013.

Nick writes character-based accessible literary fiction where he focuses on stories of human interest. He maintains he has no personal or political message to convey but his initial objective is to entertain the reader and he hopes this is reflected in his writing.

Besides being a regular contributor to literary festivals and open mics in the North East region, Nick is also a founder member of York Authors and co-presenter of Book Talk on BBC Radio York.

Also by N.E. David

Birds of the Nile (9781782791584), Roundfire.

When Michael Blake takes early retirement from the British Embassy in Cairo, he books a long-awaited birding trip. But halfway up the Nile he meets Lee Yong and things begin to change. Their tour guide Reda isn't all he seems either and when the Egyptian revolution kicks off, Blake finds himself embroiled in a tangled web of love and intrigue. Set against the background of the events of January 2011, *Birds of the Nile* is a powerful story of loss and self-discovery as three disparate characters, each with their own agenda, seek to come to terms with change. Part political thriller, part love story, *Birds of the Nile* is N.E. David's debut novel. Poignantly written, it reminds us of the complex nature of global cultural interaction and how, as individuals, we try to deal with it.

'Vivid settings, crisp writing and a highly relevant story make *Birds of the Nile* a gripping read. Egypt's great inheritance and chaotic present are brought convincingly to life, and the politics behind the uprising deftly sketched. Against this background, a haunting love story develops to an unpredictable conclusion. I have always admired N.E. David's short fiction. His long-awaited first novel does not disappoint.'

Pauline Kirk, a member of the Pennine Poets and the Editor of Fighting Cock Press

Other Works

Carol's Christmas
Feria
A Day at the Races

For more information visit the author's website at
www.nedavid.com.
You can also follow N.E. David on Twitter
@NEDavidAuthor.

At Roundfire we publish great stories. We lean towards the spiritual and thought-provoking. But whether it's literary or popular, a gentle tale or a pulsating thriller, the connecting theme in all Roundfire fiction titles is that once you pick them up you won't want to put them down.